THE SIX LOVES OF BILLY BINNS

RICHARD LUMSDEN

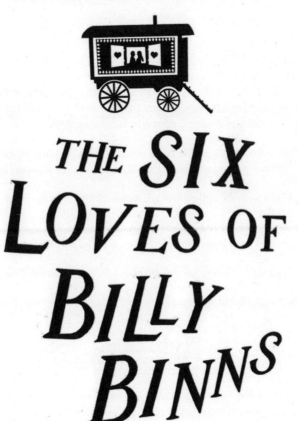

THE SIX LOVES OF BILLY BINNS

TINDER
PRESS

First published in Great Britain in 2019 by Tinder Press
An imprint of HEADLINE PUBLISHING GROUP

1

Cataloguing in Publication Data is available from the British Library

Hardback ISBN 978 1 4722 5668 3
Trade paperback ISBN 978 1 4722 5669 0

Typeset in Sabon LT Std by Jouve (UK), Milton Keynes

Printed and bound in Great Britain by Clays Ltd, Elcograf S.p.A.

HEADLINE PUBLISHING GROUP
An Hachette UK Company
Carmelite House
50 Victoria Embankment
London EC4Y 0DZ

www.tinderpress.co.uk
www.headline.co.uk
www.hachette.co.uk

For all sad words of tongue or pen
the saddest are these; it might have been.

John Greenleaf Whittier

PART ONE

One

I have to get this out.

I have to get it down before it's gone for good.

While it's still clear in my head.

While they're all sat beside me, as alive now as they were then, these people I once loved.

Mary.

Hello, Mary. Do you remember me?

You were my first, though there may have been others before you; slips of things, stolen moments behind a market stall or in the straw of a cattle barn, but nothing to match the time we shared together. That first eruption of love when the world shifts and everything glows orange.

You died much too young, of a broken heart if I remember right. Not sure if it was me or someone else who broke your heart, but we were never meant to last, you and me. Too many complications along the way, what with one thing and another.

Still, I loved you, Mary old girl.

Then Evie.

I loved you, Evelyn Ellis. For a lifetime, if I'm honest.

We were the right age for love when we started out. You were my forever girl.

A love that should have lasted to the end, but the world doesn't work that way.

I loved you from the first moment I saw you. You might say that isn't true, but you'd be wrong. I loved you then as I love you now.

These dry embers, buried deep, set alight once again at your memory. A fire that burned quiet for the rest of my life.

Archie.

My little boy.

I loved you, son, as soon as I knew you'd sparked into life. Knew you were a boy. I felt you kicking, your tiny feet.

Knew it would be you, Archie Binns. With your scruffy knees poking out of your shorts. Your pockets full of marbles; the catseye and the oxblood, the jasper, the aggie and the ruby. Your little hands.

Do you remember how we climbed trees together?

You know how much I loved you.

I'm not sure if I ever said it to you, not out loud anyway. Not in words so you could hear.

But you knew it, didn't you, son?

Vera.

I was unhappy when I first met you, Vera.

Forty-something, was I? Life was on a downward spiral, then you showed up out of the blue. You were so beautiful and you made me very happy.

4

You caused me trouble, too. I paid a price for loving you, that's for sure. For a while I was lost in the wreckage, but isn't that what we hope for when it comes to the end: to know we didn't just pass by but lived through something real along the way?

Everyone should be lucky enough to have a Vera once in their lives. Despite the trouble. Despite the price you end up paying.

To be taken to the edge and made to jump. To love until it hurts.

Mrs Jackson.

Black Betty.

Didn't think I'd ever get those feelings again, much later on in life. After Evie and Vera and the rest of them. But suddenly there you were. You brought me out of retirement, you might say.

We were old when we met. Not proper old like I am now, of course. I was still able to do something about it back when you showed up, and we made it good, the two of us, when there wasn't much pickings around.

Some lovely years together, me and Mrs Jackson.

Funny, still calling you Mrs Jackson after all this time.

Mary, Evie, Archie, Vera, Mrs Jackson.

Five of them in all.

Five loves? Is that it?

It doesn't sound much after all this time.

I recall the names, but the faces come and go.

When you first meet someone, you don't know how

long they'll be in your life for. It could be minutes or it could be forever.

You don't know when it starts.

And you don't know when it stops.

Some endings are final, others take you by surprise.

Their last goodbye.

The world drags them away and all that's left is a fading memory, turning to dust like the flesh on these old bones.

I want to remember what love feels like, one last time. To remember each of the people I loved, to see them all clearly again.

I'll start with Mary.

Get it down on paper, all the details, before it's gone for good.

While it's still clear in my head.

Two

It's 1914, and I'm as old as the century.

A boy on his bike up Shepherd's Bush Green.

Across the Goldhawk Road with the Bush Hotel on my left. The tram tracks converge and I'm bang in the centre of the world: Hammersmith to the south; north to Wormwood Scrubs; Acton to the west; Holland Park and the City to the east.

The summer air, thick and warm. The wet roads greasy now the thunderstorms have stopped.

There's been some fuss about the killing of an archduke in Austria, but that was a while ago, and the newspapers have a photograph of a boat sailing down the Panama Canal.

The bicycle wheels drop into the slots by the tracks, which Dad helped lay for the first electric trams in London. I let the tyres hum against the iron rails before jumping back onto tarmacadam as the tracks cross, where the tramcar wheels catch and shriek. Past the Empire, the Palladium Picture House. It's ten years before the big Pavilion Theatre will be built, thirty before it gets bombed in the Blitz and sixty before it becomes bingo.

I'm racing too fast through time and come back to now.

The 107 tram to Acton, crammed to the back railings,

pulls away in front of me. I swing my bike across the tracks as the tramcar picks up speed. The wires crackle and spit, drawing electricity through the pantograph on its roof as it veers left down Uxbridge Road.

I go right along the green, past the Lyons coffee house, Wellington's laundry, the cycle store, Ellis's bakery, Miles's the dog sellers. Past the Central railway station and the busy Norland Road market.

Tight on the handlebars, out of the saddle to Holland Park.

My legs push against the hill. The mansion houses make it feel like a different part of town. The chain hums in time with the pedals, left into Ladbroke Grove, standing for the climb, then down towards the railway bridge and right into Portobello to Harry Coggins' house.

I lean my bicycle against his gate, my legs twitching from the ride, and knock quietly on the front door, hoping it won't be his mum who opens it.

The latch turns and Mrs Coggins peers through a crack.

'It's Billy Binns,' she says to the shadows in the hallway behind her.

Her long black hair is tied behind her neck with a parting above the centre of her forehead. A bright red jewel hangs from one ear, a bird's feather from the other. The sleeves down her arms are long and loose, but a tight black shawl wraps across her chest like something Harry Houdini would wear to prevent escape. Even in the dimly lit hallway you can see the cleft in her lip, like a scar cutting down hard into the top of her mouth.

Harry Coggins is two weeks older than me, separated

by a century. He was born just before Christmas, 1899. I arrived in the middle of the party, early hours of January the first, 1900.

It's gone.

Like the Norland Road market, demolished for the motorway in the fifties, wasn't it?

I've lost where I was.

I remember what I'm wearing today and what I had for lunch.

I remember a cup of tea at eleven and two digestive biscuits in the saucer.

I remember changing out of my pyjamas this morning and dusky Sylvie swearing as she emptied my piss bag without first checking the valve.

I remember Sylvie is one of the carers here in The Cedars. Slip of a thing in big thick shoes. Afro hair tied on top of her head and a silver nose ring that looks like it must be uncomfortable. Nineteen at her last birthday, I think she said. I bought her a card from the shop trolley and would have stuck a fiver in it if I'd been able to find one in my trousers. I don't much carry money these days.

I remember the other carer, Ros, who's been here almost as long as me. Fifty, I reckon she is, with strong arms and a kind face. Her husband left her some time ago but she met someone else on the internet. An older gent who's a writer, apparently, though Ros says he's yet to write a book anyone can read.

You're not meant to tip the carers here, but Ros and Sylvie deserve a medal if you ask me. Not so much Gordon, who just gets annoyed with everyone, or Mrs Akinyemi, who never smiles.

I remember my dreams, but not where they start.

I recall some of last week and the week before that. Then everything goes into a haze.

Fragments of memories come looming back like red London buses in a pea-souper.

I remember my boy Archie coming to visit on my birthday, but that could have been a while ago too.

Time plays funny tricks these days.

I wait for the next memory.

I wait and I wait.

Some Christmas or other in The Cedars.

I remember because I didn't want to wear a paper hat. Gordon said, 'Wear the paper hat, you grumpy old bastard,' which isn't the proper way for a carer to speak to a resident. Gordon was unhappy since falling out with his friend who had an identical moustache and picked him up outside in a sports car each evening. Gordon said it was always me spoiling the fun by being miserable. That was a long time ago, when Gordon still had his hair on top.

All in the past now.

Water under the bridge.

I remember a tea party here where there wasn't a fuss about paper hats. The Queen sent a card even though we'd never met, and a smart-looking young man in a suit came to sit next to me for a cup of tea and a photograph.

Mrs Cutts, or it might have been Mrs Bentley, actually came over from the television set and went all giggly because he was a high-up Conservative, but his face didn't ring any bells with me.

I couldn't recall how the young man knew me, but it was nice of him to visit, being so high-up and all. Shame he didn't have time to finish his tea after the photograph was taken, but I suppose that's high-up people for you. Mrs Cutts or Mrs Bentley, whichever one it was, went back to watching the television set as soon as he was gone.

Small breaths come and go. I don't require much air these days. Just enough to keep the powdery blood pumping through the flimsy veins and that's about it. Not much longer now, I reckon.

Ba-bump. Ba-bump.

Inch after inch, slowly round it goes.

A few more trips down to the feet and back, then maybe we'll call it a day.

Long life. Nearly over. Almost done.

The sitting room is too warm and the television set too loud.

Mrs Bentley and Mrs Cutts spend all day staring up at the screen. A few other residents sit like relics in a dinosaur museum. Jimmy Parris, in the armchair next to mine, is easy to get along with when he's not banging on about the Lake District. Mrs Chaudhry and her gaggle of Indian ladies are over by the window, while Mr Ozturk combs through his hair that Sylvie washes black for him every month. Mrs Greatorex lifts a biscuit from her teacup to her mouth. I watch the biscuit break into crumbs and spill down the front of her cardigan.

There are others whose names I don't know, but we're not all here to make friends.

I'm the oldest by a long chalk. They tell me I'm the oldest man in Europe, but that only makes me feel like a boxing champion about to lose his belt.

Some reckon there's been a mistake with my birth certificate and there's no way I'm as old as they say, but you can't argue with memories.

Forgotten moments keep coming back to my mind and I'd like to get them down on paper before they go again. For Archie to know I wasn't just a bag of skin and bone who pisses out of a tube. To know I was once a proper man, despite what he thinks of me now.

Five faces in the darkness.

Each brings a tiny ache, a quiet pain just behind the lungs.

All that history.

The people I once loved. A small handful.

I try to hold them in my head, but it's like trying to catch butterflies with a torn net.

It's like they don't want to be remembered.

There were those you'd lie next to for a few moments of bliss, when nothing else matters, sweat boils on your skin and you're the happiest you could ever be. Before the chill of the real world comes back. The regrets and the guilt and the trouble brewing. Knowing it was already over while they lay cooling in the straw beside you.

But that isn't the same as love.

Archie'll know what I mean.

I've loved a few people in this long, long life and I want to remember them now before they're gone for good.

I'm a very old man and I'd like to remember what love feels like once more before I die.

To remember their faces.

To see them all, as clear as . . .

As clear as . . .

There's a word.

Ros said to keep going and not stop when you get stuck. Her boyfriend wrote a book once, so I reckon she knows what to do. She says not to worry and to fill the gaps in later.

When you're young, everything joins up in your head, then you get old and it disappears like trails of smoke.

I can feel the trails forming again.

I'll start at the beginning:

New Year's Eve, 1899.

I don't think I can remember this far back, but I remember Auntie Pam telling the story.

I'm not meant to be born for another few weeks.

Dad and Ma are at the Hampshire Hog on King Street with Auntie Pam and all the neighbours saying goodbye to 1899. Ma said the men were sour having to bring their wives with them. She and Dad argue whether the new century starts that night or the next year. Most people think the twentieth century doesn't start until 1901, but Dad reckons it starts now because nineteen hundred sounds very different from eighteen hundred.

When midnight approaches, everyone pushes outside to hear the church bells ring the new year in. People are kissing and hugging and Ma starts to feel peculiar and can't find Dad in the crowd. She gets dizzy and makes her way home.

The sun's up by the time Dad comes back the next morning, still pissed, and I'm wrapped in a blanket in Ma's arms. She said Dad's face was a picture.

Apparently he'd always wanted a boy.

I remember liking hearing this story from Auntie Pam, and sometimes think I can actually remember being born; Dad expecting an earful and finding he's got a son. Ma doing it all on her own with no help other than Auntie Pam because everyone else was stone drunk at the time.

Soon afterwards, Auntie Pam moved to Manchester with her new husband. But when I was nine or ten, she came back to the house one night. I thought I was dreaming about her and woke to hear her voice downstairs, so I might not have been dreaming after all. I got out of bed and it sounded like a row going on.

I sat at the top of the stairs.

Dad, Ma and Pam were in the parlour with the door shut. I couldn't make out what they were saying before Ma started to cry, which always happened during a row, followed by the sound of crockery smashing and Ma shouting that Pam was a *trollop*. I didn't have time to hide before Auntie Pam appeared at the front door and looked up to

14

see me sitting at the top of the stairs. I thought she'd be cross with me for not being asleep.

In the parlour I heard Dad say, 'You should have let the little bastard freeze to death.'

Auntie Pam smiled up at me. But I remember it being a sad smile, and she waved and went without saying anything else.

Ma was still crying in the parlour, but softer than before, so I went back to bed quietly and thought about which little bastard they should have let freeze to death.

I didn't see Auntie Pam for many years after that, until long after I was a married man myself. She wrote me a letter. When I went to see her, she said it was me who Dad was talking about that night.

Mrs Greatorex has dropped her teacup. The saucer clatters and rolls across the hard linoleum floor, putting a stop to these memories of Auntie Pam.

My mind is like trifle these days. A soft mess of colours, but nothing you can get your teeth into.

Nothing that stays fixed for very long.

I once had a pen, I'm sure.

A silver fountain pen. A gift, but I don't remember who from. I can still feel the weight of it in my hand, the smooth strokes across the paper.

If I could find the pen, I'd be able to write these memories down so I don't forget them, but it must have disappeared with all the other things I've lost over the years. When Sylvie has a minute, I'll get her to take me back to my room so I can look for this pen and keep going with the memories.

My only jacket hangs on the back of my bedroom door.

It takes me a while to get over to the door. I feel inside the pocket, remembering how I put the jacket on to go out into the garden not too long ago, then wiggle my fingers around until I'm sure the pen isn't in there, before going back over to the bed and sitting down to get over my disappointment at not finding it.

I'll need a moment to catch my breath after making all this effort.

This has been my bedroom since the Falklands War was kicking off, and that feels like a lifetime ago. One of the residents back then said the lower half of the walls were painted *Goose Green* and I don't think they've had a new lick of paint since then.

A small bed against the wall, with a metal hoist that Ros and Sylvie can't be arsed to use as it takes too long to get everyone up. Besides, Ros says I'm thin as a rake. Gordon says it's for health and safety, especially with some of the heavier ladies, but he isn't the one getting everyone out of bed in the mornings. A window that looks out onto Hammersmith Grove. A clock on the wall and a picture of a Scottish loch by some mountains that I stopped noticing decades ago. A wardrobe, a bedside cabinet, a small table and chair and a little sink in the corner. I watch the drips slowly fall from the tap, one then another, like life passing by. Like the small flow of powdery blood through the veins, down to the feet and back.

Down the corridor, the lift pulleys rumble and whine.

Polystyrene tiles across the ceiling like square clouds, bouncing night-time headlights from the vans up and down Hammersmith Grove off the walls.

It's been a while since I looked in the drawer in the bed-side cabinet, which is easier to get to than the wardrobe because I can sit on the bed at the same time.

In the drawer is an old Golden Virginia tin with the lid left off. It's hard opening things with my knotty fingers these days. Even now I can still smell the tobacco that would have once been in there. They stopped putting Golden Virginia in tins years ago and sold it in paper packs instead.

I used to keep precious things in my old tobacco tin but can't remember what they might have been. As you get older, you change your mind about what's precious.

Behind the tin I find my old maroon army tie, neatly rolled up.

I keep it at the back of the drawer and not hung up in the wardrobe next to my blue tie because it's a bugger to put on. The maroon tie has a single yellow flag on it. It has to be tied so the yellow flag is in the middle of the knot, which is a tall order for old fingers like mine. I gave up wearing the maroon tie with the yellow flag many years ago, leaving just my blue one with the lions or the green one I'm wearing today, which is probably my favourite, despite some ancient gravy stains down the front.

A faded brown envelope with a few old letters inside, written by me. I'm not sure why I bothered keeping those.

I've forgotten why I'm sitting here and what I'm look-ing for.

I push the maroon tie back inside the drawer and the ends of my fingers rattle something hard against the thin wood. I ease it out to the front and there it is, my old silver fountain pen, cold and heavy in my hand.

Each morning I wake with a sense of excitement at what the day might bring.

Last night, lying in bed, I could almost picture Mary, but she kept slipping from view, like the burning-out of an old photograph.

When I woke, the daylight had made a ladder of the blinds on the opposite wall, and I knew I had a clear idea where to start.

The sitting room is quieter today and I have the table by the window to myself. I pull the lid off the silver pen, press the nib onto the writing paper in front of me and scratch out an invisible line.

Ros says there might be a bottle of ink in Mrs Akinyemi's desk. Mrs Akinyemi wears a badge saying *Administrator* but neither she nor Gordon seem to agree who's in charge. Ros says neither of them are, though Gordon is always the one who ticks off Ros or Sylvie when they've done something against the rules.

Mrs Akinyemi doesn't have much to do with residents, and when she does, no one can tell what she's saying because of her strong accent and the way she never moves her lips when she speaks.

Ros comes back with a smile and shakes the silver pen like the thermometer they used to put up your arse when you were under the weather.

It still doesn't work, so she squeezes the ink until it bubbles onto the nib. She writes a solid black line and draws circles on the paper to make sure it keeps working.

She's made a right mess of my first page of memories.

I clasp the pen in my twisted fingers and write my first word like they taught in handwriting at school.

I've thought of a proper title, so that when it's finished I can give it to Archie and he'll know what it's about.

It's hard to make the pen work because my fingers won't grip tight enough. I clench it in both hands but can't get the ink to come out.

I push it down hard to force a mark onto the page.

Tap it on the table to get some bloody ink out of the damn thing onto the page.

To get some bloody ink out of the fucking pen on the bastard fucking page.

There it is, the start of the title, faint among the blotches:

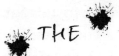

Three

I don't remember coming to bed.

It's dark outside and I might have been to sleep already.

A train rattles by in the distance. Funny how you can't hear the sound of the tracks in the day.

Sylvie took ages scrubbing with the cloth to get my inky fingers clean. No amount of scrubbing will get the black off Sylvie's hands, though there's pink on the inside of her palms.

Beautiful Sylvie.

I remember loving a girl like Sylvie, somewhere along the way.

It's hard when all your friends have gone and you're the last still alive. When no one's around to say what a decent chap you were. That you weren't always a dumb-arse who gets confused where one day ends and another begins.

Lying here, the sound of a train on distant railway tracks takes me back to the trams on the green.

A boy on his bike up Shepherd's Bush Green, over the tram rails to Harry Coggins' house.

Harry's ma opens the door. Black hair, a bird's feather

in one ear and an ugly crease in the top of her mouth like a cut made by a cheese-wire that has been left to heal.

Mrs Coggins never speaks much but says to come inside the hallway.

Harry's twin sister Peg is usually grumpy though sometimes can be nice. You never know what mood she'll be in. They don't look alike but you can tell they're twins when they're stood next to each other. Harry's dad is Irish and no one really knows what he does for a living. Harry says he finds work for theatre entertainers, though Gilbert Gelling's uncle is a ventriloquist and says Harry's dad leeches on starving turns. It isn't proper work like building tram tracks for Mr Wimpey, that's for sure. Harry's ma is from Kent. His dad came over to marry her when she was young, though she's obviously quite old now, nearly thirty apparently, and the house always smells of dogs and wet wood.

Mrs Coggins calls to Harry but he's out in the lavvy, which means I have to wait while his ma asks after my ma and dad. I say they're well thank you, trying not to look at her scary mouth. Peg walks in and says she's going next door to see Jeannie.

Harry's ma catches me staring at her mouth and bites her top lip under the bottom one. I wonder if she hides it because she knows it makes her ugly. Harry comes in after taking ages in the lavvy and says we should climb the tree at the end of his garden. This is one of the best things about Harry's house and makes up for having to talk to his odd ma.

It's his tree house, so he always goes up the rope first.

Two knots to the first branch. It's hard to let go with

one hand and grab hold of the plank with the other, especially when it's slippery after the recent thunderstorms. Harry takes his pea-shooter from the store hole in the tree trunk and inspects it as I try to get my leg up while clutching the bunch of elderberry ammo in my teeth.

Harry calls out, 'Woodlouse!' and blows one at me through the pea-shooter. It smacks on my forehead. He laughs as I struggle to hold onto the rope, not wanting to drop the elderberries in my teeth because then Harry would make me go back down to get more from the bush. When I'm up I tell him he could've had my eye out, but he says a woodlouse isn't strong enough to burst an eyeball and I don't know if he's right so I can't argue about it.

The leaves provide some cover from below. This is the best summer we've had in the tree den, mostly because of Peg and Jeannie. Peg isn't pretty but she can give you a nasty thump when she wants. She has the same dark hair as their ma, with their dad's big nose, which looks bigger on Peg than it does on Harry. Over the summer she's starting to look more like the girls that work in Glover's dairy or the bath house on Lime Grove. The shape of her chest is beginning to show beneath her clothes, which means we can make fun of her in a new way. Her friend Jeannie is a year younger but much prettier than Peg, with a bigger chest already. Jeannie has an older sister who's seventeen and isn't afraid of anything. Peg isn't grumpy when she's with Jeannie and just laughs at everything she says.

Harry brings out a cigarette he's taken from his dad's tin with a couple of matches to light it. He sparks a match against the plank, holds his hand around the flame and tells me to put the cigarette in it. The end of the tobacco glows orange and black as it burns. Harry goes first, blowing as quick as he can even though you can't see any smoke coming out, not like the four or five blows my dad gets from one mouthful. It's my turn next and I make two blows of smoke, which must impress Harry even if he doesn't say anything about it.

It feels good to be growing up.

We take a couple more sucks on his dad's cigarette before Harry crushes it out on the tree and flicks the end away. We lean back to wait for the dizziness to stop and concentrate on next door's garden. It has a short lawn and vegetable patch where Jeannie's dad grows potatoes, carrots, runner beans, peas, onions, cabbages and rhubarb. The peas are covered with netting to keep the birds off. An apple tree grows near the end of Jeannie's wall, where the girls like to sit.

Waiting for the girls to appear, Harry tells me he recently saw the remains of a dog that had been run over by a tram and sliced in two halves: head and front paws one side of the track, tail and back legs on the other.

I'm listening to his description of its innards drying red on the tarmacadam when I hear the two girls come out of the kitchen next door and walk down the path giggling. I knock Harry's arm but he pretends he isn't interested and keeps on with the story about the sliced dog, and then yawns like he's not really bothered by the sight of Jeannie and Peg walking past the vegetable patch to the bottom of the garden.

They sit on a rug under the apple tree, each eating a small bun in a cake wrapper. Peg has her back to us while

Jeannie faces this way. We're quiet in the tree den now, trying to hear what they're saying but too far away to make out words. The girls laugh and Peg looks around quick, waggles her finger into the ground and buries the cake paper. They giggle as Jeannie looks back to the house to make sure her mum isn't coming.

We know what this means.

Jeannie undoes the ties on the front of her dress.

Crosses her hands over.

Harry and I stop breathing.

She holds the bottom hem and lifts it up, arms crossed over, up to her face.

Her white underwear, pressed full with her chest.

Oh my sweet Jesus.

The girls giggle, Jeannie drops it back down and Peg lifts hers. Jeannie reaches out to touch her titties but Peg isn't turned round far enough for us to see. She's smaller than Jeannie but it's still exciting to glimpse.

It's warm lying up here.

Harry makes a noise as he swallows. Jeannie lifts up her dress again and holds it for longer this time. Beneath the thin underwear I see the dark shadow between her breasts, her arms crossed in front of her face. I try to hold the image so it stays with me forever before she lets it fall.

The girls whisper something to each other. Harry mutters that he's bored because the other day he watched Jeannie's older sister lift up her petticoat and saw her full mingey, which actually had hair on it, honest to God.

I wonder if he's made that up just to impress me.

24

Jeannie and Peg get up and walk down the garden, giggling.

It feels good to be discovering secrets about girls.

To be getting more grown up.

We lift our pea-shooters and try to hit them with our elderberry ammo before they reach the safety of the vegetable patch and disappear back inside Jeannie's house.

Ros has brought in her boyfriend's old typewriter as he uses a laptop now. She reckons it'll be easier for my fingers than a messy pen. She knows I won't go near the Toshiba used by residents wanting to surf the internet.

She brings paper from Mrs Akinyemi's office and shows me how to roll it into the machine.

I don't have any trouble pressing the keys with my fingers and remember what most of the letters are called, though some like % and & will take a little working out.

I like the sound it makes – *tap click, tap click.*

Tap click, tap click, tap click.

Ding.

I'll need a rest after all this effort.

The television set is on very loud today. Something on the news about the President of America. I wonder if there's a problem with the screen as the man's head looks very yellow, but Mrs Bentley and Mrs Cutts don't seem to be making a fuss, and they're the first to complain if it's on the blink.

I'm trying to remember school, but nothing comes to mind. I preferred bunking off to watch the airships going up and down on Wormwood Scrubs. I was twelve when Dad said it was time I paid my way. Mr Finlay gave me a job on his fish stall in Shepherd's Bush market and that was the end of my education, which didn't do me no harm I suppose.

I'm looking forward to my morning cup of tea, which will give me time to think about the fish stall. I've worked up a thirst trying to recall what love feels like.

I don't think I've fully captured it yet, but it's nice to remember the petticoats.

Shepherd's Bush market runs under the railway arches between the Uxbridge and Goldhawk Roads. In 1914, two new Metropolitan Line stations are built at each end to replace the single one running along the bridge. Trouble's brewing because the stall rents are cheaper than shop rates and the shopkeepers don't like us for taking most of the trade, but we bring in shoppers who like to walk down the market looking for bargains.

My first job of the day is to take a barrowload of fish from the cold store behind Norland Road market to the new stall in Shepherd's Bush. It's a long push across the green and a relief when the boxes are stacked up behind the trestle with the fish out ready for selling.

Clem used to deliver the fish on his horse cart from Billingsgate early mornings until his horse died, though the horse lived longer than Clem's dad, who did the job before him. Without a horse, Clem was stuck for work so Mr Finlay gave him the job in Shepherd's Bush, leaving

Mr Finlay to look after Norland Road. Mr Finlay made me Clem's barrow boy after working two years when Jack Burns had been there for four. Jack often has fish go missing when he supplies the hotels in Holland Park. Jack says they fall out of the barrow and get eaten by cats.

He's a bit simple is Jack, but he grafts hard and Mr Finlay's not an idiot.

Clem showed me how to gut the fish for richer customers who don't want to do it themselves. Sometimes, when there's a queue, Clem lets me gut the fish, although he doesn't like me speaking to customers. Clem does his patter, making comments to the ladies about their nice hair or how he'd better not wipe his hands on their skirts after he's finished with the innards. He even makes jokes about me, calling me his little kipper. If a man's paying, Clem might give them a wink and say something about his fingers smelling of fish even before the end of the day. The customers like his cheeky banter and I'm trying to learn it for the time Mr Finlay puts me in charge of the stall.

I once noticed Clem's sums were wrong as he was making a lady laugh while putting fish into her bag. I said it was less than that. Clem ignored me so I said it again and she asked him to count it back. He told her it was an honest mistake and gave her some more change. After she went, he turned to me with his filleting knife, grabbed my throat and made three swipes like I was a fish he was gutting. He went *tss tss tss* through his teeth and pretended to scoop out my intestines like I was a mackerel. He'd stopped laughing and didn't seem to be making a joke any more, even though I knew Clem was funny like that. All the

27

same, I thought it best not to mention it again when he got his sums wrong.

When Mr Edwins, the umbrella maker, made a fuss about the smell on our stall, Clem went in and dropped a few gullets behind his walking stick cabinet as a cheeky bit of fun. A day or so later, his umbrella shop was smelling bad and Mr Edwins came up to Clem and didn't stop shouting until Clem punched him and made his nose bleed. A constable came over and Clem said it wasn't him who put gullets in Mr Edwins' shop and what right did Edwins have to make accusations? It was not long after Clem had had a go at me for pointing out the lady's change, so I thought it best to tell the constable Clem was working on the stall all day and no way could he have put the gullets behind Mr Edwins' walking stick cabinet. There was no more fuss from Mr Edwins after that.

To be honest, I felt a bit sorry for Mr Edwins, knowing Clem had dropped the gullets in his shop, but it's important in life to know whose side you're on.

It's a warm Friday, summer 1914.

I'm sweating after fetching two barrowloads across from Norland Road.

The trestle's full with salt herring, cod, haddock, skate, eels, a dozen crab, three boxes of mussels, queenies and whelks.

It's a warm day and I'm about to find my first love.

I'm remembering this now because of a picture.

Practising remembering seems to make the picture come clearer.

The picture has something to do with love.

If I close my eyes, I can almost see it.

Clem calls me over to show me a drawing he saw in the Eagle on Askew Road last night. He gets a piece of paper and sketches a large V next to his fish sums and asks, 'What's it look like, Billyboy?'

He draws another upside-down V over the first, and laughs, but I don't know what it is yet. He adds a thick stick in the middle of the first V and two small circles either side.

He scribbles a small patch in the middle of one of the Vs.

He's laughing again, and I think it's a view through one of the railway arches with something in front, one of Mr Edwins' umbrellas maybe. Suddenly a lady customer asks to be served and Clem throws the drawing down while picking up his filleting knife.

'Yes, my darlin',' he says. 'So what d'you fancy, aside from me?'

I start moving empty boxes, as Mr Finlay says never to let customers see you idle. I put out the last of the herring from the melting ice and take another look at Clem's drawing, but I still can't see what it is.

It's not an umbrella because the stick would curve at the end.

I put the paper in my pocket to work out later.

And that's when she appears, walking towards me through the market.

She wears a long skirt and a blouse buttoned up to the neck, with a tie fastened at the collar. Her light brown hair pulled up behind her head, parted in the centre. I picture it falling free and spilling down onto her chest. Her dark eyebrows mirror the perfect curve of her lips while her small nose beautifully bridges the space between. She looks older than when she's under the apple tree with grumpy Peg, and for a moment I wonder if it might be Jeannie's older sister coming towards me.

She stops at Hudson's Confectionery and goes inside. When she comes out, she's sucking a large sweet. She approaches the fish stall, though no one ever browses at a fish stall unless they've come to buy fish.

'Hello, Jeannie,' I say, realising I've never actually spoken to her before, only watched her over the fence from Harry Coggins' tree den.

She gives a friendly smile but looks puzzled, like she doesn't know who I am.

Was Jeannie my first love?

I don't recall seeing her sat around the bed with the others, with Evie and Vera and the rest of them. Her face is already fading before we've even started.

Mary, wasn't it?

I'm not sure I ever loved Jeannie, with her blue eyes and her petticoat and her light brown hair. Not properly. She wasn't my forever girl, that's for sure. You only get one of those in life.

One Evie, if you're lucky.

The memory of Evie's name is like falling off a high cliff.

But she isn't here yet. It's Jeannie walking down through the market towards me, and I just want to remember what love felt like.

I don't try Clem's patter about what she fancies aside from me, or having fingers that smell of fish at the end of the day.

Jeannie says hello back and keeps walking. I feel my face go red.

I want to say she looks very pretty under the apple tree, and that it's Harry's idea to pea-shoot elderberries at her and Peg, but it's too difficult to make the words sound right so I just stay quiet. I think about asking Clem what to say, but he'd do his patter and send me away for another box of fish so he could talk to her on his own.

Jeannie goes into Mrs Chester's studio for ballroom dancing lessons.

I think about going myself. Holding her hand, seeing her face up close, then taking her to Lyons for a bowl of soup before walking up Wormwood Scrubs, where we kiss in patches of sunlight through the branches and she lifts her dress so I can see the hair growing on her mingey.

Clem smacks me round the head and says we need

another crate of eels and two dozen skate from Mr Finlay's cold store in Norland Road.

I rush to Norland Road, hoping to return before Jeannie leaves Mrs Chester's, deciding I won't tell Harry about seeing her in the market when we're in his tree den, as I like knowing things about her that he doesn't.

When I'm back, I still keep my eyes peeled for the rest of the day, knowing I must have missed her coming out when I went for the eels.

It's late that day when I sweep down the offcuts. With no running water it's a long walk with buckets from the tap and I have to brush them all the way to the gully near the Goldhawk Road.

If Clem is in good spirits he might look up to the sky and say, 'Looks like rain, Billyboy. The good Lord will wash away our fish heads and we must give thanks in church on Sunday.' Then he'll tell me to just brush them under the other stalls before the market manager sees.

Even though Clem doesn't go to church on Sundays but spends all day in the Eagle on Askew Road.

Then the boxes and any unsold fish go back to the cold storage on Norland Road, though Mr Finlay prefers us to sell out cheap at the end of the day.

On Fridays I get my wages. Six shillings for pushing the barrow and helping Clem. I used to get 10d a day but Mr Finlay put my wages up when he saw how well the stall was doing. I've seen Clem put coins into his apron instead of the leather purse on his belt, which must be the extra profits. No wonder Mr Finlay's pleased.

The wages make me feel like a proper working man.

I say goodbye to Mr Finlay and cycle through Brackenbury, under the railway bridge at Trussley Road, past Ravenscourt Park towards Hammersmith Creek. Around the back of Trafalgar Street, where rubbish gets blown up from the wharves and boatbuilding yards behind our house, thinking of Jeannie all the way home.

Ma has a big pan of water on the stove and the tin bath ready in the parlour for my Friday soak. I take my clothes off in the yard to keep the smell out of the house. Dad says one day he'll take me for a pint in the Seven Stars, but he's always gone before I get home, which is why he hasn't done it yet.

He has his bath on a Sunday.

Other days I wash from a bucket in the yard and air my clothes in the lavvy overnight. By the end of the week Dad says the smell is so bad my jacket could take a shit by itself.

I slip off my undershorts and step into the tub, sitting down quick and leaning forward to cover my bits when Ma pours in more water from the stove. Hair has started growing down there, which is something I might have in common with Jeannie, if what Harry Coggins says about her sister is true.

Ma rubs soap into my hair with her strong fingers.

I'd like to be left alone now, like Dad is when he's in the tub.

Ma rubs soap into my back and lets me do the rest. I wash my face, neck and shoulders, underarms, elbows and hands. I keep washing until the smell of antiseptic over-powers the odour of fish.

Ma goes back to her stove.

I rub the soap until it foams and wash around the old Christmas crackers, as Clem calls them. I wonder how to see Jeannie without going to Harry's house and take her up to the Scrubs for a kiss and a glimpse of her mingey.

Annoyingly, my little fellah, as Clem calls it, is getting bigger in the water.

Ma comes over to wipe soapy water down the back of my neck and I lean forward to keep it all hidden. I'm not sure if she sees the little fellah, but she quickly turns back to the sink without doing my knees and says I should do the wiping instead.

We're both quiet for a minute and I decide to get out of the bathtub. I take the towel from the pan rail to dry myself. It's a good feeling getting rid of the fish smell after a week. Ma says to go and sit with Grandma in the front room.

Grandma is very old, fifty-six I think, and hasn't been well since Grandpa died ten years ago. The other grandpa, Dad's dad, was crushed by a cart hoisted off a boat in Limehouse a few years before I was born. A month later his wife joined him in the grave when Dad wasn't much older than I am now.

Dad says it's good I don't have brothers or sisters because some of the houses on our street have twelve people in them while there's only four in ours and it's still a crush. He says he couldn't afford more mouths to feed but forgets I'm a working man too, paying two shillings to Ma's housekeeping on Fridays.

I save the rest in a tin under the bed. When I go with Dad to the Seven Stars, I'll be able to buy him and his mates a glass of beer and he'll see I'm a working man just like them.

I go back to the parlour for my fresh clothes.

Ma kneels on the floor washing my shirt and trousers over a washboard in the tub. She doesn't speak, and I know something's wrong and wonder if I should say sorry about my little fellah getting big in the bath. I put on clean socks and shoes and try to think of what else might've made her cross.

I tell her her housekeeping is next to the sink.

She usually says something about me being a working man now, but she just stays quiet and I feel hot inside my head. She turns towards me and I smile at her.

I don't see it coming.

A hard slap across my cheek.

My ear burns red and I want to cry, even before the sting lands. Soap bubbles from her hand drip down onto my clean collar. Crying wouldn't be good right now, so I keep it in.

My dirty hankie has been taken out of my pocket and left on the floor, waiting to be boiled. And I know what the trouble is even before seeing it in her other hand: Clem's drawing, picked up from the stall.

Clem laughing as he says, 'What's it look like, Billyboy?'

The paper's wet and the picture blurred. I know it can't be one of Mr Edwins' umbrellas through a pointy railway arch, and must be something to do with the grown-up world.

I want to say to Ma I didn't draw it and wonder about asking her what it is, but she's looking at me like I'm all grown up now.

She says, 'Go to your room and wait for your father.'

The night sinks by. No time goes as slow as trouble.

Gran shuffles quietly into the bedroom we share, behind the fold-up divider that splits our room in two. I don't go down to ask for supper.

I must be asleep by the time Dad gets home from the Seven Stars, because nothing gets said that night.

In the morning I walk downstairs for breakfast and Ma gives me a plate of bacon and bread without any sign of being cross. I catch her looking at my red cheek, which I've been rubbing hard since waking up to make it look extra sore when she sees it.

Nothing gets said about the picture all day, which means either Ma didn't show it to Dad or he just laughed the way Clem did.

On Sunday, Ma and I walk up Trafalgar Street and Askew Road to St Luke's Church and Ma's forgotten all about it, though I'm relieved not to bump into Clem outside the Eagle after all the fuss with the picture.

Inside the church, the congregation are singing, 'It's Only a Step to the Grave'.

Four

Sylvie puts a bowl of cottage pie in front of me, which is never as warm as I'd like.

Someone I once loved made a good shepherd's pie. Steam rising off it like mist on a hillside.

Mrs Jackson, was it?

Jimmy Parris reckons they don't actually make the food in the kitchen here, which seems daft when there's a perfectly good stove going to waste. He says it all comes out of a van in metal boxes because it's cheaper than Mrs Akinyemi paying for a cook.

Jimmy talks a lot of nonsense most of the time. You learn to take it with a pinch of salt. He's probably a good thirty years younger than me, but age doesn't make much difference when your joints are buggered and you dribble more than you eat. Jimmy's been here a while now too and I don't mind passing a quiet hour with him in the next chair, unlike most of the others in this place. Get stuck with Mr Ozturk or Mrs Bentley and you have to pretend your hearing's worse than it really is. I wouldn't have minded getting to know Jimmy when we were younger, before we both ended up here.

You learn not to make friends when someone new turns up. Like those young pilots in the Battle of Britain the older ones wouldn't speak to until they'd survived a few missions. Most people don't live too long after coming to The Cedars. When the first weeks are over, they realise the good years are done with and quickly pack it all in.

There aren't too many good years when you count them up. You get forty summers as a grown-up, and that's about it. Struggle to buy your first place at thirty. Lose it at seventy and you're not getting another home of your own after that.

Funny how quick it goes.

Jimmy's all right, though, even though he can't stop banging on about the Lake District and how beautiful it is up there.

I asked him why he doesn't move there if it's so beautiful, but he pretends he can't hear properly and tells you about the water and the fastest man in the world again.

Same old stories, over and over.

Occasionally visitors might come to give a talk, though there's a limit to the number of times you can listen to small children singing 'Little Donkey'. Bringing tins of bloody soup for harvest festival.

Mornings are best for visitors' talks. Any later in the day, they can't be disappointed if we're all dozing in our armchairs.

I remember a man coming in with old maps of west London. Seeing the gradual disappearance of fields as the nineteenth century shifted into the twentieth, when this was the edge of old London. Shepherd's Bush Green had the last patch of grass where sheep could graze overnight on their way to market the following day. The extending city, relentless and unstoppable, like waves from an ever-growing ocean.

The map man found Trafalgar Street on one of his old charts, back when Hammersmith Creek flowed from Stamford Brook, through the slum houses where I was born, past the boatbuilding wharves, across King Street and out into the Thames just beyond Hammersmith Bridge.

Trafalgar Street had gone on the next edition. After the slum houses were razed to the ground and Hammersmith Creek buried below new roads and houses. He wasn't much of a speaker, but I enjoyed seeing his maps.

It was like discovering a piece of evidence that your life actually happened.

In my seventies, after the high-rise council flat I shared with Betty was gone, I was sleeping on a bench in Furnival Gardens. One morning I looked over the wall at the Thames and saw the small tunnel in the side of the bank opening into the river. A channel of old railings buried in sand at low tide, the last sign Hammersmith Creek existed. The mouth to a busy waterway that once carried barges to and from the river. I wouldn't mind going again sometime, just to look over the wall and see if the tunnel is still there.

Maybe Archie could take me when he next comes to visit his old man. We'll make an afternoon of it. Take a picnic and a flask, maybe.

Remembering Betty Jackson's shepherd's pie makes me feel hungry. Thick and juicy it was, made with mutton, of course. I watched her grill cheese over the potato till it went brown and crispy. Gravy under the spuds kept it moist without spoiling the cheesy top. Piping hot out of the oven. Had a kick that would tickle the back of your throat, too. Her secret ingredient, she said, from her own country.

A little sauce to spice it up.

'Spicy tup,' I thought she was saying in her West Indian accent. I thought *tup* was her word for mutton.

Funny what stays in the mind. Things you'd forgotten.

Sylvie feeds me a spoonful of grey mash. A splash of tepid meat lands on the plastic bib around my neck. Sylvie says, 'Missed some!' and scoops it up into my mouth. There's a tingle in my belly at the thought of Betty Jackson that might be the memory of love but could just be cold lumps of potato going down.

I move the food around on my tongue but it feels like it's been chewed once already, so I let my mind go back to where I was, to St Luke's on the Uxbridge Road before it was bombed in the war and a new, ugly church built to replace it, to Ma singing with the congregation.

    The end is soon coming, O sinner, beware,
    For it's only a step to the grave;
    Repent, or you'll miss that bright haven so fair,
    For it's only a step to the grave.

After church, I decide to go over to Harry Coggins'

house to see if he understands the picture. Today Mrs Coggins doesn't seem quite so scary when she opens the door. I put this down to me becoming more grown up, having thought about new adult things these last few days.

Grumpy Peg is in this afternoon as Jeannie's gone out somewhere, which is both a shame and a relief as I didn't want Harry ogling Jeannie in her underwear today. Harry and I climb up his tree den and sit on the planks. Harry hasn't managed to steal any of his dad's cigarettes, which is just as well because Mrs Coggins makes an unexpected visit down the garden with a jug of lemon squash.

I say, 'Thank you, Mrs Coggins.'

Harry and I never talk about her lip, but then I wouldn't want a friend asking questions if my ma had an ugly scar in her mouth.

Besides, there are more important things on my mind.

We drink the lemon squash.

I take a pencil and paper from my pocket and start the drawing for Harry. He looks unimpressed when I ask if he can see it yet.

I draw the stick in the middle and the two small circles at the base. I do the little fuzzy scribble at the top and ask again if he gets it.

He says, 'Yes,' like it's a stupid question. He takes the pencil and draws raindrops at the end of the stick, which makes me think it might be an umbrella after all, then turns away and looks up through the branches at the sky. After a quiet moment he says, 'Have you done it with a girl yet?'

The drawing still isn't clear and I wonder if I should just say yes, but I tell him no.

To my relief Harry says, 'Me neither.'

We sit quiet for a moment. He says, 'Paddy Welsh reckons a girl did him with her hand and promised to show him her fuzzy mingey. She says he can stick it in her one day soon.'

It starts to fall into place, the fuzz and the stick.

'Paddy says there's magic skin on your hips and if you rub circles on it with your finger, it makes your cock go off.'

The thought of Ma seeing Clem's picture makes me feel sick.

Harry says we could show it to Peg, but I don't fancy talking to his sister about being a grown-up today.

In my bed later, listening to Gran wheezing behind the screen as she sleeps, I try to find the magic skin Paddy Welsh told Harry about. I move my finger in circles on my hips to see if anything happens and my cock gets bigger.

I turn on my side to stop it pressing against the bed sheet and hold it in one hand while still rubbing circles on my hip with the other.

I try to think of Jeannie but can't see her in her slip and petticoat. I remember her saying hello in the market and hold onto that memory, even if her chest isn't as big as it looks in her underwear.

I see her face, thinking this must be what love feels like.

It's getting warm under the bed sheet.

Both hands moving like when you pat your head and rub your tummy at the same time. The bedsprings squeak like in Dad's bedroom when he gets back from the Seven Stars on a Saturday night.

The memory of Jeannie getting clearer.

Her arms lifting up.

She looks back towards her house, knowing what's coming.

She laughs and crosses her arms to lift her dress.

Crossing her hands over, lifting the hem.

Right arm over the left.

Kneeling on the blanket beneath the apple tree. The skin on her neck, down to where her chest pushes frontways. The dark shadow between her curves, pressing into the white lace.

A slow wave rising.

A warmth from somewhere deep inside.

I'm scared by its promise but the moment for stopping has gone and I let myself ride on the cool wave.

A warm wetness under the blanket.

Sounds coming back.

Catching my breath as a new cold feeling sinks down through me and I wonder if I might be dying.

An emptiness in the place where the feeling just was, as if something bad has happened.

Across the room Grandma hisses angrily, 'Billy?'

I hold my breath and stay quiet.

'Billy?' she hisses again sharply, like the whip-crack of the belt she'd give when I was small and she could stand straight. 'I know what you're doing. God will send you to hell.'

I pretend to be asleep and listen to the pounding thumps of my heartbeat.

Before morning, I come up with a plan to go ballroom dancing with Jeannie and take her to Wormwood Scrubs.

I will cycle over to Norland Road as usual to help Mr Finlay unload the Billingsgate cart at five o'clock. My morning hello will not be my normal cheery one.

Mr Finlay will ask if everything's fine and I'll tell him I've been sick in the night but didn't want to let him down. I'll unload the boxes while clutching my stomach to look ill. He'll tell me to go home but I'll say I'm saving to buy a birthday present for my girlfriend.

I'll take two barrowloads over to Clem. When I return to Norland Road for the third, I'll tell Mr Finlay I've been sick again. He'll tell me to go home and get myself better. Instead, I'll have a wash in the public lavatories at the Metropolitan station.

I'll need to make sure Clem doesn't see me going into Mrs Chester's.

I'll pay for the lesson with money from the tin under my bed.

I'll say hello to Jeannie and will be standing next to her when Mrs Chester puts us into pairs. Gran once told me ballroom dancing is about flair and romance and counting in threes, all of which I've been thinking about and am ready for.

Afterwards I'll take her to Lyons coffee house on the green. We'll go to the fairground in White City and walk on the Scrubs, where I'll draw Clem's sketch to get her in the mood. We'll find a quiet place where she'll lift her slip and her petticoat and rub magic circles on my hips with her finger.

Early morning, and the plan is clear in my head.

I cycle to Norland Road for five o'clock to unload the cart for Mr Finlay.

I'm feeling ill from imagining I'm feeling ill.

Mr Finlay is sat on the side of the Billingsgate cart with his head in his hands. Boxes of fish stacked behind him in the sunlight, their dead eyes staring out from the crates.

People have been talking about the Hun marching through Belgium the last few days, though I've had other things on my mind. The Hun were told not to march through Belgium after all that business with the Archduke. It didn't mean much to me when I first heard about it, but now that my plan to go ballroom dancing with Jeannie is hanging in the balance, it's starting to look more serious.

Mr Finlay stays sat on the cart.

I'm doing my best to look ill.

I hold my tummy like I'm about to be sick, but Mr Finlay just says the Kaiser means trouble this time.

I decide to put off looking ill until Mr Finlay's cheered up a bit, and start loading the first barrow.

'Don't bother, son,' says Mr Finlay. 'Shepherd's Bush market's being used as barracks for soldiers heading off to France.'

Jack Burns arrives to load up Mr Finlay's stall in Norland Road. I wait for Mr Finlay to tell him not to bother, but Norland Road market is staying open despite the Hun in Belgium and Jack starts stacking boxes with the usual dozy expression on his face.

I ask Mr Finlay if Mrs Chester's ballroom dancing class has been turned into army barracks too, but he just says, 'Come back next week, Billy. We'll see what's happening then.'

Still working, Jack Burns grins at me.

Jack Burns, who's a divvy and steals Mr Finlay's fish to sell to doss-houses on the side.

Jack Burns, who Clem says is secretly Mr Finlay's son, after Mr Finlay knocked up Jack's ma a long time ago.

Jeannie, fading now.

The curve of her eyebrows and the rise of her little nose growing fainter.

I try to hold her here but she's getting smaller all the time, until she's nothing more than a tiny pinpoint of light, like a distant star in the morning sky.

Soon that will go too.

It may have already burned out years ago after travelling through the universe. A trick of the eye after everything else has gone, pressed onto the retina like the burning filament of a light bulb long after the eyelids have closed.

When I think of the others, like Evie and Vera and Betty Jackson, it wasn't a proper love I had for Jeannie. She was like the slow opening chords to a favourite song, a starter before the main course, an indicator of everything ahead.

This is why I thought of her just now. To remember how it felt, wanting an idea what love would feel like when it happened with the right person.

That first rush.

They can't all be for nothing, these memories.

Five

White vans are the only things moving on Hammersmith Grove. It's wet and grey out there, definitely autumn, and the plane trees on the pavement are losing their leaves.

A drip is about to fall from my runny nose, but it's too much of an effort to wipe it.

Jimmy Parris hasn't wasted any time talking to the new lady resident who just moved in. I don't know her name. She has thin straggles of grey hair and a face like a slapped arse, as Clem would have said, like she thinks she's too good for this place.

Like she didn't plan to end her days in The Cedars.

She looks proper old, like me.

Jimmy's gone to sit next to her when she probably wants to be left in peace, which is a shame as I fancied a word with Jimmy this afternoon. To see if he remembered the man with the ancient maps.

The schoolboy who comes once a week to push the shop trolley for the Duke of Edinburgh is doing his rounds today, in his shiny shoes and blazer, but there's nothing I need to buy. A small packet of tissues might not be a bad idea to stop this runny nose, but I don't have any coins with me and can't be arsed to go back to my room.

Mr Buffery is sleeping in his armchair the other side of

me. His breaths come and go in time with the passing traffic, like he's racing the vans through the rain.

I wonder if Mr Buffery is doing the same as me: filling in the gaps from long ago, retracing his steps and trying to remember what love feels like before it's too late.

Maybe when I've got all this down, some of the others in here might fancy using the typewriter, though Ros would have to check if her boyfriend needs it back.

Time is passing. I need to stop looking out at the day.

I would've liked a cup of tea but it isn't time yet otherwise Sylvie would have brought onc over.

I need to get a move on.

I press down on the chair with skeletal hands that used to be mine. I try pushing upwards, to stand under my own steam and shuffle over to the table. I raise my arms, feel the wood between my bony fingers and prepare to rise.

Something on the pavement catches my eye: a colour through the wet window.

Orange, maybe?

I'm halfway out of the chair, watching the colour take the shape of a ball, and decide to sit back down for a proper look. My arse is more bone than cushion these days. It falls into the seat, taking the breath I'd been saving for the rest of the climb.

Exhausted by the effort, I focus on the orange colour again, afraid it's been swallowed by grey light and white vans and the girl with the underwear who I'm not sure I was ever in love with.

A small boy on the pavement.

Like Archie.

As fragile on his legs as me, coat buttoned against the rain. His mother leans on the pushchair while he inspects something on the ground.

When you've had a boy of your own, you remember these moments.

I wonder what he's found? An ant or a bug scarpering from the rain perhaps. His reflection staring back from a puddle.

He holds his little hand in a fist beneath the orange ball above him.

A balloon on a string.

It hangs like a pretend moon glowing in the afternoon light. The boy's forgotten about his balloon for now. Eyes on the murky pavement below as if nothing else matters.

It's bollocks when they say youth is wasted on the young. Only a child takes that sort of interest in a speck on the ground.

His mother tugs him forward, a slow procession up the pavement. I follow their journey until a low wall hides him from view and all that remains is his mother's head and shoulders walking through the rain, an orange balloon floating beside her.

Getting up out of the chair is easier after the boy and the balloon lifted my spirits.

It'll take a while to get to the table, but I'd like to get things down while they're fresh in my head.

I'm holding them tight so I don't forget what they are when I get to the typewriter.

Ros's boyfriend says the hardest thing about writing is starting over each time you sit back down.

Watching a Zeppelin crash and burn on Brook Green, early summer 1915.

The mess of bricks and bodies.

The random injustice.

Returning with Harry to the bomb site later that night for a dig through the rubble; the glimmer of a small silver trinket, which I thought would make a good present for Jeannie until it felt like the wrong thing to be giving her and I dropped it into Hammersmith Creek instead.

Harry gets a ticket from his dad to see Marie Lloyd perform a recruitment concert at the Empire on Shepherd's Bush Green. He gets in first then slips his ticket to me through a lavvy window down the side of the Empire. I've not seen Harry much since he said Jeannie next door let him kiss her and then put her hand down his breeches in the garden.

I'm fifteen and have never been to a concert before. Harry reckons it's no big deal, but when Marie Lloyd sings through a haze of light and smoke, I'm thinking she's the most beautiful woman I've ever seen.

I tell Harry I'm thinking of joining up even though it hasn't crossed my mind until now.

Harry says, 'We're too young.'

The army barracks has closed Shepherd's Bush market and there isn't much work around. I tell him, 'I'll go if I want.'

Harry tells me I'm being a *melt*, so I push him in the chest and knock him into someone's table. He shoves me back.

I walk out of the big hall while Marie Lloyd is singing. In the foyer, lots of young men are milling around the recruitment tables. I ask the officer how old I need to be to join the Flying Corps.

He says I can sign up at eighteen and go overseas at nineteen. I stay quiet for a moment, and he asks, 'How old do you want to be, son?'

I tell him I'm eighteen.

He nods without looking impressed, even though he gets two shillings and sixpence for each new recruit, then pulls a sheet out of his file.

I write my name and address on the form. It takes a couple of goes to work out what my new date of birth should be, then I watch him stamp it.

I go back in to find Harry, but can't see him in the crowd, so I come out of the building onto the green and make my way back home instead, not sure I want to be friends with Harry Coggins any more if what he says about Jeannie is true.

A few weeks later, Ma has stood a letter with my name on it against the salt pot on the parlour table.

'What's this?' she asks when I come home.

I open the letter and put it down for her to read.

She holds her hand to her mouth and says, 'You're too young.'

I tell her it's what I want.

She starts to cry and turns to look out of the window.

She says, 'We'll see what your father says when he gets home.'

Later that night, Dad comes back steaming from the pub, reads the letter, shakes my hand and says, 'Son, you're a man now.'

I haven't seen Harry since the recruitment concert. I feel too old to sit in his tree den any more and shoot elderberries at his grumpy sister and her annoying friend next door.

Before Christmas, I get sent to Cambridgeshire to train as a cadet with No. 1 Balloon Company of the Royal Flying Corps, the air wing of the British Army. No one asks my age and I've got no birth certificate to prove it. I write no letters home as I'd only have to tell Ma I made a big mistake. At the end of April, I'm given a week's leave.

On the last day, I'm wearing my Flying Corps uniform before setting off to the South Downs for a month with the infantry, and then a boat to France. I bump into Peg on Hammersmith Grove. She says it's my last chance to see Harry before I go. I've felt sorry about our scrap at the Marie Lloyd concert. I'd also like to see Jeannie next door, as the other recruits say it's good to have a sweetheart to write to when you're overseas.

We're sixteen, Harry, Peg and me. Always the same as the century.

Peg says to walk with her under the railway bridge on Trussley Road.

She stops in the shadows and says she's proud of me. She asks if I'd like a look in her panties to remember her by. Afterwards she tries to kiss me, but someone walks under the bridge and we move away instead.

All the history in these streets.

I say goodbye to Peg on Hammersmith Grove and decide to go and see Harry in Notting Hill.

Mrs Coggins opens the door. It takes her a second to recognise me. She says I look nice in my uniform, that Harry's up in his tree den and do I want some lemon squash, which I politely refuse.

Harry doesn't mention my uniform. He says he'll only join up at eighteen if they make it law.

I ask how he is.

He tells me his uncle was shot in the Easter Rising in Dublin, defending the General Post Office against the British Army.

'Shot dead?' I ask.

Harry says he was wounded and forced to hide from the military police, who have orders to execute rebels on the run.

I tell him, 'Darker forces are at work in Europe.'

He says, 'You're talking like a cock.'

I ask what he thinks of the uniform.

He says he wouldn't wear it.

I tell him, 'Then you're either jealous or a coward.'

He says to say that again.

I tell him he's not brave enough to join.

He says, 'Fuck off out of my tree house then.'

I climb down the branches and tell Harry his grumpy sister Peg just showed me inside her panties under the railway bridge in Trussley Road and would have let me fuck her if someone hadn't walked by.

He doesn't know what to say to that.

I don't tell him I couldn't see much inside her knickers as it was already dark under the bridge, and couldn't think what to say to her about it afterwards.

Harry throws his pea-shooter at me but misses and I walk down his garden in my Royal Flying Corps uniform.

I say goodbye to his ma, trying not to look at the ugly snarl in her top lip.

She says to take care over there and shuts the door behind me.

It seems odd that Mrs Coggins is always waiting in the dark hallway, like she never knows which part of the house to be in.

Somewhere near Portsmouth, out drinking with four infantry boys from the North Yorkshire regiment.

Tomorrow we sail for France.

They rib me about the Royal Flying Corps not being a fighting unit and I rib them about their northern accents.

Me, Hoggsy, Pell, Jack Mulholland and Wilf Rutter, who everyone calls the Baron because of his Hun name. His dad's newspaper shop in Whitby keeps getting its windows smashed by locals who reckon his family are German spies. Wilf's dad had to buy adverts in the *Daily Express* saying they're a proper English family and God save the King.

We start in the Swan, then the Wheatsheaf. I stop reading pub signs after the Fox and Hounds.

One pub, then another.

Five of us drinking, pissing up country walls.

In a snug with three local girls. Hoggsy asks them to come with us for a walk.

I'm outside sucking cold air, needing to piss again. Catching up with the others but the three girls have got their arms around Hoggsy, Jack and Pell. The Baron's dropped behind and I'm thinking the two of us have missed our chance to get off with one of them. We all say we're nineteen but I reckon I'm not the only one who's lied about his age.

'You done it with a girl yet?' asks the Baron, stumbling drunk in the cold air.

'Of course,' I tell him, wondering if looking down Peg's knickers counts as doing it.

The country lane is quiet after the noise of the pub.

Hoggsy's girl is the best of the three, tall, like a willow branch, in a green summer dress. She looks too good for Hoggsy. Jack Mulholland has got his arm around the short, dark-haired girl, who's definitely better than the ugly one Pell's stuck with. Pell tries to sidle away from her but she's not letting go of her catch. He gives me a wide toothless grin, like he knows he's stuck with the fusty.

Clem always had something to say about girls like that.

It's our last night in England and we're making the best of it.

Footsteps crunch on the stones, down the quiet lane where the houses stop.

A field opens out under the black starry sky. The girls lean by a gate. The dark-haired one with Jack points to an old barn in the field. She says they want their shillings up front.

Hoggsy says it's too much, offers them eight pence and they settle for ten.

We root for the coins. Hoggsy's short and asks us to cough up for him. I'm not sure that's fair, but no one else complains.

We climb over the gate, walk down the muddy field towards the barn and up the steps to a door halfway up the wall. It pulls open and we go inside.

I'm shivering, but not from the chilly air.

The floorboards are dry and echo underfoot. The sound of animals rustling below.

The dark-haired girl says they'll see to the Baron and me when the others are done. She goes into a corner with Jack and I try not to watch them in the shadows.

Pell goes to the other corner with the ugly one. The attractive, willowy girl with Hoggsy opens a trapdoor in the floor. An animal moves about downstairs and Hoggsy says he isn't going down there.

'They don't bite,' she laughs.

'I'm fine up here.'

'It's just cows.'

'I'm not bein' watched by an animal while I'm doin' it.'

She drops the trapdoor with a bang.

I sit on the floor with my back to the wall, thinking of the boat that will take us to France tomorrow night. The Baron sits next to me with the smell of animals below getting stronger. I glance across at him.

He says, 'All right?'

I nod, and belch from too much beer.

A dusty pane of glass lets a smudge of moonlight into the chilly barn. I listen to the sound of loosened belts while nervously waiting my turn. No one's taken their clothes off yet. When the time comes, I'll want to see everything. I'll want to see her tits and her mingey otherwise it's not worth the money.

It'll be my first time and it has to be special. I don't mind going below, if that's what it takes to find out what a naked girl looks like.

Pell comes first.

Jack gives a cheer across the room and starts laughing, the pale cheeks of his arse above his trousers as he pushes into the dark-haired girl.

'Who's next?' says Pell's girl to the Baron and me while Pell does his buttons up. Her big chin drags her unhappy face forward, making her cheeks look like hamster's pouches.

The Baron says, 'He is,' pointing at me, and I can't think quick enough to say I'll wait for the pretty one by the trapdoor to finish with Hoggsy.

I try to stand but my legs have gone to sleep and I shuffle over like the animals we heard below.

I tell her I'm only doing it if we can go downstairs.

'Shy one, are you?' she says, and I know I don't like her at all. She says, 'I'm not climbing down there.'

'It's just cows,' I tell her, forcing a laugh.

She sighs, lifts the trapdoor and says for me to go first.

Jack grunts loudly in the other corner.

The pretty one asks Hoggsy, 'Is something the matter?'

I climb down and wait at the bottom of the ladder for the animals to settle.

The girl looks at me through the trapdoor then steps onto the ladder. Jack gives a noisy grunt upstairs and the Baron will be sweating knowing he's next, even though he bagged the attractive, willowy one.

I've thought about this for a long time.

The romance.

How it will be, who she is, what she looks like.

Not like this.

Knowing I have to see it through. My only chance if I don't come back from France.

She's nervous beside me away from the others. The animals have crowded into the far corner of the barn. I've only seen cows hung on hooks in the butchers' cold store. Alive, they're bigger and more frightened than I imagined.

My heart thuds and I wonder if I should tell her this is my first time, but I'd rather she didn't know that much about me.

She says, 'Get on with it then.'

I ask her to take her clothes off.

She says that's sixpence more.

I feel for the coin and hand it over.

She opens her blouse, takes off her skirt and lies back on the straw, but I've decided not to look at her face through any of this. She lies in front of me, pale on the ground.

I feel a thrill of the grown-up world, sensing the man I'm about to become but wanting to get it over with.

Her pale shape in the shadows below me. The curves of her skin and her pink blotchy flesh.

I see the horse meat for sale in the market.

I see red marks on her belly from Pell's belt buckle. I see where he's been. The noises he made. I see his toothless, grinning face and smell his odour on her neck. I see his sticky patches of spunk drying at the top of her legs.

My stomach rolls. The drink and the fear, ready to spill.

Disgust and disappointment rising in the bile.

I lurch forward and puke it out over her, sick in my nostrils, a burning ache in my throat.

She swears at me while pushing me off, wiping her skin with a handful of straw and crying as she puts her clothes back on.

One of the cows stands up behind her, looking at me through its black eye. Looking at a man face down in the straw.

Looking at me lying here and I'm thinking soon it too will be dead.

A few hours later, the five of us are sat together on a paddle steamer out of Portsmouth, hung-over, throwing up once more into the English Channel.

The cattle train through northern France smells like last night's barn. When the carriage doors are hauled open, the first thing I see is a vast pile of bloody clothes at the back of a hospital tent. The Baron nudges me and a closer look reveals a mound of arms, hands, legs and feet, hastily removed, waiting to be burned.

A stack of severed limbs, higher than a man.

A medical orderly folds back the canvas at the rear of the tent and throws a freshly sawn leg onto the pile. The limb rolls down the red mass and I'm suddenly aware how weak I really am.

I'm afraid to die this young.

Afraid I'll go home with parts of me missing.

Still a boy. Not yet a man.

And all the things I've never done.

It's late June 1916, but there's no summer in this part of the world. An endless line of pits dug into the earth. One long grave through the mud of France.

It's a bright morning next to a wood full of blood and sunlight and there are corpses piled up at the side of the road. Hundreds of thousands have already died, in places like Marne, Ypres and Verdun. Here we are now, four hundred of us marching to the Somme, a few Flying Corps cadets alongside a battalion of Yorkshire lads; the infantry friends I made in Portsmouth.

The lieutenant says we're ten miles from Bazentin Ridge, where we'll rest for the night.

Hoggsy, Pell, Jack Mulholland, the Baron and me, sheltering under a tree after a long march.

We watch the sky get dark.

The road on the other side of the trees will lead us to the front tomorrow, where we'll separate. The four of them into the mud, me floating above it.

I'll get back home in a year or so.

The lucky ones, just Hoggsy and me.

Not Jack Mulholland, Pell or the Baron, though.

All three of them dead in the next few days.

Jack Mulholland will crawl through enemy gunfire into a small trench where a British shell falls short of its target and explodes.

The lieutenant who marched us towards the front will lead the Baron across twenty feet of mud towards an enemy gun post. They'll kill seven Hun soldiers between them before getting shot by an English gunner who doesn't recognise their British uniforms.

Hoggsy will say the Baron should have put another advert in the *Daily Express*.

Pell will lie in a gully for three quarters of an hour beneath a German sentry. He'll think it's safe to glance over the edge for a recce and will get shot through the eye by the sniper waiting patiently for him to emerge. The bullet will make one small hole in the front of Pell's face and blow out the entire back of his head.

Leaving just Hoggsy and me, the lucky ones.

But now, the five of us shelter under a tree on our last night together.

Moonlight drips through the branches. Pell makes a brew on his Tommy cooker while we all sit quiet, thinking of moments from another life.

He hands me a mug, saying no Londoner ever made a decent cup of tea.

I try to make it last but it doesn't.

Pell reckons the best way to stay alive is to believe in luck. 'Some of us is just born lucky,' he says, and laughs.

I tell them I'll be keeping an eye on them from my observation balloon.

Pell tips out the dregs from his tin mug, grins through the gap in his teeth and says, 'That's us all fucked then.'

Six

Slowly the ground falls away.

The parachute harness digs into my shoulders and ribs, adding to the discomfort of the heavy flying jacket. I'm too warm now but I'll be grateful for it once we're up.

Flight Sergeant Cooper's face is not built for laughter, with heavy eyes and a big walrus moustache hiding his mouth, so it's a surprise when he tips me the wink as he bursts more flame from the burner and the earth drops from view.

He's just been promoted to captain but says to call him Flight for good luck.

I ask what happened to the last cadet.

He says, 'Same as what happened to the last captain,' and my first lesson is to not talk about what's gone before.

The basket pulls to the side in a harsh breeze, then swings back, still rising in the dawn air hanging between the kite balloon above and the cable below.

My stomach turns waiting for the first bullets to fly as we climb up, riding the early thermals.

Higher and higher, the rattle of the winch on the ground now gone.

The terror of waiting for a blast you know must come. I've trained for this above a green Cambridgeshire field, but no one there was trying to shoot me down.

An eerie silence, just the push and pull of air currents and the whine of a breeze bristling the steel cable beneath. We reach our observation altitude and the cable draws to a halt. The kite balloon holds steady above us, waiting for the day to begin.

The ground still smothered in last night's darkness.

Flight takes me through the routine. He says my young, fresh eyes are just what the doctor ordered.

The moon and stars have almost gone out.

A faint light breaks over the horizon and starts to define the land below. Flight takes out a small silver flask, offers me a sip of rum, but it's against the rules, so I decline.

He takes a swig and offers again. 'Beginner's luck,' he says, shaking the flask at me. 'Trust me, son, we'll need it.'

Voices don't belong up here.

His walrus moustache may hide most of his mouth but not the touch of madness in his eyes. He's done several months as flight sergeant in a kite balloon and it shows. Life expectancy up here is three months, so he knows he's on borrowed time. I remember what Pell said about believing you're one of the lucky ones. Flight Sergeant Cooper needs to share some fresh luck. He needs to reset the clock and get those three months back. I take a sip from the flask. The rum runs smooth down the back of my throat.

In the rising daylight I take a last glance at the map fixed to the side of the basket, then extinguish the small lantern beside it and study our sector of battlefield below. Some ground battles, like the one at Ypres, have been going on for the last two years, but our generals are confident the Somme will be regained within a matter of days.

I locate the landmarks first: the railway tracks through Mametz Wood directly below, running through Le Petit Wood at Bazentin and on to the town of Martinpuich.

Two hundred yards down the tracks I make out the first enemy line, south of Le Petit Wood; Villa trench to the north-west, the Bow and Flatiron trenches to the south-east, Circus trench a little further beyond. Another hundred yards north a second line gets dissected by the railway, with the Aston trench to the left and Forest trenches to the right. Beyond those I can make out the buildings of Bazentin and the road that bears west-north-west to Pozières.

Flight says, 'Someone's done his homework.'

He shows me where to look for the flash of distant artillery. I scan using the field glasses but he says the naked eye is more reliable if the eyesight's as fresh as mine.

I lick the last of the rum from the edge of my lips and try to forget we're a floating target suspended in the rising gloom of the French sky.

Small flashes of light off the ground beyond the little wood.

I say, 'Captain Cooper,' and immediately there's a dull crack and boom of shells from below. I don't know it yet, but this is the sound of my new infantry friends dying on the battlefield beneath us.

'See what you done now, dumb-arse,' he says. 'I said to call me Flight.'

I tell him I'll never call him Captain again.

He winks and says we need to spot where the flashes are coming from. His moustache bristles and he gives me a nod that makes me feel safer than I should, this high off the ground.

The sun climbs fully over the horizon and casts golden light on the other observation balloons a few hundred yards to our left and right, like a string of lamps hung up for target practice.

Nothing comes our way just yet.

'Lazy bastards are 'avin' a sleep-in,' says Flight Sergeant Cooper.

The sun rises another inch before its light gets sucked into thick clouds and the world turns grey again.

'Thank fuck for that,' he says. 'I'm happier when they switch the lights off.'

Figures like ants cluster on the black terrain below, too small to be real. Short blasts of fire quickly burn out. No human sound, no screams, just the solid dull boom of exploding shells.

I'm looking for flashes from a large gun beyond the ridge south-east of Pozières. Flight takes me through the noises as they happen: the sound of the big five-point-nine shells, like an express train steaming through a station; the whizz-bang of the seventy-seven millimetres, although our altitude is a little high for these; and the sigh and moan of the four-point-twos, which ring through the ear like a cymbal.

The day's brightening up again.

I locate a familiar sound among the explosions. It's been there a while but is only starting to filter through now: the barking of a lone dog, at war with all the rumpus.

My eyes follow the flat earth, charting the rise to the distant ridge, the orange glares and puffs of smoke, as I listen to the sound of cymbals, whizz-bangs and express trains.

Flight searches too, his eyes a little wilder than mine.

We look for prey like quiet birds. A shell rings across the cable below, too close for comfort, and the balloon pulls in its wake.

Flight smiles and says, 'Good, they've spotted us now.'

We don't have to wait long for another orange flare from the ground and a rising screech.

I'm stood at the edge of the basket, waiting to be smacked out of the sky.

I imagine falling, knowing I'm allowing myself the luxury of descending whole and not in pieces.

The next shell passes closer. Tension whines through the cable. The kite balloon bumps and drags as the winch below resets our altitude.

Still scanning though my field glasses, I ask Flight if they pull us down when it gets too close.

He laughs, still looking for flashes in the north-east.

I drop the field glasses and look past the buildings in Bazentin.

A tiny flash beyond the ridge, followed by another.

Flight says he can't see well enough that far away.

I focus on the map strapped inside our basket, selecting the coordinates carefully, knowing we're short of time. I call the bearings to Flight, who already has his flags out and is leaning over the side, arms wide, signalling the numbers down.

He wastes no time, quick and precise, one shape to the next.

I watch the ground crew confirm the numbers back.

The kite balloon a few hundred yards to the east bursts into bright orange flame. We watch it dissolve in fire and smoke. I picture the ground crew scattering to avoid the falling detritus, the bodies and the cable, but they're too far away to make out from here.

My hands are shaking and my feet have turned to ice.

Flight says to stay on the job.

A barrage of fire from our Lewis guns below brings me out of the blue funk. I watch the earth spit and fly thirty yards wide of the enemy guns we signalled.

I call the adjustment to Flight, who flags down the new coordinates. Another blast, closer this time.

I call a second adjustment.

Flight signals down.

The big enemy gun goes up. Ammunition fireworks.

I allow a tiny sense of victory, remembering my promise to my new infantry friends somewhere down below, unaware that Jack Mulholland is already dead.

Flight shakes my hand and says, 'There's your cherry, Billyboy, chalk it up.'

We scan the battlefield for more flashes, and Flight starts telling me about his wife and child.

This isn't what I want.

I'd like to remember what love feels like. To see Mary

again, to remember Evie and the rest of them. To be weightless and flying above the ground, but not up here, not like this.

Knowing, however, that it takes a down to come up, that good times follow bad.

So, December already, from summer to winter, six months later. Our three-month expectancy already twice survived, so we must be doing something right.

Flight and me, floating above the earth for half a year.

A love of sorts.

A different sector every few days, not that it makes much difference watching the ants dying on the ground below. Watching them smacked down and burned with fire.

The lame afternoon sun has almost given up the ghost.

A southerly wind picking up, dragging us over the battlefield below, the only advantage being able to see further beyond enemy lines. The ground black and dead. Nothing will grow here for years.

It's always cold this high, but winter is biting and no size of jacket or parachute pack keeps the chill out of the bones. We come down at the end of one day, shiver through a tiny bowl of rations, sleep for moments with the lice and the ice, locked into the cold, and come back up with the sun the next.

We scratch out the flea bites and shit out the cramps into a small bucket in the corner of the basket.

Eyes play tricks, seeing things that aren't there.

Not seeing things that are.

North of Verdun now, but everywhere looks the same these days. Trying to win back ground the Allies lost half a year ago.

Louvrement directly below, Beaumont a little further north.

Beaumont was once a nice little town apparently.

On a clear day you can see Ornes and Bezonvaux a couple of miles north-east.

The rotting bones and charred flesh of half a million men below us.

The air freezing the lungs.

Not even Flight has rum these days, but we pass the flask to keep the luck going.

We pretend and say cheers.

Lucky a long time now, and the odds are getting shorter.

'Once more round the block and we're done for the day,' says Flight with the sun going down.

He scans west to north in the darkening sky. I take east to north, then home to empty the shit bucket, feed the fleas and come back up in the morning.

New machines on the landscape: three German tanks over the ridge.

Flight signals their position and something catches my eye. I touch Flight's arm and point to the large bird circling above.

'Heron,' says Flight, very quiet.

We rarely see birds up here. There's nothing in this part of the sky for them but noise. It glides, long neck stretched and wings wide, then turns above us, just feet away. A rare moment of good fortune.

The sun drops to shine on better parts of the world and I signal down to the ground crew to haul us in. Flight says to call him Francis and picks at something in his moustache.

'Francis Randolph Cooper,' he says, like he's lord of the manor.

I laugh and wait for him to share the joke. It would be wrong, of course, after all this time together, to change our names. He's Flight and I'm Billyboy. We don't make changes. We go up and we come back down.

We don't mess with the luck.

He repeats, 'Francis Randolph,' like he's just heard his own name for the first time. He licks his lips as if he's eaten something delicious.

The winch hasn't yet started drawing us in, so I signal over the edge of the basket again.

'Francis Randolph Cooper,' says Flight.

He repeats, 'Coo-per,' stretching out his name longer than a cat's purr.

I ask if he's all right and tell him to crouch down in the basket until we're back.

He stands at the edge like Napoleon, and says, 'Gone now.'

I wonder if he's referring to the heron.

I say, 'What the fuck are they waiting for down there!'

The crack comes from nowhere and everywhere at the same time.

Hiss and boom, air and drums.

The basket tips with a jolt, swings ferociously at ninety degrees to the horizon, and my belly loses sense of where the ground is. The grey skin of the kite balloon is falling in shreds. A bright orange ball of flame ignites in a rage of heat, then disappears. The basket hangs impossibly onto thin air for the smallest fraction of time, then drops with unruly force.

Flight and me, both still alive in the basket, whole and not in pieces. I'm holding the side, hoping the parachutes are packed right, that this will be the heron's good fortune. Flight tries to grab me but is thrown clear of the basket, on his way down.

The basket tips up and I'm suspended one final moment before falling head first, feeling for my parachute cord. The shoulder straps, slackened for comfort, have slipped and the thigh hoops are down by my knees. I try to kick the harness into place. My hand finds the toggle, pulls at it, but I'm still turning as the parachute opens.

I look for the green umbrella spinning above me as the cords twist around my neck.

Knowing the choke will come before the sheet can bloom.

I wait and I wait.

It lashes my neck like a knife.

Breath gone. Tongue and eyeballs.

I bang and jolt, bouncing through the air.

The parachute collapses and spreads in a failing flutter. My legs swing full circle and hold still, long enough for the straps to slip off. Nothing to keep me up now.

I spin an arc through the air, blood up my arms from the rope cuts in my neck as the air floods into my lungs.

Free of my parachute, knowing this is how I die.

Everything is upside down. The earth the wrong way up.

Falling upwards to the ground above, the parachute cords flailing below like the trails of a jellyfish.

I glimpse Flight's parachute in full bloom. He'll see me die as I crash past on my way to the ground.

He'll see me smash and bury myself in an instant grave, two feet down through the mud.

I think of the people I've loved.

Jeannie in the garden, lifting her slip. Walking through the market to Mrs Chester's dancing lessons with a sweet in her cheek.

Peg in the shadows under the railway bridge in Trussley Road.

Harry when I called him a coward for not wanting to come here to die.

The girl in the cowshed, paid sixpence extra so I could see everything.

Braced for impact, I think of these tiny moments, knowing it wasn't enough.

The touch of death comes softer than I imagined.

No mud and dirt, no blood or crunch of bones.

I pass into a green blanket, enveloped in a cold shroud.

All the air has gone.

I'm unwrapped, then Flight Sergeant Cooper catches my arms in his hands, looks into my eyes and says, 'I got you, Billyboy, hold on, son.'

Fifty feet up, coming down quick.

Two of us hanging under Flight's parachute, my life in the grip of his palms.

His fingers slip as the ground moves underneath with the wind rushing up towards us.

Flight Sergeant Cooper's fingernails dig into my wrists, his eyes wide with the strain as I wrap my hands around his and he shouts, 'Don't fuckin' let go now.'

We're too heavy and falling fast. He grips hard and starts to laugh under his big walrus moustache as the ground races up towards us.

The crash comes like a hammer, like a collision of bells from a church roof.

An audible snap like firewood in a grate and a soft fizz passing by.

The rush of air has stopped.

The inside of my eyes shines purple, while the nerve endings in my feet play like an orchestra at the end of a concert.

We roll over in soft mud under the collapsing parachute.

The blood in my ears hisses like steam as my hands clutch the cold earth, and at last I know I am safe.

Seven

The snap was the sound of my right leg hitting the ground, the fizz was the first bullet entering the same thigh and exiting the other side. A second bullet splinters above the ankle on the same foot. I'm looking down as it happens, watching the spray of bone and blood.

Flight shouts at me but I can't hear above the noise.

I'm yanked by the arms and dragged through mud. My broken leg smacks against the ground and the pain takes me to a place where nothing is real any more. The ground drops into a hollow trench where we slide to a stop. I'm lying behind Flight with the four Canadians who pulled us here. They start to laugh at the madness of everyone being alive.

'Top jump, lads! Everything stopped, watching you come down. First peace we had all day.'

Flight touches my shoulder like my dad when he's being nice. He says something to the men and shakes their hands.

A smell I can't place.

There are tunic buttons stuck in the ground beside me, lost in the fighting. I try to pick one up as a keepsake, but my fingers don't feel anything.

The smell leads me to the meat stalls in the market when the sun's going down, when the stray dogs linger hoping to be thrown a rank cut.

The tunic is worn by a dead man sunk in the mud underneath me.

Across the gully, another man sits quiet, arms around his legs, at ease. It takes a moment to notice his head has gone. I look to see if I can find it for him and throw up where I lie.

Three Canadians move off. The fourth wraps a field dressing round my leg. He says we might be here a while, takes the rifle from the headless corpse and puts it in my hands.

'No ammo, but you got a bayonet, just in case,' he says before disappearing with the others. Gunfire cracks above us.

I'm shivering from the messages being sent through my body.

I want to throw up again but there's nothing to come out. I'm hoping it will take away the hurt from my trailing leg, but that wish fails to come true. It feels like I'm being tossed around on a freezing, boiling sea.

Flight wriggles down beside me and hugs me for warmth. His arms wrap around my chest. He holds on tight.

He tells me I have to stay awake.

He says, 'We'll be here for the night.'

The freezing night becomes morning, then another freezing day.

Sometime later it turns into night again.

I'm not sure how long I'm lying here.

I stare up at the Very lights exploding in the sky, lighting the ground for a few seconds. The fireworks fall back down, lost among shells and gunfire.

Flight reaches into his breast pocket. He takes out a pencil and notepaper and writes his address at the top.

He tells me he's writing to his wife.

He writes without stopping to think of words. They seem to come with ease. I think of his family waiting for him at home.

This must be what love is: thinking of words without effort. Saying the right thing without struggling for thoughts.

When he's finished scribbling, I watch him quietly read it back.

He folds the letter, puts it in his top pocket and offers me his pencil.

'Someone to write to, Billyboy? Your mum, or a sweetheart?'

I shake my head.

'No one's coming, Billy. We have to get ourselves home.'

The hope in his voice makes me despair.

'I'm going to look, see what's what. I'll come back. I need to look around first.'

I beg him not to go, leaving me with the headless corpse and the dead soldier with the silver buttons, but no words come.

I've forgotten how to move anything and I'm not sure what works any more, so instead I watch Flight crawl away on his belly until he's gone from view.

If I stay still, in time I might shrink to nothing.

'Billyboy . . .'

I wake in the middle of a night.

'Let's go, son.'

My leg doesn't move.

'I'll pull. Push with your good foot.'

I can't move my leg.

'We have to go now.'

I can't move my leg so I close my eyes to shut every-thing out.

He grabs my tunic.

'Billy, wake up and move your fuckin' leg.'

I'm sixteen. He's old enough to be my dad.

'Good lad, Billyboy.'

He pulls and the ground gives me up. The dead man relinquishes his grip and the silver buttons stay sucked in the earth.

The smashed bones in my leg shift as Flight pulls me away.

We drop down into another trench, to another pile of human leftovers.

Some parts are still alive.

Flight drags me behind him, one arm pull at a time. A man sits with his back against the trench wall, smiling at me. His legs are bent the wrong way out, like a stilt-walker taking a rest at the circus. I can't tell if he's dead or alive.

More Very lights shower above us.

Flight points silently to a gully on our right. He pulls me over the lip and we wriggle forward until we're almost level with the ground.

At some point of the night everything goes quiet.

Flight peers over the edge and pulls me up to show what he's looking at. A patch of ground with bushes for cover.

The silence is hard to take. I want noise to fill my head

78

with sound. Flight takes a rifle from one of the dead men. He pulls out his compass, then releases the safety catch of the rifle. He checks the chamber before quietly snapping it back, then takes the Webley pistol from his belt and hands it to me. He puts his face next to mine and speaks in a harsh whisper.

'We're going over. Hold my feet, I'll drag you behind.'

He looks across the terrain, then back at me. He signals the Hun trench alongside us and whispers, 'Keep low, hold tight.'

Each movement a blunt stab to the leg.

I clutch the pistol in one hand and hold onto his feet with the other.

Flight slides over the lip into the path of the guns.

I wait for the air to fill with bullets.

I wait for his death to come first, then mine, which I'll welcome.

My hands on Flight's boot as he pulls me along, a slow crawl through scrubland like two parts of a broken worm. Branches tear my face as my ankle hammers the ground.

Flight stops to listen for a noise.

I look to the side, afraid of movement.

We wait.

He pulls me forward again, but I'm stuck in the mud, a ring of barbed wire tangled around my knee.

Flight pulls hard. The barbs tear at the flesh in my leg but I don't sense anything above the roaring ankle. He reaches back, unhooks the wire and pulls again. This time the wire flies free, leaving just a coldness in the bones.

*

Time is passing.

A patch of burnt ground over a small ridge, a German trench on our right.

More barbed wire and a hollow in the ground to our left, a ridge into a gully twenty feet wide, away from the enemy.

Flight inches us towards the hollow. The pain in my leg comes in waves. I hope for bullets with each smothering wash.

My whole body has started shaking.

I press my mouth to my shoulder to stop the noise escaping. I want to let it all go, to call out and bring this to an end.

I decide to give up hope of getting home and let go of Flight's boot. He can go without me.

Flight looks back. I shake my head. I'm at the end and can't go no further.

He shuffles around, eyes towards the Hun soldiers, who still haven't seen us.

He tries pulling me forward with both his arms.

I dig my good foot into the ground, but he pulls again. I dig hard and he yanks me forward like a madman.

My body twists in the mud, facing the sky now, and moments later we're over the ridge and sliding down into the small hollow, away from the German trench.

We come to a stop by a thicket, a lone bush running through the middle of the gully. A hawthorn, I think, blackened by fire but showing signs of life. A thing of beauty in a frozen landscape.

The sound of our breathing comes back.

Flight tells me to wait under the hawthorn bush. He checks my pistol and wraps my fingers around it.

He says, 'No stoppin' us now, Billyboy, this close to home.'

He holds a small map of the trenches in his hand, torn and grubby, which he studies hard. I try to ask where he got it, but only a bubble of spit forms on my lips and no words come out.

He points to the other side of the gully and indicates to keep watch while he has a recce.

I try to stop him leaving. I say, 'Captain,' but he's crawling past the hawthorn bush to the far edge of our little gully in no-man's-land.

I've become old in the space of a few months. I want to go home and grow young again.

I decide to let my head go somewhere else until Flight gets back.

A tram rattles beside me up Shepherd's Bush Green, over tracks my dad laid. Cycling up the west side of the green, left onto the Uxbridge Road. Past St Stephen's Church.

I don't know if I'm remembering all this now, an old man in an armchair in an old folk's home on Hammersmith Grove, or a sixteen-year-old boy hallucinating in the mud of the Somme.

The bicycle hums comfortably beneath me over the tram tracks my father built. The whir of the chain off the pedals. A piece of grit kicks up off the front wheel into my eye and I can't see too well.

A soldier appears around the hawthorn bush on his knees, at the place where Flight Sergeant Cooper was only moments ago. His uniform is caked with mud, eyes wild with excited fury, but he's not stopping us now, not when we're this close to home.

Bang bang.

Two gunshots crack off the mud walls and a solitary bird flaps out of the bush as if it were the final straw.

I listen to it fly off with the ebbing warmth of the pistol in my hand.

The soldier on his knees, hands pressing the bullet holes in his chest.

A large walrus moustache, just like the man who caught me falling from the sky, held me warm and dragged me through mud for two days.

I'm wondering where Flight has gone to.

A look of shock and pity in the man's eyes.

This close to home.

He crumples down and rolls onto his back, blood pumping through his tunic.

Red bubbles rise and pop at the corner of his lips. I watch the effort it takes him to swallow, gulping an uphill breath.

Noises in his throat.

The tip of his tongue trying to find wetness in his dry mouth.

His eyes swivel to look at me.

Last few breaths, in and out.

He waits and he waits.

It takes a long time.

Flight Sergeant Cooper takes one last sip of air and lets it go.

Dead eyes staring up, like the fish on Mr Finlay's market stall.

I don't know where I am or what day it is.

I reach into Flight's tunic pocket and take out the letter he wrote to his wife.

I break off a small branch from the hawthorn, pull myself past the bush and up the other side of the gully. It's a struggle to move without help.

I peer over the edge of the gully at what Flight would have seen before he died: a British flag twenty feet away. A short crawl to England.

He said we'd make it back.

I'll deliver the letter to his wife.

I whistle for attention and wave the hawthorn branch. I can't think of the word for 'English', so instead call out 'London' in a harsh whisper.

A whistle comes back.

An infantryman signals to crawl towards him. I haul myself over the lip of the hollow onto the black earth.

He throws me a rope.

I take hold of the end and he drags me home.

Eight

Ros says getting old isn't for wimps.

You've no idea what it'll be like when you're young but you can't live your life knowing how you'll end up. You have to take youth for granted otherwise you'd be a pain in the arse always banging on about appreciating what you've got.

With some residents here it's easy to tell what they looked like when they were young. Mrs Elliot, for instance. Beyond the grey skin and milky eyes you can tell she was a cracker in her day. A right sort, she once would have been. Mr Ozturk still looks like a ten-year-old, though that's probably because he's kept all his hair.

Others gave it all up long ago and chose to become old. Like Mrs Bentley and her dead eyes or the new lady resident with the thin straggles of grey hair who just moved in. They stopped trying to be young and now look like they've been old all their lives.

I'm one of those, I reckon, seeing my face in the mirror these days. I don't remember what I used to look like. Same as most of us here, I suppose. Bent over like hooks, shuffling about in our wheelchairs and walking frames.

Those taut, beautiful women lost to patchwork cheeks, big hips and comfy clothes. Fit, proud men hollowed out like pea-shooters, with turkey jowls and saliva down the lapels of an old jacket.

A sorry sight, the lot of us.

I'm feeling tired today.

I wanted to remember my first love, Mary, but she's refusing to come back from the dusty corners of my mind.

A few weeks in a field hospital somewhere near Reims. Christmas is just a word in a morphine haze. Dreams of waking without a leg, haunted by the bloody pile of limbs we saw when we first got off the train.

Haunted by Pell, Jack Mulholland and the Baron.

Haunted by Flight emerging round the hawthorn bush, out of the blue like that.

Haunted by the pull of the trigger.

Bang bang.

Each time I wake, my leg is still there.

A steamer brings me back across the Channel with the other lucky ones going home. All with something missing. All with gaps to fill.

Flight Sergeant Cooper sits out on the deck under grey winter skies, a blanket for warmth, keeping his thoughts to himself.

His letter in my pocket now.

He looks out at the sea, madness in his eye, then *bang bang*, he's gone.

Getting into Felixstowe docks and seeing the terrified faces of young soldiers waiting to board the steamer back to France.

No one to greet us at the jetty.

No waving flags. Told we're not going home until we've been fixed up. Until we're not such a sight to put off the new recruits.

I'm lifted onto a carriage of broken soldiers.

The train rattles and steams. Each set of points jars my broken bones. It's an age to the next painkiller.

Several hours later, unloaded onto a makeshift platform in a field in Suffolk, into an old country house, now a hospital for recuperation.

Rows of beds.

Men in bandages, missing parts with gaps to fill.

The smell of antiseptic and piss.

Blinds over the windows so night and day are one.

Two nurses who refuse to smile and who make you move when you want to lie still.

It's January 1917 and time is passing.

Cutting back the morphine so the world comes crawling back.

Going home with a letter in my pocket.

One of the lucky ones.

Spring 1917.

History tells me the war keeps going for another year and a half, but these details have no bearing on remembering what love was like.

A train to London, miraculously two-footed, the right not so good when it rains.

At Liverpool Street I wait for the other passengers to get

off before making my way to a bus for Marble Arch and Shepherd's Bush.

I've thought about this journey, up in the basket under the kite balloon over Bazentin, in the mud of the Somme, waiting for Flight behind a hawthorn bush in no-man's-land.

Home through Bayswater and Holland Park. Wondering what Harry Coggins is doing now. Aware of a distant falling-out, but it seems inconsequential in the face of everything. A childhood spat, easily fixed when I find the courage to see him.

Past Norland Road market, busy with shoppers despite what's happening elsewhere. Past the daytime drunks sleeping in the spring sunshine on Shepherd's Bush Green.

The market still closed.

A Metropolitan train thunders over the bridge on Goldhawk Road.

A pile of rubble in the middle of a terrace like the gap in Pell's teeth.

It takes a while to get my legs out from the seat at Paddenswick Road. The bus driver shouts, 'I haven't got all day.'

Slow steps to Trafalgar Street.

It was never this far before.

A gentle rain starts to fall, a thin film of grease on my hands and face.

My crutches tap and slip on the cobbles beside Hammersmith Creek.

Sharp pain in my right leg from walking this far. The

front door of the house is bolted inside. I bang the knocker but no one comes.

I make my way back up the street then down the alley behind the houses.

One of my crutches slips on the cobbles but I jam the other at the wall to stop me falling.

I'm trying to recall which is ours but the houses have lost their shape.

A gatepost holds me up.

I call out for Ma.

Flight Sergeant Cooper floating in the basket beside me.

No stopping us now, this close to home.

My crutches slip again and I'm dropping down without my parachute.

No warm shroud, no arms to grab me.

Down onto cold stones.

It feels slow but happens fast.

I reach for the hawthorn bush, but there's just a green gate and a brick wall. A patch of nettles and a smear of dog shit.

Loose stones and broken glass pepper my cheek.

This will have to do.

I close my eyes and at last I'm home.

I'm trying to remember home.

The place you feel safe when you're small. Before the world drags you up and you start to make one of your own. When you buy curtains for the first time and plant tomato seeds in your greenhouse. You dig carrots and potatoes and feel like a proper grown-up, with your own patch of soil to work on. A tiny square of earth that's yours.

If you're lucky, you share it with someone, and when they're gone, when that love is over, you must start again.

Coming home to the one you love. Where everything is as it should be.

I wake in my father's armchair.

Ma found me face down in the alley. A neighbour told her a stranger had been acting suspiciously by the front door. Her eyes are wet from crying. She looks older since I went away.

A message has been sent to my dad in the pub, but it's dark by the time he gets back. He stumbles into the sitting room wearing the same jacket and tie.

Ma says, 'Look what the cat dragged in.'

Dad shuffles in the doorway, wipes his forehead and says, 'Another bloody mouth to feed.'

Grandma died while I was away but no one in my house writes letters so it's news to me.

Ma asks what it was like but I'm my father's son and no beans are spilled.

Dad tells me I'll need to work now I'm back.

Ma says I've only just got home.

We sit in silence listening to the ticking of the clock until I decide to go to bed.

After Gran died, they rented out my room to one of Dad's relatives, a second cousin he bumped into in the Seven Stars, apparently, though Ma never heard Dad mention a second cousin before.

Ma brings out the small partition kept in the outhouse since Gran died and gives it a wipe-down. An hour later, a large man crashes drunkenly into the bedroom. He drops his breeches and shoes on the floor and clatters into bed. I listen to the sound of his snoring, like the rumble of a far-away train.

Summer 1917 and bombs are falling.

Liverpool Street station is demolished by German planes, killing a hundred and sixty people.

Destruction is normal and we're becoming immune to the numbers.

Mr Finlay has gone from Norland Road market and word is Clem's in prison, but there's plenty of rebuilding work and I'm already walking better.

Dad isn't happy when Ma tells him to ask about a job at George Wimpey's for me, until he realises it would mean a little more money in the house for food.

We walk together down Hammersmith Creek in the early-morning sunlight, past a barge unloading crates onto the wharf. It's the only time we've walked a distance together as two men and he doesn't speak the whole way. Along Glenthorne Road and up to Wimpey's yard on Hammersmith Grove.

I'm happy to be able to show my dad I can work hard

too. Maybe take him for a beer in the Seven Stars when we finish for the day.

The manager gives me a solid handshake as Dad heads over to his gang waiting by the cart with the asphalt burner. He shows me into the hut with photographs of Hammersmith Town Hall, and the White City stadium they built for the 1908 Olympics.

The manager tells the ladies to show me the ropes. I ask when I can go out with the cart, but he says he's got enough labourers and my dad told him my leg wasn't up to scratch in any case.

The ladies say it'll be nice to have a young man about the place. Through the little window I watch Dad loading up the aggregate.

Time goes slow inside the hut.

The office ladies sit and potter like well-dressed ferrets.

A noise in my head I can't get rid of.

I stamp the morning post and carry tea to the ladies in the other hut. I refill the paraffin lamps and screw the pencil sharpener down to the table. Loose files go into boxes in the cupboards.

By quarter past eleven I've done my tasks. I fetch the dirty teacups from upstairs and give them a clean. One of the ladies brushes glue from a large tin onto the back of new regulation posters.

I reach across to pick up her empty cup and saucer. The smell of glue like cordite from a gun with the teacup frail in my fingers. I watch it fall like it's something from the future. A time will come when it will hit the ground and smash into pieces.

BANG

He comes from nowhere on his knees, like an enemy, out from behind the hawthorn—

CLICK

The chamber turns, finger on the trigger—

BANG

Stop him before he stops me—

CLICK

The chamber turns, he goes down slow.

No stoppin' us now, Billyboy.

Warm oil on my palm from the gun.

Flight Sergeant Cooper brings his hands up to stop the blood.

He looks into my eyes, knowing he shouldn't have come out quick like that.

This close to home.

His last words.

I stagger into the sunlight, down the steps and across the builder's yard.

Up Hammersmith Grove to Shepherd's Bush Green with the daytime drunks and a bottle of rum from somewhere.

A policeman finds me later that evening and brings me home.

Dad comes back from the pub yelling that I made a tit of him in front of his boss. He says, 'What sort of man are you?'

I want to tell him I'm the sort of man who fell out of the sky, got caught by the arms, and dragged through the mud by my flight sergeant, who called me Billyboy and then pulled me home with his feet. Who stepped out too quick from behind a hawthorn bush after writing a letter to his wife, which I've kept in a tin upstairs.

Instead I keep it all in.

Instead I make a promise that when I have my own son, I'll tell him everything. I'll put it all down on paper for him and let him decide the sort of man I am.

I take out Flight's letter to his wife from under my bed but it feels too soon to open up a wound like that. First I have to find Harry Coggins. At seventeen, we're both still too young to join the army, but I wonder if he's changed since I last saw him.

I take the bus to Holland Park and walk through Portobello without my stick because I don't want to look like I've come for sympathy.

There are boards over the windows of Harry's house and a pile of rubble out front. Two planks of wood across the gate in front of the door. I climb over and peer through the boards. The front wall is there but the roof has gone. The stairs are standing, leading only to clouds. Just light and rubble where the rest of the building used to be. I can see all the way through to the tree at the rear of the garden.

The upstairs windows are as cold as Harry's mother's eyes. The back walls open, like Pell face down in the mud.

A woman stops to ask if I'm all right, but I'm not in a place for bad news so I walk back down the street to go home.

Time is passing.

A warm evening, and the White City fairground is open for summer, unfazed by the horrors in the rest of the world.

Harry once told me fortune-tellers were a con, that his dad employs them in his fairs and circuses. They eavesdrop on punters before coming in and get colleagues to ask questions on what they'd like the fortune-teller to talk about: a dead relative or something about their future maybe. Most people just want to hear about tall dark strangers and true love because they wish their lives would get better.

Harry said people who go to fortune-tellers believe in it the way others believe in God.

Behind the merry-go-round I spot a small caravan next to a horses' paddock. A painted sign outside has a picture of a woman with long dark hair and a crystal ball. A veil over her mouth makes her look mysterious. The sign says, *Be amazed by the world-famous Madame Rosa.*

I knock on her door and a foreign voice says to come in.

It's dark and warm inside her tiny wagon. Curtains are drawn across the small window and a candle flickers on the green baize table in front of Madame Rosa. She wears her veil that reveals just her eyes, framed by her long black hair. A kettle simmers on a small pot-bellied stove. She looks like she's already seen something terrible and tells me to sit down.

She says to cross her palm with silver.

I put a coin in her hand.

She asks why I've come.

Through the grille in the roof of the caravan I can see a tiny slice of sky. I tell her I want to know my fortune.

She doesn't ask my name but stares at the lines on my palm.

She says, 'You will live a very long time.'

She tells me I've lost many friends and my heart is full of sadness. She knows because her heart is full of sadness too.

I ask her why her heart is full of sadness.

She hesitates a moment, then tells me she lost her children, her eyes fixed at me over the veil.

She turns over my other palm and counts the lines out loud.

'One. Two. Three. Four. Five.'

She waits before she speaks again.

'Five lovers,' she tells me.

I wonder which country she's from.

'You will live a very long life, Billy. And in that time you will love five people.'

Lying in my bed that night, my dad's drunken second cousin snoring on the other side of the room, I twist my foot around the bed sheet and think about those five people I will love. Who they are and what they're doing now.

I think about why Madame Rosa would tell me about the sadness in her own heart, and how she knew my name.

The next evening, she's sat in her little caravan with the candle burning, like she hasn't moved since the night before.

'Both of them?' I ask. 'Harry and Peg?'

She sits in silence.

'Mrs Coggins? Are Harry and Peg both dead?'

She wipes a tear and drops her head into her hands in silence.

I tell her about seeing the bomb site when I went to find Harry.

She speaks in a whisper, as if the fake accent was the part of the disguise making her brave. 'Harry went missing in action six months ago.'

She looks up at the tiny grille in the roof and says he joined up after I'd gone.

Jealous or a coward.

'I was in the hallway with the letter in my hand, saying he was missing in action near the Belgian border, when a bomb from a Zeppelin fell through the roof. Peggy was in the sitting room at the time.'

Her voice matter-of-fact, eyes dead over the top of her veil.

'If it had exploded, it would have killed me too.'

Both on the same day.

I want to ask if she's only become a fortune-teller since losing her children. If it's true that I'll live a long life and love five people, or she made that up to please me.

A knock on the caravan door. She walks over, opens it a little way and tells a young man with bright red hair to come back tomorrow.

He mutters something quietly and goes.

She follows him out and comes back with her painted sign, shuts the wagon door and asks if I'd do something for her.

She asks me to read her fortune.

*

The lid of the tea tin shows a man with rosy cheeks and a wide grin. His face is red, like Dad's when he's back from the Seven Stars, with a tunic fastened all the way up his neck.

I wonder if there's a letter in his pocket.

She tells me to spoon tea leaves into the pot and pour in water from the kettle.

The teacup is white, with small pink roses on the side.

I pour in the tea and watch the leaves settle. I put the pot back on the stove and sit in front of her. She looks unhappy in the candlelight and I'm not sure it's a good idea to be doing this for Mrs Coggins.

She drinks the tea and tips the dregs into the saucer.

I'd like to make it better for her and think about what she'd like me to say.

'What do you see, Billy?'

Should I give her hope that Harry's alive or tell her people only ever come back in pieces?

'What do you see?'

'You already know, Mrs Coggins. You don't need me to tell you.'

She looks at me with eyes of fury and loss.

I hold her gaze and then look for shapes in her tea leaves.

I start getting hard in my trousers.

Peg and Jeannie, in their slips and petticoats under the apple tree.

'Tell me what you see.'

Flight Sergeant Cooper in the basket behind her.

A shape begins to form in the leaves.

'I see a large bird. A heron. It's looking for something on the ground below.'

Her eyes cold over the veil. She says, 'Good.'

I look harder, wanting to get this right.

'Its wings are spread wide.'

She takes a deep breath, in then out.

'I can't see what's on the ground.'

'How does this bird make you feel, Billy?'

'I'm happy it's there.'

She touches the back of my hand and says, 'We can see better in the darkness.'

She snuffs out the candle with her fingers.

She tells me to stand beside her.

I walk around the table next to her.

Her hand brushes my leg and she looks up like it wasn't an accident.

Mrs Coggins undoes the buttons on my trousers, puts her hand inside and holds me in her fingers. She starts to rub me slowly, not fast like I do it, which gives me time to think about these new feelings.

I want to tell her this is my first time, not counting a drunken fumble with an unhappy girl in a cowshed, but she puts her finger to my lips.

I reckon she wants to think how important this moment is for her too.

I try to pull my trousers down but she draws them back up, looks at the door and says quietly, 'In case we need you dressed, quicksticks.'

I try to kiss her but she turns away and my teeth bang into her cheek. I realise how clumsy I am at this.

She stands, perches against her table and lifts her skirt. My bad ankle tenses with the strain.

She squeezes hard where the skin pulls back. My eyes water and I don't want her to think I'm crying. She puts me inside her. I want to tell her how important this moment is for me but she holds my head against her shoulder, which stops me making any sound.

Flight Sergeant Cooper is on the other side of the table. I close my eyes but he holds tight under the parachute and won't let go.

I got you, Billyboy.

A long way down to the ground.

Bang bang.

On my feet, pushing inside Mrs Coggins, but the pain in my ankle takes my head somewhere else.

A sound buried deep. I'm not sure if it's me or her.

Mrs Coggins stops moving but I can't stop the pain.

Another cry from far away.

'It's my fault,' I tell her, tears starting to fall. 'I made Harry go.'

She holds the back of my head and tells me to shush.

The crying comes in sudden heaves. She smothers my face in her neck and wraps her hand over my mouth to quiet the noises. She quickly pulls my trousers up before the caravan door opens. A man with dark hair and a beard peers into the darkness.

'Mary?' he calls.

She looks at Mr Coggins and says, 'It's Harry's friend Billy, back from France. Poor love didn't know.'

Mr Coggins closes the door without another word.

She waits for the hush.

My heart beats loudly and Mrs Coggins reaches into my trousers and starts rubbing me again with her hand.

'He won't be back now,' she says, pushing me onto the floor of her little wagon.

'Mrs Coggins . . .'

'Call me Mary,' she whispers.

She pulls my trousers down to my ankles, crouches over me and lifts her skirt at the front with my knees pressing against her back.

I see her face better now with the weight off my ankle. She looks beautiful from here.

She guides me in with her hand then sinks down onto me. I've seen this silhouette before: Clem's drawing of two Vs, her thighs and mine, the stick and the fuzz.

She takes off her gypsy veil.

Her face looks different now. Even the ugly snarl in her mouth looks beautiful in the dim light. The moon is framed in the grille in the caravan's roof above her. It glows behind her head like a halo.

In a moment, the thought occurs: I'm only seventeen years old and after Mary Coggins I will only have four people left to love over my long, long life.

The next day, I buy a small bunch of pink roses from a flower stall in the market, like the ones painted on her cup and saucer. At the fairground, Mrs Coggins is busy reading someone else's fortune, so I wait near the horses' paddock for her to finish.

Sometime later, the red-haired young man who knocked on her door yesterday comes out of the wagon. He glances around before heading off through the fair. I wonder what fortune Madame Rosa told him.

Mrs Coggins likes the flowers but has a headache today. I tell her I'll come back later, but she's gone when I return.

I wait an hour in the moonlight before walking home, past the scenic railway and the big dipper, back under the tall white arch on Shepherd's Bush Green.

When I return to the fairground the next day, the wagons and horses have gone, leaving piles of rubbish on the open field.

It's a shock to see dry yellow patches on the grass like wide graves. I find the place where Mary's caravan used to be and sit on the dewy ground to feel close to her again.

Did she leave because of me? Maybe it was too soon to kiss her, when she turned her face away. It occurs to me that maybe we don't share the same longings, so I look through the rubbish to see if she threw away the roses I gave her. Harry said fairs and circuses were always on the move. She may have already written me a letter saying where she'll be but won't know where to send it.

Watching the rubbish blow across the empty field, I realise I might have fallen in love with Mary.

I stand looking up at the sky, trying to work out exactly what this means, and conclude it has something to do with wanting her to be free of sadness.

That I could be the one to take that away from her.

To make everything good again.

To show her what sort of man I am.

*

My first love, Mary Coggins.

Looking at the sky, I get a clear sense I'm not in fact looking up, but instead peering down into the clouds at the wider galaxy beneath me, just gravity sticking me to the bottom of the earth like glue.

A tiny speck on a rock, spinning through space. A single grain of sand on a long beach that stretches as far as the eye can see.

There's an inevitability about what will happen now.

How life unfolds and the choices I must make.

A plan emerges.

A plan to bring us together and make everything good.

I write a letter to Mary telling her I will go back to France to search for Harry and bring him home.

I have no address to send it to, but it feels good putting the plan into words.

Recalling it now helps me remember what love feels like.

Nine

The black sun burns cold in a Belgian sky and I'm slipping in the blood of the horses.

I've run out of morphine from the dead soldiers' packs and the pain is rising. A few days ago I burst my blisters and couldn't get my boots back on over my swollen feet. Since then I've been walking in three pairs of socks, which are wet solid and I daren't take them off again.

Some of the horses are still alive, their intestines hanging out through the gashes in their flanks, cut by the fleeing Hun soldiers to stop them being used. One struggles to stand on its legs. It refuses to lie still and die but its eyes are elsewhere and it needs to be put out of its misery.

I whisper quiet words in its ear, stroke it calm and then shoot a bullet through its head. It collapses for the final time and my corporal shouts, 'I'll fuckin' have you for wasting ammo.'

I tell him, 'Yes, sir,' but he's new to this and hasn't seen the things I have.

It's the end of December 1917 and I'm still one of the youngest here. I signed up again the day after writing to Mary, not to the Flying Corps this time, but to the infantry to follow in Harry's footsteps. My leg didn't worry the medical officer, who was more keen to test me for madness after my previous medical discharge. I answered all his questions with a no and he stamped 'PASSED' on the form.

One month later, a steamer to Cherbourg.

Here now, in winter again, with the dead horses. Back to keep my promises this time.

I ask each company if anyone knows a Harry Coggins. On one occasion I'm led to a hospital tent, to the bedside of a soldier with that name who has lost his memory, and my heart beats fast picturing Mary as I walk him back home through White City, but the man in bandages isn't him.

New Year's Eve.

At some point in the night it will be 1918.

After trailing an enemy patrol through dark woods close to the Belgian border I've become separated from my division and stumble across a grey building with bars on the windows. The doors are wide open. I wander through the small rooms looking for prisoners in the cells thinking this is how I'll find him, but the place is empty.

I come out into a yard with a small fountain. At the end of the yard is a gate into an orchard of fruit trees under a white moon.

Someone is singing the French words to 'Auld Lang Syne'.

I creep forward towards a wall.

Slow steps.

Crouched down against the other side of the wall, a soldier is drinking a brew of tea.

He looks up at me, the cup already to his lips. He nods hello.

It takes me a moment to realise he's German.

In the same moment he shrouds his eyes, realising I'm his enemy.

My rifle is slack in my arms, his down by his side.

Neither of us move.

We wait and we wait.

There is kindness in his eyes.

He offers me his brew, which doesn't seem such a ridiculous idea, that we might sit down together next to an orchard and find a way to get along in all the madness.

His smile widens at the corners of his mouth.

Mine does the same.

The tune of 'Auld Lang Syne' starts up again, and another soldier appears from behind a tree, doing up the buttons of his trousers.

He sees me by the wall and starts shouting in German. He hoists up his rifle.

I tell him, 'No.'

He cocks it to fire. It locks. He cocks it again.

I turn to run behind a tree for cover, ducking through the branches as a volley of bullets zips by, shredding leaves and splinters of bark around me.

I drop into the undergrowth and crawl around the side of the building where the woods get thick again.

More gunfire in the trees.

An old naked man, bony and tall, stands up from the undergrowth. Straggles of long grey hair flap around the sides of his otherwise bald head.

I wonder if I'll be like him one day.

I crawl further away, around the edge of the deserted building in the woods.

A woman in a thin smock leans against the concrete wall, tapping her head against the stone.

The shooting has stopped but I can hear soldiers whispering a short distance away.

A large lady, as unsteady on her legs as the injured horses, wanders out of the trees repeating, '*J'ai froid. J'ai froid . . .*'

I recall seeing an old asylum on the maps and realise its patients must have been let free when the fighting came close. I crawl away in my socked feet, slowing as I go.

A British medic cradles a young dark-skinned woman in his arms against a tree. They look like lovers. Her eyes are open and she wears the same flimsy gown as the woman tapping her head on the stone wall of the building.

I ask in a whisper if they need help. The medic has been shot through the head. Even in death, he refuses to let go of his young companion.

She looks at me but doesn't register my presence.

There's blood on my hands from the side of my belly, which I didn't feel when the shooting started. It seems superficial rather than anything to worry about.

I dig through the medic's bag for phials of morphine and syringes packed in cotton, along with bandages and iodine.

I ask the woman how she's feeling, but she doesn't answer.

She doesn't flinch when I take her wrist and tap it until a vein appears, then inject enough morphine to help her through the night. I put the cap back over the needle and tell her help is coming.

I put the phials of morphine and the syringes into my backpack and crawl away, leaving the woman tight in the arms of the dead medic.

Everything is quiet now I'm on my own again.

I dress the wound in my side with a little iodine, wrap a bandage tight around my waist and rest up for an hour. I take out my notepaper to write to Mary again.

Starting is always hard, but someone once said to just get on with it even when you don't know what to put. They said never to read the words back once they're written down.

But first I wipe my arm with spit and leaves until a branch of blue veins emerges on my own skin. I tap the syringe and squeeze out the first drops of liquid to clear the air bubbles. My fingers are frozen but my thumbs still work. I search the scar tissue for a fresh bit of skin and push the point of the needle into my vein. The flesh resists and pinches like a tiny balloon, then relaxes as the needle slides through.

I can't feel it go in.

I can't feel anything.

Over the last few weeks I've calculated the right amount of morphine to inject to ease the pain without putting me out of my misery, for I have promises to keep.

And miles to go.

The stars are luminous and wild in the black sky.

A voice calls through the trees.

I ignore it, sharpen my pencil on the bayonet, grateful for a sweetheart to write letters home to.

The stars glow weak in the sky above Hammersmith Grove, barely filtering through the blanket of gloom off the yellow street lamps.

I switch on the bedside lamp and swivel my feet off the side of the bed until my toes touch the cold floor.

The bedside drawer is in easy reach.

Something became clear and it won't wait until morning.

I take out the old faded envelope at the back of the drawer and pull out the soft grey sheets of paper, browned like lightly done toast.

I uncurl the creases with my old fingers and can just about make out the words.

September 14th, 1917
Dear Mary,
    It don't seem right calling you Mrs Coggins. It's months since our time in the caravan. I came to find you the next day but you'd already gone. You never said you were going so I think it was as much of a surprise for you as it was for me.
    I miss you and think of the next time we can lie together.
    Your Billy

I turn to the next page behind it.

October 2nd, 1917
Dear Mary,

London seems like another world. I feel so far away from you, like I was never there. Do you remember our time together?

I wish I'd kissed you but you turned your face away at the wrong moment. Sorry if it wasn't the proper thing to do. I'm thinking what it would be like to kiss you now.

Billy xx

Footsteps bang down the landing outside. The old floorboards creak and swoon. Tabor, I reckon, on his night duty, stretching his legs to see if any of the residents have escaped into the forest outside. The heavy footsteps halt outside my bedroom door before starting up again, heading away towards the lift at the end of the hallway.

I hear the drone of the pulley as the counterweight falls and the lift rises.

The lift doors open and close, and the mechanism drones back to silence.

Under the light of the bedside lamp I unfold the next letter.

October 20th, 1917
Dear Mary,

I've been very lucky today. I reckon it's because you were thinking of me.

Our orders were to run across a long field towards an enemy gun post. I crawled over the ridge, put my head down and ran as fast as my ankle would let me. Halfway across my helmet came off. I stopped to pick it up but thought of you and decided to keep going without it as I knew you were thinking of me at that exact moment too. I knew I'd be safe as long as you kept thinking of me, Mary. The air was hot with metal as the bullets flew by. I never ran so fast in my life, thinking every step would be my last. Men were falling all around me but I just kept going, knowing you were still thinking of me. A few of us, the lucky ones, reached the gun post and dealt with the enemy pretty smartish. I felt happy to be alive and I was laughing when we got there and couldn't stop laughing. Anyone watching me would think I was mad.

Over a thousand Englishmen died in that field today, Mary. Your love kept me safe. Thank you.

Billy xx

I look inside the old brown envelope for her replies, but there's nothing else in there.

November 30th, 1917
Dear Mary,

I'm bivvied in a pigsty in the ruins of a farm with snow falling. We spent the last few days stuck here trying to get over the hill at the top of the field. All the pigs are dead from the mustard gas and lie rotting in heaps on the freezing ground. When the alarm went up I heard a pig squealing nearby. In my gas mask I could hear the noise of it dying in pain. I kept listening until it started calling out for help. I crept out of the bivvie through the pig shit, if you'll excuse my language, Mary. When I finally found it, I realised it wasn't a pig at all but one of our lads crouched against the wall of a barn. He'd lost his gas mask, was covered in blood and struggling to breathe through his swollen throat. His skin was purple in the yellow mist and his red eyeballs bulged out. He tried to grab the mask off my face but had no strength left in him. It was too late to help. I could see he was dying so I helped him like I helped the horses.

After my night with you in the caravan I knew I had to come back. Because of all the things I've done wrong. It's my fault, you see. About Flight. And Harry missing in action. I tried to tell you when we were together but I couldn't find the words. I told Harry he was a coward for not wearing the uniform and he joined up to prove me wrong.

I want you to know I came to look for Harry and I'll write to you when I find him safe and well.

I wish I was back there with you now.

Billy xx

The paper is soft and frail, like it's already turning to dust in my fingers. There's one more letter inside the envelope. I unfold it nervously, hoping it will reveal the promise I kept to Mary, but it's a strange, rambling, hallucinatory tale about floating over a battlefield in a hot-air balloon

111

made of canvas backpacks. Harry eventually emerges as a dot of light under a hawthorn bush and I come down to him in my home-made balloon, fix him into the straps and bring him home.

It reads like the ramblings of a man out of his mind on morphine.

I feel the old paper in my fingers like the wing of a dead butterfly.

Maybe not all promises can be kept after all.

Maybe not everything has a happy ending.

But then . . .

Maybe it did happen that way. Among the madness perhaps I managed to build a balloon out of backpacks, held to the ground with guy ropes, fuelled by the heat of a burning fire.

Maybe it's one of those strange memories that becomes real the more you wish it. Even when you're sure the world doesn't work that way.

Ros says I've been sat at the table for too long today, which is not good for my back.

The sound of the typewriter keys is annoying Mrs Bentley and Mrs Cutts, who are trying to watch the television set and keep looking over at me with their lips curled. *Tap tap tap*.

Ding.

I quite fancy having my hot chocolate now, but Sylvie won't bring it round until I'm in my pyjamas. Sometimes Sylvie forgets about the hot chocolate if there's lots on her plate.

Is that another day gone already?

Ros says not to read back what you've written because

it never looks like you hoped, then you give up and don't bother writing any more. She says you just think it's all a load of shit and never get it finished.

That's what her boyfriend says anyway, though I reckon they're both too old to be calling him a boyfriend. He's nearly sixty apparently. And Ros is pushing fifty, so she's no spring chicken.

She says he's not a proper writer in any case, just does books for the university that no one ever reads.

We didn't get much of a chance, did we, Mary?

A love of sorts, but hard to know what it is when you're young.

I wonder if my letters would have brought you any comfort in your final years, even if I'd been able to send them. But without a forwarding address they just stayed in my tunic pocket and never got posted to you.

By the time I was home, you'd put yourself out of your misery.

Left your little wagon in a field somewhere, went back to Notting Hill to the garden behind your old bombed-out house and climbed the tree where Harry and I would watch Peg and Jeannie in their underwear next door. You tied a rope to a high branch and that was that.

The letters are all faded now, but I can still make out the words, and it's good to have something to remember you by.

Yes, that's what it'll be, this small ache deep in the middle of my bones.

The old, cold dregs of love.

PART TWO

Ten

The mist dissolves in the air.

I count the seconds from my last breath to my next.

It's a bright October morning but the blue sky is full of the promise of winter, like a silvery chill has been laced through the sunlight.

Some of the chill might be due to thinking about Mary Coggins.

I wait for the next breath to come, for my lungs, soft as old balloons, to draw in another rush of cold air.

I wait and I wait.

I never used to wait this long when I was a young man.

When the fire alarm rang this morning, heads turned from the television set and tutted in annoyance. Gordon emerged flapping from his office like a hen while Ros and Sylvie began wheeling out the residents and asking those with better legs to make their way outside.

I'm old and dry like straw. I'll burn quick and easy when the undertaker's fire catches up with me. I thought about letting the flames take me now, but a fire engine arriving is the most exciting thing to happen here since Mr Mablethorpe, a retired piano teacher, was asked to leave for having sex with some of the elderly ladies. The women seemed happy enough, having invited Mr Mablethorpe's attentions in the first place, but it was their families who insisted on his removal.

Sylvie pushed me down the ramp at the front of the building, which gets the best of the morning sunlight, where I'm now enjoying the warmth under a blanket.

Two fire engines race up from Hammersmith and park in the street. The doors open, a blur of yellows and blacks jump down and run into the building. You forget how it feels to be strong.

My arms are shivering in the chilly air but I'm grateful for the sensation of being alive away from the relentless heat of the television room.

Mrs Bentley and Mrs Cutts are sat with their faces shut, snorting through their noses like two angry bulls, unhappy to be missing the thin man in the suit who likes to shout at people.

Jimmy Parris hisses at me from his wheelchair. It's awkward to turn and face him. He hisses again.

I crane my neck but I'm blinded by the sun's rays. The light feels good on my face.

'Billyboy! Let's fuck off while we can,' he laughs. 'Taxi to the station, train to the Lakes, nice pint by Windermere.' He laughs again. 'Or steal a car and do a Thelma and Louise off Beachy Head.'

I've no idea what he's talking about.

Ros and Sylvie are giggling with the firemen. Sylvie's untied her hair, which she hardly ever does indoors. She looks older with it hanging free.

One of the firemen is a lady.

It turns out the alarm was set off by Gordon burning

toast in his office and the engines leave as quick as they came. I enjoy a few more rays of sunlight before Ros wheels me back into the fetid warmth of the television room.

Jimmy Parris hisses again, 'Missed our chance, Billy-boy. Have to tunnel our way out now.'

Ros says, 'Find me a shovel and I'm coming with you.'

Much later, with the television set on loud again and the lingering smell of wet vegetables, it's like the excitement of this morning's fire alarm never happened.

Where am I?

Back in time, trying to remember who of the five comes next.

Her face falls into view, like clouds in a dream.

Evelyn Ellis.

Evie for short.

I loved you very much, Evie.

You were my forever girl. With your big eyes and your clear skin and your slow blink like you were still thinking about what was said long after the words were over. Beautiful and heartbreaking.

Your eyes searching above whatever you were looking at, as if the answer was always to be found further up in the sky. Your lips a gentle curve, like a sideways S, a softly undulating sine wave in a joyous science experiment.

Kindness in your eyes.

Your black hair in waves down your neck. A ribbon across the top, worn with a silver leaf-shaped hairpin your gran left you when she died.

You were funny and bright and good. You spoke well,

not like posh people, but like it wasn't a bad thing to be from Shepherd's Bush.

We took our time, Evie Ellis, you and me. To court and get married. There was no rush because it was all ahead of us.

We took our time before Archie came along.

Another alarm goes off in the distance. Not from Gordon's office this time but further down the street. A car or house maybe. Someone up to no good.

Everything has alarms these days.

I hear it through the faint ringing that washes through my ears day and night.

I let the alarm grow tired until my mind filters it out and I try to think of Evie floating back towards me, somewhere down the market stalls.

Late spring, 1921.

Three years of gaps to fill in, but only history's scraps come to mind.

Europe coming back into line after the war. David Lloyd George saying it can never be allowed to happen again, despite Dad reckoning he was always a friend of the Kaiser's, the Half Moon and Seven Stars his trusted library where all the information in the world gets found.

A letter from Auntie Pam saying her husband in Manchester died, but Ma refusing to let her visit and Dad coming back from the pub hammered and trying to be chirpy after seeing Pam's letter on the table. He tells Ma the advantages of living in modern post-war London. 'Wages for workers, health benefits!' while she scrubs sick off his trousers and works them through the mangle. 'Even the King's making friends with the working class.'

Jack Burns running the fish stalls now, Mr Finlay's retarded offspring who pushed the barrow at Norland Road and nicked fish to sell to doss-houses. He's grown gruff and thickset over the years, solid as the wheels on a Billingsgate cart.

I watch Jack Burns in Norland Road giving his clumsy patter to a woman buying skate wings. When she's gone, I ask if Mr Finlay is still around. He takes a moment to remember me, then says Mr Finlay fucked off years ago.

I ask if there's a job going in Shepherd's Bush now the barracks have gone. Jack Burns spits on the ground and says Mrs Cumbernauld works it since Clem disappeared. He says times are hard and he'd heard my leg was no good in any case.

He then asks me to lug six boxes of mussels over from the cold store. I do it in one haul and he says he'll see about getting my old job back working the barrow for Mrs Cumbernauld.

Mrs Cumbernauld is a rough bull of a woman. She wears a man's trousers and jacket, with a flat cap over her short hair. She swears more than Clem did and does her fair share of shifting boxes when I bring the cart over from Norland Road. Mrs Cumbernauld doesn't do tittle-tattle, but once said that Jack Burns wasn't the only secret child fathered by Mr Finlay, who got chased out of town by an angry husband wielding an axe.

Most of the old traders have gone since the war. It feels like a new world is starting over.

The new fish stall is further up towards the top of the market, between a cloth seller and a homeware stall loaded with pots and pans. A greengrocer opposite, and a clothes shop with hats and ties in the window under the arches.

Mr Edwins' umbrella shop is still where it used to be, though Mr Edwins looks old and never says hello when he shuffles past in the mornings. The sweet shop is still there too, down towards Goldhawk Road, though Mrs Chester's dancing rooms are home to a pet store with birds in cages, rodents, tortoises, kittens and dogs in kennels, which you can smell from several stalls away.

A steady stream of customers for fish.

I see the same faces and sometimes it's hard to remember all that happened since the last time I was here.

After the morning rush, Mrs Cumbernauld goes for a smoke, leaving me to run the stall while she's gone.

I'm on my own when a beautiful young woman with a wave of black hair and eyes like pools of dark water walks up and says, 'Four penn'orth of whiting and half a pint of winkles, please.'

I try to reply using some of Clem's old banter but nothing comes to mind, so instead ask, 'What can I get you, love?'

She looks puzzled and says again, 'Four penn'orth of whiting, please, and half a pint of winkles,' before looking back at her shopping list.

There are flowers embroidered in her white lace skirt.

122

Her shoes have a black and white check across the toes and a small heel that taps on the cobbles as she turns to view the greengrocer's stall opposite.

I weigh the whiting, making sure not to give her coley or pollack, and ask how many eels she's after. She says it's winkles she wanted. I give her a pint.

'I only asked for half.'

I tell her the winkles are a present if she comes back to see me again soon. She pays, her eyes blinking up above my head, like she's working out if we're speaking two different languages.

She asks for her change, which I've forgotten about.

Fumbling quickly for coins, I drop them under the counter, bend down to pick them up, bang my head on the trestle table and knock a pot of jellied eels over the cobbles onto her shoes. She looks at me like I'm an injured puppy that needs putting down, and I tell her, 'Well, that all went very well!'

She laughs with kindness in her eyes and it's the most beautiful sight I've ever seen.

I ask if she'd let me buy her a cake in Lyons coffee house to make up for the mess on her shoes but she says she has to be getting home and goes.

The following week, after seven days watching out for her, I see her walking down the market again.

'Four penn'orth of whiting and half a pint of winkles?' I call out. 'And I promise not to chuck them over your shoes today.'

She laughs once more, and a beam of sunlight radiates out of her.

She isn't shopping for fish, but says yes to a cake in Lyons coffee house.

A hand on my shoulder.

Jimmy is asking me about something.

Out of the window the day has turned grey, as if autumn has quietly robbed the last blue sky of summer.

I turn my good ear to catch what Jimmy is saying.

Something about canasta in pairs with Mrs Chaudhry and another of the Indian ladies.

It's a struggle to hold cards these days, and I can never remember if it's spades or clubs or whatever they're called.

'I'm meeting Evie in Lyons coffee house,' I tell him.

He laughs and says, 'Suit yourself, Billyboy.'

Scrubbed up on a cool, bright Saturday afternoon, April 1921.

Walking the north side of the green like it's the top of the world. A tide of men in blue and white scarves heading to Loftus Road for the afternoon.

I'm early, find a table at the back of Lyons coffee house with a view of the door, read the menu and wonder which cake she'll ask for, not even minding if it's the expensive French gateau at the bottom of the list.

The hour comes and goes.

A middle-aged woman in a black hat sits nearby with her niece, working silently through slices of Victoria sponge, which neither seem to be enjoying.

I look up each time the door opens, but it's never her.

Two men in the booth beside me discuss whether the split of Third Division teams into northern and southern leagues will affect Rangers' chances next season.

The serving lady returns twice for my order. After an hour, I order a toasted teacake to save face.

She brings it on a china plate and I watch the butter melt through, glancing at the door each time the bell rings.

The dream of Evie Ellis dies with each tearing of the bun.

I pay the bill, button up my jacket and plot my unhappy exit from the busy tea room.

A young woman sits with her back to me in a booth near the door, an abandoned teacake in front of her. As I pass, she jumps in surprise and says, 'I thought you'd changed your mind.'

The pools of her eyes are big enough to swim in.

She wears a dress the colour of mint, speckled with a print of tiny blackbirds and buttons down the front.

'I didn't see you,' pointing out the table at the back of the room. 'I got here very early.'

'I got here early too,' she replies. 'You look very smart. I thought you'd stood me up.'

I try to tell her that would never happen, but instead ask, 'How was your teacake?'

'Terrible!' she laughs.

'Mine too,' and she laughs again with a slow blink of her eyelashes, like the flutter of soft feathers.

We decide we've already spent long enough in Lyons coffee house and walk up to the fairground to stroll past the old palaces and canals at White City.

On the way I make a silent, solemn vow that I intend to keep forever.

Jimmy and Mrs Chaudhry are making a lot of noise playing cards, having been joined by Mrs Subram and Mrs Nagpal. One was a dancer in Bollywood and the other's a right stuck-up so-and-so from Perivale.

The sound of other people's laughter is always hard on the ears when you're trying to fill the gaps in your own head.

I think Mrs Subram was the one in Bollywood. I've seen a photograph by the door in her room of when she was young and she certainly looked a cracker back then. It's easy to spot when you're shuffling down the corridor if her door is left open, though I expect she put it there so everyone can see how fetching she used to be.

Jimmy is starting to get on my nerves, carrying on with all the women in here. One minute he's sweet-talking Mrs Gibson, the new resident with the thin straggles of grey hair, the next he's playing cards with three Indian ladies like he's Lawrence of Arabia.

Mrs Nagpal is smiling at him across the card table.

I'm not sure I've ever seen her smile before.

How easily we could have missed each other. A lifetime lost by one slip of the eye. We walk side by side in perfect step, freshly minted like the green of Evie's dress, past the white palaces and canals, the glamour of the old buildings fading now.

She asks where I live.

She's in Brackenbury, in a well-to-do house off Hammersmith Grove.

She asks about my parents.

Her father is the Ellis of Ellis's bakery. There was a brother and a sister once, though not any more.

I ask if her brother was in France.

She shakes her head.

I ask about her sister and she says, 'Can it be a subject for another day?' and we listen to the sound of our footsteps on the old gravel pathways.

'You were in France?' she asks.

'Once or twice,' I tell her.

'You have the air,' she says. 'And a gentle limp when you walk.'

'Only if it's about to rain.'

She laughs, her voice like honey, and brushes close beside me.

'Make sure you tell me,' she smiles, 'and I'll know to bring a coat.'

I already feel she has seen my weaknesses and I'm preparing, happily, to throw in the towel from the corner of the ring.

I ask if she's chilly.

She says she's comfortable.

I tell her she can wear my jacket if she's cold.

She tucks her arm though mine, says, 'You're a proper gent, Billy Binns,' and we keep walking over the old stones in silence.

When she lets go, she holds her hands in front of her like she was born to carry a bouquet.

She asks who my best friend is. I'm already thinking *You are*, but it's much too soon to put that into words.

I tell her about Harry Coggins, missing in action, presumed dead. How we argued and fell out over nothing. How I failed to find him when I went back.

These are things I've never said out loud before. They emerge into the real world leaving a cavernous space inside me, a dusty old attic with the windows thrown open and new air rushing in for the first time.

I tell her about the man who caught me falling from a balloon, who brought me home safe, but spare her the details about his letter and our misunderstanding by the hawthorn bush.

I don't tell her about Mrs Coggins, as some things are best kept packed in boxes.

The flutes of a barrel organ chime through the evening air as the big dipper rises in front of us.

I ask about her favourite pastimes.

Evie says, 'Fairgrounds, dancing . . .'

I reach down to soothe the ache in my leg and tell her she might have to find someone else to go courting with.

She laughs and says, 'In that case, I might have to give up dancing,' looping her arm through mine again.

128

I hold her eyes, counting the heartbeats, and look down at our feet, the same slow pace, one foot then the other. The sight of the fairground ahead of us, knowing I've found my forever girl.

Forever girl.

Much too soon to say that out loud, too. Knowing from old promises that words are meaningless until they are made good by actions.

The fairground lights are coming on as the sky turns deep blue and dark orange. The last of the low sun shines against the old stadium and dies on the arms of the Flip Flap ride.

I buy tuppenny tickets for the big dipper and we sit at the front of the little train.

It's a long, slow climb to the top.

Up and up it goes.

Looking down at the lights below.

People like ants. I've seen that before but this is not the time for those kind of memories.

Evie laughs nervously and grips my hand. She says she's changed her mind but we know it's too late for that. The cars climb up the rickety track and she nestles her head into the warm harbour of my neck.

This.

This is what it's like.

The smell of her skin.

She is everything beautiful in the world.

I'm lost in the aroma, and far ahead in the future, a distant version of me whispers, 'This . . . this is what it's like.'

An old man in an armchair thinks, *If it all ends now, it's worth it for the smell of her skin.*

Near the top of the big dipper she says, 'Don't let go of my hand.'

I tell her, 'I won't,' and it's loaded with the weight of everything to come.

She whispers something else I don't catch because the girls behind us are screaming.

My skin prickles nervously in the cool air as we rattle steadily upwards and come to a stop.

A dog barks somewhere down below.

We're at the front of the roller coaster, looking down with a chill in the bones at how far we've come already.

Evie and me.

And then.

We wait.

We wait . . .

And then we fly.

Over the tracks. Down in a rush of air.

Screams behind, stomach still at the top.

A glance sideways at Evie, eyes open, mouth wide.

The clatter of wheels.

The cars take another swift rise, a tease to hold off the final drop.

Evie's face as we fall again, wind-blown, full of wonder, over much too quick.

The dipper comes to a halt and the screams become laughter.

Evie looks at me with total joy.

We climb out of the carriage and another couple take our seats at the front of the train.

We walk back through the fairground, listening to the

sound of the big dipper rattling up into the sky once more. A whole carload of other people's stories waiting to be told.

She smiles and lets go of my hand.

Evie Ellis puts a small amount of distance between us.

We walk towards a stall where I buy three hoops to throw over skittles, and fail to win her a goldfish.

Eleven

We used to keep goldfish in a tank here but they caught a fungus and died one by one. Eight or nine there were at first.

Gordon scooped them out with a ladle from the kitchen and carried them at arm's length into the staff toilet, emerging moments later with his face still curled in disgust.

When they'd all been flushed, the tank was replaced with another armchair in the sitting room, not unlike when a resident dies here. One of the undertaker's boys comes to take away the body and free up another place to sit.

We find our spot in here and stick to it. Creatures of habit, the lot of us. Jimmy Parris likes the armchair where the fish tank used to be. Mrs Bentley and Mrs Cutts always stay below the television set.

Jimmy is having a sleep, a book about lifeboats closed on his lap. He'll be exhausted from all his carousing at the card table with the Indian ladies.

I'm thinking about Ros saying she'd want to escape with Jimmy and me. Maybe she's not as settled with her gentleman boyfriend as she lets on. And she'll be too old for the young firemen she and Sylvie were giggling with.

Maybe we're all trying to escape from something.

Other people's lives always seem settled when you don't know much about them.

I shuffle myself up in the chair as Sylvie holds me under one arm and plumps the cushion below with the other.

Jimmy opens his eyes after his nap.

I'm feeling anxious about the people I once loved. Five, was it, the gypsy woman said?

I thought I could see them all clearly, but now I'm not so sure if I remember who they were.

Evie for sure.

I remember Evie.

And Mary, lost in the hallway of her house in Notting Hill.

There was my boy, Archie, with his filthy knees and a pocketful of marbles.

Two others whose faces escape me now.

I might ask Jimmy Parris if he can remember any of the people he's loved over the years.

Leaning towards him, I try to speak, but either I'm not good at words today or he hasn't put his hearing aid in. He shakes his head, says he can't tell what I'm saying and goes back to his book about lifeboats.

I ask him again.

He says, 'What's that?'

I ask how many people he's loved in his life.

He brushes his white moustache with his thumb and takes a sip of tea, removes his glasses and rubs his eyes.

Ros is on the other side of Jimmy's chair, giving out pills to the Polish submarine captain whose name I can never remember. She says Jimmy can't tell what I'm saying. She puts her head close to my lips and I summon the strength to ask one last time.

Ros rolls her eyes and says, 'Don't get him started!'

She repeats my question to Jimmy, who laughs, brushes his moustache again and says, 'Oh hundreds, Billyboy!'

Time is passing.

In a finger snap, the memories of Evie leap from a spring evening riding the big dipper in White City to Christmas Eve on the Uxbridge Road, later the same year.

We've kissed in stolen moments, Evie and me, but nothing more. We wait for the rest because it's the right thing when you're decent and know what's precious and worth holding out for.

Until tonight.

This is new and different. Rich in the promise of what's to come. It has a rawness and edge that could light a bonfire on a cold night.

During the midnight service we hold hands in the freezing pew of St Stephen's Church. She keeps my fingers tight in her gloved fist as the herald angels sing. The fist only peels open for prayers. My prayer gets answered and after the final Amen she takes my hand again. We wish the vicar a happy Christmas and come out into the thrill of falling snow.

This allows me a few extra minutes to walk Evie home because no decent father-in-law begrudges a young man a late-night snowball fight with the girl he will one day marry.

There's just enough fresh snow on Lime Grove to roll a snowball off a wall. Mine misses her by a long mile, though I wasn't aiming it close in the first place. Evie scores a direct hit on the back of my coat.

She laughs and says, 'You're not allowed to turn away.'

I tell her, 'I'm no fool.'

She says, 'You're a fool for me,' and smiles through the falling snowflakes. In the silence there are words we don't need to say.

Her smile fades and she looks like an entirely different woman.

She steps into a quiet alley with a gaze that demands I follow, and then turns back to face me. I'm not the one to bring us here. I promised I'd take her straight home after church.

There's mischief in her eyes and the sound of merry-makers up Lime Grove.

She leans against the wall in the shadows with snow-flakes on her shoulders and gives me another look that makes me think there's already enough trouble in the world without women wanting equality and making decisions for themselves.

I say, 'Aren't you cold?'

Her eyes look up at the falling snow and back into my bones. I'm weightless, caught in the deep space of her eyes.

A current sweeps me out and I can't find my feet.

Her hand on my arm.

She tells me to kiss her.

I whisper a yes.

Our warm breath forms a rich single cloud, her face just an inch away.

She waits to be discovered, like distant land on a freshly inked map.

Her eyes close and we kiss.

In the gentle wilderness after our lips part she whispers, 'All yours.'

All yours, Billy.

And I know, burying roots in the earth beneath me, she will always be my forever girl. Her essence like a silver pearl. The secret middle no one else will ever get close to. She is offering me the rest of our lives and I'm the luckiest man in the world.

A snowflake lands on the edge of her eyelashes. She blinks it away.

I'm on a planet as distant as the moon and everything has changed.

I reach for another kiss but the moment has passed and it feels somehow misappropriated.

My hand weaves between the buttons of her winter coat and brushes the side of her hip.

Her smile says that's enough.

I delay my hand a moment longer, feeling the warmth of the cotton beside her skin.

She says, 'Happy Christmas, Billy.'

Our kisses melt with the snowflakes and we should be getting back.

We return to the planet we came from, having just glimpsed it from far away.

Good girls don't rush these things when they're decent and proper.

I take my hand out of her coat and bring the warmth to her cold cheek.

We walk out of the alley, down Lime Grove to the Goldhawk Road and back to her parents' house in Brackenbury.

Her father clasps me on the shoulder and says, 'Good man,' offering a glass of port from his decanter before I go.

I say goodnight to her mother and father and make my way down Hammersmith Creek, to Ma in the parlour and Dad who won't be home for a good while yet.

The snow is starting to settle.

In spring we'll have courted a year and I'll be able to ask Evie's father for his permission to marry.

A smell of fresh-baked bread, but I don't know if it's a distant memory or real life.

Jimmy Parris said they don't use the kitchens here for baking so I reckon it must be a memory.

Sometime before my proposal, I left the market stall and started working for Evie's father, Irwin, doing night shifts at his bakery on the corner of Loftus Road, overseeing the bread and buns being made for the following day.

He gave me a small office and a silver fountain pen on my first shift.

A Parker pen, I'm sure.

Ma was impressed by my new job but worried she'd

have to meet Evie's parents because they came from a different world and lived in a well-to-do house in Brackenbury. Mostly she was nervous about Dad, if he'd show up drunk in his vest and breeches like the first time I brought Evie round to Trafalgar Street.

Dad didn't reckon the bakery was man's work, though he didn't seem to mind meeting Evie, or eating the fresh muffins I'd bring home for his breakfast at the end of my shift.

'She's too good for you, son,' he said after the first time I brought her to the house.

I remember the weight of the pen and the smell of fresh bread in the mornings, walking down Trafalgar Street with a warm loaf under my arm.

The ovens are on through the night, manned by a small team of four bakers. My job is to make sure everything runs smoothly.

I clock on at five in the afternoon before Irwin leaves for home. He returns at six the following morning. He says to take an hour's nap when everything is quiet, but I find it hard to sleep while the bakers are working.

After some nights, the flour dust and sweat leaves a light batter on the skin like a congealed perfume, but the smell of pastry and bread, and a warm office, is luxury after working the fish stall in the market.

On Saturdays I dress smart and walk Evie through Ravenscourt Park. Sometimes we take a bus to

Chiswick House to feed the ducks with the crusts of an old loaf.

Sunday lunches at her parents' house in Brackenbury after church, or Trafalgar Street if it can't be helped. Dad makes fun of Ma for bringing out the good tablecloth and her mother's cutlery box while he sits in his braces reading the paper after we've eaten.

It's 1922 and we're a proper couple, Evie and me.

Ma comments on it being a year since we started courting and Dad says, 'Leave it alone, woman,' from behind his newspaper.

At Evie's house I watch her pedal her mother's sewing machine, feeding material through the needle. She makes me a waistcoat embroidered with a lime-green silk lining, and a handkerchief onto which my initials are monogrammed.

BB.

To thank her, I pick some wild flowers from Wormwood Scrubs that she knows all the names of.

Do you remember this, Evie?

The smell of bread and the beautiful waistcoat you made me, with the embroidered green silk lining?

The monogrammed handkerchief?

I could only give you small things in return: a ribbon for your hair, wild flowers. I was saving up for a life together.

All mapped out, as clear as . . .

As clear as . . .

It's June 1922, and everyone is waiting for me to do the right thing.

Even Mrs Cumbernauld in the market says, 'You not asked that lovely girl yet?' when I'm buying mussels with Evie out of earshot. 'She's much too good for you, sunshine. Pull your finger out before it's too late.'

The following week I'm outside Mr Ellis's office at the end of his day. My shoes are brushed army-bright and I've washed the pastry crumbs from the corners of my mouth. I've put on a few pounds these last few months. Ma reckons it suits me, but if I add any more weight I'll need to buy a set of new clothes.

Mr Ellis steps out of his office. I'm always surprised how tall he is when he's standing up, his neck elongated by a stiff collar and tie. A thin nose and long cheekbones highlight his kindly face, though it's probably fair to say it wasn't a misfortune Evie inherited her looks from her mother.

He sees me loitering and asks if I'm unwell.

I tell him I'd like his advice on a certain matter.

He looks at his pocket watch and says he has to check the oil tank at the back of the factory yard.

I follow him though a nightmare of pipework, my heart beating quickly and a film of sweat on my brow. He taps a troublesome gauge and waits for the needle to correct itself.

'So then, on what certain matter would you like my advice?'

I take a deep breath but the words fail to materialise.

He pockets his watch.

I tell him, 'I've been wondering if we should start making bagels.'

He says, 'There's not enough call for Jewish food in west London at this time.'

He taps the faulty pressure gauge once again and asks, 'Is that what's on your mind?'

I tell him he's probably right about the bagels.

We go our separate ways and it's another two weeks before I find the courage for a second attempt.

Sunday, July, mid morning.

Evie and her ma are visiting her aunt and won't be home for another hour.

Mr Ellis answers the door and, before I can speak, explains where Evie is, says to make myself comfortable until she returns and disappears into his study.

The sitting room is heavy with dark wood. The steady knock of the grandfather clock marks each passing second before death.

I look at the painting of Evie's grandfather above the fireplace – a man important enough to commission his own portrait with his loyal otterhound. The dog has been depicted with a sweetness missing in Irwin Ellis's father. I look at the two faces for a minute, the old man and the dog, knowing this is now the time.

I walk into the hallway and knock on the door of his study.

141

Mr Ellis says to enter.

I close the door behind me and stand on the rug in front of his desk.

'I need to ask you something, sir.'

He slots his pen into the ornate holder at the front of his desk, dabs the blotter over the page he's been writing and pushes it carefully to the side. He leans forward with a steely gaze not unlike the portrait of his father and says, 'It's not about bagels again, is it, lad?'

I wonder what happens if he refuses.

I wipe the sweat from my hands onto my good trousers and start to form the words through a mouth dry as sand.

'No, sir. I've come to ask your permission for Evie's hand in marriage.'

Twelve

How sorry I am for my mistakes, great and small.

Those tiny lapses in judgement.

It hurts to recall the pain and anguish I caused along the way.

I still don't know what God is, after all these years. I've never been one for churches.

But I think, at last, I understand forgiveness.

Gordon and Mrs Akinyemi are rowing in her office. They snipe at each other most days but this morning it's gone medieval, as Jimmy would say.

Something about a car parked at the front of The Cedars.

Mrs Akinyemi has started leaving her little Renault in the space reserved for an emergency ambulance, which Gordon isn't happy about.

Mrs Akinyemi barks back against Gordon's angry yelps.

He says, 'How would it be if we all parked in the ambulance spot?'

Mrs Akinyemi says, 'Gordon, you don't have a car.'

He tells her, 'That's not the point.'

She says, 'It's only while my husband is ill.'

Gordon replies, 'He's been ill for a bloody long time,' which probably isn't the best way to win his argument.

He comes out of her office and stomps into his own, banging the door loudly behind him.

Mrs Akinyemi walks unflustered through the television room as if the row never happened. She has a face I wouldn't recognise without her spectacles and always wears a crucifix over her blouse and matching cardigan. I used to be impressed how she made her hair look identical every day until Sylvie said it was a wig.

I wonder if the crucifix means Mrs Akinyemi is good at forgiveness.

Sitting here, in the quiet after the row, thinking about Archie.

I may have forgotten his birthday once or twice over the years and I'm worried this is why he hasn't come to see me for a while.

Not since November, I think, though I'm a little hazy on the dates.

Having Archie on my mind reminds me how everything gets done for us when we're born, then we grow up and learn to do things for ourselves. We live for fifty summers or so, if we're one of the lucky ones, then time catches up and we gradually find our way back to helplessness again.

How short life is.

How quickly time passes.

My pads need changing.

Each day I feel a little less able than the one before. My food is a wet mash intended merely to slip down easily. I still enjoy a good cup of tea, mainly down to the sugar in it.

My mouth was once a playground of adventure:

144

Mrs Jackson's curry goat with allspice berries; the soft earthiness of asparagus in warm butter; the sweetness of a perfect peach; the heady flatline of the first gin and tonic of the day; malt whisky, aged a fraction of my own time, harsh and soft in the same mouthful, slipping over the tongue like ball bearings cast of iron and peat.

This memory of tastes explodes in my head and fades like a firework, like the final twitches of a hanging man. Sweet and sour, heat and chill, sugar and salt. Frozen in the mess of wires somewhere in the far corners of my mind.

They come back to life in tiny moments.

Irwin Ellis sucks unsuccessfully on his pipe and relights it with a match. He holds his thumb against the packed tobacco, emitting clouds of smoke into the room, finally convincing himself it's alight.

In the silence around the drawing on his pipe, I'm wondering if I only imagined asking him the question about Evie; that he's still waiting to hear what I'm doing in his study in the middle of a Sunday morning. I feel like I'm skating on a frozen lake with no control over the direction I'm heading.

He takes the pipe out of his mouth.

'Well. There are some questions I need to ask you first, Billy. Before I can answer the one you asked me.'

The tobacco cloud smells sweet and nutty.

'Firstly, what are your prospects?'

I ask him to repeat the question.

He looks puzzled, then says it again.

I tell him I have a good job which I'm very grateful for. I hope to impress him over time, preserve the good name of Ellis's bakery and do all I can to keep Evie in the manner to which she's become accustomed.

Irwin Ellis sucks on his pipe again.

I look down at the floor, which feels wrong, so I look directly into his eyes but can't hold his gaze, so I look at the wall behind him instead.

I'd imagined having his answer by now, a simple yes or no, but the wait goes on.

He says, 'When did you speak to her about this?'

'Pardon, sir?'

'What did she say when you popped the question?'

'I haven't asked her the question yet, sir.'

He looks confused. 'She doesn't know?'

'I thought I was meant to ask you first.'

'You haven't actually asked her to marry you yet?'

'I've never done this before, sir. I thought I had to ask you first.'

I'm stood to attention in front of him and wonder if every man's marriage proposal is as painful as this.

Irwin Ellis asks me, 'So what happens now if I decline?'

The walls are starting to fragment around me. I fight the urge to run away.

I look Mr Ellis in the eye. 'If you decline, sir, I'll make her run away with me and just do my best to make her happy for the rest of her life. I'll love her with all my heart until the day I die.'

Mr Ellis stares me down.

He gets up out of his chair, high on his long legs, and

walks around his desk like a giant insect. I've never seen him angry like this. He's at least a foot taller than me but the only thing I can do is stand my ground and look him hard in the eye.

He stops in front of me, a curl forming at the edge of his lips.

Irwin Ellis grabs my hand, shakes it firmly, and with a smile as wide as a saucer says, 'Congratulations, son. I can't think of a better man to marry my Evie.'

She's surprised to find me waiting in the sitting room when she returns with her ma.

I don't recall the lunch we all ate together.

Maybe we skipped lunch and Evie and I went straight for a walk.

Maybe we ate lunch, her father and I quietly harbouring our secret while passing the potatoes.

Lovely gravy, Mrs Ellis.

I don't recall the lunch but I remember Evie's father sending the two of us out of the house for a walk and some air.

We're strolling past the railway arches in Ravenscourt Park.

I'm about to ask her underneath the blossom by the small lake but it's busy with dogs and people, so we loop around the water again, holding our breath as we pass the tuberculosis hospital in Ravenscourt House and walk back once more towards the railway arches under the Metropolitan Line.

Evie asks why I'm acting strangely.

I comment on the blossom already starting to fall.

Evie stands in the sunlight, I'm in the shadow of the arch.

She says, 'It doesn't stay on the trees for long.'

I'm trying to unstick the words, twice in the same day.

Evie bends down and scoops a small handful of the pink and white blossom. I tell myself if she says yes I'll come back to collect some for wedding confetti.

She inspects the tiny flowers in her hand.

I bend down on my knee.

She turns to see what I'm doing.

With her hand still full of petals, she lifts it up to her mouth in shock.

I'm deep in her beautiful eyes, swimming in the life ahead of us, and the words slip out like the easiest thing in the world.

'Will you marry me, Evie?'

Her eyes fill with tears. This time she doesn't look up to the sky for an answer. She beams the brightest smile and says, 'Of course I will.'

I hold on tight as she cries.

A train rattles above us and a breeze blows through the arches, bringing more of the blossom down.

Evie wipes her eyes and says, 'Can we go back now so you can ask my father?'

I tell her his permission is already granted.

Evie makes another splutter of tears and some of the petals spill from her tiny fist.

Evie's ma is thrilled, though she claims she had an inkling after her husband and future son-in-law's odd behaviour at the lunch table.

Evie's father pours out a good malt whisky for the husbands and a sherry for their spouses.

The world has already changed.

Later that afternoon, I walk back to Trafalgar Street, heavy with the smell of effluent off the Creek.

Ma hugs me and sheds a tear.

Dad says we'll struggle to survive the coming economic depression.

I go to sleep with my head full of blossom, already stored in a pouch at the back of my clothes drawer for the big day, and dream of sleeping in a large bed with Evie once we are married.

I wake in the middle of the night feeling for the comfort of her warm skin next to me.

I try to wrap my arms around her to steal a little of her heat, then realise she must be up and about, a cup of tea in the kitchen maybe, doing the crossword to keep the four-in-the-morning demons away when they come bringing trouble.

Archie is snoring in his bedroom across the landing.

His tiny breaths in and out.

In and out.

I try to get warm, wishing Evie would come back to bed before the creamy white glow of the street lamp goes and the day starts proper.

The yellow light outside hauls me into a different century.

A bang in the corridor, voices and footsteps, and the lift doors opening and closing down the hallway.

Tabor's voice, his deep accented rumble, and the whispers of a man alongside him.

A delivery is most unusual at this time of night.

Then I hear the wheels of a trolley rattle by and I know
that one of the residents has died.

I map my way around the sitting room to consider the
most likely: Mr Buffery with his hacking cough, I reckon.
Some of the other faces come to mind. I'm not great with
names but the faces I still do well.

Our time here almost done.

My thin blood turning to powder, the last few laps
down to the feet and back.

I think about getting up and shuffling to the door to ask
Tabor who's copped it. But the air is cold on my thin shoul-
ders and I pull the covers up over them instead to remember
Evie from the dream.

Sometime later, the sound of the trolley wheels again,
weighted this time, hushed across the carpet.

A final journey out.

It won't be long before I do the same.

Evie is at her ma's sewing machine, pedalling fast then
slow, feeding material under a warm lamp.

The soft clatter of the needle.

Her total immersion in the task fills me with joy.

She looks up and smiles. 'I'll make a mistake if you
keep staring.'

I look away but can't help looking back over again. She

doesn't tell me to stop watching this time and smiles because she knows I still am.

A painting of three children on the wall behind her.

The eldest, Evie's brother, killed by a horse delivering his father's bread when he was thirteen.

A sister who didn't make it through childhood.

Evie, the survivor.

She never knew them, she says, but it feels like they're here.

One evening, Mr Ellis told me about Evie's brother and sister dying, then said he hoped I might run his business one day.

Billy Binns the baker and Evie the baker's wife.

We arrange the wedding for May the following year, 1923.

Our kisses are careful, but charged with a memory of the one we shared off Lime Grove that snowy Christmas Eve. Saving ourselves for marriage because it's the right thing to do when you're decent and proper. Even when we're alone in a quiet house.

The promise of what's to come.

My history buried now, undiscussed. I suspect she knows but doesn't ask because she's not that sort of girl.

Her beautiful eyes, a little sad at the edges sometimes.

Not submitting to temptation, with a wedding just months, then weeks away.

Dad is helping build new roads around the twin towers at Wembley Stadium. Ma is still anxious about meeting Evie's parents, while Dad does his best to make sure it doesn't happen until the wedding day.

A new law gets passed letting women divorce their

husbands for adultery, leading to jokes in pubs about having to be careful who you fool around with.

Evie and her ma strike lines through the wedding list as the time draws near.

The church, the priest, the guests . . .

Evie's aunties in charge of the flowers.

The reception in the banqueting room of the Clarendon Hotel on Hammersmith Broadway.

A charabanc to take everyone from the Uxbridge Road to Hammersmith, with a crate of ales and a lap or two around the green first.

My suit ordered from Mr Putter the tailor on Uxbridge Road.

Her dress sealed away in a wardrobe at her house.

The honeymoon reservation.

The list goes on.

Mr Ellis gives me two tickets for Jack Jackson's Rag Pickers at the Hammersmith Palais and says I should take Evie out dancing to ease the wedding pressure and hear the new music from America.

A warm Saturday afternoon in February. The sort of day that makes you believe spring is on its way. I'm wearing an old blazer, patched and darned by Ma, a striped shirt too large at the collar and trousers from the jumble, with a straw boater bought for the occasion.

Evie's ma opens the door and says Evie has influenza. She reads my disappointment and says, 'Better now than May, at least.'

I ask to see her, reckoning she might still be persuaded, but Evie shivers under a blanket, her pale skin wet and sore.

She says to go to the Palais by myself.

I tell her I'm not going without her.

She says I must, if I promise not to dance with another girl.

I tell her she already knows I can't dance to save my life and have no intention of letting anyone else find that out. 'In any case, these trousers are too big and will fall down if I do.'

She laughs, her cheeks flushed with fever, and says she's got me a present she was saving for our wedding but it looks like I could do with them now.

I unclasp the lid of a small jewellery box, it springs open with a soft click and I unwrap the pale cloth around her grandfather's silver cufflinks embedded with the blue and white glaze of a nautical flag.

Evie slots them into the cuffs of my second-hand shirt.

I don't want to go out without her but she says to come back tomorrow to tell her all about it, and we say goodnight.

Over the last two years, I've cultivated an idea what her skin looks like beneath her clothes, even when she's ill, even shivering in a blanket for warmth.

My undiscovered world.

I'm happy to wait.

Her ma closes the door and Evie waves at me through the gap in the shutters of the sitting room window.

Hammersmith Broadway is bustling with Saturday night-life, and surprisingly warm for February.

A tram rattles by as I walk up to the Palais de Danse, an

ice rink before the war, then a factory making wooden aeroplane bodies, which were carted to Wormwood Scrubs to have their wings fitted.

There's a buzz in the street and two tickets in my pocket.

The crowds arrive, dressed to the nines, seasoned revellers and first-timers ready for an evening of Dixieland jazz.

I already know it will be worthless without my forever girl, so I look for a pair of strangers to give the tickets to. Everyone I approach already has their own, so I give up and walk against the tide to go home.

On the corner of Hammersmith Broadway, I glance through the doors of the Clarendon Hotel and imagine walking into our wedding reception in just two months.

I buy a pot of hyacinths, rich with purple scent, from the flower seller behind King Street. Evie will chide me for not using the tickets but be secretly pleased I came back with flowers for her instead.

I walk past the Albion on Overstone Road on the way to Evie's house.

A man steps out of the pub, tanked. He whistles at me in my striped jacket and straw boater and calls out, 'La-di-da!'

I try to ignore him swaying on the pavement.

'Billyboy!' he shouts. 'You didn't 'ave to buy me no fuckin' flowers.'

Thirteen

Clem has filled out these last eight years.

He carries the weight of middle age but still has menace at the corner of his eyes. He stands me a pint in the Albion and the years catch up.

Time in prison for robbery and an assault he didn't do, though there were plenty of others he got away with so fair's fair, he says. He was drafted into the infantry on an early release and served in Flanders, on which he's as vague as me. Now works unblocking shit and dead rats from the sewers and says Saturday's the only day he looks human.

I tell him I'm getting married in a couple of months and he shakes my hand and orders two gin chasers for the ale.

I buy us another pint with a gin top. After the next I mention Evie being ill and not going to see Jack Jackson's Rag Pickers at the Hammersmith Palais. Clem says we should go to celebrate my nuptials.

I say he's not dressed right and he says this is the most right dressed he ever gets.

The Palais has an ornate frame in the middle of the hall around the dance floor, which is thick with couples as the Rag Pickers play behind it. The rest of the room packed with tables for those sat drinking.

The music is fresh and full of life and I'm happy Clem made me come back.

Women in bright-coloured dresses with collars and beads, flapper-style, hair bobbed flat. Men in striped blazers, waistcoats and bow ties, several in identical straw boaters to the one I lost in the Albion after many ales and gins with Clem.

Ragtime sounds like it's from another world, which I suppose it is.

Clem swiftly takes two full glasses of gin from a table without being spotted and finds two seats on the far side of the dance hall. We down the stolen drinks and he pulls out a bottle from his inside pocket to refill our glasses as we sit watching the bare shoulders of women dancing with their partners.

There's joy in the music and disappointment Evie isn't here to share it.

Clem stands and knocks into someone's lady but claims he meant no harm and her boyfriend lets it pass.

I'm talking to a woman in a black dress which blooms into bright flower-heads and tassels over her knees. A string of beads around her soft neck and hair the colour of straw. She's sweet enough but not as pretty as Evie. A few years younger maybe, with the look of someone who wants to dance on a Saturday night.

I tell her, 'I like your dress.'

She says, 'I borrowed it for the night,' and does a twirl, making the tassels fly and fall like descending birds.

She's all dressed up but speaks rough. She asks, 'Ain't I seen you sweeping the platform at Hammersmith station?'

I tell her I'm the manager in a bakery and ask if she likes ragtime.

She says, 'Don't mind if I do,' gives a little curtsey and laughs, and I find myself walking her to the edge of the dance floor.

A hand pulls me back sharp. 'He's taken, luv,' Clem says to the girl. 'Got a wifey waitin' for him at home.'

She shrugs and walks back to her group of friends. I tell Clem to fuck off, we were just going to dance.

'No such thing, Billyboy. You want to be careful.'

I tell him, 'Just because you haven't picked up anyone yourself yet.'

He laughs and says he's getting the eye off the wife of a bloke he used to be in prison with.

I move towards the girl again but Clem grabs me hard and says, 'I'm serious, don't balls it up.'

I tell him he's the one getting the eye off another man's wife.

He says he's not getting married in a couple of months, and in any case, his mate won't be out of prison for ten years.

I'm feeling gin-soaked and alive. I look for the girl in the crowd.

'Listen to me, Billyboy. You always were a bit of a twat, but I like you so I'm goin' to tell you what's what. If you want to get married, forget doin' the other shit.'

I'm still looking around the dance floor when Clem slaps me hard across the face.

The sting reddens my cheek.

The room swims and I look into his eyes, at the bleak history buried deep.

'Think about other women much as you like when you're married, Billy. You won't get through it otherwise. 'Cause there'll always be a girl who takes your fancy.'

The floor is bouncing to the music.

Clem's hand grips the lapel of my blazer.

'But once you got someone on the side, touch her, kiss her, whatever, it'll dig away at you. It'll keep diggin' because do it once and you'll do it again. You'll keep doin' it 'cause you think you got away with it last time, but it'll eat you up. There's blokes who can tup girls on the side, Billy, but you ain't one of 'em.'

I ask, if he knows so much, how come he's not married with a family.

''Cause I'm a cunt, Billyboy, and you ain't like me. Think you can handle it but you can't.'

He slaps my face again, softer this time, more like a friend.

'You want a good marriage, Billyboy, remember what I'm sayin'. That little tart you was just moonin' over. Go home, picture her tits in your face, her wet minge on your little todger and toss one out.'

He laughs now, lets go of my lapel.

'Knock one out to get her off your mind, an' then get back to your wife. You'll thank me when you're old and still married.'

He takes another glass from a nearby table, downs the drink and leads me out of the Palais with the ragtime still ringing in my ears.

We're on the pavement in the cold night air and it feels like February again. We stand for a minute in silence, then shake hands. Clem gives me a toothless grin, says we must do this again sometime and wanders off into the darkness.

On the corner of the Broadway, I wait a moment to steady my head, remembering the purple hyacinths I bought for Evie but not where I left them.

Two girls are walking down the pavement, arm in arm. One is the girl in the black dress with flower-heads and tassels.

We say hello again and she unlocks arms with her friend.

The fresh air is making the street spin.

I ask her which way they're going.

She says, 'This way.'

I say, 'I'm going this way too.'

We walk towards Hammersmith Bridge without asking each other's names and turn right along the path by the Thames.

Her friend is suddenly not there any more.

A deep chill makes me shiver.

She says, 'It's got cold again.'

I give her my blazer and she tells me I'm a right gentleman.

We're in a dark alley not far from Hammersmith Creek with a breeze cutting in off the Thames.

We kiss hard and fast in the shadows.

My hand on her chin, pushing her head back against the brick wall, knowing Clem has it all wrong.

'Fancy cufflinks,' she says.

I decide not to think about the cufflinks.

She lifts the hem at the bottom of her dress, her hand full of flower-heads like a bride's bouquet. It rides up over her hips.

I unbutton my trousers which fall easily to my knees. My cock's already hard and my head thrilled at all of this.

She tells me everything's fine, that I'm not her first. I slip quick and easy inside her. She lifts her knees around me and I hold her there, my hands under her backside, pushing against the wall to keep the weight off my ankle.

Evie's face appears, her kind eyes wide and full of wonder, but I shut it out, knowing this has nothing to do with her.

A bit of fun with a girl whose name I don't know, a farewell to other lives before a long and faithful marriage. I'm happy Evie will be the one remaining love, despite what Mrs Coggins once said about having five.

Knowing she would never cheapen herself like this girl is doing. Sat at home saving herself for me.

The girl stays quiet and I feel the warm rush. We stop moving and the cold comes back.

She asks for a handkerchief to wipe the mess.

I'm reluctant to hand it over.

She says, 'Quick, it's drippin'.'

I give her my handkerchief and she wipes the top of her legs. She looks at the initials on the fine cotton, hands it back and says, 'Thank you, BB.'

She pulls her dress back down and I belt up my trousers in awkward silence. We step out of the shadows, she gives me back my jacket and I make my escape up Hammersmith Creek.

Back at the house, recalling Clem's words, I reckon I've learned an important lesson: we only gain knowledge through experience rather than heeding other people's advice.

Trying not to make any noise, I splash cold water on my face in the parlour, then wash the smell of the girl off the top of my legs. When I get into bed, I shut my eyes to stem a burning sadness knowing I'll never let anything like that happen again.

The room makes a few turns as gin belches sting my throat. I fall into a shallow sleep and dream of Evie shrouded beside me in a small boat on a long voyage.

Her big eyes, bright and wide and beautiful.

At some part of the voyage I lean over the rail to be sick. The feeling passes and I sleep soundly afterwards, warm and safe beside the forever girl of my dreams.

Fourteen

The cold light of day smudges the arm of the small crane above my bed. I already know Evie isn't here beside me.

I roll back the covers and raise myself up, swinging my legs off the mattress into the slippers left on the floor. It takes time to get my dressing gown on before groping for the arms of the stroller next to the bed.

A gentle push forward and I'm up.

A few seconds to settle my balance.

Nothing in the day to rush for.

When the blood in my ears stops spinning, I start the slow lunge to the bedroom door, one leg, then the other, a lift and shuffle of the frame, step by step.

Ros says I'm bloody-minded when I want to be.

It's important not to give in. When I feel the dark shadow waiting, his breath heavy on my cheek, arms open, ready to smother me.

On other days I might drop into the wheelchair and wait for Sylvie to take me to breakfast. Some days I don't even bother to get out of bed at all, waiting instead for a speedy end to this last, sorry descent. This slow fade that begins with the first aches of middle age and ends with the uselessness of now.

These last few steps towards death.

Waiting a long time now.

It'll come soon enough, I reckon, but not today.

At breakfast I stick two fingers up at the yoghurt and dried fruit, to the Weetabix and warm milk too, and ask instead for a runny egg and pork sausage.

I imagine the egg freshly laid that morning, a warm yolk ready to erupt like a small volcano, the sausage browned and juicy with a slice of soft bread to mop it up.

A pale egg arrives in a puddle of water. I chase it around the plate with a spoon. The promise of a runny yolk isn't fulfilled; instead a yellow crust even the knife won't damage. The sausage swims on the plastic plate like a damp pink turd.

Sylvie says she has sad news.

The memory of the Hammersmith girl by the river has left me unsettled and I've forgotten about the quiet commotion in the night and the trolley wheels in the corridor.

She tells me Jimmy Parris passed away in his sleep.

After breakfast, I sit at the table with Ros's typewriter. Some new memories are coming to light that I'd like to get down before they fade in a lost corner of my mind.

Tap click. Tap click.

Ding.

After a while, having forgotten them again, I move back to my chair near the window. The television set is on quiet this morning, out of respect for Jimmy.

His armchair where the old fish tank used to be remains empty for a good hour or so before Mrs Gibson, the new

163

lady with the thin grey hair, decides a suitable period of mourning has passed and takes it before someone else has the same idea.

I decide not to say anything in protest.

None of it matters, of course.

These are the petty moments of daily life.

Being new, Mrs Gibson might not be aware how it works here when someone dies.

None of it's important, I suppose, when there's memories to get lost in.

I would have liked to escape with Jimmy to the Lake District when the fire alarm went off. Taken a train and enjoyed a pint in his favourite pub by the water.

Maybe he didn't pass away in the night after all, but stuck a fiver in Tabor's pocket, made a break for the border without telling anyone, and is now sat looking at the lake with a glass of beer.

Sentimental bollocks, of course.

A happy ending to an unhappy tale.

Gordon will be making a call to Jimmy's relatives or writing them a letter to say sorry for their loss.

As he'll do for the rest of us soon enough.

That's what happens when families move around and live in faraway places. Easy to lose touch these days.

Last thing you want is to be a burden to your kids.

Gordon and Mrs Akinyemi seem to have patched things up after arguing about the parking space and are talking politely outside her office. Gordon keeps touching her arm and smiling while he's speaking, though it's always impossible to tell what sort of mood Mrs Akinyemi is in.

Maybe Jimmy's death has reminded them of the import-ant things in life.

Jimmy's family haven't called to see him for a while. They'll have to make the arrangements now.

Archie knows what to do when my time comes.

I don't want any fuss.

Not at this age.

I think everyone here is surprised it's not me who passed away in the night.

What's that joke about being old? Looking for the obit-uaries each morning, and if you can't see yours, you must be still alive.

When he next comes in to push the shop trolley, I'm wondering about asking the Duke of Edinburgh's school-boy to get a message to Archie for me. I could write a letter and ask him to send it as everyone here's always busy and you never know if the post gets overlooked.

He'll sometimes read the paper to a few of the residents when he's done his rounds. Gordon says he's only fifteen, though I'm not sure what the Duke of Edinburgh has to do with it. Maybe it's a punishment, made to sell mints and puzzle books to old people, though I can't think what he might have done to upset that posh oaf. He should come here himself rather than send some poor school lad to do his bidding.

I'm not even sure if the Duke of Edinburgh's around anymore. He wasn't looking well when I first moved in here and he might have been dead for years.

At least Archie will know what to do when my time comes. We've been over it before, but I might go over it again when he next calls in. Better to have it sorted and know what's what before it happens.

With the ashes or whatever. Where to scatter them.

Under that tree.

The weeping willow we planted.

Stanton Moor, was it?

Not that I mind really. When the time comes, he can find any spot he likes and throw me to the wind, doesn't make much difference, I suppose.

I still can't picture that woman I met in the Hammersmith Palais. The good-time girl who cheapened herself going with men whose names she didn't even know.

Hard to respect a low girl like that.

It might be that egg I had for breakfast, but thinking of her now makes me feel queasy.

I can remember the thrill, getting frisky in an alley by the Thames, but not much else about her.

Not a proper love like Evie.

A mistake perhaps, but a valuable lesson learned.

I wonder what might have happened to that Hammersmith girl afterwards and the sorry life she went on to have.

A month before the wedding and Evie's mum tells us to get out from under her feet.

We walk up to collect my wedding suit from Mr Putter's on the Uxbridge Road and Evie helps me choose new shoes to go with it. The suit is a perfect fit, though the shoes pinch across the toes, which is only to be expected as it takes years to break in a good pair.

We discuss decorating the flat off Askew Road that Evie's father bought as a wedding gift, with a wage rise that means I'll be able to afford the mortgage. We talk about the children we'd like to have, both of us keen on a large family. Sunday lunches around the dining table, the warm hearth in winter.

Evie asks what we should plant in our tiny garden, but a strange mood has been growing between us.

She asks what the matter is.

I tell her nothing.

She takes my hand and suggests a walk to the Easter fair in White City.

We walk past the old exhibition halls and palaces, derelict now. The canals have drained away, leaving only a maze of muddy ditches filled with rubbish left by travellers passing through.

Holding hands with Evie, trying not to think about the Hammersmith girl. I put the strange mood between us down to wedding nerves.

Approaching the fairground, she asks again if something's worrying me and I snap at her for always repeating the same question.

She says she's sorry and asks me to win her a coconut.

The bearded man takes my ha'penny, hands me three leather balls and moves to the side of the stall.

Five poles in the ground with coconuts on top.

I've never tasted coconut before.

A sudden breeze whips the side of the canvas.

Evie asks, 'Which one are you aiming for?'

I say, 'I'm shutting my eyes and hoping for the best.'

She laughs, touches my arm gently and for a moment this touch helps me remember what love feels like.

I take the first ball and gauge its weight. Aiming for the middle prize, I pull my arm back to throw.

It misses by a whisker and smacks into the canvas at the back of the stall.

A young boy and his father have come by to watch.

My second throw thumps the wooden frame at the corner of the tent with a loud smack.

I want to win for Evie, to make amends for what happened with the Hammersmith girl. To restore the silent vow I made the day we met in Lyons coffee house, on the walk to White City. To be a good man always and forever, till death us do part.

One last ball to throw.

I choose the coconut to the left of the middle this time.

Pull my arm back with nothing in my head but winning it for her.

The ball makes a perfect arc.

It cracks hard against the coconut and bounces off the prize.

I look to the man who says, 'Tough luck, son. Not hard enough.'

I tell him the coconut must be fixed to the pole.

'You need to throw it harder, mate.'

I tell him I won the coconut fair and square.

He takes money from the young father with the boy. I tell him it's a cheat. The man on the stall says they won't come off if you throw like a girl.

The young father laughs.

Evie taps my arm and says we should go.

I tell the stallholder I know he stuck the coconuts to the poles and it's a con like everything else in the fairground; skittles lined up too close for the hoops so you can't win a goldfish, and fortune-tellers who lie.

Evie says, 'What's wrong, Billy?'

I shrug her away.

The man on the stall calls out, 'Son!'

He lifts the coconut out of its cup and waves it around with a grin before dropping it back into place.

By the mud bank of an old canal I tell Evie this was never built to last.

She touches my arm and says she knows it's hard but I can tell her anything about the past if I want.

I say, 'Thank you,' but she doesn't know how wrong she is.

Our long shadows are getting sucked into the black pool of evening and she kisses me on the lips. The kiss should be bliss but it brings back the cold sweep of the river.

I concentrate instead on the smell of Evie's cheek. The rub of her nose as our heads turn slowly through the kiss. My hand on the small of her back. Arms by her sides, chaste, unhurried.

Shutting the Hammersmith girl out.

Letting this moment be Evie's, pure once more.

Her fingers reach into my hand and I don't understand why everything has to be saved for marriage.

I slide my thumb over her fingernails, sharp like a blade.

Through the kiss, my other hand brushes the back of her neck below her hairline, above the collar of her dress. It's a hidden part I've never considered before and resolve to give it my full attention when we're married.

Her fingers touch the bones of my ribs through my shirt. A small collision of teeth and her smile that says don't worry, we're young, we'll learn all this in time.

Our long journey of discovery ahead.

The soft breeze of her breath on my cheek as our mouths close.

My eyes open at the same time as hers and I struggle to contain the wild thump in my chest, remembering the soiled handkerchief that cleaned up the mess.

Thank you, BB.

Evie tells me she loves me.

We make our way back across the green, still carrying my wedding suit and new shoes. I try to hide the bubbles of tears in my eyes and wipe them away before they become real in her world.

She says, 'I wish you'd tell me what's wrong.'

I wonder if now's the time to give up one of my secrets.

I think for a second about a full admission.

Instead I choose to fasten my buttons tight.

Fifteen

When they finally set me alight, I will catch fire like straw.

My blood like powder in the veins doing a last few laps down to the feet and back. I'm brittle and dry, more like a prehistoric bird than a man now. Grey sand, the only thing left for Archie. The cool dust of a long, long life.

Windermere or Coniston, was it, where Jimmy wanted to be scattered?

Two weeks since he died and I've kept my buttons tight all that time.

Left the typewriter alone and let the days come and go.

Gordon says there's a store in the basement under Mrs Akinyemi's office where jars of old ashes are kept, still waiting to be collected by the families of old residents.

Everyone's far away nowadays, spread across the world.

Gordon says Jimmy's family aren't making the trip for his ashes and won't give an address where to post them. One of his children said to scatter him here with his friends.

Today started out nice, sunny and cold, but by lunchtime the wind picked up and it feels like October now. Windows are rattling and a car alarm down the street has been shrieking for a while.

The rain that was forecast has held off so we'll go ahead with Jimmy's memorial after all.

Sylvie's back from the Iranian grocer with biscuits and two packets of fondant fancies.

The television set has been switched off as a mark of respect, though Mrs Bentley's not happy about it.

Mrs Gibson is sleeping in Jimmy's armchair where the fish tank used to be, a newspaper folded on her lap beneath her old twisted hands. Everyone seems to have already forgotten it was Jimmy's chair.

Mrs Chaudhry's put a coat on over her sari in readiness. She goes into the small garden at the back with Gordon holding the ashes. The garden backs onto a factory shed with a blue tarpaulin whipping hard against its roof.

Everyone knows Mrs Chaudhry had a soft spot for Jimmy Parris, which Sylvie would tease him about. The bushes are bent forward in the breeze, not unlike Mrs Chaudhry.

Inside, the other Indian ladies are wearing bright-coloured saris. We had a few words about Jimmy in the sitting room before Gordon disappeared for twenty minutes to put his green duffel coat on. Through the window, I can see Gordon holding Jimmy's urn while trying to stop the strings of hair blowing off his bald top.

I don't remember losing my own hair. All I'm left with now is a round bare skull like an egg with a shade of bristle where grey used to be. I recall, late thirties maybe, noticing a steady greying in the mirror and realising life was on the wane. White hairs at the temples. Watching the

172

whiteness spread around the sides and over the brow. Before you know it, the barber's asking what you'd like to do with the tufts, then, soon after, it's gone.

Your threescore and ten goes quick.

That was decades ago and I shouldn't still be here, remembering those who never even made seventy: Harry Coggins and his sister Peg, Flight, Mary, Jack Mulholland, Pell and the Baron . . .

I've had more than my fair share.

What did Ros say; how getting old isn't for wimps?

Mrs Bentley has put the television set back on even though Gordon and Mrs Chaudhry haven't scattered Jimmy in the wind yet.

On the screen, a row of people press buttons that light up, but other than that, nothing much seems to happen. I don't understand television programmes these days.

Outside in the garden, Gordon is losing the fight to keep his hair in place while Mrs Chaudhry attempts to take the lid off Jimmy's urn. Ros has gone out to help. She walks Mrs Chaudhry over to the rose bushes, Mrs Chaudhry tips up the jar and Jimmy's remains fly into the wind. Some of him gets blown over the back wall and onto the blue tarpaulin roof of the big shed next door.

Gordon walks over to Ros while Mrs Chaudhry gives Jimmy's urn a final shake. A lump of ashes blows back over Gordon, who hurriedly tries to brush it off his face and the front of his green duffel coat.

A few moments later, Gordon comes back inside with his mouth pursed, still swiping ash from his hair. Mrs Chaudhry looks like she's been crying.

Sylvie and Ros hand out cups of tea and Jimmy's favourite pink and yellow cakes.

A shame he's not here to enjoy one.

Afterwards, Sylvie clears the plates while singing along to music in her white earbuds.

Mr Ozturk says Sylvie'll go deaf if she keeps wearing those things, and he should know. Gordon is always yelling at Mr Ozturk to put his hearing aid in but he says it wastes the battery.

Chewing slowly on my cake the colour of cherry blossom, I think about Jimmy Parris and how far he might travel in the wind, which is blowing up a gale out there.

Maybe he'll make it to the Lake District after all.

Less than two weeks to the wedding, and it's harder to look Evie in the eye. She keeps saying she's worried about me and I tell her not to fuss.

I imagine how beautiful she'll be walking down the aisle on her father's arm.

My forever girl.

We stroll through Wendell Park, the air rich with cherry blossom. She asks if I've lost the monogrammed handkerchief she embroidered with my initials as she hasn't seen it lately.

I've not thought about the Hammersmith girl for at least an hour, and the sudden idea of her makes me want to be sick and confess everything. Telling Evie this close to the wedding doesn't feel like the right thing to do, so I deflect the memory by unburdening one of my other secrets instead.

'There's something I want to tell you.'

Her lips form their soft little curl and her eyes look up above me, wondering what might fall. We sit on a bench, her hands by her sides, and I explain that pocket handkerchieves always make me think of Flight Sergeant Cooper, who saved my life in France. I tell her he wrote a letter to his wife just before he died, which I took from his tunic pocket but never delivered.

'You still have the letter?' Evie asks.

I tell her it's under my bed.

She says she's very proud of me for being brave and telling her.

She looks me in the eye, her hand tight on mine. 'Take it to her, Billy. To Flight Sergeant Cooper's wife. It'll be good for both you and her.'

'It was seven years ago, Evie. I left it too long.'

She shakes her head. 'If it was me, I'd want the last letter you'd written, even if it was seventy years.'

We sit silently on the bench watching a male pigeon strutting after a female, neck feathers splayed out wide.

'Don't think bad of me,' she says, 'but I thought you were going to say you didn't want to marry me any more.'

I tell her I love her and want to marry her more than anything.

She says, 'I can come with you, Billy, to see Flight Sergeant Cooper's wife, if you like.'

'Thank you,' I tell her. 'But it's something I need to do alone.'

Metropolitan Line to Baker Street.

His letter in my pocket.

Change for an Amersham train to Metro-land, carrying a small bag with two gifts inside.

A sick feeling in my gut passing the Wembley towers as the city gives up to green fields. Through Harrow on the Hill to Pinner with a street map bought from the station.

I'm expecting Metro-land to look like the pictures in estate agent windows, all sunshine, cows and bicycles, but estate agents will do anything to sell a house. Built for commuters who want a London home in the countryside, Metro-land feels like its poor cousin sent to the doldrums. The city on the horizon with its aftertaste of hops and coal dust. I miss the beaten rugs down alleyways and the stench off Hammersmith Creek.

A slow procession of identical front doors, too far apart and shut to the outside world. After an hour on foot, I come to a gate in a hedge and finally put an image to the address Flight Sergeant Cooper scrawled on the envelope in a muddy ditch all those years ago.

Shivering down the pathway, I think about turning round, walking back down the lane and dropping the letter into a bin but before I reach the knocker, a middle-aged woman opens the door, already angry at the stranger on her garden path.

I say my name but it doesn't change her expression.

Offering my condolences, I tell her I've brought a letter her husband wrote before he died in France.

A man calls out, 'Who is it?' and the woman replies, 'Some bloke reckons you wrote me a letter before you was killed in the war.'

He emerges with his fist raised, saying he's sick of tinker's tricks to sell their filthy wares, and tells me sod off quick before he lamps me one.

His fury absolves some of my guilt about the Hammersmith girl, knowing I can go back to the bustle of London and a good marriage to Evie with my debt now paid. I turn to leave, but the woman changes her tune and says, 'Who exactly did you come to see?'

She then recalls a Mrs Cooper who lived in the house when the war finished and goes to find the address, not too far away, she thinks, while her husband stands furious on the doorstep, not quite keeping up with events.

This time I know the woman who answers the door is Flight's wife. She's pretty, but life has knocked the edges off her. When I open my mouth to introduce myself, a deep choke sucks the air from my lungs.

I stutter on her doorstep, my eyes wet and brimming.

She takes a deep breath and says, 'It's Billy, isn't it?'

She looks past me to the greater world beyond, as if by some chance I've brought her husband back after all these years. She says she hoped I might turn up at some point, that Francis always mentioned me in his letters but she presumed I was killed in action too.

She hugs me for a moment and says, 'Thank God you're alive,' before breaking away again and holding down the rising pressure in her chest.

I can handle her upset better than my own, and we stand in silence until she says to come inside.

When the front door is closed, neither of us know what to say.

She tells me she doesn't have long.

I follow her into the living room and we sit in armchairs in silence again before I remember the two gifts I bought from Shepherd's Bush market that morning for her and her son, who I reckon will be nearly eight. She takes the toy train and the bunch of early rhubarb, and I'm thinking her house feels too quiet for a home with a boy in it.

Mrs Cooper wipes a stream of tears from her eyes with a tiny cloth. I tell her that her husband was a fine man who saved my life after falling out of the balloon and then pulled me through no-man's-land for two nights when I'd been shot in the leg.

I tell her I was with him when he died.

She smiles bravely but keeps her lips tight to hold it all in.

She says I would've been a great comfort to him at that time.

More tears drip from her wet eyes. I find her a smile in return.

'I stayed with him to the end, Mrs Cooper. He looked right at me.'

I decide not to say the other things I'd planned, like it being a waste of life or that I'll never forget him.

I start to tell her he was like a father to me but it's not a sentence I can finish out loud, so we just sit quiet as the small clock on the mantelpiece chimes three in the afternoon.

Mrs Cooper says she'll have to be getting on.

I tell her there's something else I meant to give her and take out the folded envelope. The ink on the front, legible amidst the stains, reads, *Cherry, my love.*

She holds it without looking down, her face turned away, biting hard into her bottom lip. She tries to say something but no sound comes out.

I stand to go, apologising if coming to see her was a bad idea.

She looks at me with eyes as kind as Evie's and says it was the best thing she could have wished for.

I tell her how I'd sit watching Flight write letters to her. And hoped I'd find a love like that to write letters to one day, someone who'd be out in the world thinking of me.

I tell her I'm sorry.

She shakes her head, looks at the clock.

I tell her I'm very sorry.

I want to keep saying I'm sorry until she knows what happened under the hawthorn bush in a muddy hollow in France, but the front door opens and closes, followed by heavy footsteps across the hallway into the sitting room.

An older, thickset man stands in the doorway, red-faced, leaning on a stick to catch his breath. My first thought is he's Mrs Cooper's elderly father who she cares for in his old age.

'Didn't know we were expecting visitors?' he says from the doorway.

'Hello, sir,' I reply.

'Billy was with Mr Cooper in France.'

The man stares at me, crosses over to the hearth

without a handshake, bolts up phlegm from his throat and spits it into the fireplace.

Mrs Cooper lets the silence settle and says, 'This is my husband, Thomas.'

I tell him I hope I'm not intruding.

'He brought a toy train for Albert.'

I'm about to mention the letter, but Mrs Cooper gives me a look and I realise it's already pocketed inside her apron, so I decide to keep quiet about it.

The red-faced man glowers at me and says, 'I'm off upstairs. Finish what you came to say. When I come back down, I want you gone from my house.'

Mrs Cooper is already wiping her cheeks clear and tells him I was about to leave in any case.

I pick up my small bag and listen to the footsteps creaking across the upstairs landing, followed by the slam of a bedroom door.

'I'm sorry,' I say for the final time.

Mrs Cooper whispers, 'Thank you for coming.'

I tell her I'm sorry not to have met her son.

She glances upstairs and says her husband thought a growing boy would do better at boarding school, especially now there's another on the way. She puts her hand across her belly and the rest of her story becomes clear.

At the door, she touches her apron pocket and whispers, 'Thank you for this,' before failing to hold back a loud sob, like the bark of a straining dog fighting to get free of its chain.

A tiny piece of grit in the eye, blown in after Mrs Chaudhry was out scattering Jimmy into the wind, maybe.

The old pipework is knocking behind the walls as the boiler kicks in, winter on its way.

Time is passing.

It could be the next day, or the day after, I suppose.

It could be a Saturday, one week before the wedding.

Walking out of Mr Ellis's bakery on Loftus Road, another night shift over. The May sun already high above the green as I walk down the Uxbridge Road, past St Stephen's Church, knowing soon I'll be a married man.

A list of vegetables in my hand to save Ma a trip out later, not as good on her legs as she used to be.

Footsteps behind me.

Two young men cross the road to Lime Grove before looking back. I recall them waiting on the other side of Loftus Road when I came out from work.

I tear a crust off the fresh loaf under my arm. The bread is warm and sweet and chewy.

A tram rattles by towards Acton.

The two men stand talking as I pass Lime Grove and make my way to the market to pick up Ma's list and say hello to Mrs Cumbernauld on the fish stall. She can't help making a comment about the women's movement before I walk down to the Goldhawk Road, where I see the same young men following again.

They're mid twenties. The taller wears a white shirt

and black trousers, thick hair on top, shaved around the sides, with a padded face the colour of off milk. The other is shorter and stocky, cloth cap and finer features. The sleeves of his shirt rolled up under a waistcoat buttoned tight against the trunk of his body.

'Binns?' the shorter one calls.

I search for history in his face but nothing comes back. I ask who's asking.

'Come with us.'

His accent is rough, local, but I don't think we've met. His eyes are cold and offer nothing good. I say I'm not going anywhere if I don't know who they are.

He says we can walk or get the bus to Acton.

Propelled by fear and sensing few other options, I run a few paces around the corner up Titmuss Street, but they are onto me in seconds. The tall one grabs my collar, spins me to the pavement and swings a punch at me on the ground.

They pull me up and slam me hard against a wall. People are taking no notice just a short distance away on the Goldhawk Road, and I'm thinking my mistake was to run into a side street.

I say, 'Why do I have to come to Acton?'

'You'll find out.'

I try to push past them, but they muscle together and force me back against the wall. The short one opens his waistcoat to show a blade handle in the belt of his trousers.

The day is warm and bright and sweat is running under my collar.

I decide to stop thinking about escape until a better opportunity arises.

Neither of them speak as we cross the road, flanking me as a bus approaches. We get on and they sit me against a window, looking out, the tall one next to me with the short one directly in front.

Maybe they've cased Mr Ellis's bakery for a robbery and singled me out as an inside man. Or it might be a prank by Clem, the week before getting married. Two ex-prison mates drag me to a pub where he'll be waiting with a gin and ale.

'Is it Clem?' I ask hopefully.

Neither of them look at me.

Past Stamford Brook Road and Turnham Green, where they rise from their seats and bustle me onto the pavement. We walk up Swan Lane, past the pub and onto Acton Lane, into a maze of slum houses and lean-tos waiting for demolition, ripe with the smell of piss.

Some boys kick a stone against a wall.

Through the maze with no idea how I'll get back. The tall one stops by a broken gate, torn from its hinges. He shoves me into the yard towards the back door.

It opens an inch on my first knock. They nod at me to go in.

My eyes adjust to the darkness. A stout woman with thick shoulders, a little younger than Ma, is stood in the tiny kitchen brandishing a rolling pin like a weapon. A large crack runs all the way down the small window.

'Upstairs,' she tells me, watching me walk up the creaking steps.

I can hear the two men talking in the yard outside. If this was a robbery, it would have happened by now.

Two doors off the landing. One closed, the other ajar. A faint sound of crying inside.

I knock quietly on the open one and go in.

The room is packed with dark furniture end to end. The crying comes from a small bed on the far side of the room. Two bunks on the other, separated by a curtain hooked to the ceiling.

A girl sits on the bed, head forward. Straw-coloured hair hangs over her face, lank and unwashed. A frayed bed sheet over the window keeps any sunlight out of the cramped room.

She lifts her eyes, her face wet with tears, like someone I can't place, another girl I once knew.

I chase the memories and wonder if it's Harry's sister Peg, not dead after all, come back from the shadows of the railway bridge in Trussley Road.

'I didn't know how to find you,' she says.

A voice I've heard before.

Memories roll in waves to the shore, steam trains converging at a busy junction, and in a few seconds everything will become clear.

'You said you worked in a bakery. I only had your initials.'

Evie's handkerchief.

A chill off the river on a dark night.

She says her brothers have been looking for me these last two weeks. 'There's a lot of bakeries in west London.'

I have questions but already know the answer.

She looks up again.

The remaining light gets sucked out of the room when she tells me, 'We're going to have a baby.'

Sixteen

There's a phrase, something like:

An old man's memory can't be trusted. Or: *Never trust the memory of a very old man.*

Something like that. I'm at the typewriter trying to recall the exact words but making a ham fist of it, as Dad would say.

Sometimes I hit a seam when everything flows like water from a pipe. At others I can only remember fragments, pieces of a jigsaw that mean nothing to me, like I'm recalling the tale of an entirely different person.

The lamps in the sitting room are on. The stormy sky has brought evening a little early. A flash of lightning in the windows is followed quickly by the rumble of thunder.

One of the Indian ladies says it'll be Jimmy making his way to heaven. Another – Mrs Subram, I think – says, 'And not being let in!' which makes the others laugh.

It feels too soon after the memorial to be making jokes about Jimmy's death, even if it's a while since he died.

I've lost my sense of time.

How quickly it passes these days.

Mrs Subram's joke about not being let into heaven is exactly what Jimmy Parris would've said if he were here, with the thunder and lightning. He'd have been the first to laugh. It just sounds different coming from a woman, especially an Indian lady, I suppose. Thinking Jimmy would have approved, I let myself have a chuckle at Mrs Subram's joke, even if it's a while now since she said it.

I'd like another look at that photograph on Mrs Subram's wall when I next go past her room. Very glamorous she was, back when she was a Bollywood star.

A right sort, you might say.

Shame more people don't hang pictures up where everyone can see, but I'm not sure it's allowed here, not in the sitting room at least. It'd be good to be reminded how everybody looked in their heyday.

The submarine captain is muttering in his own language. Mrs Bentley dunks a biscuit in her tea but leaves it in too long, and when she lifts it to her mouth, it crumbles into her lap.

It's disgusting watching old people let themselves go. That's why I wear a tie and get a proper shave once a week. It's important to keep up standards.

Gordon laughed when he once saw me cleaning my good shoes with a tissue and said there wasn't much mud on the footrests of a wheelchair, but Sylvie had promised to walk me round the green the following day and I wanted to look my best for her.

Lovely Sylvie, with her filthy laugh and a ring in her nose you'd think would draw her eye each time she looks down. Never had much luck with men, she says, but she's young and seems to have a different boyfriend every week.

Hard to imagine Sylvie growing old, hunched over a wet biscuit like Mrs Bentley.

It was a shock remembering the Hammersmith girl saying we were going to have a baby. I'm sure it all got dealt with somehow, but it's not something you want to dwell on when you're trying to remember what love was like.

A shame, all the fuss she had to go through to get it sorted.

We learn from our mistakes I suppose.

Looking back now, I might be confusing the Hammersmith girl with someone else. My mind could easily be playing tricks on me.

That's why I want to get these memories down for Archie, before I become properly senile and can't recall my own name. Like Mr Buffery, who just sits in the corner all day coughing and dribbling.

It'll take a while to get it all down at this rate. When it's finished, I might let Ros have a look at the pages, before I give it to Archie, of course. To prove I wasn't always a bag of dried-up skin and bone who pisses out of a tube. Something for my boy to remember me by when I'm gone.

I'll put a few words for him at the beginning, before the title.

A dedication, Ros says it's called.

Tap click, tap click, tap click.

Tap click.

Tap click, tap click, tap click, tap click, tap click.

Tap click. Tap click

Ding.

Something simple, so he knows it's for him.

`for Archi e`

Silence in the girl's bedroom, like a blanket muffling the sound of the outside world.

'We can't have a baby,' I tell her.

She wipes a train of snot from her nose.

I tell her I'm getting married to my fiancée next week, that I'm on my way to lunch with her parents after dropping off Ma's errands and taking a quick nap after my night shift.

I'm thinking how to get past her ma and two brothers downstairs and never coming back here again.

'Besides, you're wrong,' I say. 'It must be someone else's.'

She says, 'Your initials were on the hankie.'

I can just about remember being inside her those few seconds, with a cold breeze off the Thames. Not long enough to make a baby, certainly.

I remind her she was stood up at the time, that I saw her wipe everything clean with the handkerchief. She'd said so herself.

She doesn't reply and just sits looking very young on the bed.

I'm thinking how else to persuade her. 'It must be another man you've gone with. It can't be mine.'

'The other men didn't do it up me,' she replies. 'Ma says the night with you was the middle of my monthly cycle, when it's most likely.'

I don't understand what she's talking about but feel the walls closing in. I need to get back to Evie, where everything makes sense.

'No,' I tell her firmly, the way Dad would say it. 'You're not tricking me. I'm marrying a decent girl. You need to find whoever else you've been with, or get rid of it.'

Her blue eyes are wet with crying. I'm not sure I ever noticed her blue eyes before. She says, 'It's yours, Billy.'

It was a tiny moment in an alley, barely worth remembering. I even took Flight Sergeant Cooper's letter to his wife to make up for it.

'Ma says you need to make an honest woman of me before Pa finds out about the baby.'

Fury and injustice rising, somewhere deep, talking to a girl who isn't listening to what I'm saying.

I think of Mrs Cumbernauld at the market and these modern ideas that let a young woman talk to a man like this. If I were more like Clem or my father, I'd probably knock some sense into her, but that isn't me.

Instead I let the fury burn, and shout that I've got nothing to do with her fucking bastard baby. I tell her I'm marrying Evie next week and this talk has to stop, it's her fault, and goodbye.

I leave her room and walk downstairs as quick as I can, but the stocky brother is blocking my way. I try to push past but he grabs my collar, his fingers pinched into the skin of my neck. He punches me hard in the mouth, shoves me back upstairs and throws me into the bedroom.

He stands in the doorway. A metallic taste of blood on my tongue as my lip swells.

He looks to his sister and says, 'Is it sorted, you little whore?'

She shakes her head and mutters, 'No.'

He jabs me in the chest with his finger, tells me to fix it before her dad gets home, and leaves the room again.

A sick feeling in my gut that I'm not even sure is the result of getting punched. Again I tell her, quieter this time, 'We're not having a baby.'

She says, 'You're its dad.'

I'm swimming in a dark place, slipping under the surface, fighting for breath.

'I can't,' I tell her, desperate now. 'I'm getting married. You have to get rid of it. Jump down the stairs and make it fall out.'

She says, 'I tried but it don't work.'

Slipping under.

'I missed my bleed,' she says, tears rolling down her cheeks. 'I don't know what to do. Ma says if I'm carryin', you need to get it fixed.'

Lots of women trick men into marriage but I can remember enough fragments of my own life to know it doesn't pan out that way.

Just five loves whose faces came clear to me that night.

Mary, Evie, Archie, Vera, Betty Jackson.

The Hammersmith girl, for sure, isn't one of them.

I tell the Hammersmith girl about Mrs Cumbernauld at the market, who will know about helping women. She can speak to her tomorrow about sorting it quick, but must tell her ma we're not getting married.

She wipes her eyes with the back of her fingers, filthy with black dust, and I'm thinking Evie's hands would never get that unclean. She stops crying and I feel like I've knocked some sense into her without using violence.

I tell her goodbye and she looks lost on her little bed. There's no sign of the easy woman in the black dress with flower-heads and tassels I met that night in the Hammersmith Palais.

I leave the room as kindly as I can. Her brothers watch me on the stairs. I tell them everything's sorted.

One says, 'It better be,' and I avoid looking him in the eye, passing through the gloomy hallway into the dark kitchen.

A big man with pockmarked skin and a scar from his cheek to his neck stands in the doorway, the light from the broken window behind him. Her ma is still in the corner by the stove.

The man drops his cap on the table. His voice is low and soft with menace. 'Apparently you want to talk to me 'bout my daughter?'

His wife says the two of us should have a word in private.

There's still the tang of blood in my mouth and I wonder if I should take my chances and run. Instead I plot a wiser move, and hold out my arm to shake hands. 'I'm Billy. Pleased to meet you, sir.'

We sit in the front room, saved for best, just the two of

us. He's taken his jacket off but his frame is too big for the armchair.

He says, 'Somethin' to ask me, then?'

I tell him I've spoken to his daughter and there's clearly been a mistake.

He looks down, says, 'I said, you've got somethin' to ask me?'

I tell him again there's been a misunderstanding. My fiancée is waiting for me, we're having lunch with her parents today before we get married next week. I say the mistake's been cleared up with his daughter and I'm sorry for any confusion.

He looks at the door.

The antimacassars on the back of the armchairs make me think of Auntie Pam, and I wonder how she is in Manchester since Ma made it clear it was best if she wasn't invited to the wedding.

When he speaks, it's barely a whisper.

'Listen, sonny. My wife thinks I'm some sort o' cunt who don't understand what my daughter gets up to.'

Every word he says is a threat.

'My wife can think what she do. That's how it works in this 'ouse. But you don't think I'm some sort o' cunt too, do you, sonny?'

I explain again about the misunderstanding, but he stops me with a small lift of his finger.

'I asked if you think I'm some sort o' cunt.'

I tell him no, I don't.

'So. Somethin' you need to ask me?'

I tell him thank you, but I don't have anything to ask him at all.

He says, 'You're not listenin'.'

He gets out of the chair and walks towards me. I stay sitting to avoid a confrontation. He puts his thumbs into the straps of his braces, reeking of sweat and violence.

'My daughter's upstairs in a state, is that right?'

I tell him she's upset, but we've spoken and she's much better since we agreed there's been a mistake.

He asks if I've been with his daughter this last couple of months, and I tell him it was only a brief – I search for the right words – *time together* that we had. I try to say it's not possible I'm the father of her baby as we were standing up at the time and she wiped off the mess with my handkerchief straight away, but these are not words for an angry father of an easy girl you spent a few minutes with by the river.

'So for the last time, sonny,' he continues, his quiet voice taking root in the wooden floor, 'what is it you want to ask me?'

I'm staring at the empty fireplace.

A small clock ticks away the promise of my happiness and I realise the only way out of this room is forward.

He goes back to his armchair.

I'm thinking this'll all be over once I've spoken to Mrs Cumbernauld.

I listen for any sound outside the room saved for best, but nothing else is happening out there.

My other world is disappearing.

He taps his leg, waiting.

I ask for his permission to marry his daughter.

Seventeen

I'm late meeting Evie and her parents for lunch at the restaurant, still wearing my work clothes from the night before.

No one mentions my bloody nose and fat lip.

It's a subdued affair. I sense Evie's told them about my visit to a dead friend's wife and everyone is treading on eggshells.

Everything stays calm until Irwin chokes on a cherry stone during pudding and has to be upturned over the back of a chair and slapped vigorously by a doctor sitting, as luck would have it, at a nearby table. The good doctor and his wife are invited to our wedding the following weekend as a show of gratitude for saving the bride's father's life.

Walking home, Evie says, 'You're quiet again today.'

I tell her, 'I can't wait to be married.'

Her mum overhears and tells her to stop worrying, saying it's groom's nerves and Irwin was just like this before their wedding.

It's Tuesday morning and I'm to marry Evie in four days.

I come out of work after a long night, half expecting another visit from the two brothers, but it's the

Hammersmith girl who is waiting for me on the corner of Loftus Road.

I've never seen her in daylight before.

I bustle her away from the bakery, afraid that Evie's father is watching, and ask why she's come to my work.

She says, 'A wife can visit her husband, can't she?'

Then she says, 'That was meant to be a joke.'

I walk briskly towards the market, hoping she won't keep up with my pace.

So much history in these stalls under the railway arches.

She catches up and starts to cry again, which almost makes me feel sorry for her.

I give her my handkerchief so she can wipe her tears and neither of us mentions the last time I did such a thing.

The street is busy with morning people. I ask if she wants some coffee. Knowing the market café will be busy, we walk along to Lyons instead and take a booth in the corner. I sit with my back to the room and order coffee for two and a toasted teacake for her, which she eats hungrily.

'I can't marry you,' I tell her.

'I know it's not what you want,' she says. 'It's not what I want either.'

'But your dad . . .'

She looks across the room with a shrug, as if she has her own thoughts on the matter.

'You don't want to get married?' I ask.

'I don't want to be carryin'. Not till I'm with the right person. I just don't know how to . . . I need you to help me get it sorted.'

A beam of sunlight draws angles through the window

of Lyons coffee house. Evie's face comes into view and a small ray of hope in the sorry tale.

The sunlight passes, stolen by a cloud.

'You don't want the baby?' I ask. 'You'll give it away, I mean?'

She looks at a picture of a volcano on the wall. Then says, 'I don't love you, Billy. I don't even know you. You said you knew someone who could sort it, for good.'

Dregs at the bottom of my coffee cup.

Women are always more complicated than they seem.

Four days, before marrying Evie at eleven o'clock on Saturday.

I pay for the coffee and we go to Shepherd's Bush market to see Mrs Cumbernauld, but Jack Burns is working the fish stall when we get there.

The Hammersmith girl, whose name I still can't remember, is behind me. I wait, hoping Mrs Cumbernauld will stride up with a crate while Jack Burns rows with an unhappy customer.

We walk up to the arches, to the rear of where Mr Edwins' umbrella shop used to be, where Mrs Cumbernauld goes to smoke with the other market women, but she's not there either.

Returning to the stall, I ask Jack Burns where Mrs Cumbernauld is.

He grins and says, 'Aye aye, girl trouble, is it?'

I tell him to fuck off.

He tells me Mrs Cumbernauld's over at Norland Road today.

Everything used to be simple back when I was fetching

boxes for Mr Finlay over to Clem's stall. We walk past Lyons coffee house again, past the arch to White City and over to the Norland Road market.

I tell the Hammersmith girl to wait while I go behind the stalls to the cellar store where Mr Finlay used to keep ice.

The raised trapdoors are open next to a pile of broken wooden crates. Down the stone steps I hear Mrs Cumbernauld cursing in the darkness, her large frame emerging into the light, hot and flustered, a small cigarette tight in her lips.

She sees me, dumps an armful of old wood and says, 'Fuckin' Jack Burns. Gets me doin' all the shit he should be doin' 'imself.'

I tell her I'm in a predicament.

She brushes damp splinters from her big arms.

I say I'm hoping she can help, as a woman.

Mrs Cumbernauld spits on the ground and says, 'Don't know what you're talkin' about, Billy.'

I tell her it's women troubles that need sorting urgently.

She says, 'It's men who cause women troubles in the first place.'

'I thought you'd be able to help.'

She looks at me with a sideways eye. 'You're getting married soon?'

'On Saturday.'

'You got no worries then. Tell everyone it was a good honeymoon.' She laughs. 'Few raised eyebrows when it pops out in eight months, but no one minds that.'

'The girl with the troubles is not the one I'm marrying.'

198

She relights the end of her cigarette. 'Billy Binns. I didn't have *you* down as no fuckin' idiot.'

She picks a flake of tobacco off the end of her tongue.

'You want it over?'

'We both do.'

Mrs Cumbernauld clocks the Hammersmith girl behind me. I turn and see her watching from the back of a stall a short distance away. Mrs Cumbernauld says, 'I don't have nothin' to do with any o' that business,' and walks back down the steps of the old ice store. 'Not worth the trouble.'

I tell her we don't want trouble, which is why we've come to her.

She stops on the stone steps. 'No trouble for you, Billy Binns. It's them like me they send to prison.'

'Please, can you help us?'

'Sorry, Billy.'

The Hammersmith girl has come over. She says, 'I don't know what else to do.'

Mrs Cumbernauld shakes her head. After a silence she turns and says, 'I may be able to advise. *Advise*, mind! There's one or two married women I've *advised* how to regulate their monthly cycle, but I don't do nothin' else. Is that clear?'

I recall the Hammersmith girl saying something about a cycle and feel like we're getting somewhere. 'That's what we need, Mrs Cumbernauld. Advice. We need it quick.'

She steps closer, looks at the Hammersmith girl and asks, 'How are you, love?'

The Hammersmith girl nods but doesn't speak. Mrs Cumbernauld puts a hand on the young girl's cheek.

'You're too young for this,' she tells her. 'It's easier for married women who got a family and can't cope with having no more. Who can't tell their husbands. If it goes wrong, they lose the baby, damage their insides maybe, but they already got their kids. Somethin' goes wrong for you, you're childless for good.'

'Mrs Cumbernauld,' I say quietly. 'We came to get—'

'Quiet!' she barks at me. My body is fired with useless anger, wondering what the world would be like if every woman spoke to a man this way.

She turns back to the Hammersmith girl. 'If you want my advice, love, it's a big mistake what you're looking for. Riskin' your health and your future. It'll stay on your mind forever. 'Ave the baby. It'll be hard, yes, its father will probably sod off for good and your family'll want nothin' to do with you. But there's help if you know where to look. Not much, granted, but you're young an' strong. An' at least you'll grow old not regrettin' what you did when you weren't more than a kid yourself.'

I bite down on my tongue, furious about coming here and seeing how the suffragettes are out to destroy the world for men.

Evie's beautiful face fading from view.

Her kind eyes a disappearing dream.

I look for my exit from the Norland Road market. For the excuse I'll make to Evie when I ask her to run away with me this afternoon. To trust me and not ask questions. To leave London together, go somewhere far away and never come back.

I look at the girl I fucked against a cold wall for just a

few seconds some weeks ago, who ruined the rest of my life. She stays locked in Mrs Cumbernauld's grip, eye to eye.

The Hammersmith girl says, slow and measured, 'Thank you, Mrs Cumbernauld, but I don't want this baby. I want it gone so I can get on with my life. Please can you help me?'

Mrs Cumbernauld nods slowly. She loosens her grip on the girl's shoulders, smiles kindly at her and says, 'All right then, love. This is how it's goin' to happen.'

Eighteen

Evie opens the door.

She's surprised and pleased to see me.

We go into the sitting room and I tell her I've found a gift that will bring us a great deal of happiness in our married life but don't have enough money to pay for it right now. I was hoping to borrow twelve pounds and two shillings from the money her parents have given us to buy furniture for our new flat.

She asks what it's for exactly and I tell her I can't say yet as I want it to be a surprise.

She says it's a lot to spend on a surprise and I tell her I'd rather not spoil it by saying.

I've tried to borrow money from elsewhere to pay Mrs Cumbernauld's friend for her services. My father just asked if I thought it grew on trees. I decided against approaching Mr Ellis for an advance and searched a few pubs for Clem to see if he knew someone who could lend it to me.

Evie asks if I'm sure about this, and I tell her she won't regret it. I feel myself getting frustrated at her reluctance to trust me on this important matter.

She says, 'You're not in trouble, are you, Billy?'

I tell her she just needs to trust me and all will be well.

She leaves me alone in the sitting room. I stare at the painting of the brother and sister she once had. It must be a relief for the dead, not suffering the worries of life any more.

A few minutes later she returns with the notes and coins, which she counts slowly into my hand. Again I tell her not to worry. Her lovely eyes look wounded, which makes me even more keen to protect her from the agonies of the world.

Walking away from Evie's doorstep, I repeat my silent promise that nothing like this will ever happen again.

It's Wednesday morning, after work.

Time is pressing like a squeezed accordion and there's still so much to do.

I emerge into sunlight from Mr Ellis's bakery, take the tram through Holland Park towards Bayswater, get off at Lancaster Gate and walk through the back streets towards Paddington. The Hammersmith girl is waiting by the water fountain a short walk from St Mary's Hospital. She looks like a street urchin in a dark blouse buttoned half-way up her pale wrists and a plain skirt that looks like it's been used to wash floors.

All the appeal of her that evening at the Palais has gone. She means nothing to me now, stood there haunted, cold and lost.

We walk the cobbled streets under a grey gloom at the back of the hospital. Past the wharves, to the rows of dwellings in a maze of alleyways, with a familiar stench off the Paddington canal.

I can tell she's afraid.

She says it's the right thing to do, though it sounds like she's reminding herself. When she says the same thing a few minutes later, I raise my voice and say of course it's the right thing, before blaming my mood on two days without sleep.

We share a cigarette beside a barge getting unloaded at the wharf and the mood lightens a fraction.

I tell her I'm sorry.

She's sorry too.

She says, 'I just want it done.'

I tell her, 'You're very brave.'

She blows out smoke and says, 'I don't have any choice.'

It takes a while to find the right address.

The door is opened by a middle-aged woman with a small child on her hip.

The woman says Mrs Winter isn't here yet and to make ourselves comfortable in the parlour.

A fire glows weak in the grate.

'I want to get married one day too,' the Hammersmith girl tells me with a bite in her voice. 'To have my own family. That's why I'm doin' this. So I can have one when it's right.'

Sat across the parlour, she looks older than her years. She rubs her hand on her belly, over the growing baby inside that'll soon be gone. Nothing left but these troublesome memories and a chance of happiness for us both.

'I'll tell Ma I lost it and she'll deal with my dad. No one'll care when it's forgotten.'

I look at my shoes, thinking of the new pair waiting to be worn for the first time on Saturday.

My wedding is in three days.

There's a quiet knock at the door and a voice says, 'Sorry I'm late.'

Mrs Winter is a small, harsh woman with cold eyes and an unfriendly nature.

She used to be a nurse, a good one Mrs Cumbernauld said, until she was caught stealing medicine from the hospital pharmacy.

She says most ladies she helps are married with children of their own, and the Hammersmith girl is very young for menstrual suppression, which are words I'd rather not hear. She says Mrs Cumbernauld convinced her it's in the best interest of the Hammersmith girl to be regular again. She's also aware we need to complete the procedure in the next couple of days, so I can walk down the aisle on Saturday knowing *before God* there is no such impediment to prevent me marrying my wife.

She asks me to wait in the other room as a man doesn't need to be present for the talk about bringing back regularity, but I feel it's only right to show support to the Hammersmith girl. I'm also worried Mrs Winter will try to persuade her against it if I'm not in the room.

The Hammersmith girl says she'd like me to stay, and Mrs Winter reluctantly agrees, claiming it's a first. She explains she won't be able to help if I become squeamish, which in her experience most men tend to be.

She looks me in the eye at every mention of unsavoury details, as if she's trying to make me queasy to prove her point.

More than once I struggle to hold my stomach down.

She tells us the old technique of a hot bath, plenty of gin and a self-inflicted tumble downstairs is a myth that brings little chance of success; that we're lucky we found her, as other women offering this service are still using veterinary medicine. She'll take us through the process today to get started and we come back tomorrow to complete the business.

She says the chance of success in anti-suppression is increased if the lady avoids food and water for twenty-four hours to be in an ideal state for receiving the purgatives that will initiate the removal of the obstruction.

Mrs Winter removes a large church candle from her cloth bag and places it on the table. I wonder if she's about to do a religious ceremony as part of the service when she opens a small jar of grease and instructs the Hammersmith girl how to smear her lower region with it, insert the candle as far as possible to encourage a widening of the cervix, and to repeat this action once every hour until morning.

I'm regretting my decision to stay in the room.

Mrs Winter reminds the Hammersmith girl to do this throughout the night to prepare for the procedure tomorrow, and I sense her satisfaction in the discomfort she's causing me.

After the hourly widening of the cervix, tomorrow morning she'll give the Hammersmith girl a tincture to drink, containing the correct balance of ingredients to bring about her regularity. There will be discomfort for a few hours while the lady absorbs the ingredients, resulting in the restoration of a monthly flow onto towels she'll leave us with. She'll return later to inspect the towels and the expelled matter.

After that she'll need to widen the cervix with her instruments to inspect the area inside, and all remaining organic matter can be cleansed with a small scraper called a curette and washed clear with a – Mrs Winter fixes me with her cold eyes before speaking the words – *vaginal douche.*

She says the patient will need a day or two to recuperate and that it's normal to experience a lot of soreness *down there*, as well as a tug of emptiness – touching her chest – *up here.*

While packing her bag, she asks if we have questions, then tells us to meet her here at eight o'clock tomorrow morning.

She repeats that it's not necessary, or indeed desirable, that I attend. She says men tend to get in the way and women are better equipped to deal with these matters alone, but I have to see this through.

I feel discomfort at what the Hammersmith girl must go through to get this done and try to catch her eye to show support, but she refuses to look at me.

It'll be difficult to forget some of these details when sharing a marital bed with Evie, but that's a small price to pay for being a bystander in all this.

I want it over, then we can all get on.

Mrs Winter bustles to the door like an uptight fist, and is about to leave when the Hammersmith girl asks what's in the tincture she must drink.

Mrs Winter says it's her own tonic, developed over the years to bring good results.

The Hammersmith girl says she'd like to know, out of interest.

The nurse looks like she's not used to being challenged. She takes a moment before saying, 'I take an ounce of pennyroyal, which is a herb like spearmint. It's a small, safe quantity but would be toxic in a higher dose. I combine it with several drops of turpentine to form a safe diarrhetic compound that affects a woman's lower regions and helps clean out the impurities in her uterus. You drink the small cup I give you and we let nature take its course.'

The Hammersmith girl says very quietly, 'Thank you, Mrs Winter. I just wanted to know.'

Mrs Winter touches the Hammersmith girl on the arm. 'You're a smart young woman who made a bad choice.' She suggests doing the first insertion with the candle right away. The more discomfort she can bear now, the greater the relief tomorrow. She looks at me and says to give the girl some breathing space, and then she goes.

I wait in the sitting room on the other side of the closed door, listening to the soft cries of pain from the Hammersmith girl sat alone in the parlour, as she starts the process of bringing her regularity back with the church candle.

Nineteen

Back to the alley behind Trafalgar Street.

Dad comes out of the back door and says it's time we had a man's talk about being a good husband, and the only place for that's the pub. Ma scrubs the back step with a wire brush, trying not to look like she told him to do it.

I tell him I have to sleep before going to work that night, and he says I'll need to be more of a man than that once I'm married.

We walk up to the Eagle on Askew Road. I buy two pints of light ale and we stand in a thick cloud of silence and tobacco smoke as he downs his beer.

'Tide's out,' he says eventually, waving his empty glass and looking for someone he'd rather be drinking with.

I buy him another pint, still only a few sips into mine, and ask what advice he has for being a good husband.

I can't recall any of his words.

I'd have liked to know what he thought.

Maybe he spilled a few pearls of wisdom, which might have been helpful a couple of months earlier, before meeting the easy girl in Hammersmith Palais, but I don't reckon so.

I watch him share racing tips with a man stood over a paper down the bar. For a moment he looks animated, talking about a racehorse, someone I don't recognise, but he returns to silence, peers into his diminishing beer and becomes familiar again.

I consider what might happen if I told him I'd knocked up the Hammersmith girl, taken Evie's savings to pay for her to get *regular* again; had messed everything up and didn't know what to do. If I were to ask for his help, give him the chance to unbutton his own secrets, open the gates and find some common ground. Two men putting it to rights over a pint. I'd forget about work tonight and we'd get pissed together after a lifetime of silence. Make everything good between us. Listen to him say it will all blow over with the sands of time.

But the man with the racing paper is talking about the ground being good to soft and I'm alone at the bar lost in clouds of smoke while the landlord joins in and says what a pain in the arse wives are.

I tell my dad I have to be getting to work.

He says he's staying for one more and asks me to stand him a couple of shillings before I go.

It's a long, slow night shift before Thursday.

I wait for the Hammersmith girl near Paddington station. She's already half an hour late and I'm convinced she's changed her mind about having the baby when I see her walking towards me, pale and still wearing yesterday's clothes.

We say a quiet hello.

After today, we'll not see each other again.

She's had a rough sleepless night, which I assume can't have been any worse than mine until I remember the church candle.

I ask how she is and she says she wants it over so we can get on with our lives. I take her hand and she smiles with an unbearable sadness as we walk past the wharves and the barges under the shadow of St Mary's Hospital.

Mrs Winter opens the door and scolds us for being late.

The woman with the child on her hip has left for the day.

A kettle of hot water simmers on the stove and a small fire burns in the grate.

A pile of towels next to the chair and a metal bucket on the floor.

Mrs Winter's cloth bag is unfolded on the kitchen table.

A box of small phials and a teacup and saucer.

Mrs Winter pours hot water into the teacup and measures out liquid from two of the phials.

The Hammersmith girl asks me to wait outside as she wants to speak with Mrs Winter before she starts. My eyes are dead and heavy.

I step out.

Despite the promise of spring, it's cold away from the warmth of the small fire. The sky is dark behind the walls of the grey hospital. I think of the Hammersmith girl inside the little house, drinking Mrs Winter's tonic from the teacup, and the potion starting to work.

The pennyroyal and turpentine.

The anti-suppression, to bring back regularity.

I long to see a full blue sky after the weekend.

Evie's face slips into view and soon all this will be a bad memory, dissolving into history like a teaspoon of sand in a bucket of seawater.

The front door opens and Mrs Winter says to come back inside.

The Hammersmith girl looks at me.

Mrs Winter waits for her to speak.

'Sorry. I can't do it, Billy.'

My eyes search for the empty teacup, to know the tonic is already working to free the tiny problem growing in the Hammersmith girl's belly, but the cup is still full and steaming.

'I can't . . .'

Mrs Winter turns her back to us, starts folding up her towels and putting the phials back into the cloth bag.

'I'm going to keep the baby.'

A cloud of noise in my ears, like the wash of sound I will constantly hear when I'm an old man.

'You can't keep it,' I tell her. 'I'm getting married in two days.'

'I'm keeping the baby, Billy,' she says again, quieter now. She runs her hand over her belly the way expectant mothers do.

The ringing in my ears is consumed by the sound of the outside world crashing back in.

I slam my palm on the table, upsetting the last of Mrs Winter's phials, and shout, 'We're here now and you'll damn well do it. You've got your whole life to have a baby and I'm getting married this weekend.'

Mrs Winter says to keep my voice down.

I feel the rage of the powerless.

I shut my eyes. The terror gushes up like the blood from the bullet holes in Flight Sergeant Cooper's chest.

'Please,' I beg her. 'You have to stop it now.'

'I might never carry again.'

'You have to. Mrs Winter, tell her she can't have this baby.'

Mrs Winter says, 'It's for a woman to choose.'

'I don't love you,' I tell the Hammersmith girl. 'I love Evie.'

'I don't love you either, Billy, but this is how it is.'

I scream at her that she's throwing away our lives, destroying any happiness we might have. I call her a name I'm not proud of, but there's a few times in life when no other name will do.

Mrs Winter says, 'Stop it now.'

The Hammersmith girl says it's what she wants.

I tell her, 'Your dad'll kill me if I don't marry you.'

The room falls quiet.

'Better do it quick then,' says the Hammersmith girl. 'Before my belly starts showing.'

Twenty

Another day of spring sunshine and I'm thinking it's the wrong kind of weather for what's to come.

It's Friday.

Walking up towards St Stephen's to meet Evie for our last appointment with the vicar before the service tomorrow. The ground pulls heavy on my boots, like wading through quicksand. Willing it to suck me under.

Searching for the first words I'll say to the girl who'll arrive with her eyes bright and leave with her world torn apart.

Knowing I was on the verge of having everything I ever wanted.

One of my legs buckles at the door of the church and I think I'm going to be sick, though this could easily be from other memories racing at me now like a ball through skittles: the sight of the heron before the balloon fall; Pell lifting his head to peer over the edge of his bunker with the sniper waiting for him on the other side; calming the horse with a gash in its flank, standing and falling . . .

These last few seconds.

Standing and falling.

Holding on before the inevitable.

Evie Ellis is walking towards me right on time, with the

best smile on her face. She wears a new dress the colour of summer: a field of yellow, with a pink check and matching buttons, and the same shoes with black and white squares across the toes that I first threw jellied eels over two years ago.

A small bag over her arm that brings fresh agony, knowing I'll never hold her hand again or feel her fingers in mine.

In that moment, a sudden elation. A refusal to believe this is over.

I give myself a few extra seconds for the world to find some magic resolution.

A brief stay of execution in which I will find the answer to make everything good again. My last chance before breaking both our hearts.

She stops in front of me, her graceful arms warm in the sunlight, pale against her tiny sleeves.

She says, 'I love you, Billy Binns.'

The seconds ebb away and no resolution comes.

Dead silence.

'There's something I have to tell you, Evie, before we go in.'

Words in motion, building up speed like a train from a station. Unable to stop now.

A small cloud arrives on her brow. A sign of the weather to come.

'We'll be late for the vicar,' she says.

'I have to tell you something first.'

'It's too late to change your mind, Billy,' she laughs, trying to make the cloud disappear.

It's the hardest thing to smile back.

She looks into my eyes and her smile fades.

'What's wrong, Billy?'

I'm fighting to hold back tears, but the world is shrouded in a dark mist and I've no option but to let the first one roll.

I say, 'I love you, Evie Ellis, in a very particular way.'

And then I tell her, my words falling like shells.

From somewhere high up, I watch the commotion on the ground below.

I don't hear the explosions but I know the exact moment they land.

I watch them detonate.

A shock wave blasts through the streets. From here, north to Wormwood Scrubs, south to the river, east to Acton and west to Holland Park.

I think I can see Evie in the desolation but it doesn't look like her any more. My forever girl left unrecognisable, shattered.

The light in her eyes has gone.

Those kind eyes.

I look up to the sky, the spire of St Stephen's Church the only thing left standing in the ruins. It blocks out the sun climbing up behind it and blinds everything else from view.

The silhouette of the spire burns into my retinas like a photographic negative.

I'm happy to suffer the blindness. Not to have to see this any more.

Thankfully it puts an end to the sight of my forever girl caught in the heat of an unforgiving blast.

Twenty-One

With a few extra quid in his pocket to oil the clerical wheels and publish the emergency banns that afternoon, the vicar, a man seemingly untroubled by the paths of right and wrong, is happy to accept the name alteration on tomorrow's wedding service.

There's little point in changing the hymns, but I do make sure Evie gets removed from each part of the service and replaced with the name of the Hammersmith girl.

I'd like to remember her name.

To refer to her in another way.

I decide against mentioning the change to Ma and Dad that evening and let them find out tomorrow instead.

My stag night is spent alone, drinking myself into a stupor in a rough little alehouse near the Creek, before singing bawdy songs with the bargemen about my impending marriage.

I get home when the sun comes up. Ma is worried about

the state of me. I go to bed for an hour and wake up feeling worse.

I put on my new suit and the cufflinks from Evie's grandfather with the blue and white flags. I button up the waistcoat she embroidered with the silk lining, knot the tie and tuck it down the front before squeezing my feet into my brand-new shoes.

The leather squeaks as I walk; I'm grateful for the blisters cultivating below my ankle and across my toes, desperate for a physical pain to absorb the inner one.

Ma asks what's wrong, but I can't find the words.

Dad is unhappy about having to put on his new second-hand suit.

I'm not able to keep breakfast down and drink water to counter the ale consumed with the bargemen. Setting off up Trafalgar Street, I stop twice to piss in the alleyways on the way to St Stephen's.

The bright early-morning sunlight has gone, swept under black skies by the breeze of a coming storm.

Only a few pews on the right side of the church are taken. Some long-forgotten relatives and one or two of my father's drinking mates, only here for the free beer afterwards, uneasy in their Sunday suits.

Word has got to most of the Ellis family, though a handful of the uncontactable are now being turned away from the church gate.

The Hammersmith girl's family have taken their pews: her mother, father and brothers, wearing slightly better versions of the clothes they woke up in. Her father glowers at me as I walk down the aisle to sit next to Ma.

She attempts to straighten my jacket, tells me Evie's family don't look a bit like she imagined and asks if Evie is all right.

The Hammersmith girl's brothers whisper to each other. The taller one looks over at me and laughs in a way that isn't befitting of the occasion.

Her father stands and walks slowly to the back of the church like it's a chore as the vicar steps forward, uneasy in front of the rabble before him. He invites us to stand for the bride. Heads turn as the Hammersmith girl walks down the aisle arm in arm with her imposing father.

She's wearing a cream wedding dress that once belonged to an elderly relative, hastily altered by her mother, and carrying a small bunch of wild flowers in her hand.

Ma turns in shock but I refuse to catch her eye.

The bride completes her long walk down the aisle and gives me a nervous smile, which I'm not sure how to respond to.

Last night's ale has me unsteady on my feet.

I turn my back on everyone and shut out the whispers.

When the vicar asks if there's any known impediment why the two of us should not be married, I hear snorts of laughter from the bride's pews.

Time passes.

Words are spoken.

We are pronounced man and wife, though I don't accept the offer to kiss the bride as I'm not even sure it's something we did by the Thames just a few weeks previously.

We walk out of the church, where the clouds have opened, and wait under the small canopy to shelter from the pouring rain.

I tell Ma this isn't the time for questions.

My bride's brothers shake my hand. The tall one says I made a wise choice and he'll fuck me over if I ever give her cause to complain.

Her father calls me son, but not in a friendly way.

Dad shakes my hand while looking puzzled at the floor, awkward in his badly fitting suit. Ma dabs her eyes in the line next to him.

I introduce my father to hers and they shake hands warily, like dogs sizing up their chances in a fight.

Dad says it's all so quick anyone would think she was in the family way, and Ma gives him a look I've never seen before. I try to convey an apology but now she's the one refusing to catch my eye.

Rain pours off the edge of the church canopy.

It made sense to use the church for the service but it would have been unseemly holding the wedding party at the Clarendon Hotel as Mr Ellis had planned, so an arrangement's been made for the back room at the Railway Arms near the corner of Shepherd's Bush Green.

I give my new father-in-law the last of Evie's furniture money to pay for the sandwiches and free bar so his daughter can have the dignified wedding she deserves.

I look to where Mr Ellis's charabanc would have been parked to take everyone past Lime Grove, where Evie and I shared a kiss that snowy Christmas Eve, and force myself not to remember what love feels like.

I've no overcoat to put over the shoulders of my new bride, nor an umbrella to shield her from the downpour. She accepts a brolly and mackintosh from some chivalrous relative and we set off on the five-minute dash through the puddles towards Shepherd's Bush Green.

It quickly becomes clear that neither of us can walk fast in our new shoes, so we submit to the rain and the slippery pavements. I can feel the angry blisters swelling against the merciless press of fresh leather.

We slow to a casual stroll, her borrowed coat wrapped tight around her, my new suit drenched from the storm, the shirt sticking to my skin like glue.

I ask how she is.

She says she's fine.

I wonder if we should at least hold hands, but I'm not sure either of us are ready for that level of intimacy yet.

Water drips off my ears and the end of my nose.

It's difficult to see through the downpour, the rain bouncing hard off the ground and firing back against itself. Tiny droplets smack into the tarmac as a shallow lake forms across the Uxbridge Road.

The street is empty of witnesses to our first stroll as newly-weds.

Not even dog walkers would be out in this.

I see figures in doorways sheltering from the storm, waiting to brave the next part of their journey. Momentary visitors to shops looking to buy nothing more than a break from the rain.

I think of the flat I won't be living in, hollow and without furniture. I think of the family who accepted me as their own. Of the girl who embroidered the lining of my waistcoat and gave me her grandfather's cufflinks.

Saving herself for me, for this, our wedding night.

Saving herself for the rest of our lives.

A tram rattles by towards Acton. Sparks from the wet cable like tiny flashes of lightning in a black sky.

I think of Mrs Cumbernauld tipping water off the tarpaulin sheets above the market stall with the stick of a broom.

It's a surprise to see a solitary figure out in the street, making no attempt to get out of the rain.

The young woman stands idly on the pavement opposite Lime Grove, as soaked as we are now. An umbrella over the top of her head keeps her face hidden from view, but I already know who she is.

The shape through her clothes, imagined a thousand times.

All my thirst for that knowledge, which would have been granted today.

She tips the umbrella back in her right hand to see better. Her left arm tight to her side, like she's carrying the weight of a small invisible object.

Her wedding finger.

We catch eyes for the smallest of seconds.

A tiny moment that will stay with me for a lifetime.

I look at her, seeing all the way down to her bones, and silently plead for her to walk across the road and save me from this now the formalities are out of the way.

To let her know it's not too late. That we can still make it good, despite what conventions or unmarried mothers or their ignorant big-fisted families or marriage certificates may say. To spend the rest of our lives happy together and steal them back from the foolish errors we once made. That I'll be sorry for this even when I'm an old, old man. That I'd rather die now than live with this pain for all the years to come.

I look at her, wishing it to come true, but the wish doesn't work.

I've no choice but to turn away from Evie, from my forever girl, and look down at my new shoes, bought for the woman on the wet pavement at the other side of the road.

I walk on, my bride somewhere beside me, knowing Evie is still watching. Knowing she'll keep watching until we turn the corner at the top of Shepherd's Bush Green.

I try to look back to wave, but I'm afraid it might be the last time I ever see her. And only then, at the corner of the green and the Uxbridge Road, do I hear for the first time since leaving the church the peal of St Stephen's bells ringing out.

Ringing out through the noise of the storm and the quiet of the wet deserted street.

Ringing out.

As clear as a bell.

PART THREE

Twenty-Two

Wrapped up against the late-October chill with a blanket over my legs, being pushed out in the street by Sylvie.

Beautiful Sylvie with her big eyes and her nose ring and her dusky skin, from some exotic part of the world.

Penge, I think she once said.

She pushes me up Hammersmith Grove to the traffic lights, onto Shepherd's Bush Green, and we stop outside a shop with an electric sign that lights up in the shape of a red and blue chicken.

It's good to get out of The Cedars and see a bit of life.

She looks through the window and says we're going inside.

At the counter she talks to a tall black man she pretends not to like but I reckon has a soft spot for.

I can't tell what they're saying to each other until he asks if I'm her grandad.

She says, 'This is my mate Billy, from the home.'

He says, 'How you doin', Billy?' and then keeps on talking to Sylvie, so I just sit still without trying to think of a reply.

This row of shops has changed since I was a boy. Lyons coffee house has gone, Wellington's laundry, the cycle store, Miles's the dog sellers . . .

Next to the Underground station, near where Norland

227

Road market used to be, I remember a footbridge that looked like a train, spanning the road to the old precinct, long before the big new shopping centre went up, where the old white palaces and canals were built for the first millennium. The Flip Flap and the roller coaster long gone too.

Two millenniums I've seen in now. One's more than enough, thank you very much. *Millennia*, Gordon said the plural was, but he can be a tosser sometimes.

They built the white palaces and canals for the first one, and a big lemony dome for the second, somewhere out by the docks it was, near where *EastEnders* starts.

Sylvie's still talking to the tall black man in the chicken shop about some programme on the television set where British people show off their talents.

Opportunity Knocks, maybe, or *Stars in Their Eyes*.

Mrs Jackson and I enjoyed *Opportunity Knocks* on Saturday nights, when we weren't out gallivanting. They should bring those old shows back someday. Better than the nonsense they have on now that Mrs Bentley and Mrs Cutts like to watch.

Sylvie orders a bag of popcorn chicken and a big chip, which doesn't sound enough for a growing girl.

She laughs at something the man says, then abruptly announces we're going and pushes me towards the door.

He says, 'See you roun', Billy. You got my number, yeh, B?' which sounds like a pleasant way to say goodbye to a new friend.

We cross the road onto the green, past the skateboarders by the swings near where the drunks used to sit.

A young boy on a bike, around ten years old I reckon,

though it's hard to tell children's ages these days, long blond hair sticking out from under his crash helmet and a gap between his front teeth.

He makes me think of Archie.

My boy.

Almost caught sight of him again for a moment there, his scuffed knees and knitted tank top. I knew he was going to be trouble the moment I held him after he was born, while his mum took a breather for a minute or two. His cheeky little face smiling up.

Something good to come out of it all.

I can see the edge of his nose and the shape of his head. I just can't see all of him yet. He'll show up in his own good time, I expect.

It's been a while since he last called by to take me out for a picnic.

When you think about it, he may well be dead now. Adding up the years to work out his age.

Twenty-three, was I, when he was born?

Which would now make him . . .

Too late in the day for those kind of sums, I reckon.

We all have to go sometime.

Like Jimmy Parris.

At this age, the inevitability is no longer shocking.

My little Archie.

Come where I can see you, my boy.

Come into the light for a few moments at least.

We'll remember the good times we had together.

Our honeymoon is one night in a bed and breakfast guest house in Mortlake, in a room next to a travelling salesman who makes lewd jokes about being kept awake by a creaky bed.

Neither my new bride nor myself are keen to be alone together just yet and accept the landlady's offer of a hot Bovril in the sitting room, to listen to the wireless before going up. The Ku Klux Klan are lynching Negroes in the southern states of America and a theatre in Berlin has been attacked by Nazis. In London, the new Wembley stadium has been heralded a success after hosting the FA Cup final without falling down.

We finish our Bovril in silence.

The travelling salesman shakes my hand and says, 'I'll leave you lovebirds to it,' and goes upstairs, grinning as he walks out of the room.

When his footsteps on the landing have settled, we head upstairs and clean our teeth separately in the small bathroom down the hallway. The Hammersmith girl is already in bed when I return, and I slide under the sheets next to her after switching off the lamp.

We lie motionless and silent, unsure how to proceed, before the Hammersmith girl turns to face me and asks if I feel different now, being married. I sense she's trying to instigate more of what got us here in the first place, but it doesn't feel appropriate now there's a baby growing inside her, and I tell her I'm tired after the wedding day and turn over to shut my eyes.

In the morning, we're woken by a severe knocking on the bedroom door.

The landlady is accompanied by a policeman, awkward in his tall hat on the landing. He's sorry to interrupt us this early in the day but has come to inform me my father died in the night.

I should feel something about his death, but it comes as a relief.

It means I have an excuse to escape the Hammersmith girl for a good few days at least.

The cold seeps in under the blanket.

The trees on Shepherd's Bush Green look like they shouldn't be growing here. A struggle of nature.

Given a choice, they'd have planted themselves up on Wormwood Scrubs at least, if not out of town somewhere, away from the traffic and the dirty air.

Like the willow I watched grow over the years, though I may not have remembered correctly the sort of tree it is. A weeping willow, I think. Its thin branches spread wide like the hairdo of one of those sixties glamour ladies, round like a helmet, flicking out at the sides.

Like children, it's hard to imagine the size they'll grow one day.

I wonder if this melancholy, this dampness in the root of my bones, is because of the weeping willow.

Living back on Trafalgar Street with Ma, my new wife and a child on the way. The house is oddly dark under the shadow of my father's ghost.

Scattering his ashes in Kensal Green cemetery because there isn't enough money to pay for a grave.

Working night shifts in the railway tunnels when the trains stop running, the first job I can get after coming back from honeymoon. Laying concrete under the tracks for the electrification of the Underground lines. Back-breaking hours, shovelling stones in a tunnel filled with soot, not being able to stand straight at the end of the shift.

Around four each morning, I remember the smell of fresh bread and the warmth of the ovens. I remember the life I once had, away from the rats and the cough and spit of dust.

Walking home in early light, filthy black. A plate of last night's leftovers, then falling onto Gran's old mattress on the floor next to my single bed where the Hammersmith girl sleeps with her growing belly. Light coming in through the small window, with the noise of the waking world.

Later in the day we might take a short walk down Hammersmith Creek together in the last of the daylight before I go back to work to wait for the trains to stop.

Ma sleeps in the sitting room now, her old bedroom rented by a succession of travelling road workers earning money to take home at weekends. The promise of Dad's savings long gone after it turned out he'd spent it all at the bookie's.

I think of Evie on her own journey every day. Months after the wedding, I recognise her on the Uxbridge Road and hide in a doorway against the red bricks, heart thudding in shame. I don't see her again after that, imagining her gone to another part of London, choosing to believe our paths might one day cross again, somewhere along the way.

The days are getting shorter, just a few weeks before the Hammersmith girl is due in November.

Home late one morning with a bag of shopping for Ma, she says an elderly aunt of the Hammersmith girl is upstairs dangling crystals over her belly to find out if it's a boy or a girl.

I knock to enter my own room and exchange a few tense words with my wife, who doesn't wish to be disturbed while her aunt does the business over her bare stomach.

The old woman has a dark shawl and untrusting eyes, a thread held in her fingers on which a crystal sparkles in the dim candlelight.

The Hammersmith girl's belly is stretched tight, like a small mountain. The skin almost translucent, held taut over the shudders within, as if an alien life-form is forcing itself into view.

A holdall of baby clothes against the wall: hand-me-downs from the musty lofts and wardrobes of neighbours, mothballed and mildewed, belted shut for good luck until the time comes.

The elderly aunt says it's going to be a girl, who will suffer unless my wife moves back to her parents' house to have the baby. She says her own kind should be looking after her while she's labouring.

She persuades the Hammersmith girl to pack her few clothes and leave with her that afternoon. The old lady tells me to bring over the bags and hand-me-downs later that day, with one small suitcase of my own, and it seems the idea had been discussed long before I came home.

Ma says, with her husband gone too, she'll miss the noise of us all footling about the house.

Later that day, carrying the bags as instructed, I close the door of Trafalgar Street behind me, and only ever come back again as a visitor.

The slum houses off Acton Lane itch with the patter of mice.

The Hammersmith girl's bedroom has been given over to the two of us, soon to be three, and her brothers' bunk beds have been crammed into the downstairs room once saved for best.

I'm greeted upstairs by her father, who says I must pay him weekly board and lodging for the lot of us, as she's my responsibility now.

Twenty-Three

I'm thinking about my plan to ask the Duke of Edinburgh's schoolboy to post a letter to Archie for me and have it ready by the time he next comes to push the shop trolley or read the newspapers, when the new lady leans over from Jimmy Parris's armchair and says, 'You've got a nice face.'

It's the first I've heard her speak. She adds, 'It's about time we said hello.'

There's light in her eyes today. Ros said she's almost as old as I am and in an acute stage of dementia, but she appears perfectly fine to me.

'Mrs Gibson,' she tells me, by way of introduction.

'Billy,' I reply, wondering if I should try to shake her hand.

'I once knew a Billy,' she says. 'A sailor in the wartime who might have stolen my heart if I hadn't stood firm.' She laughs. 'And kept his wandering hands at bay.'

He gave her jewels that turned out to be stolen in a robbery and she had to hand them to the police when they came to arrest him. 'He was a right wrong 'un,' she tells me, laughing again and enjoying filling in the gaps.

She went on to marry an insurance clerk, a good man who gave her two lovely children before he was struck by lightning in the garden.

Everyone has a story to tell.

She says her great-granddaughter is coming to do the ladies' hair. She has a salon and a big house in Brackenbury, where Mrs Gibson lived when she was young.

I tell her I once knew a girl who lived around there, and the memory of Evie makes me wish I could sit peacefully on my own for a moment.

She speaks too quiet for me to follow all she says, and I wonder if Ros might be right about Mrs Gibson not having all her marbles when she tells me Brackenbury houses are getting sold for two million pounds.

She asks if I have family and I tell her I've a son who I've lost touch with over the years.

'They move away,' she sighs. 'It's what happens when you build aeroplanes. They make people think the world is smaller.'

I'm enjoying my talk with Mrs Gibson, though I'm not sure how much we're following each other as I only catch a few words of her sentences, and when I reply, she looks like she isn't listening to me at all.

In one of her silences I tell her about Archie and how much trouble sons can be, but you never stop loving them despite everything.

I tell her about the good times we shared when he was small, which is fresh in my memory.

About the marbles in his pockets: the catseye and oxblood, the jasper, aggie and ruby.

I make a decision to spend some time later, when Mrs Gibson has left me in peace, to remember the games Archie and I played together: the marbles; the Bayko signal box;

the pick-up sticks and ball games; flying kites on Worm-wood Scrubs and camping in the New Forest.

I'm pretty sure it was the New Forest we went to, just the two of us, to get out of the flat for a day or so.

Taking the train with two rucksacks and a heavy old tent. Pitching up near a beach where the trees stopped. The blue sky and yellow sun. Cooking beans on the stove with a loaf of bread to dunk. Giving him his first beer around the fire and seeing his lips curl in disgust.

We'd talk long into the night, him and me, about how I tried to save my friend Harry Coggins in a hot-air balloon made out of backpacks. Archie would listen, staring at our little fire. We made the most of our trips together before coming back to London, to the silence and rows between me and the Hammersmith girl.

We were living in a tiny flat on Coningham Road at the time, which was all we could afford after moving out of her parents' house. We stopped talking after the first couple of years, me and her. It was better to live in silence than argue all the time, causing gloom around the dinner table.

So I'd take Archie camping, down to the New Forest.

I'm sure it was the New Forest.

I realise I've not been listening to anything Mrs Gibson has been saying these last few minutes, lost in my memories of Archie instead. It's a shame we haven't seen eye to eye these last few years.

'Look at this,' she says, unfolding a newspaper on her lap.

My eyes try to focus on a page of holiday adverts, but the print is too small.

'All the places you can go: India, Australia . . .'

I tell her several residents here have family in Australia, and Canada too.

'Peru!' she says.

I agree there's lots of holidays in the newspaper today.

She turns the page and says, 'Cambodia, Vietnam, where they kill everybody. They drink blood out of their skulls in churches and have a crackpot dictator who the Americans have been trying to bump off for years.'

Having stopped reading the news a long time ago, I'm not up to speed on crackpot dictators any more, though I can inform her there's been some talk of a bridge of trees over the Thames.

'They build all these aeroplanes so people can go off to fancy places. It makes them think the world is smaller, but it's the same size it always was. It just makes people want to go far away from home, from where they're loved.'

I was thinking Ros was right about Mrs Gibson losing her marbles, but it's difficult to disagree with the things she's saying.

Her rheumy eyes, misting over now.

Remembering those far away, I expect.

Maybe she's thinking about her wartime sailor with the wandering hands who once stole her heart.

We sit quiet for a moment, exhausted by the conversation.

The light outside is calling it a day. It'll be November soon.

I want to sympathise with Mrs Gibson, looking lost in Jimmy Parris's chair beside me, but I'm tired, my mouth is dry and I've no strength left for words.

Instead I lean towards her as best I can and pat her

hand gently, then we both sit looking out of the window at the angry sky.

Time is passing.

A freezing night in November, 1923.

I stand out in the tiny back yard, looking up at the stars.

A few whizz-bangs and crashes of light above the maze of alleys, but fireworks will never please me.

The elderly aunt is in the bedroom with her crystals while the Hammersmith girl's ma prepares towels and bowls of warm water.

The two brothers are bare-knuckle fighting in the yard and challenge me to a bout.

I tell them no thanks.

One of them smacks me lightly across the jaw to draw me in, but I tell him to fuck off back to the pikey farm he came from, and he lays in with another punch, harder this time.

Their ma opens the bedroom window and throws a mug down, which smashes against the bricks. She yells, 'Quiet down,' and slams the window shut.

I walk into the alley behind the slum houses, lost in my own misery.

The brothers are laughing, goading me back.

Dim shadows move in the upstairs window and I know by morning I'll be a father.

Twenty-Four

Ros says the Duke of Edinburgh's schoolboy is called Thomas.

Apparently he's from round here but doesn't speak like it. He sounds like he's got a mouthful of plums, which is probably the Duke of Edinburgh's doing.

It's hard to believe he's the same age as we were in France. He doesn't look like he'd survive two minutes over there with his spotty neck and school blazer, although I expect none of us looked like we'd survive two minutes either when we were his age.

Some of us didn't, of course.

Still, it makes a change to see a young face around the place, and he doesn't always hold a little telephone in front of him like most kids on the pavement outside.

He reads the newspaper aloud in his plummy voice to three of us sat near the window overlooking the back garden. Mrs Chaudhry looks like she's thinking about something else and Mr Ozturk, whose English isn't good at the best of times, nodded off as soon as he began.

The newspaper stories all sound glum, but it's good to hear a different voice talking in here. People are angry with immigrants, the same town keeps getting bombed in the Middle East and an American soldier can't decide if he's a man or a woman. Queens Park Rangers fail to get any mention, as usual.

I remember watching games at Loftus Road over the years. Good to have the company on a Saturday afternoon, same old faces every week or two. A pie and a pint in the stands and a bit of banter about who's shit at kicking a ball.

I saw some of the greats before the fun went out of it: Arthur Jefferson, Tony Ingham, Harry Brown in goal, Stan Bowles.

The schoolboy keeps reading the newspaper but I struggle to concentrate on most things outside my head these days. I remember going to Shepherd's Bush library near the market in the mornings to save the cost of buying a paper.

Ros is slow bringing the tea round today. I fancy a hot drink and a biscuit. A little sweetness to brighten up the afternoon.

I might have nodded off, just as Archie was asking if we'd like to hear the obituaries.

He turns several pages and says, 'Here we are. Births, marriages and deaths.'

Mr Ozturk tells him not to bother with the first two and get straight to the deaths.

They're always about somebody who made a mark on the world.

I thought it was Archie reading the newspaper for a moment there but it must have been the schoolboy.

Thomas, I think his name is.

He reads the obituary for an Austrian musical

conductor in his eighties, which makes me think about driving a bus through the Blitz with that clippie I took a shine to.

Vera, was it?

She comes into view again, but it's too soon to think about her as I'm still trying to remember Archie and why his little face hasn't come clear like Evie's and Mrs Coggins'.

I listen to Thomas reading about the Austrian conductor who made his mark reinterpreting Bartok, but it's all a lot of twaddle to me.

That's the thing about other people's lives. They never mean much unless it happens to be someone you once loved. Otherwise nobody really cares.

I'm not sure I ever made a mark on the world when it came to it. Apart from the fence I once named in Chatsworth House in Derbyshire.

A wide rolling landscape packed with trees.

I was older then, after all the fuss that happened with Vera.

Moved away from London for several years, working on the land, digging ditches and driving tractors for the Duke of Devonshire. Building fences for horse trials each summer, for country folk in green jackets and wellies. The tall fences looked terrifying, stood by them. The horses were big too, though I'd already seen a few of those up close in France.

Each week the foreman would set the task of building new jumps over the course, which were given names: The Log Jump, formed of three large tree trunks dragged up the hill by tractor and fixed onto stanchions; The Hawthorn, a hedge grown over a wooden frame, stacked with earth and shrubs, though I tried to avoid working on that one as certain memories will never let you go.

We dug a wide ditch and built a water jump, imaginatively called The Water Jump. Another we named The Duchess, after the Duke's wife. We said this was because it flowered majestically throughout the year, though the real reason was it got jumped twice on the same course, after a story going round at the time.

One fence we constructed out of planks on a timber frame, angled like a window blind, five feet high and twelve feet wide. No one could think of a good name and I suggested we call it The Racket Fence.

Many years later they were still calling it The Racket Fence, so I suppose you can say I did make one small mark on the world.

There were lots of trees on the Chatsworth estate but I don't remember putting in a weeping willow.

That must have been somewhere else.

Stood out in the rain digging a hole wide enough, a pile of fresh earth shovelled to the side and a small bag of compost spread amongst its roots to help it grow.

Saplings one minute, proud and tall the next, like your children.

And here he is.

Little Archie running up in his shorts, knees dirty from playing in the mud on Wormwood Scrubs. Marbles jangling in his pocket, the silvery chink of glass and the sliver of pretty colours: the catseye, the oxblood, the jasper, aggie and ruby.

His little tweed jacket much too big for him, sleeves stitched back by his ma for room to grow. Shorts hoisted up with braces. You couldn't afford new clothes when they grow so quick.

A fleeting glimpse of my little boy.

His dirty collar, neck stained black with grit. Scrubbed clean once a week in the bathtub and filthy moments later.

Never saw his ears clean once, I reckon, not while he was growing.

Here he is now.

His little face coming into view.

After the Austrian conductor, there's a few words about a young nurse killed helping others in a war who didn't get a chance to live a proper life.

The last of the deaths reported in the newspaper is someone who used to be on the television set in the seventies, but they're ten a penny these days and keep dropping like flies. No one cares much about them either, although Mrs Chaudhry's perked up, opening her eyes for the first time since Thomas started reading aloud.

He finishes the obituaries and goes back to pushing the shop trolley around while I try to muster strength to ask him about getting a message to Archie.

Mrs Subram is taking ages buying tissues to put up the sleeve of her cardigan.

The Duke of Edinburgh certainly gets his money's worth out of the poor lad. I watch him travel slowly around the room, trying to catch his eye again.

Listening to the newspaper reports has given me an idea about a way to find Archie's whereabouts.

Somewhere behind Acton Lane, down a warren of lean-tos and alleyways, I stumble across an old pub, a sawdust dive with piss-pots under the bar and paraffin lamps hung up to illuminate the gloom.

I'm stood with a tankard of ale. A blind man next to me at the bar, seven sheets to the wind, white eyes rolling steadily from side to side.

I stand him a pint and tell him I'm expecting my first child.

He says, 'My sympathies!' and raises his jar.

His pint still in one hand, he takes his cock out with the other and pisses furiously into the pot by his feet. The spray hits and misses the tin in equal measure, splashing over my shoes and the damp sawdust. The piss goes on and on.

Two men lean against a pillar next to the blacked-out window. It could be night or day out there. Another man walks out of a secret hidden door in the back wall. When it closes, it's impossible to see it there.

The landlord tips the slops under the barrel into a tankard and takes it to the man who came out of the secret doorway. He takes a long swig, already unsteady on his feet.

Having finished his piss, the blind man downs the rest of his ale and knocks the jar on the bar to demand a refill but doesn't offer me one in return.

A young woman comes out of the secret doorway. She has a red ribbon in her thick curly hair. At first sight she looks as filthy as me after a night in the railway tunnels, but as the dim light adjusts, it's clear she's dark-skinned. She wears a man's threadbare woollen jacket over a creased button-shirt, open at the collar and frayed at the cuffs, with clogs on her otherwise bare feet. She looks around the room and I'm struck by how beautiful and unhappy she is.

She goes behind the counter and comes back with a large enamel jug. She kneels beside the man she followed out of the secret door, picks up the piss-pot at his feet and empties it into the jug, then bashes the tin pot down on the stone floor and does the same with the next.

She looks like something from another world.

She walks towards me, picks up the pot directly below the blind man and tips it into the jug with the rest.

I can't take my eyes off her. She says something down on the floor but I'm not sure what it is. I say thank you even though it's not my piss she's emptying. She mutters a few more words and carries the jug out of the back door of the pub.

The landlord leans over the counter and says, 'Six shillings and you're next,' in his broad Irish accent.

I count the coins left over from my wages, having not yet paid board and lodging to the Hammersmith girl's father for the week. I consider going with the dark-skinned girl in the back of the pub but then think how it will feel to be a father myself, determined not to make any more mistakes like the one that landed me with the Hammersmith girl in the first place.

So I say goodnight to the blind man, who's taking another long piss into the empty pot at his feet, before heading out and walking back to see if my young wife has given birth to our child yet.

I open my eyes and the schoolboy with the blazer is tapping me on the shoulder.

'Excuse me, sir,' he says in his plummy voice. 'The lady said you wanted something off the trolley?'

He struggles to understand my whisper.

Mrs Chaudhry puts her ear close to my lips and writes the words down in a corner of her puzzle book to help explain what I need.

Archie Binns.

Archibald in full, though no one ever called him that.

Never had a middle name, did Archie. Arrived so quick we didn't have time to think of one, we used to say.

Born sometime in November, 1923.

Can't have been many boys called Archie Binns in Shepherd's Bush at that time. The lad might be able to find something in the births section of the newspaper from back then, in the library maybe.

He could even ask the Duke of Edinburgh to help, if he's of a mind.

Mrs Chaudhry repeats it to the young man and asks him to find an address so I can send Archie a card.

I'm grateful for her help, as it's exhausting explaining things to someone you don't know.

There's more details I don't bother with, like not being able to remember the Hammersmith girl's name, or holding out much hope of finding him, if I'm honest. Not the age he would be now, even if he was still alive.

He won't be far off getting his own postcard from the Queen.

The Hammersmith girl long gone too. Can't even remember when she died, so there's no chance of any help from her.

It'd be nice to remember her name, though, after all she went through at the time. All the trouble her father and brothers caused her.

Water under the bridge now.

She gave me a son and you can't hate someone forever when they've given you that.

Not forever, that's for sure.

Bygones be bygones.

Sleeping dogs lie.

I don't bother asking Mrs Chaudhry to explain any more, such as it being a long time since Archie dropped by to take me for a drive, or out for a picnic with a tub of egg and cress sandwiches and a flask of sweet tea, made by his wife, I expect. I don't recall his wife ever coming to visit much, though she must have done once or twice over the years, I suppose. Can't recall her name either, but that's not a surprise if I'm struggling to remember the Hammersmith girl.

Something lovely about a picnic. Finding the perfect spot and throwing the rug over the grass and sitting down next to the daisies. These days I'd get myself down all right; it's the getting back up that's the problem.

We'd be better taking folding chairs in the boot of Archie's car, or finding a seat to sit on.

Lovely to find a bench in some beautiful spot, next to a river maybe. With a few words on the back in memory of someone who once loved to sit there.

A dedication.

For so and so . . .

Everybody wants to be remembered.

Twenty-Five

The lady hairdresser looks familiar.

I feel like I've seen her somewhere before, which isn't likely, of course. When you've seen so many people over the years, it's no surprise everyone reminds you of somebody else. It's hard enough keeping track of those you loved without thinking who other people remind you of.

Sylvie says it's Mrs Gibson's great granddaughter, who owns a hair salon in Notting Hill that celebrities go to, including one of her big brother's housemates, whatever that means. It might be that she reminds me of Mrs Gibson, which is why I think I've seen her before.

Mrs Gibson has made herself popular with the lady residents by getting her great-granddaughter to come and do the ladies' hair, even if she never stops banging on about aeroplanes making the world smaller.

It's difficult to tell people's ages these days, but I'd say her great-granddaughter is approaching middle age, though she still looks quite well-to-do. Ros says she's charging five quid for a quick hairdo, which sounds a lot of money to me but Ros says it's good for a professional. There's a list for any ladies who want an appointment and Mr Ozturk was one of the first to go on it. I reckon he's the only man here who still has a full head of hair, and that includes Gordon.

Nice for Mrs Gibson to have family dropping in to see her.

Something to show for the years.

Her great-granddaughter is an attractive young woman, and speaks nicely to the ladies, asking about their families and what their favourite holidays were.

It can do wonders, someone speaking nicely to you for a few moments about your memories. Not like Tabor on his nightly rounds, who calls us coffin-dodgers or the walking dead.

I've not seen Tabor for a little while. Sylvie said he'd gone to prison for a stint, but I'm not sure if she was pulling my leg.

The television set is on loud again.

Hearing aids screech and whine like midnight cats.

The snipping of scissors and endless chatter about holidays.

It takes an age to catch Sylvie's eye and get her to wheel me to the lift and along the upstairs corridor, back to my room for some peace and quiet. She pushes me up to the small table with the typewriter and closes the door when she goes.

I look out at the pavement below. A woman with a dog on a long lead waits as it crouches under a tree. The dog paddles back towards her as the lead magically shortens and they head down Hammersmith Grove.

A helicopter throbs over the roof like a giant insect and a group of teenagers slope up the road as if they can't be bothered to move, schoolbags slung over shoulders.

All of them taking youth for granted.

251

Living their own lives.

They don't see me up at my window watching them.

No one passing ever looks into an old folk's home.

Afraid of the future, maybe. Afraid to consider what they might themselves become one day. They make sure to look away quick and hope being old isn't catching.

I push my fingers onto the metal keys to get more memories down on the fresh paper Ros brought from Mrs Akinyemi's office.

Tap click tap click. Tap click.

Ding.

Good to keep the old mind working.

Not give up on it all just yet.

In the parlour, I ask the Hammersmith girl's ma what's happening upstairs and she says not to get in the way and throws a pail of water into the yard. The elderly aunt with the crystals is stomping down the stairs, complaining about her feet. She says, 'It's nearly time.'

The Hammersmith girl's ma says she'll go to fetch the neighbour then.

I go upstairs even though she said not to get in the way.

There's no reply to my knock on the bedroom door. I open it slowly and see the Hammersmith girl lying on her side.

I ask if it's all right to come in.

She tells me, 'I'm scared.'

I sit next to her on the edge of the bed and neither of us say anything for a while.

I ask if she still thinks it's a girl.

She does a few funny breaths, which make me think she didn't hear my question properly.

I tell her I still think it's a boy, but don't mind what it is as long as they're both well.

Her two brothers are having another fist-fight in the back yard. Laughter and the slap of punches carries up to the small room.

I tell her I can't wait to meet whoever it is.

She asks, 'Have you been drinking?' but says it with a smile like she doesn't mind.

She says, 'I'm afraid I'll bleed to death giving birth, like my sister did.'

I say I never knew she had a sister who bled to death.

I brush the strands of damp hair off her face. Her skin feels hot against my fingers.

She lifts her dress to look at her naked belly. It's a shocking sight, tight as a drum. It feels like you might see the baby inside if you stared hard enough.

I ask if I can stroke her belly, but she says no.

Another strand of hair falls across her face. She doesn't say not to move it, so I gently brush it back behind her ear and think this is probably the most intimate we've ever been.

The elderly aunt bangs her way up the stairs and brings a fresh bowl of water into the room. She looks disapprovingly at me sat on the bed. I'm thinking our quiet moment together is over now, but the aunt puts the bowl down and stomps back onto the landing.

I want to tell my young wife I'm sure everything will be

fine and she won't bleed to death, but I've learned not to make promises that can't be kept.

I want to talk about the night we met in the Palais nine months ago. To say, 'Who'd have thought a quiet stroll by the Thames would end like this,' but it's something we've never talked about before and it feels wrong to bring it up now.

My shoes are caked in piss and sawdust from the bar. I should have taken them off before walking into the room where my wife's having a baby, but it's too late for that now.

I want to tell her I've changed. I'll be a good husband and father and do them right, and maybe we'll grow to love each other like a proper husband and wife.

She says, 'Can you stop touching my hair.'

I want to say everything will be different now, that the baby will bring us closer, but it still sounds wrong in my head so I just look at her instead.

She asks me not to look at her because she's a fright.

She grimaces like something's pulling her from the inside, then moans long and slow, her eyes tight against the pain.

The aunt comes back with a toothless woman who speaks in a low growl like a drunken man. She says, 'Are you widening?'

The Hammersmith girl sighs and says, 'I don't know.'

The woman says, 'It's time,' to the Hammersmith girl's aunt.

My wife says, 'Not yet.'

It's surprising how women can communicate without making any sense.

254

The toothless neighbour growls at me to myself scarce.

At the door, I turn for a final look at my wife on her back. Her belly looks ridiculous in the light from the paraffin lamps, stretched taut and blue-veined. The aunt pulls the thin dress down over her stomach and rolls up her sleeves. She tells me to go and I'll be sent for in good time.

I think of the promises I've made and the man I will soon become.

Some mornings I wake and it takes a moment to realise I'm still alive, especially when I've woken up once already and nodded off in front of the television set.

I wonder how Mrs Bentley and Mrs Cutts manage to stay awake in front of it all day.

My back aches. A dull throb in the base of the spine behind where I imagine my kidneys lie rotting.

A crackle in my left ear. I press the soft skin below the temple, just above where I once had sideburns, and the membranes bubble and spit as if the small bones within have dissolved and turned to jelly.

I'm disintegrating at a rate of knots. Soon I'll be nothing more than grey skin slouched over an armchair in the television room while a thin man in a suit shouts at a fat lady in sports clothes for sleeping with her brother.

When the body dies, I hope the mind goes with it. No spirit left wandering the ramparts. There's no pleasure in the thought of surviving as a ghost. Living for eternity with the regrets you made.

The life you lived.

What will Archie make of mine when I finally get it all down? Piecing together these tiny fragments of history and the people I once loved.

Seeing it all at the end of a long, long life and deciding what sort of man I was.

Mrs Gibson is over by the bookshelves today, an empty chair next to her, which is normally Mr Ozturk's but he's gone to hospital this morning to have his verruca lanced.

I ask Sylvie to take me over to the empty chair. She whispers, 'Still got an eye for the ladies, Billyboy.'

Normally I enjoy Sylvie's lewd banter, but I don't care for her tone today. I've woken feeling blue and wonder if this is the beginning of the end, as Jimmy Parris called it. He'd cheerfully tell anyone complaining of a new ailment that it was the beginning of the end. It annoyed some of the residents here as most days begin with a new ailment.

The thought of Jimmy lifts my spirits, and I wish it was him I was sitting next to instead of Mrs Gibson.

I ask her how she is today.

She says, 'You have a nice face.'

I remind her who I am again.

She says she knew a Billy once: a sailor in the wartime who would touch her up in Shepherd's Bush market. Gave her jewels he'd nicked before running off with a floozy.

I ask when her great-granddaughter will be here again to do the ladies' hair, but she looks puzzled. 'That lady who cuts hair?' I remind her, but she doesn't seem to know what I'm talking about.

She taps the newspaper in her lap and asks if I've seen all the places you can fly to nowadays and how small it makes the world.

It was probably a mistake to ask Sylvie to sit me next to Mrs Gibson, so I decide to keep quiet and spend the rest of the morning in my own head, remembering games I once played with Archie instead of trying to make conversation with a madwoman.

I remember the signal box we built from a Bayko kit: a Bakelite tray with small holes for long pins. You slid tiles between the pins to make walls. You could make all sorts of buildings, but Archie only ever wanted a signal box to pull his little train past.

Flying kites on Wormwood Scrubs.

A game with a small ball, called sevens, a sequence of catches against a wall. One was simple throw and catch. Two was a throw and a bounce, which you did twice. Three was a throw and three claps before the ball came back.

Four . . . I can't remember what four was now.

Five was a bounce off the ground and back up off the wall. Six was six throws against the wall with a catch in the opposite hand. Sevens, to finish, if you still hadn't dropped the ball, was a hard throw to the ground and a bounce off the wall with a clap and a turn before catching.

Thinking about it now, it sounds like a girls' game, but I remember watching him play it for hours in the yard outside the kitchen.

Pick-up sticks on wet days, or a jigsaw.

We played card games once his hands were big enough to fan the cards and hold them. Newmarket: betting a matchstick on four horses before each round and one for the kitty. The kitty got taken by whoever went out first.

This is what I should have done a long time ago: remembering the good moments with Archie.

I recall one time he went off somewhere with his mum for a day or two maybe, and came back with a present he'd made for me: a small gauze-like sheet of soft yellow fabric onto which he'd sewn, in thick colourful wool, the stick figures of a man and a boy in front of a house with a red sun shining above it.

Underneath the embroidered picture he'd stitched the words *For My Dad*.

I'm not sure I was very grateful for it at the time. It seemed more the sort of present a girl would make for her father rather than a boy, and when he handed it to me I don't think I gave it much attention for that reason.

But I remember it now and wish I'd treasured it more carefully at the time.

Folded it up and kept it safe in my Golden Virginia tin.

I'm grateful for all these tiny moments we had together.

Just him and me, before it all went wrong between us.

Building signal boxes together and throwing a ball against the wall in the back yard.

It goes quick, childhood.

Feels like an eternity at the time, but it's gone in seconds.

I can sense the happiness in all of this, sitting here now, remembering what love feels like.

Twenty-Six

We've had lunch.

Something soft, meant to slip down easy. A beef stew, Ros said, but I'm not sure there was much beef in it. Rice pudding for afters.

I'm having a quiet moment now, looking at the purple filament in the bulb of the lamp behind where the fish tank used to be. Close your eyes and the colours stay with you, like old moments of your life coming back. Then they fade and the brightness you saw goes dark.

Gordon sits on the empty chair next to me.

'How are you today, Mr Binns?' he says.

I'm stuck between thinking how I am and trying to remember the last time Gordon sat down and spoke to me when he wasn't snapping about something.

I'd like a shave as it's been a while and Sylvie's been too busy. Though I'd rather wait for her to scrape me with a razor than let Gordon do it so I keep quiet and give him a silent nod instead.

He makes a comment about me being the oldest resident in here for ages now and how lucky they are to have me brightening up the place.

He asks if I'm comfortable slouched over and leans me forward in the chair to plump up the cushion, but when he sits me back it's less comfortable than it was before he started messing.

'Aren't we lucky,' he says again.

He looks around the room for a moment, lifts the newspaper left under the lamp by Mrs Gibson then puts it down again.

'Isn't the news awful,' he says. 'They should tell us things we want to hear, not just the bad stuff.'

I remember the feel of a newspaper, dusty ink rubbing off the pages.

Gordon says, 'Well, this is lovely, having a little chat.'

He looks out of the window, then leans forward to speak a little quieter. 'Oh yes. I should just mention a few changes happening over the coming weeks. The Cedars has got new owners and we're waiting to see how it all pans out. Just having a quiet word now so no one has to worry if they hear any rumours, till we know what's what.'

You'd think this place was owned by Ros and Sylvie, or Mrs Akinyemi and Gordon, as they're the only ones you ever see working here.

'The new owners have asked for staff appraisals. They're sending out forms so you can tell them what you think of us. All confidential, of course.' He laughs. 'We don't get to see it. You can fill it in online, or post it in an envelope if you prefer.'

He looks like he's growing his little moustache again, with a goatee beard under his chin.

He says, 'Well, I can't sit here chatting all day,' with

another small laugh. 'Back to the grindstone,' as he gets up and walks into the corridor.

You never get much post here these days, and if you do, it's usually someone trying to sell you something.

Maybe the new owners will want to brighten the place up. A lick of paint on the Goose Green walls, or fix the broken tiles in my bedroom ceiling perhaps.

I'm looking out for Ros, to ask if she can put me on the hairdresser's list the next time the lady comes in, thinking maybe she can get a message to Archie if the Duke of Edinburgh's schoolboy can't do it, when he suddenly appears with the shop trolley across the room.

Thomas glances briefly at me and then moves off into the corridor.

I'm not hoping for much luck with Archie, but he might have family somewhere, even if it's abroad. Someone I could send a fiver to every now and then. Not for them to worry about me or take me out for a picnic even, just to let them know I was once a man who lived a full life.

A Christmas card once a year, maybe, to hear about what they're up to. I'm not looking to visit or anything. Travelling is no fun at this age.

Besides, I'd miss Ros and Sylvie too much.

I'd miss my armchair and seeing all the life down Hammersmith Grove.

Everything I have is here.

In Shepherd's Bush.

I'm trying to think about Archie, but the memories only

come in short doses, like bursts of muddy water through a blocked pipe.

Back through the alleys.

A black moonless sky and stars out over London. Somewhere nearby, a fox is stealing into a chicken coop. A commotion of wings and the cursing and banging of pans.

Back to the sawdust pub behind Acton Lane to steady my nerves and get the warmth back into my hands while a pack of men get pissed before facing another night at home with their wives and children.

I see the man I could easily become.

My father's son.

The beer slips down easy. A malty numbness dulls my veins and I wonder how long it will be before Archie gets born.

When the glass empties, I buy another.

I'm losing track how many I've had.

There's a crowd at the counter. The landlord doesn't change his expression and keeps the beer coming. I'm not sure I could stand if the pillar wasn't holding me up.

Someone with a cap pulled low asks what I reckon Hellcat's chances are, but I've no idea what he's talking about. He says I'm the only one who hasn't.

A dog fight about to happen in the back yard.

He says the Staffie is favourite, but word's out he's got worms and been starved by his owner. They reckon he'll drop quick if the fight lasts. Hellcat's a young local bull with a vicious temper that's already maimed three kids and taken a lump out of its owner's arm.

Good odds, he says.

I ask what the odds are.

He asks what I'll be putting down.

I count the week's board and lodging in my pocket.

He says, 'You'll be takin' home six months' wages.'

I think about the presents I could buy for Archie, a kite or a bicycle maybe, or a necklace for his mother.

The down payment on our own house, even.

Something to show them I'll be a good father.

A hand falls on my shoulder.

The Hammersmith girl's brothers drag me out into the freezing air, back through the maze of slums and lean-tos, letting me stop to puke over the icy cobblestones. One of them says, 'You're meant to wait till the bairn's born before wetting the baby's head.'

In the back yard again, the crunch of broken pottery under my shoes, I wipe my mouth on the sleeve of my jacket to make myself presentable before meeting Archie for the first time.

From inside, the harsh call of a woman's agony. The Hammersmith girl's father steps out of the kitchen pulling on his jacket. He says he's not listening to any more of this shit and heads off down the alley.

I walk into the kitchen and stand by the small coal stove to warm my hands. It's an odd moment, waiting for your child to arrive, knowing life will never be the same again.

Her ma comes down to refill the bowl with water from the pan.

I ask how she is. Her ma tuts and says, 'Getting there.'

Another loud moan from above, then the toothless neighbour growls instructions downstairs, her voice rumbling through the floorboards.

One of the brothers says something from the kitchen door and I don't catch that either.

My head throbs from the beer but I feel better after spilling some on the walk home. Her ma goes upstairs with the fresh bowl of water as another guttural cry rattles the dimly lit kitchen, and I'm wondering why they've brought me back to the house much too soon.

Spinning forward through time.

Climbing a tree with Archie, watching the little fellow become a man.

He's wearing a blue school blazer, braided with a light blue ribbon, identical to the one worn by the school lad who comes to push the shop trolley and read out the newspaper obituaries.

I can't remember him as a baby, just a few moments of growing up. I've seen a few babies over the years and they mostly look the same, but I'm struggling to remember Archie when he was like that.

I can't make out his face, like Evie or Mary Coggins or the Hammersmith girl even, and I never properly loved her. Their features are easier to recall the more I think about them, like Mary Coggins' cleft lip, or the way Evie looked above your head and up to the sky with her kind eyes.

But those loves came with conditions and I realise Archie never had those. It was a simple bond between father and son, the love of a child by its parent, and yet his face struggles to come into view.

When it does, it quickly fades, like a burning photograph.

He grew up in front of me and I can't now picture the boy.

Maybe I didn't love him as much as I should, especially at the beginning. It's hard during those first years when they're small. It's the mothers they respond to. Hard to love them, or even find them vaguely interesting, when they just lie there crying all day.

Maybe for a time I blamed him for trapping me with the Hammersmith girl. You grow to love them, for sure, but maybe he was more of a burden to me after he'd forced Evie to stop loving me, and that's why it's hard now trying to recall his little face.

A fresh wave of car lights washes through the thin blinds and travels across the ceiling tiles.

I'm trying to keep this in order so Archie can make sense of it all when he reads it.

I spin forward through time again, away from the unhappy kitchen, to a tree I once helped Archie climb.

When he was bigger and started to become interesting.

An oak or a chestnut it would have been, with a solid thick trunk, good for clambering up and looking down at the world below.

My hands cup together so I can give him a leg-up to the first branch.

He puts his muddy shoe in the crook of my fist and I

hoist him upwards. He springs easily up two more branches, knee first, pulling himself onto it, then to a fork where the main trunk splits. He shuffles along the branch and calls me to follow.

Last time I climbed a tree was in Harry Coggins' garden.

I work my way up slowly, shuffle my arse along beside him and ask if he's all right.

He asks me the same.

There's an apple in my pocket. I take out my pocket-knife and cut it into quarters, and we sit crunching it on the long branch.

He asks when he can have a pocketknife of his own.

I tell him when he's old enough to use one properly.

He says, 'I'm old enough to use one properly now.'

I ask what he knows about the birds and the bees.

His face curls in disgust, like the time I gave him his first beer, and he says he doesn't want to be having this talk now.

I remember sitting on the branch next to him but not what I said about the birds and bees.

Something short and vague, I hope. Nothing to disturb the boy. Not what you'd say if you were talking to a man in a pub, maybe.

I think it made sense to him. Doing my fatherly duty and explaining what happens when time comes to consider getting married.

Passing on what I knew of women's matters and the moon and whatnot.

He sits quiet for a while, looking unhappy at what I've just told him.

A young couple walk along the footpath below us.

We watch them on the ground. They stop under the tree directly beneath us, glancing back along the footpath to make sure they're not being watched before starting a kiss.

It's an awful sight to see. Archie and I both sit quiet on our branch, embarrassed, hoping they won't look up.

The kiss goes on for ages.

I'm hoping it's not going to get any worse, knowing what young men can be like when they get a woman on her own somewhere quiet.

Archie takes aim with his apple core and throws it down at the couple before I can stop him.

It rattles a branch and hits the ground but the couple don't break from their embrace.

When their kiss finally ends, they set off down the path again.

Archie looks at me like I deliberately put him through this ordeal.

The sight of two young people kissing has stopped me wanting to give any more advice about the birds and the bees.

I finish my last slice of apple and shuffle back to the trunk, climbing down slowly through the branches.

When my feet are on the ground, I look up.

Sunlight blazes yellow through the leaves.

We walk in silence down the footpath. I decide the time has come for Archie to have his own pocketknife and give him the one I brought to cut the apple.

His little face opens up.

Happiness in his eyes.

And it's this that gives me the smallest memory of his face, and how it feels to love someone without conditions.

A last push from the upstairs bedroom and I can't look her brothers in the eye.

The low scream fills the little house, followed by a shriek of what sounds like relief from one of the older women.

I want to go up to greet my newborn son but decide to wait until the women have cleared the mess up there first.

Time passes.

I wonder if it's not a son but a daughter waiting for me. I listen for the sound of crying, thinking I'll know which it is from the wail, but everything stays hushed.

The toothless neighbour calls to say come up now.

I pace my steps quietly, not wanting to disturb mother or child.

The door is ajar.

I peer inside.

The Hammersmith girl is lying back on the small bed, her face red and wet in the light of the paraffin lamp. She looks like she's been dragged out of a river after a fight.

It takes a moment to realise the bundle of rags in her arms is our baby.

Her ma is by the window, wringing out a towel into an enamel pot.

The Hammersmith girl says nothing to me.

Still wringing out the towel, her ma says I should hold him.

My little boy.

I take the bundle in my arms and peer into his tiny purple face to say hello.

He doesn't make a sound.

I walk over to the window to see him better.

A half-moon is rising over the alleyways, the stars bright against the coal-black sky.

There are lots of things I want to tell him.

That this is his world and he will make his mark on it.

There'll be lots of people he won't like and a small number he'll love, but it's the ones he loves that matter.

When he's older, we'll sit on the branch of a tree together eating an apple and I'll give him his first pocketknife.

That we might fall out from time to time and lose touch as the years go by, but it won't matter as I'll always love him in a way he'll only understand when he has a son of his own.

But it doesn't feel right saying these things out loud to a newborn son with a tiny purple face, while his mother lies in bed like she's been in a brawl and his grandmother squeezes blood from a wet towel.

I put the bundle of rags back into the Hammersmith girl's arms.

Another enamel basin has been pushed under the bed with something inside. I pull it out to look. It contains a large jellyfish with a coil of bloody rope and smells of flesh and garlic.

I drop it with a clatter, trying not to let my stomach turn.

The Hammersmith girl opens her eyes in shock as her ma scuttles across the room to push the basin back, and I'm a little ashamed that the first words my newborn baby hears from its father are 'What the fuck is that?!'

Dinner is soup with peas.

It spoons easy from the bowl and slips down warm and wet, followed by a small wrap of soft cheese on a cream cracker.

I might ask Sylvie about getting a new tie when we next go to the green, as the one I'm wearing today is badly stained with gravy.

My throat feels sore after doing my best with the cracker. It doesn't take much to fill me up these days. I used to have an appetite like a horse, but now I only pick at things like a small bird.

A couple of spoonfuls of warm custard would go down a treat, but it's never something that gets served with cheese and a cracker.

After dinner, Mrs Gibson sits next to me again. If I were a younger man I'd be thinking she was a little keen maybe.

There's a light in her eyes that wouldn't have been unattractive when she was younger.

I ask if she enjoyed the soup with peas.

She says I have a nice face and thought it was time she said hello.

She speaks like there's something in the back of her throat that needs coughing up.

I tell her, 'It's me, Billy.'

She goes quiet for a moment and I tell her I'm having a blue day trying to remember what love feels like.

She says she used to know someone called Billy before the war, but he knocked her up and stole a load of necklaces. 'A right wrong 'un,' she laughs. 'You always fall for the ones who break your heart.'

She asks if I have a family and I tell her I've got a son but I'm struggling to remember his little face. She tells me she has a great-granddaughter who's a hairdresser and comes to do the ladies, as well as Mr Ozturk, who has a fine head of hair.

She says he has a nice face too and turns over her newspaper.

'Look,' she says. 'We've all been priced out of the area. My great-granddaughter lives in Brackenbury now.'

I tell her I used to know a girl in Brackenbury.

She says young people can't afford to live there these days as all the big houses go for millions, bought by Russian gangsters for their prostitutes to live in. She says they come on aeroplanes, which make the world smaller every day. 'Even Shepherd's Bush market is changing. They want to make it posh like Brixton,' she tells me.

It's hard to disagree with anything she's saying.

'And when they do,' Mrs Gibson continues, 'where will all the blacks buy their funny little vegetables?'

Ros has her coat on, ready for home, with a carrier bag of shopping beside her. Cooking a chilli with garlic bread for her boyfriend tonight, she says.

She sits in the chair next to me, where Mrs Gibson was sat earlier.

I wonder if she's about to say he wants his typewriter back.

Instead she starts talking about the schoolboy in the blazer who's been coming every week for the Duke of Edinburgh these last few months.

It was his last day today.

Thomas, his name was. You don't hear the name Thomas much these days. There were a lot of Toms and Tommys at one time, but names go out of fashion and then come back when they've been forgotten.

Thomas told her I'd asked him to find Archie's address.

I didn't have him down as a snitch.

You can't trust kids these days. Talking to the care workers behind your back.

Ros says I have to stop asking everyone who comes here to find Archie for me, and speak to her or Gordon about it instead.

I tell her it's a while since we went out for a picnic. He'll want to know how I'm doing and I don't want him to worry.

Ros touches my hand and says Archie was stillborn.

Choked by the cord while his mum was giving birth.

She tells me he died the same day he was born, in November, 1923.

She tells me his birth and death certificate are kept in the office whenever I want to look at them again.

November is always a difficult time of year.

Fireworks going off in gardens.

Kids roaming the streets, along the landings, dressed as ghosts.

Mischief night, they call it.

Knocking on the doors in the tower blocks and running off. Setting fire to newspaper filled with dog shit and posting it through your letter box. Pressing the bell and running away, leaving you to stamp it out on the carpet.

I look up through the branches to see his little face in yellow sunlight again.

Dirty knees and a pocketful of marbles.

The catseye, the oxblood, the jasper, aggie and ruby.

Rattling around next to his pocketknife, chinking against the glass.

Sitting up there talking about the birds and the bees.

I try to see his little face, climbing higher up the tree, but I keep losing sight of him in the leaves.

You love them, always and forever.

You don't ever forget.

I wouldn't mind looking for the tree we planted.

The little sapling we put in for him.

Dug a hole in the ground, placed it in there gently. Fed the roots with compost, filled the hole and gave it water.

Stood in silence for an hour or two, just thinking.

Me and the Hammersmith girl.

Alice.

Grown good and proper now, I reckon.

A weeping willow, I'm sure.

PART FOUR

Twenty-Seven

Mary Coggins.

Evie.

My boy Archie.

Their faces appear like fireworks above the rooftops, leaving a silhouette of fluorescence on the back of the eye and a trail of smoke that disappears in the air.

Vera and Betty Jackson in the shadows.

Ghosts, the lot of them.

Mr Ozturk is playing patience with a deck of cards while the submarine captain sits with his mouth opening and shutting like he's chewing on an invisible stick.

Seven rows of cards on a tray across the arms of Mr Ozturk's chair. He turns the top card over in each pile.

Two of hearts.

Eight of diamonds.

Nine of hearts.

Black eight, clubs or spades, I forget which they are.

The other black eight next to it.

Ace of hearts.

Black seven.

Mr Ozturk gets distracted by the television set.

Meanwhile, the black seven will go under the red

eight, a black eight under the red nine and the ace starts a suit pile.

Mr Ozturk stares at the screen and I wish he'd get on with his game. Three new cards to turn over but he's more interested watching an excited lady show a large man and woman wearing football shirts around a house overlooking a bright blue sea.

He points at the television set and says, 'Yugoslavia!' but he must be mistaken as I don't think it's been called that for years.

'Look,' he says to the submarine captain, who doesn't stop chewing his invisible stick. 'Where they killed my wife and brothers.'

I'm not sure if Mr Ozturk is all there, as it would be a coincidence if the television set was showing the same house where his family got murdered.

He looks back at the cards on the tray without moving the ace, the black seven or either of the two eights. Filling in the gaps in his history like the rest of us, I reckon.

Watching his silent newsreel passing through time.

My own newsreel spins forward, like at the pictures, waiting for Vera to appear.

Trying to remember what love was like.

To bring her back to life like Evie. Like Mary Coggins and Archie. Tiny details down the wires from some distant corner of the mind.

Where was I?

1924.

The weeping willow left to grow. The raw black soil

278

will have sprouted new grass to hide its wounds in the earth. Some places are too hard to return to, so I let it battle with the wind by itself and keep moving forward in time.

The images pick up speed as the years go by.

1925 . . . A miners' strike and economic depression that my father saw coming, born out of the wisdom of the Seven Stars. The first television pictures. London double-deckers with roofs to keep out the rain.

I almost see Vera, but it's still too soon.

A woman swims across the English Channel. It's not Mrs Cumbernauld but there's a look of her in the photograph.

1927 . . . An American man flies across the Atlantic to Paris in the *Spirit of St Louis*. Pictures with sound. The Thames floods its banks just before young women get the vote at the same age as men, though the Hammersmith girl reckons politics is too complicated to understand.

A woman flies across the Atlantic too, but no one likes a show-off.

On through time and I still can't see her face.

Wall Street crashes and Britain feels the pinch, but a letter comes from Auntie Pam in Manchester, with a cheque for £100 following the death of her second husband. It's enough for the deposit on a small flat with a garden in Coningham Road for myself and the Hammersmith girl.

'Natural causes this time,' she says in the letter, after her first husband was murdered by a gang in Salford.

I stop working in railway tunnels and get a job driving buses, still preferring nights because life is easier for my wife and me if we're awake at different parts of the day. For the first time I have a home of my own, even if the Hammersmith girl and I rarely speak inside it.

Ma gets a cheque too, but she returns hers to the address in Pam's letter.

An earthquake halts the Panama Canal's shipping lanes, which I remember opening when I was a boy riding my bicycle over the tram tracks on Shepherd's Bush Green.

On through years of marriage.

1932 ... 1933 ... Adolf Hitler on the rise. I stop myself from racing forward too quickly because we know how that turns out. Chamberlain's *peace in our time* and Churchill's *nothing to offer but blood, toil, tears and sweat.*

The Sydney Harbour Bridge and the Empire State Building.

The London Underground map appears and I still marvel how it joins up in the real world.

A pattern of coloured lines, but still no sign of Vera.

George V becomes George VI, interrupted briefly by Edward VIII when his many affairs catch up with him, which Ma has something to say about.

The Spanish Civil War.

The *Hindenburg*, Spam and nylon.

On we go, the flickering newsreel speeding by.

The Hammersmith girl and I silent now, listening to the radio at eleven o'clock on September 3rd, 1939: ... *no such undertaking has been received and that consequently this country is at war with Germany.*

A warm Sunday in the garden listening to birdsong. The last of summer's tomatoes in the greenhouse. I put the small crop on the kitchen table. The Hammersmith girl smiles briefly and says, 'Those smell nice.' It's a rare and pleasant exchange between us but nothing to remind me now what love feels like.

Churchill will say, *We shall fight on the beaches*, but my fighting days are over.

I look back at the playing cards on Mr Ozturk's tray once again and it's here I find Vera's face, waiting patiently for me all along.

The eight and the eight, side by side.

Acton Green, Shepherd's Bush, Marble Arch, Piccadilly Circus, Westminster, then Vauxhall, Clapham and Tooting.

The ace and the seven.

London Bridge, St Paul's, Oxford Circus to Shepherd's Bush. In rush hour, on to Old Oak Common, East Acton and Park Royal.

The 88 and the 17, my old bus routes.

Hair the colour of autumn, chestnut red, spilling under her hat, already tilted like a carefree showgirl as if her evening is in chaos before it's started. Red on her lips and black around her eyes, like girls are wearing these days.

Her dark uniform: bright silver buttons, skirt down to her knees, navy-blue stockings and black shoes. White shirt and black tie. A bag on each shoulder with brown leather straps crossed over: one for change, the other her ticket box. Pale green canvas straps of her gas mask, discarded under the stairwell at the rear of the bus as soon as we're off.

Her eyes are green too, a shade darker than the canvas straps. A bright, intelligent face and a smile which suggests trouble's only a short distance away.

I watch her in the mirror above the windscreen as she taps the bell rope.

One for stop. Two for go.

Three remaining playing cards on Mr Ozturk's tray: two, eight and nine.

289: all night from London Bridge, through St Paul's, Holborn, Marble Arch, Shepherd's Bush, Acton, Ealing and out to Southall.

Through the fires of the Blitz.

Funny, what stays with you, washing up in waves.

Fossils among the grit.

Mr Ozturk turns back from the memory of a murdered wife and brothers and comes back to his game.

He puts the seven under the eight and turns over a queen.

Takes out the ace to start a suit pile and reveals a three. Doesn't see the eight that goes under the nine and turns three cards from the remainders.

I leave him to his game, with Vera now beside me for company.

I loved you, Vera.

I loved you very much, though you brought trouble with you.

It came in one of those bags over your shoulders, I reckon. Impossible to resist a spot of trouble sometimes.

I have to get this down.

I have to get it down before it's gone for good.

Twenty-Eight

I'm forty-one.

February, 1941.

My lips look skinny and pale in the men's washroom mirror in the Wells Road bus depot. The grey is spreading across my temples. A gentle sagging of skin around my jaw and neck. Lines around the eyes and cheeks like furrows in a flat field.

I'm not a young man any more. I've become old after eighteen years of marriage to the Hammersmith girl.

My hair needs a trim. It's greased with Brylcreem and the ends curl out like John Wayne as the Ringo Kid.

I'm hoping my new clippie will be anyone but the attractive girl with chestnut hair the colour of autumn. I'm happier without the distraction of beauty.

Women are more forward these days. Wartime gives them a sense of purpose and a willingness for adventure that I no longer wish to keep up with.

The memory of Evie keeps me faithful to the Hammersmith girl, despite the lack of words between us. Our paths cross outside the tiny bathroom when it can't be avoided, or in the kitchen, on the way to the greenhouse.

We sleep in separate beds.

I doubt anyone could make me happy again, not since Evie disappeared nearly eighteen years ago.

I see beautiful petals around me but leave them for others to pick. My conversational skills are gone, withered like the pale vines of last summer's crop.

At least you know where you stand with tomatoes.

Mr Oldhouse, the depot manager at Wells Road, assigns the new crews. He says I'll have to keep my eye on this one, and tells my new clippie with the chestnut hair to straighten her tie as she picks up her ticket box.

I curse my bad luck.

She looks nervous and just laughs when the other drivers say I'll have to check her little box at the end of the run, and I'm thinking she won't last one night once the bombs start falling.

The smell of the oil engine beside me in the cab of the red STL double-decker, stripped of its fineries for wartime, mesh over the passenger windows.

I watch Vera take her first fares. The click and wind of the box spitting tickets. She punches a hole through the boarding stop.

She's late twenties, I reckon. I'm as old as the century, weathered as the Blitz. I'm like the bombed-out town we live in; she still has the flame of youth. Her fresh skin like cream, mine silted by middle age.

She forgets to signal go. At this rate it'll be morning before we make it to London Bridge.

I look through the little window behind me, down the lower deck.

'Two bells?' I call through the window.

She's trying to untangle the strap of her money bag.

'Get it together, love,' I shout down the bus. 'I'd rather be a moving target than a sitting duck.'

A couple of passengers laugh, and Vera blushes then spills her change bag onto the deck. She taps twice on the bell cord as the passengers help to pick up coins and I quickly regret humiliating her before we've even left Shepherd's Bush Green.

Across town to London Bridge, waiting for planes. Through Holland Park, along Bayswater Road, Hyde Park on the right, dark and wide. The street lamps unlit down the middle of Oxford Street. Rubble and small stones crunch under the tyres. Each day reveals wounds from the previous night raids.

Past Maynards and Palmers stores. Past Boots and the Grosvenor Court Hotel. The window aprons outside John Lewis are being drawn in for the night. Past Tottenham Court Road and the chilly patch through St Giles, built on an acre of plague pits, before the streets warm again in Holborn.

The Cittie of Yorke pub with its three-sided clock.

My father once said the best pubs were the ones you had to pass by.

Past Chancery Lane station, where Clerkenwell families are queuing to sleep on the platforms below.

The city stone turns grey as darkness falls.

Ludgate Circus, the Stock Exchange, and our first pass of St Paul's. I see Vera checking it's still there through the small hole in the mesh window.

The fuel ban keeps motor cars off the streets and the journey's quick when it's like this.

I start to imagine her sat next to me, listening to my guided tour of the city. Glimpsing bomb damage at Mary-le-Bow on Cheapside, home of the cockney bells. Christopher Wren's monument to the Great Fire of London before the Thames. Tower Bridge looming in the shadows downstream as we cross the water to London Bridge, and I realise I've talked more to an imaginary Vera these last few minutes than a whole month with the Hammersmith girl.

Coming back through Shepherd's Bush Green, we cross the old tram tracks laid by my father half a century ago, rusting in the tarmac since trams were replaced by the trolley buses, sucking power from the tram cables overhead. Past Coningham Road, where the Hammersmith girl will be sitting alone, or listening to the wireless with her ma in the evening, on to Old Oak and Park Royal.

A quiet sadness passes deep through my bones.

It fades at the sight of Vera on the lower deck and leaves a sense of disappointment at how life turned out, like ash after a fire.

Back through the City again, the sky lit by distant burning. My ears tuned for the drone of aircraft over the rumble of the bus engine, unable to take my eye off the new clippie in the mirror, walking the aisle behind me.

In the depot at midnight we sit with mugs of tea from the urn, sweet with sugar to keep the cold at bay. This close, she might be a few years older than I first thought, early thirties maybe.

She asks about the changes I've seen since I first started driving a bus.

I tell her I'm not that old, and she laughs.

Then, to fill the silence, I tell her about automatic traffic lights and Belisha beacons. Fixed stops every few hundred yards keep the roads moving. I explain at some length until I feel I should stop.

She says, 'What do you like doing when you're not driving?'

I resist telling her I'm married, and *tomatoes* doesn't feel like the sort of answer she was hoping for.

I say, 'I'm not sure I do anything.'

She laughs again because she thinks I'm joking.

I ask Vera what she likes, and she says, 'Butterflies.'

Her father left her his collection when she was a girl and she's been fascinated ever since. She says their pupae travel on food around the world, which is how they migrate. A red Jamaican Shoemaker recently hatched on bananas in Covent Garden market, while a black-winged Brazilian Julia turned up in Rotherhithe. They mate with common local breeds, in which, she imagines, they remain a glamorous novelty.

Vera says butterflies have different meanings in other cultures. In Japan a swarm is seen as a sign of danger, but a single one means your *forever love* will arrive.

I sip the lukewarm tea, not minding the bitterness it leaves at the back of my throat.

She tells me the Greek word for butterfly means 'soul'.

In some places people worship the caterpillar as a symbol of rebirth, while in parts of England they kill the first butterfly of spring for good luck.

I can't work out if the fifteen-minute tea break goes slowly or very, very fast.

Boarding the double-decker for the rest of the night, Vera says, 'Remind me what we do in an air raid.'

I tell her not to worry, how the bombs always fall elsewhere, but her hands are shaking and I realise how well she's been hiding her fears.

I explain that we're meant to drop our passengers at the nearest Underground station. During the first bombings last September, the bus would empty immediately but the stations only accepted those who'd already booked a ticket for the shelter. Now most passengers choose to stay on the bus and keep going through the raid instead.

Vera says, 'It'll be easier when it's real, and not in my head.'

It'll be easier when it's real, and not in my head.

An understanding lies outside my grasp, but I don't have time to absorb it, as the history is coming back like it's real and not in my head.

Vera taps the rope, twice for go.

Her shape more familiar with each passing mile.

No lights in the road, cloaked for protection against the sky. Smoke hangs low over the city.

The slow rumble of buses passing in the opposite direction, my eyes focused on shapes looming out of the darkness, only ever a few seconds from collision.

When Vera loses sight of the stop, the passengers boarding call it out for the benefit of those inside.

At Lancaster Gate we stop for a roadblock and step out of the bus to stretch our legs. The sky suddenly clears, like it's been wiped clean, to reveal bright stars, beauty above the chaos.

She points out some of the more difficult constellations and I choose not to mention kite balloons in the last war.

Her warmth a footstep away.

A small bruise on her cheek, hidden with make-up. She says it's from lifting a scuttle down from the top of the coal bunker.

I tell her it's barely visible, even this close.

She says, 'I can be right clumsy sometimes.'

At the end of our shift, the sun rising over the City, we shake hands and bid each other goodnight.

The next evening Mr Oldhouse puts us back together again and my heart soars and sinks in equal measure, seeing the trouble ahead like enemy planes over the city.

Two weeks later, I still haven't told her about the Hammersmith girl.

Vera has her back to me in the Wells Road depot, talking to another clippie by the tea urn, and I hear her say the words *my husband*. It sounds like something from another language.

She senses a shift behind her, turns to see me a few paces away, then drops her eyes quickly.

From then on, everything looks like trouble.

Sylvie sits on the side of the bed with her blue gloves on, holding a small pair of snippers. She's cut my nails since they stopped sending a nurse to do it, and while lacking a gentle touch, she doesn't seem to mind the task too much.

She says it's like chopping through leather.

Funny how nails keep growing long after the hair has given up.

The Hammersmith girl would cut them with scissors for me, back when we were first married. I've done it myself ever since until it became too difficult to reach down that low.

Sylvie tells me about her boyfriend, an older married man who keeps saying he's going to leave his wife for her. 'Believe him when I see it,' she says.

One evening he fell asleep on the sofa, she tells me, and Sylvie painted his toenails red. He woke late and Sylvie had run out of varnish remover, and he went mental about having to hide his toenails from his wife. Sylvie told him to wear socks in bed when he got home.

She's laughing, but it's not hard to think she doesn't have the life she wanted.

She asks if I'd like her to paint my toenails red too.

I tell her go on then.

She laughs and says I'm wicked, then takes out a small red pot from her pocket and does all the nails of one foot, then the other.

She says she's only doing one coat as the varnish isn't cheap.

When my eyes are tired, it's hard to see colours but I can definitely make out red at the ends of my feet.

The varnish smells like metal.

Sylvie says I've got nice toes and tells me she'll be back to put my socks on when it's dry, unless I'd like to keep my slippers off for everyone to see.

I tell her to come back soon for the socks.

She says, 'This can be our little secret, Billyboy.'

I look at my newly painted toenails, ripe as the colour of young blood.

I'm sure there's an old bus ticket in my tobacco tin. I don't know if it's one of Vera's, but I'm sure I kept an old ticket in there. The date will have faded now, like most of these memories.

Twenty-Nine

The black cushion offers small comfort to a cold arse against a hard metal seat. I press my foot on the heavy brake and take the engine out of gear.

Looking for planes through the top of the windscreen, black with soot, listening for the distant rumble.

Fresh gaps of bombed-out buildings like missing teeth in a giant's mouth.

Vera taps the glass at the back of the cab, head tilted like she's being modest. She asks if everything's all right.

We're stopped on the Bayswater Road.

Her beauty in shadow and a kindness in her eyes that makes me think of Evie if I'm not careful.

I tell her I'm listening for planes.

She says, 'We're better off as a moving target than a sitting duck.'

A number 12 trundles by on the other side of the road, going to Harlesden. It emerges from blackness and disappears as steady as it came.

I can't see the driver, just a coat, hat and scarf bundled up for the night. No friendly word, side to side in the middle of the street. No quick hello and the state of the roads coming up.

'Are we off?' I ask her.

She says she's tapped twice, more than once.

I look at the sky, pitch black.

We're still carrying passengers at this late hour. Offices stay open all night to avoid rush hours, working late in a city that never sleeps.

I tell her the bell might be faulty and we'd best get a move on.

She taps the rope twice with a look in her eye and says, 'It's working now.'

Past Marble Arch, Oxford Street, grey and dark.

Vera working the upper deck.

No children, she said when we talked in our last tea break. Not yet anyway, although she says her husband isn't very keen.

These days my wife and her husband get a casual mention from time to time, though we don't dwell on the subject long.

She'd like children when the war's over but says she's not getting any younger and thinks she's running out of time. Her husband, ex-army who now works behind a desk, reckons there's too much uncertainty in the world to start a family.

She's yet to say his name.

I think of the Hammersmith girl, asleep now, cold cuts on the shelf left for the morning. Our separate lives, night and day. Happy to keep it that way.

A line of passengers in Holborn waiting to go south of the river.

An orange glow down Red Lion Street.

A fire truck sweeps past and everyone glimpses

someone else's horror, grateful our names weren't on that one.

The crunch of masonry under our wheels and I'm expecting the drag of a puncture but we keep moving.

People running across Leather Lane. Shouts and the roar of nearby flames, with the drone of planes rumbling high above us, an air-raid siren in full wail.

I pull over and the bus half empties. I watch some of the passengers walk briskly towards the Underground station at Chancery Lane.

Vera wishes them, 'Get home safe.'

I open the cab door and step down to inspect the bus for damage.

More fire trucks sweeping by.

I tap on the engine grille for good luck, a recent superstition I can't break. I've started doing it before each run and mid journey too. I talk to the engine like a friend, thinking a kind word won't do us no harm.

Vera has stepped off the bus. She says, 'I thought you were doing a runner.'

I tell her, 'Don't be a cheeky sort.'

She puts her hand on her hip and says, 'I know how you like it when I'm being a cheeky sort.'

Adrenalin through our veins after the falling bomb. It's a brave exchange we wouldn't normally make.

She looks at the pavement with a sudden sigh of despair and says her mum's bracelet has broken.

She picks it up off the ground, beautiful in her unhappiness.

I say, 'That can be fixed.'

She gives it to me. I turn the silver chain's charms and trinkets over in my fingers.

I tell her, 'I'll put it in my pocket to keep it safe.'

She says, 'Maybe we could all get in there.'

There's a look in Vera's eyes like Bette Davis in *Jezebel*, and it's this that brings the memory of her face into sudden focus.

Vera.

Your green eyes and chestnut hair the colour of autumn.

The apples of your cheekbones and dimples like pips that stay fixed even after you've stopped smiling.

Your delightful clumsiness.

Your voice, Camden-born and no messing, tells me there's still passengers on board, to get back in the cab and move my arse to London Bridge, quicksticks.

Mary, Evie, Archie my boy, Vera . . .

Four of you, back to help me remember what love feels like.

A traffic policeman says Holborn Viaduct is closed, diverts us down Fetter Lane, Fleet Street and Ludgate Circus until we're back on the route where passengers are waiting to board near St Paul's.

They get on; others get off and walk up to Clerkenwell.

A 289 coming the other way.

We drive towards it.

I glance at the dome, Hitler's prize, but the firefighters have been told never to let the flames get close.

The street crashes sideways.

The pit of my stomach lurches upwards and a light comes and goes like the bursting of a sun. Steam explodes through my ears and I can't suck my eardrums back out.

Thunder shudders through the bus and the street shakes itself back into place.

The wrench of metal and the high-pitched ripple of a glass waterfall.

It could be minutes before any sound comes back.

My foot is still pressed hard on the pedal but the world has stopped and we're not moving any more.

Smoke pouring under the cab. Vera is knocking on the panel behind me but I can't make out what she's saying.

I glance behind, my shoulders numb. Something isn't right in the lower deck. The passengers are crouched across the seats. I look outside but all I see is smoke and a hash of mangled metal strewn across the road.

Vera asks if I'm all right and I tell her of course I am.

There's no sign of the passengers I saw walking towards Clerkenwell just moments ago.

I tell her to hit the bell when she's ready, but she's crouching down beside one of the passengers, so I take the opportunity to get out and inspect the vehicle again.

After some difficulty with the door handle, I open the cab and step into the road.

A large block of stone is jammed into the engine grille. I try to pull it out, thinking it might be warm, but it's cold to the touch.

I pull hard but it doesn't move.

I step around the side of the bus. It looks like someone has taken a can-opener to the upper deck, and I realise the hash of smoking metal in the road is the remains of the roof.

The smell of diesel and burning flesh.

Tiny stones crunch under my feet. There's a chill around my toes where the leather of my right shoe flaps open like the mouth of a fish.

I'll have to take it to the cobbler next to Mr Putter on Uxbridge Road to see what he can do, but I reckon the pair might be ruined.

I sit down on the pavement and lift the open leather flap, wondering if my toes are still inside.

The sock is torn and there's blood around the toenails, but I count them.

One.

Two.

Three.

Four.

Five.

Same as the number of loves Mary Coggins told me I'd have, in her gypsy caravan many years ago.

Vera sits on the pavement and asks if I'm hurt.

I say, 'Are we meant to have five toes?'

She says, 'That's right.'

'That's good then.'

'Can you walk?'

I tell her I can do better than that, I can drive, though I might need a minute to get the masonry out of the engine before continuing down Cannon Street.

Vera tells me to stay sat while she sees to the passengers.

I tell her we're behind schedule.

She asks if I can stand.

'Yes, but these shoes are ruined.'

I get up and turn around to demonstrate my wellness.

She says she needs help with the injured.

I ask if she knows where the top deck has gone.

She says, 'Seven passengers were up there but none survived the blast.'

The unlucky ones.

I tell her I'll do whatever she needs.

I follow her to the back of the mangled platform and step on. The lower deck has been twisted around like a half-chewed jujube. There's blood in the wooden grooves of the floor and sounds of dying I'm already familiar with.

Vera works with an impressive coolness, wrapping bandages and giving kind words to those on the floor.

She says nine passengers were on the lower deck. Four on the left are all dead. On the right, one is unconscious, another has a broken arm and head injuries. One other is bleeding, which she's bandaged with torn clothes and the straps of her gas mask case, cut with her knife. Three say they can walk.

A lady off the street says the ambulance can't get through.

Vera says we need to get our passengers to hospital.

Two young men turn up with a wooden board for a makeshift stretcher.

Vera tells them to lift the unconscious man near the front.

He stays quiet as we untangle him from the twisted guts of the lower deck and carry him out into the road. He opens his eyes and makes no sound other than to tell us he's cold.

Vera takes off her uniform jacket and puts it over him.

He says, 'That's better.'

The sound of the world is coming back. Fire truck bells and the roar of flames from the glow behind us.

A number 13 to Golders Green has stopped down Cannon Street. I tell Vera we can get the driver to turn around and take us back to London Bridge. The man on the stretcher lets out a sudden moan. Vera calls him by his name and says he'll be fine.

I suppose we all make promises we can't keep.

The air sticks heavy with the smell of the oil bomb, its acrid taste at the back of the throat.

The bus driver, hands on the wheel, doesn't return my wave.

His passengers have all gone but his engine still ticks over.

Vera gets everyone onto the back of the bus as I tap his window, but he makes no attempt to look at me, as if I'm not really here. My head's full of clouds and I wonder if I died in the bomb blast, caught now in a half-state between life and death.

Vera calls, 'We need to move.'

The driver keeps looking forward.

I open the door and put my hand on his arm. His head tips back against the rear panel and rolls to the side. Blood from his hairline, down the left side of his face.

His eyes open, dead to the world.

Only then do I notice the windscreen has gone. Shards of glass over his legs.

Vera calls again, urgent now.

I pull the driver gently forward in his seat, shift my arms under his and hoist him down from the cab, over my shoulder.

I carry him across the road and lay him down gently on the pavement.

An elderly lady crouches beside me. She asks if he's all right and I tell her no such luck.

I ask if she'll stay with him until the ambulance comes.

She says, 'What's his name?' but I can't even give her that.

I walk back to the cab, brush the broken glass away with my sleeve and climb in.

It takes a nine-point turn to avoid the wreckage in the road. One of the front tyres has shredded and the wheel churns noisily on the tarmac, the steering almost impossible to control. We shudder down Cannon Street, past Monument, not stopping for passengers.

The wind blows in where the windscreen used to be. Over London Bridge with plumes of grey smoke rising above the burning city.

The Thames, dark and forbidding.

I drive the crippled bus past Tooley Street to the terminus at London Bridge and switch the engine off, the rush of steam still hissing in my ears.

Vera raps hard against the panel to ask what I'm doing.

I explain it's the end of the route, ten minutes for a brew and a quick lavvy break.

'Billy, we need to get the passengers to hospital. Drive us to Guy's.'

I explain we can only carry passengers on the route displayed on the destination roller.

'If you don't drive us to a hospital now, at least two of these passengers will die.'

'Sorry, it's against company regulations,' I tell her.

She looks at me through the glass panel. I wonder if it only stayed intact because the driver shielded it from the blast when the windscreen blew in.

Vera puts her hand on the glass behind me and looks me in the eyes.

A kindness I have seen before.

Her thumb and fingers spread wide, a motionless wave, like an open starfish, fingerprints magnified against the tiny pane.

A lifeline across her palm. Her future mapped out, like mine was all those years ago. I wonder how many lovers Vera will have, hoping it might only be one more.

The station manager is not in his booth.

I turn the key and the engine coughs back to life. Fragments of broken glass crunch on the pedals.

I drive up to the turning circle and out of the terminus.

Left, away from the river, through a series of wrong turns in unfamiliar streets, south London not my territory. Most of the east never made much sense to me either, beyond Limehouse and Poplar. I don't mind the north, Holloway and Hampstead, but I'll always be a west London man.

I ask pedestrians for directions, carving the tarmac

302

with the bare wheel, the front of the bus tilted like an old dog on an injured paw.

It takes a while to find the hospital, eventually turning down a side road for an ambulance to pass. It takes every bit of shoulder muscle to steer us up onto the kerb. I scrape a wall, dead slow, and come to a halt jammed against a street lamp with the hospital entrance in sight.

I tell Vera it's the best I can do, and go round to help carry the wounded the last few yards.

Vera cradles the head of the man on the makeshift stretcher. She looks up at me and gently shakes her head.

His final breaths.

A sound that stays with you forever.

He dies in Vera's arms and I think about Flight Sergeant Cooper's wife, hoping she found happiness with her new husband in Metro-land.

Later, we walk back to the depot at London Bridge. I explain to the station manager what happened near St Paul's, the number 13 we commandeered from the dead driver and had to abandon in a side street near Guy's Hospital.

He says to go and fetch it back.

I tell him I don't think I can drive any more tonight, which escalates into a row, him shouting that I'll lose my job for unauthorised use of a transportation vehicle.

I tell him to stick his job up his arse and walk away.

Sitting on the grass on Primrose Hill, watching the sun come up with Vera after a long walk back through town.

Putting off going home to cold cuts on the parlour shelf.

I let slip that I know where she lives in Chalk Farm after seeing her walk there one day.

She says, 'Have you been spying on me?' but not in an unfriendly way.

I tell her, 'I can't not see you any more.'

She stays quiet and I think I've said too much.

A dog barking somewhere down the hill below. The view of London from Primrose Hill can be spectacular, though today it looks beaten. We huddle for warmth under our coats while the rising sun reveals the smoke and scars of another bruising attack. Six months of nightly raids by German planes. Other cities are getting it too, though London feels like the jackpot. There are shards of glass in my arms while a dull ache plummets from my head into my back and ribs.

The lucky ones, I suppose.

Maybe we were thinking of the people we loved and that's what kept us safe.

Sat close, I notice another dim bruise on the left side of Vera's face and red marks on her neck. I ask how she got them but she says not to fuss. After a silence, she says she took a knock in the close shave near St Paul's.

It's late. I walk her to the end of her street, the other side of Primrose Hill.

'Sorry I asked you to drive to the hospital. All that trouble with the manager.'

I tell her she's the best clippie I ever worked with.

She smiles awkwardly, bites her lip and says, 'I get embarrassed if someone is nice to me.'

There are things I want to tell her but don't know where to start.

She asks me not to walk any further in case her husband sees.

'I wish everything was different,' she says.

I watch her by the front door but she doesn't turn to wave.

When the door closes, I walk away with my hands in my pockets to keep out the morning chill and find the broken bracelet her mother gave her, cool against my fingers.

I consider getting it repaired, the joy of taking it to the jeweller's for her, but it feels like a dangerous step towards an intimacy we cannot have.

Better just to give it back now.

To get rid of it and move on.

I walk up to her front door.

The innocent returning of something she lost at work.

To glimpse her world for a moment, and maybe even the man she married, with a clear conscience and nothing to hide. To view the goodness they share and stop myself falling in love.

To let my feelings die before the flame gets truly lit.

I pause by the step. A bridge between two worlds.

I raise my hand to knock and hear voices at the back of the house. A man shouting and Vera's muffled response. I can't make out the words. Another furious outburst by the man and the smashing of crockery against a wall.

I've heard cups smash before, and will do so again.

Silence follows, the quietness more disturbing than fury. I put my ear to the door to listen for Vera's voice.

A sound of crying maybe, but that might be my imagination.

I raise my knuckles once more to tap, to ask if everything's all right, but that feels more intimate than the offer of a broken bracelet kept safe in my trouser pocket.

Instead I walk away from Vera's house, back to Regent's Park for a bus to Lancaster Gate and Shepherd's Bush Green.

Back along the Uxbridge Road with forty years of memories under my feet. Down Coningham Road to the small flat I share with the Hammersmith girl.

The hallway smells of cabbage. Two slices of cold gammon and a couple of boiled potatoes on a plate on the cold shelf, but my appetite has gone. I take off my shoes with the gaping hole in the leather, tread quietly into the bedroom and get into the single bed without undressing, across from the other small bed my wife sleeps in.

She faces the wall on the other side of the room. Soon after I'm home, she gets up to start her day.

I wonder about pushing the two beds together sometime. If we could reach out and hold on to each other, would it all come good? If I brushed her shoulder with my fingers and whispered a thing or two, and we turned to face each other, could we be like a proper man and wife?

Or is this the only way we'll manage to get by?

I lie under the sheet and blankets, thinking how Vera manages to get by too.

Her bruises.

The way she taps the glass panel with her head tilted, just enough to keep them hidden from view.

Her *clumsiness* . . .

We manage, and we stay quiet.

We don't change.

My headache's raging now and a pain grows in my toes, some of which I fear are broken.

I close my eyes hoping I might dream of rescuing Vera from her violent husband.

Thirty

Hello, Billyboy.
Vera, you've come back.
Not Vera.
The Hammersmith girl?
How quick we forget!
My boy! Step into the light, son, I can't see your face.
Your forever love.
Weren't there five of you? Five, Mrs Coggins said.
What do you want, Billyboy?
I'm afraid I'll still be alone when I get to the end.
You had your chances.
Didn't turn out like I thought.
You're telling me.
Mary Coggins, Evie, Archie, Vera and Betty Jackson.
All gone now, are they? All of them left you behind?
Everyone's dead, apart from me.
We had some good times.
I can't see your face. Who are you?
You tell me, Billyboy, it's your dream!

The boiler has just switched on and the central heating pipes are groaning in the walls. Early risers stumble in the corridor while delivery vans race down the street outside.

Dementia. Alzheimer's. Amnesia.

Lots of fancy words these days for losing your marbles.

Live through the Blitz and no amount of dementia will see those dates off. September 1940 to May 1941. I was already middle-aged back then.

The numbers are easy.

It's not dates I want to recall, but the feelings.

Vera, are you there?

Take me away from this, seeing my days out in a grey block down Hammersmith Grove.

Are you there?

I'm sure I loved you very much.

Let me remember how it felt to love you one last time.

'Let's get you sorted, Billyboy.'

Sylvie hoists me off the bed into a wheelchair.

For a moment I think my toes are covered in blood from the blast but then remember Sylvie painted them with varnish last night.

She tells me I'm a proper dandy.

She fills the sink with warm water and wipes my face with a flannel.

The water isn't as warm as I'd like.

She wheels me into the day room for a small bowl of porridge.

I sit quiet and try to remember Vera.

Jamming a bus down a side street near London Bridge didn't lose me my job. That happened after being arrested for stealing another, kidnapping Vera and driving up north so we could be together.

'Where are you going?'

'They haven't told me.'

'How long for?'

'I don't know.'

The Hammersmith girl cuts up a turnip from the garden for a stew.

'Evacuees, somewhere up north,' I tell her. 'I'll need my ration book. Will you be all right?'

A light rain tapping on the window.

She scrapes chopped turnip into the pan.

'I might knock on Mr Hooper's door when I've made this. Take him up a plate for his dinner.'

It's a month since Mr Hooper lost his wife, who was visiting her sister when a bomb fell in Godolphin Road, two streets down.

'I'll leave money on the side to tide you over.'

It's the most we've said to each other in weeks.

The Hammersmith girl looks at me across the parlour.

'I worry about you, Billy.'

'I know you do.'

She looks out at the rain.

'I wish everything was different,' I tell her.

I arrive at the Wells Road depot two hours early, take a key from the rack in Mr Oldhouse's office and walk out past the clippies' room, into the garage. I climb into the cab of a double-decker with a full tank. When Mr Oldhouse disappears inside, I turn the engine over and drive onto the Goldhawk Road. At the corner of Shepherd's Bush Green, I pull over and wind the destination roller to *Not in Service*.

My small rucksack, stowed under the seat, has a clean shirt and tie and my best pair of shoes, a flask of tea, some water and a few items from the larder.

Driving a bus is easy when you don't have to stop for people.

Notting Hill, Paddington, up the Edgware Road.

London is bracing itself for another night, but we'll be out of the suburbs by the time the planes come.

Regent's Park, Swiss Cottage, across to Chalk Farm. I park at the end of Vera's street wondering what it might feel like to kiss her.

I wait and I wait.

I know the time she leaves for work and recognise her shape as soon as she steps onto the pavement, full and compact, like a tightly packed suitcase fighting to keep a promise not to burst its buckles.

Chestnut hair tied up beneath a headscarf and a handbag over her arm.

She picks up her pace and still hasn't noticed the red and cream double-decker parked on the road. I climb down from the cab and stand on the pavement as she approaches.

She slows and her face opens into a smile that can't disguise the bruises from the previous day.

311

I tell her, 'We've been given a top-secret mission up north, for a couple of days at least.'

'Evacuees?' she asks nervously, knowing I took children and teachers to other cities when the Blitz started.

'We'll find out soon enough.'

I tell her she'll need a few extra clothes and a blanket if it gets cold. 'It'll be a change of scenery for us both.'

She says, 'My husband won't be pleased. He isn't back from work yet.'

'Can you write him a note?'

The worry on her face turns to excitement and she says, 'How long to get my bag ready?'

I tell her five minutes.

She hurries back to the house. I open the panel inside the cab, wind the roller to *Special* and wait for Vera. Fifteen minutes later, she's back with a big coat and a small suitcase.

'I left a note on the table saying I'm on a top-secret mission for a couple of days, but didn't mention the north.'

I tell her she did well.

In her hurry she forgot a blanket, but I say there's one next to a picnic I've brought for us, and we'll need to get going before dark.

She says, 'This is all very exciting,' and I almost take her hand but it feels too soon for that.

The world opens and London becomes a memory as evening draws in.

I think of seeing Ma the previous day, taking her rations and some extras to her Peabody flat in Fulham. Trafalgar

Street and Hammersmith Creek now just another layer of history buried under London's thick crust. Telling her I was going away for a few days and wasn't sure when I'd be back.

She said, 'Take care, love. Your father will be home soon,' and I sensed, at sixty-four, this could be the beginning of her end.

Auntie Pam's address in my pocket.

I watch the land change, an evacuee myself. Glimpsing Vera in the mirror, sat alone on the lower deck.

Headlights stay off, even out of town. Road signs have been taken down and only the milometer shows how far we've come. Shifting between exhilaration and fear with each passing mile, knowing it's already too late to turn back.

Thirty-five gallons of diesel in a full tank.

Six miles per gallon, at thirty miles per hour. We won't make Manchester on a single tank but should reach the other side of Derby. I stop to ask a man walking his dog beside the road if we've passed the RAF airfield at Wittering yet, and he makes a joke about being very lost in a London bus.

Vera looks at the wide fields in moonlight through the hole in the mesh but it feels like some distance has already grown between us.

After Melton Mowbray, I pull into an empty lay-by to suggest we use the facilities. She asks where the facilities are and I tell her it's the hedge beside the road, hoping she'll laugh. She looks troubled and I force myself to think this is still a good idea.

313

I go behind the hedge and piss against a tree trunk. The countryside looks peaceful under the moon and stars but the call of late birds and wind through the leaves is unsettling. Vera says she'd rather hang on for a proper lavatory. I tell her there won't be anywhere open till morning and she'll be more comfortable if she goes now. Reluctantly she disappears through the gap in the hedge. She comes back looking bashful but admits she'd been holding the urge for a couple of hours.

It's nearly midnight and I suggest we sleep here to avoid running out of diesel in the dark. We share the bread, corned beef and an apple cut into quarters with my pocket-knife. Vera finishes the tepid tea from the flask.

Cold April air blows through the open platform. I tell her to take the blanket upstairs to get some sleep. I rest my head against the cold mesh on the lower deck with my jacket buttoned tight. Sleep comes in fits and starts, my mind racing, knowing Vera and I will already be missed back at the depot in London.

I wake in the early light, having only slept for minutes.

Three Bedford trucks roll by, the first of the day's army lorries.

My back aches, hunched over in the cold air. Stretching out, I stumble to the stairs to call up to Vera.

I call again, louder this time, then take a few steps up, but she's not there.

Off the platform into the empty lay-by, knowing she's escaped, wondering when she saw through the story about a secret mission.

There's no clue to say which direction she's gone. If she'd chosen to walk back towards Melton Mowbray, the army lorries might have picked her up. If she'd gone in the direction we were heading, they would have passed her now.

Back in the cab, I turn the engine over and work out my choices: back to London to take the flak, or on to a new life without her, in which case I'd do better to abandon the bus and go on foot.

Vera emerges through the gap in the hedge.

She sees me and waves. 'Not going without me?!' she calls, playfully troublesome. 'I could really do with making myself beautiful.'

I tell her, 'You're beautiful as you are,' and she gives me a smile I can still see when my eyes are closed, which make me think I might be remembering what love feels like after all.

When she's back on the lower deck, she taps the bell rope twice and I think this is the happiest I've been since kissing Evie Ellis on Lime Grove on a snowy night twenty years ago.

An hour later, near Nottingham, we pull into a garage with a small café and order bowls of black pudding hotpot and two mugs of steaming tea. We sit in the corner of the café by a window, unable to see through the filthy glass, and Vera says, 'This is the life.'

After finishing the hotpot, the mugs of tea still warm in our hands, I ask how she met her husband.

She says how good-looking he was. He wooed her briskly and proposed when war was inevitable. They married quick, two years ago, but stopped seeing eye to eye soon after their wedding.

There's a bruise and a small swelling on her cheekbone under her eye, which I want to brush softly with my fingers, but this is not the time or place.

She gently angles her head away from my gaze and asks how I met my wife.

There are details Vera doesn't need to hear. I tell her I was engaged but it didn't work out and I met the Hammersmith girl soon after.

She asks if we have children and is surprised when I say, 'One.'

'Boy or girl?'

I tell her his name.

'How old is he?'

I wonder how tall the weeping willow will have grown over these years, the promise to return to it unfulfilled.

In the long silence, Vera reads the tea leaves at the bottom of her mug and says she's sorry.

I wipe condensation off the grimy window as a truck pulls onto the gravel outside.

Her warm hand touches my fingers.

'I shouldn't have asked,' she says.

I shake my head and smile, wishing I could put the mug down and take her hand in mine.

She catches me looking back at the bruise below her eye but this time doesn't turn away, holding it proudly towards me like a battle scar.

We keep our eyes on each other much longer than we should.

I tell her, 'We must be getting on.'

Thirty-One

The garage attendant asks to see my transport papers.

I show my bus driver's card and more than enough cash for a full tank, but he won't give the fuel without official authorisation.

Vera watches from the lower deck.

I explain how my depot manager said to show my driver's card but didn't give me transport papers when I left London. I ask if news of the Blitz has reached this far north.

He says they've got enough troubles of their own without worrying about London.

I tell him if he doesn't let me have the fuel we need, he'll be helping Hitler undermine the war effort.

He says he's got strict orders about rationing and turns to walk back to his little booth. I'm wondering if Vera should have spoken to him instead.

I ask if there's another petrol station nearby where we can buy diesel.

'Not officially,' he says.

'How about unofficially?'

'That'd be against the law,' he says.

'You don't give me another choice.'

He smiles and says there's a farmer up the road who's

rumoured to sell black market diesel, but I didn't hear that from him.

I get back in the cab wondering what Vera made of the exchange.

His directions make little sense, and we're soon bouncing slowly down a lane full of holes, branches scraping the Hovis advertising board on the side of the bus, until we come to a locked gate with no farm building in sight.

Reversing slowly, I see an old lady working in the field, suspiciously eyeing a red double-decker on a farm track in the middle of nowhere. I decide not to ask if she knows where to buy black market diesel.

At the end of the lane, Vera taps on the panel and says, 'Let me help.'

She fixes on her clippie's hat and jumps off the platform to walk into the road. Through the near-side mirror I watch her stop an approaching truck with an outstretched hand before waving me out.

The bus bounces back onto tarmac.

She checks the road ahead and waves the waiting truck past. The driver leans out, sounds his horn and makes a lewd comment at her. Unruffled, she steps back onto the open platform and taps the bell rope twice.

She walks to the front of the lower deck, knocks on the glass behind me and calls through, 'This is all very exciting.'

We're refused diesel at each garage we stop at, and I realise I didn't think the plan through well enough before leaving London.

Past Derby, on the road to Buxton, the needle twitching towards empty.

Through Cromford and Matlock Bath.

At Darley Dale the engine splutters as the last sips of fuel pass through the carburettor.

I turn off the main road and over a small railway bridge as the engine begins to choke, spotting a coal dump next to the road. We coast silently across gravel, the engine finally starved, and come to a quiet halt behind a cover of trees.

The noise of the road is replaced by birdsong and a distant hammering of metal.

Vera knocks on the glass panel again but doesn't say a word.

I'm considering coming clean, telling her the mission was to rescue her from her violent husband, and me from an unhappy marriage, when smoke appears above the trees and a train whistle shrieks on the other side of the coal dump. I have the urge to grab her hand and run for the train, wherever it may be going, but our new life can't be rushed. Apologising for not bringing the right papers, I assure Vera it'll be fine after I've made a telephone call to London. She doesn't ask any difficult questions, just quietly gathers her small suitcase and we leave the bus parked under the trees.

It's late in the afternoon and neither of us have eaten since breakfast in the roadside café. There's no tea bar at Darley Dale station, so I seat Vera on a bench with the bags while I approach the stationmaster, who tells me the next connecting train to Manchester via Buxton isn't until morning.

I ask to make an important telephone call to London regarding wartime matters but he says the telephone is strictly reserved for railway business only.

I tell him the north is full of the most unhelpful people I've ever met, and ask for information on local guest houses. He directs us to his sister's place in Stanton, a half-hour walk up the hill, which he offers to call and book on our behalf.

'Not on the telephone strictly reserved for railway business, I hope?' I ask, but he fails to see the funny side.

When I tell Vera we'll be staying in a guest house overnight and taking a train to Manchester in the morning, she asks, 'Will the bus be all right here?'

'Safer than in London,' I reply, but she doesn't see the funny side either.

We pass a pub overlooking a river, the Square and Compass, that Jimmy Parris would approve of. Past a lead factory where the hill gets steeper, to the tiny hamlet of Stanton Lees. I ask for directions to the Derwent View guest house and a lady says we want *Stanton in Peak*, which is another mile or so over the hill. I quietly curse the stationmaster, whose idea of a thirty-minute walk differs to ours, even without dragging a rucksack and suitcase uphill.

Vera stopped talking to me a while ago.

We eventually arrive in grim silence at the Derwent View, shivering from the cold air, with blisters from a long walk in bad shoes.

Mrs Critchlow has been expecting us since her brother, the stationmaster, called to reserve the room. She's extremely short, with beady eyes and a faint moustache that makes her face look like a Yorkshire terrier. Over her high-collared blouse and tweed jacket she wears a string of pearls and a large crucifix out of proportion with the size of her body.

I tell her we're heading to Manchester on wartime business. She watches us the way an executioner measures up prisoners for the gallows and solemnly scratches the information into her guest book with an old pen. I give a false surname and address and Vera doesn't look at me when I refer to her as my wife.

Unimpressed by my details, the landlady tells us to follow her upstairs to the room.

Once the bedroom door is closed and Mrs Critchlow's stern footsteps have retreated down the landing, Vera hisses at me to explain what's going on.

This porridge is cold and lumpy.

I used to enjoy going to see films during the Cold War. Often I went to the pictures just to get warm and save on the heating bill.

I played no part in the Cold War. I was too old for wars by then.

I liked spy films at the time, with twists and turns you didn't see coming: double agents, an umbrella tipped with poison, hidden microphones in flowers pinned to lapels, police vans listening to secret conversations in hotel rooms, fingers in dials and lips to the receiver, tapes stopping and starting whenever the telephone was lifted to record every word.

I imagine the spools turning now, deep in the wires of my old mind. Playing back the memories from long ago, like the time I ran away with Vera.

Remembering what love feels like.

All the details about how we fell in love are flowing today.

I just want to keep going.

Mrs Akinyemi wants me to sign a piece of paper, but I'm not going to let her or this cold lumpy porridge put a stop to the flow.

Vera wants a straight and honest answer.

I look out at the green hills and tell her that secret messages from Germany have been decoded revealing Hitler's plans to increase bombing over the north of England. We've come to help evacuate children like we did in London. 'They helped us at the start of the Blitz and sent buses from all over,' I tell her. 'Now it's our turn to help them.'

After a moment she says, 'I knew it'd be something to do with children.'

She smiles briefly, then continues, 'So why won't they let us have diesel?'

'We didn't get the papers in time.'

'You'd have thought they'd want to help save their own children.'

I tell her they haven't been told yet to avoid a panic.

'Why are we going by train then?'

'It's drivers they need. They've got enough buses to get started.'

Vera sits on the bed and takes off her clippie's hat.

Now would be the time to kiss her. To come clean, even. To hide where no one knows us.

'Billy. Why did I come too?'

She looks me in the eye. I'm stood by the door with the rucksack and suitcase between us. She waits and she waits.

I undo the top button on my shirt and think about saying, *Because I wanted to rescue you from your violent husband.*

The light is dying outside the small window. I'm tired from the drive and not sleeping. From getting us here. I'm tired but she deserves the truth.

'I don't think your husband treats you very well. I wanted you to come. I thought you needed a couple of days away.'

She's sat on the end of the bed, hands upturned on her knees. She touches a recent bruise, covered with make-up. I wonder how it would feel to take her in my arms, but we're both good married people and infidelity doesn't come easy any more.

She says, 'Where will you sleep, Billy?'

'On the floor, if that's all right. Just one night.'

She looks at the threadbare pink carpet and doesn't reply.

Dinner at Mrs Critchlow's table is no joyous affair.

Vera and I sit opposite each other eating liver and onions, the meat as tough as the boots rotting in the hallway, while Mrs Critchlow stands over us asking questions.

She knows we're lying.

Vera stays silent through the inquisition while I create a new history.

'Where did you get married?'

'Finchley,' I answer, hoping she's never heard of it.

'No one gives you the time of day down there,' Mrs Critchlow replies. 'Which parish, exactly?'

Vera refuses to look up. I pick the first saint that comes to mind, hoping it might deter further questions.

The landlady's lips curl in permanent disapproval. She tells us how rude everybody is down in London.

I'm still chewing the last obstinate onion, with Vera's knife and fork laid side by side in the gravy like dead soldiers as I excuse the two of us from the table with a plan to visit the village pub for a nightcap.

Mrs Critchlow gives Vera the eye and says, 'I didn't have *you* down as a drinker.'

I steer Vera upstairs, across the landing and into our room. When the door is closed, she bursts into tears and says that was the worst experience of her life.

I touch her arm and tell her I'm sorry.

She attempts to blow her nose quietly and says, 'Give me the Blitz over dinner with that horrible woman any time!'

We share a smile.

I ask if she'd like to come to the pub with me.

She says, 'You're not leaving me here alone with that b—'

It's the first time I've heard her swear, though she doesn't say the word out loud.

We pick up our jackets, shut the bedroom door behind

*

us and tiptoe downstairs, where Mrs Critchlow is already guarding the door.

'Don't be late!' she barks. 'I go to bed by nine and won't be making Bovril after seven.'

Vera's first gin goes down as quick as my pint and we're onto our second without asking.

'Like a proper couple,' I tell her.

She chinks her glass against mine, which feels like a step in the right direction.

The Flying Childers is quiet. Two farmworkers stand by the counter with their own silver tankards. It's hard to imagine London right now, Underground stations packed with people bedding down in the fetid air, and we drink to the city never being defeated.

After our third glasses, Vera says her husband has some good qualities and not to judge him on his temper, which only comes on when she does something foolish.

Some of the locals play a noisy game of skittles on the table behind us. They nod but no one says hello.

Warm in the glow of the alcohol, I realise Vera and I have already come a long way since we left London the previous evening.

When we return to the guest house, shortly before nine, Mrs Critchlow reminds us we're too late for Bovril and breakfast will be served at seven sharp. We bid her good-night and both have a sense she's been snooping around the room while we were out.

Vera cleans her teeth in the small sink and asks me to

turn the other way while she gets into bed fully clothed. She hands me one of the pillows and turns aside to brush her hair.

I clean my teeth in silence too, and wrap myself in the blanket from the bus on the carpet, curled up below Vera's feet on the bedroom floor like an old dog in his master's bad books.

Vera blows out the candle and we bid each other an awkward goodnight before lying in silence, both unable to sleep.

Outside, the sound of animals killing each other.

Not much different to us really.

At some point before the sun comes up, I fall asleep and dream I'm a very old man living in a grey room down Hammersmith Grove. My teeth and hair have gone and I'm surrounded by elderly people, trying to remember all those I once loved.

Thirty-Two

Early-morning light smudges the tiny window.

I stand to allow my ankle to reconcile its first steps of the day. Vera is awake and already spruced, sat up on the bed.

I ask how she slept.

'Fine,' she says and we leave it at that.

Breakfast is as chilly as last night's dinner.

Vera and I return to the room to pack in silence.

I put Auntie Pam's letter into my jacket pocket. We go downstairs to settle up with Mrs Critchlow, who bids us a cold farewell, then start the long walk down through Stanton Lees to Darley Dale, Vera always a few steps behind me.

At the station, I buy our train tickets to Buxton and Manchester.

When the train pulls out, we get a view of the Hovis sign on the side of the bus parked next to the coal dump, though neither of us break the chilly atmosphere to mention it.

The scenery changes further into the Peaks. A wide-open landscape, green and pleasant, clear air bringing the rolling horizon into sharp focus. Hillsides sliced with dry-stone walls, deep valleys woven by a dark river. Occasional dwellings like toy houses, any of which would do me for the rest of my days. Two older passengers share the compartment, their dialect soft and lazy after the sharp patter of London tongues. The warm green light mellows the chill between Vera and me and the mood lifts, like the hills, closer to Buxton.

Two hours to wait for our connecting train. Over hot tea and soft pastries from the buffet, Vera surprises me with an uncanny impression of Mrs Critchlow that leaves us wiping tears from our eyes.

She goes to the ladies' while I sit on a bench and imagine telling our future grandchildren the story of how we fell in love. She returns with a spring in her step and the bruises softening on her beautiful face.

'How are you?' she asks.

I think I'm well.

'So then, Billy Binns, what really happens in Manchester?' she asks.

I take out the letter Auntie Pam sent when war broke out last year. *Come and see me if it gets a little hot down south.*

It's too early for the whole truth, especially with the mood lifting, so I just tell Vera we'll visit my Auntie Pam and wait for more instructions.

With time to spare, we leave the station. It feels like Buxton has been built of nothing but cold grey stone and hoisted up into the clouds. Vera sees a silver butterfly pendant with blue wings on a chain in a jeweller's window. It's beautiful but much too expensive to buy for a friend.

I remember choosing Evie's wedding ring all those years ago.

The trouble that came with the Hammersmith girl.

I remember the weeping willow.

Knowing all these moments have led me here, to now, to a blue and silver butterfly in a Buxton shop window.

A long, slow route to happiness.

A connecting line through the gaps that make us who we are.

Tiny moments holding us together like pendants on a chain.

Tiny moments.

Clear as a bell.

They disappear like breath on a cold day.

Trying to find some warmth in my old bones.

Mrs Akinyemi returns to her office with a paper I've just signed for her. The television set shows an overly cheerful woman bringing a cake out of an oven, displaying too much cleavage for her age.

Mr Buffery is asleep by the doors out to the back garden, the hack and rattle of his cough at peace for the time being. Mrs Gibson snores gently, a magazine open on her lap showing a photograph of blue sky and a sunny beach, and I wonder if everyone here is just pretending to be asleep so they can fill in the gaps in their own past.

We tap on the jeweller's door.

It's opened by a well-dressed man as chilly as the Buxton air.

He says, 'Are sir and madam looking for a ring?'

There's enough oil in his manner to start the bus we left back at the railway station.

Wanting to avoid any more awkward conversations, I ask about the necklace with the pendant shaped like a butterfly.

He says the wings are made from Blue John, a precious stone only found under local hills.

Vera holds the necklace against her clippie's uniform.

She says, 'It's beautiful but we'll have to think about it.'

I'd like to buy it for her with the diesel money but need to keep the adventure going a while longer until Vera sees where her future lies. There'll be time for buying beautiful things after we've broken our vows.

In our new lives in a new town.

The train steams into Manchester.

It's a short bus ride from London Road station to Salford, back amongst the noise and smog of a city once more. Vera and I sit on the lower deck like aliens from another planet. The unfamiliar streets quickly reveal the same desolate scars as home. Manchester has taken it badly too.

The lady behind us gives directions to the address on Pam's letter. The dialect has changed again: soft, slow Derbyshire vowels giving way to punchy northern urgency. I wonder if people in cities have to talk quicker, afraid the world will rush on and leave them behind.

We get off at Pendleton, walk down Littleton Road, along Romney Street, up to Milnthorpe Street, taking in the whole new world.

The streets remind me of the old houses down Hammersmith Creek. Remembering Auntie Pam by the front door when I was sat up the stairs, when Ma called her a trollop and Dad said she should have let the little bastard freeze to death.

Terraces of two-up-two-downs. Back yards with alleys for rubbish and late-night trouble.

A gap where Pam's number should be.

A warden patrols the street while a gang of children rummage through rubble between the houses standing either side. A fraction of the upstairs floor clings onto the side wall, spewing split timbers and twisted metal cores through broken brickwork.

I stand on the pavement with Vera, hoping we're on the wrong road.

Vera doesn't know what to say.

A neighbour comes out and asks if we're family. She says, 'It happened two nights ago. They were such a lovely couple.'

She says to come in for a cup of tea.

We follow her into her house opposite the bomb site and wait in silence while she puts the kettle on. Over a warm tea, the neighbour asks if it was Ron or Mavis I was related to.

Puzzled, I tell her it was my Auntie Pam.

The woman takes a moment, then says, 'Pam? Not Ron and Mavis?'

I nod. She exhales like she's been winded and says Pam sold the house to Ron and Mavis just a few months ago, when it all started. 'Sold it for a bargain, she did. Wanted

331

to get out quick and move to the Peak District. I've got the address somewhere. Give me a minute to find it.'

She comes back with an address in Bakewell, which I remember passing through soon after Darley Dale.

We laugh nervously, considering the ill-fortune of the dead couple who survived just three months in their new house, but there's a limit to the grieving you can do when people are dying all over. You celebrate good luck when it happens.

Vera and I return to London Road and catch the last train back to Buxton, where I pay for two single rooms at the Palace Hotel and lie in bed thinking of Vera in the room next door. When sleep finally comes, I dream of Mrs Critchlow stood watching over me while I dig Blue John out of an underground cave with my bare fingers.

At breakfast, Vera reckons my wife and her husband will be worrying about us. I tell her I'll buy her a train ticket back to London if she's anxious. She says she'll think about it but doesn't mention it at the station when I ask for two singles to Bakewell.

Pam shares the same doleful eyes as Ma but wears make-up around hers, which Ma always considered slatternly.

Her grey hair is better cared for and a small kiss curl makes her look younger than her years. She wears pearls and a zebra-print dress mismatched with house slippers, as if she's off out somewhere but hasn't quite finished getting ready. The noticeable difference between the sisters is Pam looks like she married better.

It takes her a moment to recognise me before a smile opens up and she welcomes us into the small cottage with a warm hug.

She refers to Vera as my *lady friend* and says I have to stop calling her Auntie now we're all getting old. We spend the rest of the day catching up and Vera quickly relaxes in Pam's company.

She asks after Ma, and I explain how her health is failing. Pam says, 'That woman put up with so much from your dad over the years,' but we leave it at that for now and I feel a little disloyal seeing Pam after she and Ma haven't spoken all this time.

The next day we all walk around the cattle market and eat Bakewell pudding in a tea room. I thank her for the money she sent me after her second husband died, which paid the deposit on the flat in Coningham Road. Pam says it was nice to get my letter and she wished Ma had cashed her own cheque too.

She tells us a little about her three husbands: the first, who got involved with the wrong sort and was then murdered in Salford thirty years ago; her second, who inherited his father's cotton mill in the Peak District and died several years later. She felt it was only right to share the money around. A period of solitude followed before she married her third, a policeman who quickly ran off with some of her savings and a dolly bird.

When the bombing started, Pam knew she had to sell the house in Manchester straight away. She could have got more money for it but wanted to leave quick.

She has enough left, she reckons, to see out her days here. Vera says Bakewell is so pretty she can imagine living here herself, which makes my heart soar.

Back at the cottage, Pam cooks a thick stew for dinner and calls it tea. I ask what the fuss was about the night I watched her leave from the top of the stairs, and Pam says it was a misunderstanding between her and Ma, which has gone on for years.

'Your father was a tinker back then. He'd been carrying on with a couple of local girls and your ma thought I was one of them.'

I ask if she remembers him saying, 'You should have let the little bastard freeze to death,' the night they had their row.

She says Ma was a bit of a tinker too and Dad said she tricked him into getting married, that I'd been a surprise while they were courting. Pam says my dad was like a puppy who snapped whenever he felt trapped in a corner but never meant the things he said.

'All water under the bridge,' she says and changes the subject.

Pam says what's between Vera and me is private and she's seen enough of the world to know not to ask questions. She says we look like a proper couple, and she should know after having three husbands, two of them in the grave.

The next day Vera is suffering from women's ache and Pam tells me to make myself scarce for the afternoon.

It doesn't feel right being apart from her for the first time in five days, but she's in good hands with Pam, and

I've learned it's always better to be away from a woman when she's in her monthly mood.

There's bliss in the root of my bones.

Disappointment too, remembering these people I once loved.

Never quite how you imagined.

Life is what happens when you're planning other things, somebody once said.

You can't always get what you want.

An old song plays in the back of my head.

Vera's face comes into sharp focus then fades like the tune that was here just a moment ago, when I thought there was so much more of her to come.

I tell them I'm out for a long walk over Chatsworth but head instead to the railway station.

Up through the hills once more, into tunnels and over viaducts to Buxton, smoke bashing the carriage windows.

Out through the station past the buffet where Vera and I laughed at her impression of the landlady whose name I'm already struggling to recall, and straight to the jewellery shop.

Using the diesel cash and other money I'd been saving, I buy the butterfly necklace with the Blue John wings for Vera.

It's late afternoon by the time I return to Pam's cottage, where Vera is feeling much better. After dinner, the three of us play Newmarket with matchsticks. One for a horse and one for the kitty. I remember teaching it to Archie once he was able to fan the cards in his small hands.

Vera wins handsomely, lending me matchsticks when my own pile has gone, much to Pam's amusement. Afterwards Pam goes to bed, leaving the two of us alone.

Vera sits on the settee next to me and puts her arm through mine.

'I want to be like Auntie Pam when I grow up,' she says.

Without using words, I tell her I've fallen in love with her.

I think about giving her the small box in my jacket pocket, but I've already worked out a good plan for that moment.

Vera looks into my eyes, says she feels safe up here, and I think she might be falling in love with me too.

The three of us take the bus from Bakewell to Stanton Moor, where Pam wants to show us the Nine Ladies stone circle. She sits beside Vera in front of me.

I'm enjoying looking at the back of Vera's neck when she turns to point out the guest house we stayed in, which feels like a lifetime ago.

The bus drops us near the top of Stanton in Peak and we walk up the hill. Auntie Pam links arms between us and says she's not getting any younger. We follow her over a stile at the edge of Stanton Moor and she exhales after the exertion of the climb.

The stones are smaller than I expected but form a quiet circle filled with magic.

Pam tells us they were young women turned to rock for drinking and dancing on a Sunday when they should have been in church.

Their names long forgotten.

Nine of them in all.

I'm not one for churches but I say a quiet prayer to whatever god is here. The god that turns nine ladies to stone, I suppose.

I take out my pocketknife and make a small cut across my thumb.

I offer this sacrifice to ask that Vera be mine.

I taste blood off my thumb and hope she knows this is love.

Vera says, 'You're quiet!'

Pam says, 'This place does that to a person.'

I finish my prayer and say, 'Amen.'

Pam walks out of the stone circle.

Vera puts her arm through mine and says, 'Can we talk later, when we're alone?'

'Of course,' I tell her.

I lose myself in her eyes for a moment.

She says, 'You've made me very happy.'

The three of us walk across the open plain where the wind blows hard, to a large rock called the Corkstone stood twenty feet out of the ground. It looks like it was thrown down by an angry god. Foot-holes have been carved into it with iron rungs to grab onto. As a boy I'd have been up it like a shot, but at this age I prefer to stand at a distance and admire.

We walk back to the road, where Pam's knowledge of the bus timetable is accurate to the minute.

That evening, Pam goes to bed early.

Vera and I play Newmarket again but it's not as good with two. I wonder if now's the right time to hear what she wants to tell me, but decide to let her do it whenever she's ready.

Vera asks about other parts of the world I'd like to see when the war's over.

I tell her I've already seen enough of the other parts.

She wants to visit India and the Far East and reckons I'd like it too. I picture us under the raw Indian sun surrounded by colours, by flowers and light, sipping gin beneath the blazing blue of a wide open sky, knowing I'd follow her wherever she wants to go.

She puts her cards down and calls it a night.

I wait for her to speak.

She stands and stretches the way people do when they're ready for bed, then walks around the card table and sits again on the settee beside me.

Her frame is small next to mine but big enough to fill my whole world.

Her hands clasped together in her lap.

I can see this going one of two ways.

Then she says, 'You can kiss me, Billy, if you'd like.'

Thirty-Three

Clattering teacups and the smell of old people.

Sounds come and go.

The history and the here-now.

You can kiss me, Billy, if you'd like.

The words reverberate around the sitting room, through the television chatter and the noise of the vacuum cleaner while Gordon clears the mess of crumbs beneath Mrs Cutts's chair. They come back off the walls like a pinball bouncing around a bagatelle. As if Vera is here with me now among the decrepit and the nearly-dead.

I hear her words.

But I don't lean in to kiss her.

The offer hangs for a moment like the promise of Christmas Day.

Instead I say, 'I'm sorry. The truth is, we haven't been sent on a secret mission.'

She says, 'I know, Billy.'

'I stole the bus to take you away from your husband.'

'I know.'

She strokes a finger on my chin, stubble growing after

not shaving these past few days. A disguise that will be the new me.

I tell her, 'I've fallen in love.'

She brushes the start of my young beard.

'And I don't think I can live without you.'

Her finger gently moves across my cheek, over my forehead, down to my lips. No one's ever touched me like this before.

She says, 'I will always love you, Billy, in a very particular way.'

A shiver of words from another life.

She smiles, but her eyes are as sad as a service for a dead friend.

Silence rolls out between us like a carpet, unwrapping motes filling the air with the dust of dreams.

She turns her head and says, 'You're a good man,' though I'm not sure that's true.

She stands up again and goes to the door by the stairs.

I tell her to wait.

She turns.

The burning log spits out a spark of flame, which dies quickly on the fireside rug.

I stand up and take out the box from my jacket pocket.

Do I see out the rest now, while the thin man in a suit shouts at a heavily tattooed woman on the television set, or dwell here for longer?

You can kiss me, Billy, if you'd like.

I wasn't a good man and I knew it.

I remember the angle of her head, opening for the kiss.

Her chin tilted towards me, my hand on the small of her back.

Her bruises fade like magic as I lean in and think of our own little cottage in the hills, with thick walls to keep the world out and an old dog sleeping by a fire.

A light-show of stars in a black sky every night.

The kiss goes on, sweeter than seaside rock.

The press of my hand on her skin.

Facing each other as we sleep.

Lying in at the weekend, a walk around the Nine Ladies on Sundays, our very own church high up on the moors where promises are kept and prayers are answered.

Her eyes closed to the rest of the world.

I see her like this and seal it like a photograph to keep forever.

The photograph burns out like the embers spat from the fire with a sudden rapid knocking on the door.

Wishing I'd kissed her, at least, like she asked.

It takes a moment, under the blanket on Auntie Pam's sofa, to work out where I am and whether it's the end of a night or the start of a day.

Pam is first to the door, voices on the other side. Vera behind her in a borrowed nightgown. Pam whispers something but the voices have no intention of keeping quiet.

Four men: two police, two in the uniform of the Civil Defence.

341

One of the policemen tells me my name and informs me I'm being arrested for abducting a young woman against her will and the misappropriation of a London bus.

Vera puts her hand to her mouth but doesn't speak any words.

Pam asks where they're taking me.

The policeman says to get my things.

Auntie Pam turns away and walks into her kitchen.

I begin to undo everything that was perfect. The agony of betrayal. Pulling every thread, even the good ones. Unravelling the perfect moments over the last few days to consider when the call was made.

Vera looks at me and mouths, 'Sorry.'

Going to Buxton for the pendant. Two of them left alone when she had her monthly ache. Pam will have asked what was going on and Vera sent a telegram to her husband.

Vera shakes her head and says, 'I didn't want it to be like this.'

I'm looking for things to put in my bag, but there's nothing I need any more and the policemen aren't in the mood to wait.

Four men bustle me out of the house. The first crack of morning opens at the edge of the black sky.

I turn to see Vera in the doorway, wrapped in Pam's nightgown. Her eyes wide open as if in shock, but I don't believe that for a moment. One hand over her mouth, the other fingering the delicate chain and Blue John butterfly wings on her pale neck.

Gordon says this would be easier at the table, but we'll see how we get on in the armchairs. He rests his clipboard on his legs, opens an envelope and takes ages fussing around for his glasses, so I slip back to the police van heading for London.

No window. I'm chained to a grille and forced to keep my arms lifted to stop my wrists chafing on the cuffs. My head is cut from a hasty transfer from the cell.

Arriving back in town, stiff from the journey, trousers piss-wet to add to the shame.

The black city after green hills, thinking for the first time London doesn't feel like home.

A quick trial.

They give me a lawyer but he doesn't speak well for me.

The diminutive Mrs Critchlow makes a righteous appearance, her head barely visible over the witness box. She confirms I stayed in her guest house with false details and knew I wasn't to be trusted.

Vera stands in the box and says I told her we were evacuating children from the north.

I'm sure this isn't the last time I see her, though it's difficult to concentrate on memories with Gordon talking in my ear.

He says, 'You've still not returned your appraisal, so we'll do the form now.'

Maybe I do get to see her again, when I come out of prison perhaps.

Loving her a good few more years, I'm sure.

In court there are fresh marks on her face the colour of aubergine. She denies I caused her bruises and says she fell downstairs when she got home. In the corridor afterwards I hear a policeman say, 'If she was my wife, I'd have belted her for not coming home quick too.'

Three years for taking the bus and abducting a female.

When the sentence is read out, I'm thinking it'll be Wormwood Scrubs, near where I watched the airships rise and fall with Harry Coggins when we were boys, but it's used by the army now and they send me to Wandsworth, to a wing with prisoners waiting to be hanged for treason.

May, 1941, listening through the window bars to bombs falling at night, for a while at least.

Gordon says, 'Regarding your overall care at The Cedars, would you say you were: one, very satisfied; two, satisfied; three, neither satisfied nor dissatisfied; four, dissatisfied; or five, very dissatisfied?'

Getting old is like being trapped in a cell. At least then I could walk outside for an hour each week.

I don't want to remember prison. It's not the sort of

thing a son wants to read about his father, but there's moments of kindness coming back which I'd like to recall.

Time is passing.

I wanted to remember what love was like but I'm not sure I've long left, so perhaps I should settle for remembering kindness instead.

Locked up for six months now, the fetid air of summer gone. Winter brings a new cellmate, taller than me, with an open face and a shaved head.

At first we circle like hawks waiting to dive on dead meat, not giving anything away. Days without speaking, sharing a shit-pot. Rotten food and stomach bugs. It's a week before we even say our first names.

Time is passing, slowly now.

The good days go fast and the painful ones drag.

Then something changes and he asks me how old I am. I'm forty-one. He'll soon be thirty. Kurt speaks good English with a foreign accent.

We start talking when darkness comes.

He was arrested for espionage but the warders have already told me that. They've told me to keep my ears open before they hang him, to knock time off my own sentence if I hear anything useful. To spy on the spy.

Lying on his concrete slab across the dim cell, feet poking from the end of his blanket, Kurt asks what I'm in for.

I give him the short version: a girl I loved, stealing a

bus, going to Derbyshire to find my aunt, and a few bliss-ful days with Vera, but I reckon it makes me sound like a lovesick youth.

He wants more details.

I whisper in the darkness. I tell him about Evie and the Hammersmith girl. Riding my bicycle across the tram tracks my father built in Shepherd's Bush Green.

I tell him about Auntie Pam and the Nine Ladies, how I'd like to go back to Derbyshire one day and leave London behind forever.

Kurt makes an occasional sound in the darkness to show he's listening. He questions certain moments and laughs when I do Vera's impression of the landlady.

I tell him about my eighteen-year marriage to the Hammersmith girl being over on numerous grounds but adultery not being one of them.

I tell him I never kissed Vera, even when she asked.

I tell him everything.

Sometimes we laugh until tears roll down our faces.

A guard rattles the bars of the cell door and hisses at us to shut the fuck up.

When I'm finished, Kurt tells me how he came here. It's a more interesting story than mine and takes several nights because whenever he talks about Gertrude he has to go quiet for a while.

In those moments I let him lie silent on his concrete bunk, filling the gaps in his own memories, and know not to ask anything else until he's ready to start again.

I'd like to recall it now because I think it helps me remember what love was like.

Besides, I'm not really listening to Gordon and his list of questions about being dissatisfied. I vary my answers by giving different numbers, hoping he'll leave me in peace to think about Kurt in the prison cell.

His father ran a metalwork shop in a small town in Czechoslovakia near the German border.

At sixteen, Kurt was an apprentice in a car factory before going back to work for his father. He started a business renting out motor cars that his dad helped set up, but it collapsed and he couldn't pay off the debts. He tried to join the Czechoslovakian army and was rejected on health grounds. 'Flat feet,' he said.

It was 1935 and Hitler was on the rise. At twenty-four, Kurt saw trouble looming in Europe and applied for an American visa. The embassy said he would get one in a year or two, so Kurt joined a merchant ship bound for Indonesia and came back to Hamburg twelve months later.

For three years he worked in the engine room on a steamer that sailed between Hamburg and New York every four weeks. In New York he fell in love with a girl called Gertrude. When she told him she was pregnant, Kurt decided to make one final trip to Hamburg to say goodbye to his family, then jump ship in New York and settle down with Gertrude and their baby. It was August, 1939.

Kurt takes a moment on his cold bunk. I listen to the sound of his breathing in the din of a prison night.

I wonder if he's had enough memories for now, but he goes on, his voice soft in the darkness.

Europe declared war with Germany and the voyage to New York was cancelled. He spent two months travelling through Poland, Lithuania and Sweden on false papers, heading to Scotland to find a merchant boat that would take him to America.

His false papers were discovered at the Norwegian border by the Gestapo. He was arrested and sent to a concentration camp in Germany.

Across the dark cell, Kurt asks if he's boring me.

I tell him it makes pilfering a bus to Derbyshire sound like child's play.

He says it's always hard to understand anyone else's life, and I get a sense of how small the world is.

I ask him to keep going but he stays quiet this time and we both lie on our cold bunks listening to the sound of the outside world until sleep comes.

The next night he says just enough about the concentration camp to describe what it was like, which I don't need to think about here.

After a month in that place he was recruited by the Abwehr as a Nazi spy. The alternative was suffering a slow and certain death as a prisoner. They took him to The Hague, then Hamburg for his training. Each day he regretted not jumping ship in New York when he had the chance.

He was introduced to another trainee spy called Jakob

who was being parachuted into England to send reports about the British weather.

Kurt was relieved when he heard this, believing it would be possible to see out the war in England and then find a way to Gertrude and his young son in New York. But his hopes were dashed when he was given his own mission some weeks later: to meet with a spy in London who the Abwehr suspected was now a double agent working for the British. Kurt was to find proof and then assassinate him before escaping back to Germany.

He falls quiet again.

There's a limit to how many memories can be recalled in one sitting.

In prison I keep an eye out for Clem, hoping I might one day spot him across the yard, but you keep your eyes low. You learn to not see things. To keep it all to yourself.

When night comes, Kurt and I speak in whispers, words spilling out to keep the scuttling rats at bay.

Kurt was in a plane flying over London around the time I stole away with Vera.

I think of us back then, our paths set to meet.

He watched the approach over the city, saw the Thames snaking through.

Saw the Houses of Parliament and St Paul's Cathedral.

Saw bombs fall from the other planes around him.

Watched the sparkles below.

Felt the bump and grind of flak.

Felt the plane bank right and was ejected over London Colney, north of the city.

It was his first jump out of a plane. He'd done it once from the top of a tower, but only in daylight.

He thought it was the beginning of the end.

Wind rushing by, the tug of the ropes.

I tell him I parachuted once and it didn't end well.

He says at least I lived to tell the tale.

He came down waiting for the bullets that would kill him while he hung under the ropes of his parachute.

Felt the rush of air as the drone of the aeroplane faded.

Heard a barking dog somewhere on the ground below.

We have much in common, Kurt and me, and I'm already thinking he is not my enemy.

He landed at the end of a farmer's field, just missing a small copse of trees. It took a moment to work out none of his bones were broken and another to roll the wash of silk in a tight ball.

He smoothed the marks in the field where he'd landed and hid in the copse of trees, shivering all the way to morning.

His instructions were to go immediately to an address in central London to meet the spy, who'd been told to expect a friend.

Using the spade in his backpack, he dug a hole to bury the parachute. He also buried his radio transmitter, which he'd say got broken in the fall, along with his pistol, as he had no intention of shooting anybody.

When the sun came up, he sipped water from his bottle, ate two pieces of dried fruit and practised his English accent out loud.

He spotted a small farm building in the distance. His compass had broken in the descent and he decided to wait another day to take his bearings from the sun. By night-fall, he'd still not stopped shivering.

He hid under a bush and forced himself to sleep for minutes at a time, until the sun came up the following day.

He waited four more days without moving, sipping water, until his dried fruit was gone, too scared to leave.

He thought about giving himself up to the police but knew the punishment for spying was death. Offering his services as a double agent would, at best, get him sent back to die in Germany.

On the fifth day, he finally left his sheltered copse of trees and set off with the morning sun. He kept out of sight of the farm buildings until coming to a road, then headed south towards London.

He reckoned he'd be there by the end of the day.

A mile or two down the lane a lorry driver stopped to ask directions. Kurt did his best to reply in English. The lorry driver thanked him and went on his way.

Soon afterwards, a policeman on a bicycle stopped, claiming a foreign man had been seen walking down the road. Kurt presented his forged papers, then his own out-dated passport, realising the names wouldn't match. The policeman took him to an office, where he was interrogated by government officials.

He told them his real name and claimed to be an illegal immigrant fleeing the Nazis, and was sent to a detention camp, where he was interrogated without sleep for several days.

He maintained his story until a man was brought into the room. It took him a moment to recognise Jakob, the young spy he met in Hamburg, sent to England to file weather reports. Jakob identified Kurt as a member of the Abwehr and Kurt was forced to admit why he was there.

Time passes, waiting for his trial to be held in secret.

The sounds of London through the cold window bars, muted by thick stone walls.

I wonder if Kurt is drawing me in. Looking for information to influence his sentence. Planning to give me up, like Vera and Auntie Pam did. He'll know I've been told to report on him and this might just be a game to hasten our own ends. To see who gives the other up first.

I wonder what information I could tell the guards to reduce my three years. To help me get out early.

I look at his silhouette across the cell, wondering what Vera is doing right now.

We talk until late. Quiet whispers brushing off the stone walls like soft mice.

He believes he'll be found guilty of espionage and sentenced to hang.

I tell him that won't happen.

He asks if Vera might be waiting for me when I get out.

I tell him that won't happen either.

He says he can't stop thinking about Gertrude in New York, and the young son he's never met. Soon he'll be old enough to start climbing trees.

Both of us quietly lost in our own futures.

I say it's cold.

He says, 'Two blankets are better than one.'

We huddle together against the chill of the dank wall.

Moments of kindness, like the flare of a match in the middle of a long storm.

A shared geography, unspoken then, which I'll say no more about.

Thirty-Four

Gordon looks at me, waiting with the pen in his hand.

I ask him to repeat the question as I was just remembering an unspoken moment of kindness from the past.

'Which staff member would you give special mention to, and why?'

This needs careful consideration.

Both Ros and Sylvie are kind. They treat me well, get me up in the morning, bring my tea and spoon my food. Gordon is mostly fine too, though he stays in his office most days and flaps like a hen sometimes. I remember he spoke unpleasantly to me once about a party hat, several years ago.

Mrs Akinyemi is nice too, when she's not arguing with Gordon. She brings paper for the typewriter when I'm trying to put these memories down.

No one ever has a decent word to say about Tabor.

I lean forward so Gordon can hear me. 'Ros,' I tell him.

He rolls his eyes.

'And Sylvie,' I add.

He mutters, 'For God's sake,' under his breath but my ears are working well enough today to hear him.

He says, 'There's only space for one.'

I don't understand what he means.

'You can only put one name down, Mr Binns.'

I tell him, 'Ros and Sylvie.'

He says, 'You can only put one name in the box. There's no space for two.' Gordon points down at the form to prove his point. I can't make out the words but the space looks big enough.

I tell him, 'They're only short names,' but he doesn't seem to understand.

So I try to choose whether it's Ros or Sylvie that should get a special mention. Ros is always kind and gentle, and looks tired when she talks about her writer boyfriend. I reckon she's not as happy as she makes out; I remember how she said she'd tunnel out of here with Jimmy and me the day the fire alarm went off.

Then I think about dusky Sylvie, with her nose ring and her cheeky laugh and the men who don't seem to treat her very well, how she cuts my toenails and clears up the mess when the valve on my piss-bag breaks.

I reckon Sylvie could probably do with a special mention on the form, but it seems wrong to put her down without Ros, so I just shake my head and look out of the window.

Gordon puts a line through the box and looks quite pleased with that.

Time is passing.

An unremarkable Christmas and a long winter after Kurt has gone.

Two years still to serve. Nothing to tell the guards to

bring my sentence down. Given another chance for early release if I agree to fight for my country in Europe.

I tell them all my wars are over.

One hour of exercise in the yard each week. Talking to a younger prisoner whose name I don't recall.

Sometime later he'll get me a gun when we're both out of Wandsworth. We'll meet in a pub in Turnham Green, walk to the common by the railway, where he shows me how to load it. An ex-army pistol with the serial number filed away. Six bullets, which he drops into my other hand. He offers to sell me more but I'll only need one. Two at most maybe.

All still to come.

I'm walking around the prison yard when he asks if I heard what happened to the Nazi spy on death row. I only knew Kurt's appeal had failed and that he'd never get to New York to meet his young son.

I think of Archie with his scruffy knees, playing marbles.

We circle the yard in the bright winter air. The prisoner speaks in whispers as he repeats what the guards told him.

'Fifteen seconds it's meant to take, that's all.'

He shakes his head.

'Fifteen seconds,' he says again.

We're not meant to talk in the yard.

'Hangman fucked it, the guards say.'

'They let him go?' I ask with hope in my voice. 'He got away?'

I see Kurt walking off the boat in New York, back to his girl and his little boy with their arms outstretched, and for a moment, at least, I think I remember what love feels like.

They tell me I have a visitor.

I shuffle into the room and sit by the small table. It's almost a year and I've never had visitors before. Suddenly I'm aware how I look after all this time in prison.

I've lost weight. My face a death mask under the beard. The trousers, big when they were issued, now hang even looser off my hips.

People amble in. I'm looking for a face I recognise.

My letters to Ma have gone unanswered. A reply from one of her neighbours said she was struggling to remember names. I wrote to thank her for keeping an eye and promised to see her when I was out.

I wonder if this visit is to do with her and prepare myself for bad news, thinking she'd have ended her days disappointed how low I'd sunk.

For a moment I let myself think it might be Vera coming to make everything right, to tell me she's left her violent husband and is waiting for me, but I'm surprised to see the Hammersmith girl walk over and sit at the table.

It's a shock how pleased I am to see her. How well she looks, despite everything we've been through. I tell her, 'It's good to see you.'

She says, 'I made you a cake but the guards took it.'

She tells me about Coningham Road and a broken pane of glass in my greenhouse, how it's a shame not to see tomatoes growing there any more. She says her two brothers have been given medals after the siege of Tobruk in Libya. When she asks what it's like in here, I'm not sure I can explain it to her.

The conversation quickly flounders after a few minutes, subjects washing up like driftwood on a rocky beach.

We sit quiet.

I ask why she's come.

She says, 'Because I'm your wife.'

After a silence she says, 'I've been taking Mr Hooper some dinner every day. I knock on his door and take a tray up for him. Sometimes I sit and we talk while he eats; other times I leave him in peace.' She smiles sadly and fingers a button on her cardigan. She says, 'It's nice to have company.'

She looks at me for a moment, then away across the room.

'When I leave him in peace, he puts the tray back outside the front door the following morning with a little note saying thank you.'

I tell her she doesn't need to explain anything else.

We sit in silence for a minute before she says, 'Never was much of a marriage, was it, Billy?'

I think of those promises we made when we were young.

'I thought it'd grow into a kind of love,' she says. 'Being thrown together like that.'

There's a small window high up at the far end of the room.

A tiny rectangle of sky.

Kept my vows to her though, not like I did with Evie. I kept my promises to the Hammersmith girl, despite everything.

358

I thank her for coming to see me but reckon it's best if she doesn't come back again.

She wipes away a tear and says, 'I just feel sorry for you.'

The window is too small to make out if it's clear sky or clouds up there.

She says, 'Maybe it's time.'

She stands up at the table in the visiting room.

I wish her well and she walks away. I don't think I ever see the Hammersmith girl again.

Maybe I do see her again.

Maybe we pass each other down the market once or twice, many years later, withered by age, unrecognisable.

Maybe our paths cross on the green and we stop for a talk, a kind word about the past, and look fondly back on the marriage we attempted all those years.

It's difficult to remember what she looks like now. I see her for tiny moments and then she's gone. The Hammersmith girl, slipping away, like the rest of it.

Archie made it worthwhile, of course.

Maybe he'll know what happened to her. Maybe they secretly kept in touch over the years.

I'll ask him, when he next comes over to take me for a drive somewhere.

Time doesn't make much sense any more.

Minutes, days, weeks, months and years.

I count time in seconds now.

Ba-bump, ba-bump. The thin, powdery blood passing through the veins, down to the feet and back.

I can't even recall when I first started trying to get these memories down.

All the people I once loved.

To remember what love was like.

I'd like to have it finished before Ros's boyfriend asks for his typewriter back.

So I can give it to Archie when he next comes for a picnic.

Thirty-Five

April, 1944.

No time off, despite the good behaviour.

Out of prison, onto the streets with a year of the war still to come.

I go to visit Ma for the first time in three years. She looks old and frail and doesn't remember who I am. Most days I call by with her shopping and to clean up after her, but she usually thinks I'm the man from downstairs.

One day in August I bring her a loaf of freshly baked bread. She smells the end of it and says, 'Oh, Billy, what are we going to do with you!'

She dies in her armchair that night.

I'm not quite sure what to do with myself the next day, so I go to the pictures to see a Walt Disney cartoon called *Bambi*, which probably isn't the wisest choice to make that afternoon.

Where next from here?

Not back to the Hammersmith girl, who's taking dinners up to Mr Hooper in the flat above.

Not back to the old house in Trafalgar Street, Hammersmith Creek long flattened beneath new houses and roads.

An emptiness with Ma gone. Wondering if the

dementia helped her forget the disappointment I turned out to be.

I start work for George Wimpey, digging roads like my father once did, and it feels like I've come full circle.

March, 1945.

I lie on an old mattress under a greatcoat for a blanket, in a numberless house on a nameless road in Queensway, with holes in the ceilings and walls. A few of us in a road workers' squat, using floorboards and broken armchairs for firewood.

The smell of the oil bomb ingrained in the blown plaster won't be gone until the whole row gets knocked down. There's still signs of the family that once lived here: a sock and a broken plate buried in the dust.

We stay until the floorboards are gone then look for another ruin to carve up, washing at the public baths every week.

In the pocket of an old pair of work trousers I find a woman's bracelet with charms and trinkets. The chain is broken and needs repairing.

I know what I must do.

Later that day I walk through Paddington, over the canal at Little Venice, through Regent's Park and up to Chalk Farm. I wait on a bench near where I parked the stolen bus that afternoon and read a newspaper taken from a bin until she comes out of her front door a couple of hours later.

She's still wearing a clippie's uniform: the dark tunic and skirt with bright silver buttons. Her hair looks less like autumn now under the cap worn straight, as if she's learned a lesson or two over the passing years, and I wonder which driver she rides with.

I walk across the street and she turns to see me. I've changed over the past three years. The unkempt beard on my sallow cheeks. I look older and more frail with fifty on the horizon, sensing the downward spiral to come.

It takes a moment for her to recognise me. As I get closer I realise she's aged too. Her face has puffed out. Beneath the make-up a purple bruise darkens her left eye and there's a broken patchwork of veins across her cheekbone. Her top lip looks swollen and sore.

She looks like a neglected doll at the bottom of a toy box.

I say, 'Hello, Vera. How are you?'

She turns back to look at her house and asks, 'What are you doing here?'

'I don't want to cause trouble.'

She says, 'Wait,' then sets off again along the pavement. I follow a few paces behind. She turns the corner and crosses the road before stopping.

'He doesn't like me talking,' she says.

I ask if that's how she got the black eye.

She says, 'I fell in the bathtub, I'm such an idiot.'

I remember my prayer to the Nine Ladies on Stanton Moor.

'I'm not sure that beard suits you,' she says, trying to smile.

A lady passes by on a bicycle.

'Billy, I always thought you deserved an—'

I stop her with a shake of the head, reckoning it's all better left unsaid.

Vera looks down the street. Through the colours on her face I see the old Vera.

She says, 'I like to think of you.'

I close my eyes because I don't want to hear any more.

She looks down at her shoes.

'Off to work?' I ask.

'He'd rather I didn't. I only do it when they're short of a crew.' She looks back up at me and this time we hold each other's gaze.

'I found this and thought you'd like it back.'

She lifts her hand up like an orphan looking for food and I carefully tip the chain into her palm. She turns the charms and trinkets slowly with her thumb.

'Your mum's, I think you said.'

She touches a finger to her eye.

'I wanted to get it repaired for you.'

She says, 'You gave me more than my fair share of jewellery.'

Another silence, and we should probably leave it at that.

She glances down the street again. When she turns back, the magic has gone and we both know it. I turn and walk away without saying goodbye.

At the corner, I look back. Vera hasn't moved, her hand still holding her mother's broken bracelet.

We both stay like this for a moment. Maybe she's remembering the cottage in the hills we once spoke of. The warm hearth and the bright stars overhead.

She lifts her other hand, her fingers spread wide like a

starfish; like her hand on the glass at the back of the driver's cab the night we were hit on Cannon Street.

I return the motionless wave, a mirror to her.

Our silent goodbye.

There's a small ache growing through my middle, not unlike the indigestion I used to get after Mrs Jackson's spicy food. I loved the taste, even if it played havoc for a day or two.

Sylvie takes me to my room for a lie-down after lunch.

She says, 'This isn't like you, Billy.'

When I'm in bed she asks if I'm all right in a less jokey way and I tell her I overdid it answering Gordon's form.

'It's all bollocks,' she says. 'Ros says the writing's on the wall for all of us,' which I don't really understand, and she leaves me in peace.

I lie waiting for the ache to go but it nags like a cartoon fishwife, so I pull the bell string and wait for Sylvie to bring me back to the television room for the rest of the afternoon.

After giving Vera her bracelet and sitting back on the wooden bench, I watch a man walk out of her front door. He's close to my age, late forties maybe. Well-trimmed moustache, double-breasted suit and trilby pulled low over his brow the way Americans wear them. Good-looking, as Vera once said.

He doesn't notice the shabby figure sat on the opposite side of the street as he walks by. He gets to the end of the road, walks past the spot where I spoke with Vera an hour or so earlier, then turns the corner onto King Henry Road beside the railway line. I follow him, slowing my pace when he's in sight and speeding up when he's out of view. Over the bridge and across the road past Chalk Farm station. He walks up Haverstock Hill into Steele's public house on the main road.

I order a light and bitter and sit across the bar looking at the stained-glass window and listening to him talk with the landlord, his trilby on the counter next to his glass.

It's easy to hear the conversation in the quiet pub and Vera's husband seems pleasant enough. When the landlord goes to serve another customer, I move to the bar and stand a short distance down the counter.

He says spring is in the air and reckons the Germans are on the defensive now, and the fighting will soon be over.

He smiles when he speaks.

He offers me a drink, and it feels wrong to refuse.

I make up a name. He tells me his.

He doesn't look like the sort of man to hit his wife and I wonder if I've followed the wrong person here.

He asks if I heard that Princess Elizabeth had joined the army as a truck driver and reckons she'll make a good queen one day.

I tell him I work on the roads and he says, 'You chaps have your work cut out.' He says *chaps* like he's pretending to be someone he's not. He used to dismantle bombs before the war and now works for the government. 'Bloody pen-pusher these days, sorry to say.'

'Safer than your old job,' I tell him.

'I'd rather take one apart than be in the office when it falls,' he replies.

I buy his next pint and we discuss the V-2 rocket that killed a hundred and thirty people when it fell on Stepney a couple of nights ago.

I say, 'You're either one of the lucky ones, or you're not.'

He asks if I'm married.

I tell him I've not seen my wife for over two years and he says, 'You're better off without one.' He laughs, tells me his wife works nights on the buses so he has to get his own dinner. He takes a long, slow sip of his pint.

An undercurrent flows beneath his words.

He leans back against the bar and faces out into the room. The knuckles on his right hand are red and covered in grazes.

I sip my drink.

I say, 'Looks like you've been in a fight.'

He says, 'What?'

'What happened to your hand?'

He says, 'It's nothing. Scraped it on a wall.'

The landlord is stood behind him. 'He's being modest,' he says. 'This gentleman walked into a house where an unexploded bomb had fallen. Found it in the rubble, took off the plate and defused it before it went off. Daft sod. They're giving him a medal for stupidity!'

Vera's husband deflects the landlord's praise. 'It was jammed in a tight spot,' he says, rubbing the scabs on his knuckles. 'Had my tools with me. Didn't think about it. One of the lucky ones, as you say.'

I finish my drink, make my excuses and head back to the Queensway squat, conflicted by the meeting with Vera's husband.

I wonder how much history we invent to join the gaps when none of it makes sense.

Two weeks later, walking across Shepherd's Bush Green on a bright day in April, an old man dressed for a funeral ambles towards me. He says my name, asks if it's me, and I recognise my old manager from the Wells Road bus depot.

'How are you, Mr Oldhouse?'

We shake hands.

'You missed it,' he says.

I don't understand what he's talking about.

'Rum do,' he says after a pause. 'Wondered if you'd be there.'

'Be where?'

'The clippie you were soft on. After she gave you all that bother.'

A heartbeat.

A breath.

A chill in my veins.

'Vera?' I ask.

'Just buried her, not two hours ago.'

The world keeps spinning but I hold still a moment. A thud in my chest like when the bomb landed.

'You didn't know?' he asks.

I say no, but I'm not sure the word comes out.

'Terrible business. She fell down the stairs at home apparently. Broke her neck and that was that.'

I'm trying to catch up with the earth moving beneath me and I don't hear anything else he says.

A few days later, I get a message back from the young prisoner I met in Wandsworth and make my way to Turnham Green.

After jail, anything is easy.

The gun is wrapped in an old oilcloth.

The bullets cold and heavy in my other hand.

On the common, he shows me how to load the cylinder with the arrogance of youth. He doesn't ask if I've done this before.

He empties the cylinder.

I practise pulling the hammer and squeezing the trigger as a train rattles over the tracks.

Click. No bang.

He wraps the pistol in the oilcloth; I hand over the agreed sum and put the gun in the pocket of my greatcoat.

He drops six bullets into my left hand, goes without a goodbye, and I wonder if this will be one of those secrets that must be carried to the grave.

Thirty-Six

Sylvie wheels me to my armchair but the submarine captain is sitting in it.

In my armchair.

No one ever sits in someone else's armchair if they're still alive.

We have our place and we stick to it. There has to be order when you can barely remember what day it is.

I stare daggers at the submarine captain but he just looks out of the window, sucking a boiled sweet and unwrapping another from the packet.

Sylvie puts me beside Mrs Chaudhry instead. Mrs Chaudhry says a van just knocked over a pedestrian outside The Cedars. The submarine captain heard the commotion and moved to my chair to get a better view of the road while Ros went out to help.

I'm in time to see the blue lights of the ambulance arrive, though the view is definitely not as good from back here. It's typical, the moment you go for a lie-down, you miss all the excitement.

I wonder about the person lying in the road out there.

How life changes in an instant.

I hope they're not too young, having already lived a good life, and have some idea what love feels like.

I go to Steele's public house for an hour or two after work each day and sit away from the bar with a view of the door, waiting to see if he comes back.

He walks in several days later.

I don't say hello this time, but quietly put my coat on and leave the end of my pint on the small table.

He stands talking with the barman as I pass behind him unseen, his thin moustache trimmed tight above his upper lip. He reminds me of that actor in those swash-buckling films who got into trouble for messing about with young girls.

I pass some time near the bridge by the corner of King Henry Road waiting for the street to clear, a thick smell of pollen in the air.

The clouds keep the stars and moon hidden. When the pavement is quiet I walk up by the houses, listening to the sound of my own footsteps. A quick check behind me and I duck through the broken slats in the wooden fence and stand under a tree looking back for sight of Vera's husband walking home.

I take out the ladies' headscarf I found on a bench in Regent's Park and wait in the scrubland behind the fence.

I wait and I wait.

The oilcloth weighs heavy in my greatcoat pocket.

A rope has been hung from a tree for kids to swing on, which makes me think of the man I once met in a Wandsworth cell.

I tie the headscarf around my face, over my nose and mouth, like John Wayne as the Ringo Kid.

A man walks up the pavement but it isn't him.

I crouch among the briars and put my eye to the small crack in the fence to look down the road again.

I take out the oilcloth and unwrap the gun.

The chamber clicks open.

I slot the bullets into the cylinder.

One, two, three, four, five.

You will love five people.

I remember Mary Coggins in her little caravan, a veil across her face like I'm wearing now.

I contemplate leaving one of the chambers empty to give him a chance, but this isn't a game. I load the last bullet, lock the cylinder and put the gun back into my pocket.

An opportunity to make something good.

I shut out the memory of Kurt but the rope swings in the breeze and I'm haunted by those fifteen seconds.

Albert Pierrepoint sized him up the night before the hanging. He watched him on his final walk around the exercise yard and calculated the length of the rope required for a perfect drop.

A swift break of the spinal column at the third vertebra and instant death.

A dark art, well practised, done with mercy.

He's got it down to fifteen seconds.

Fifteen seconds, from the moment Pierrepoint steps into the cell.

He asks the guards to have the prisoner seated facing away from the door so they don't see him come in. He swiftly binds the wrists of the condemned man with a leather strap, walks him through the door into the gallows chamber next to the cell.

They're usually surprised the gallows chamber is just a door away.

He attaches the hood and noose and pulls the lever to open the trapdoors.

With mercy.

Fifteen seconds, from the door to the drop.

The cell door opens and Pierrepoint sweeps in holding the leather strap to bind Kurt's wrists, but the condemned man is stood facing the door and the hangman already knows this will not go to plan.

Kurt sees him coming, already up on his feet.

He charges at the opposite wall and smashes his head against the bricks. Two warders can't stop him. They pin him to the floor so the hangman can fasten the strap behind his back.

Kurt gets lifted onto his feet. He gives a loud cry and summons the strength to tear the wrist straps apart.

The guards have never seen that before.

With his hands free, he runs around the cell like a demon, lashing out at the warders, his screams heard all the way down death row. More warders rush in and it takes four of them to force him to the ground while Kurt calls the name of his girl in New York.

Gertrude.

Two more leather straps are fitted to his ankles and wrists but Kurt's thrashing around enough to prevent them dragging him to his feet for another two minutes.

Pierrepoint and four warders shuffle him through the door into the gallows chamber.

He says he's not a spy.

He begs for mercy.

He's moving too much to stop the hood being put over his head.

He tells them he has a son.

The hangman gives up on the hood and tries to put the noose around his neck.

The guards stand clear of the trapdoors but Kurt muscles himself away before Pierrepoint can pull the lever.

They get him back on the mark.

He moves away again.

They put him back on the mark.

He throws himself to the side and screams, refusing to stand where the world will suck him down to his death.

Time is passing.

Sixteen minutes since the hangman walked in.

Sixteen minutes of Kurt's screams, on and off the trapdoors, until the hangman judges his moment and pulls the lever.

The floor opens but Kurt takes flight like a bird.

He flies up, not down.

He springs off the floor in a final act of defiance.

Up he goes, higher and higher.

Lifts himself off the ground, flies out of the door and over the walls. Rises like a balloon on a thermal of warm air, into the sky and back to his forever girl.

I see the trilby first over the fence.

Vera's husband walks up the pavement, shuffling home to make his own dinner.

A loaded pistol in my greatcoat pocket and a scarf over my nose and mouth like some Wild West cowboy.

Like Mrs Coggins in her veil all those years ago.

The rope sways in the gentle breeze.

No one else on the street.

I wonder about forgiveness. Letting him pass. Letting him be one of the lucky ones.

He's almost alongside when he stops to take out a cigarette.

I'm surprised he can't hear me breathing, watching him through a crack in the fence, my heart thudding like a ticking bomb.

He flares a match down the side of the box.

Lifts it to his cigarette.

Scabs on the knuckles of his hands.

You can kiss me, Billy, if you'd like.

I step through the gap in the planks, swifter than a hangman on a good day, grab him around the neck with the pistol in his face.

He drops his cigarette in shock. I drag him swiftly through the fence and push him onto his knees, his trilby rolling towards the railway lines, holding him there so he can't get up.

I was going to do this in less than fifteen seconds, but time is passing.

Instead of just pulling the trigger I say, 'Make a noise and you're dead.'

Listening for footsteps in the street, but the world carries on as normal.

He says, 'Take my money.'

I should pull the trigger.

His eyes search my face through the scarf.

I tell him to look away.

He drops his gaze and says, 'What do you want?'

I watch him kneeling in the briars, hands above his head, scabs on his knuckles.

He says, 'Please.'

I say, 'You're not so brave now,' looking down at him below me.

In Harry's tree watching Jeannie lift her petticoats, arms over her head.

Under a hot-air balloon with Flight Sergeant Cooper, watching out for Pell, Hoggsy, Jack Mulholland and the Baron somewhere below.

He spits and says, 'If you wanted to kill me, you'd have done it by now.'

He starts to stand.

I tell him to stay where he is.

He says, 'Fuck off an' shoot me then.'

No more *you chaps* and it sounds like the real him.

I put the pistol between his eyes and he sinks back to his knees.

Again he says, 'What d'you want?'

I tell him, 'This is for Vera.'

He spits again and smiles, his eyes as dead as she is.

He says, 'You were one of the blokes she was fucking!'

I pull the hammer back with my thumb and squeeze my finger against the trigger.

His arms up, palms towards me.

'It should be me pointing a gun at you.' He laughs, hollow.

The Blue John butterfly flashes against her pale collar. The shallow dip beneath her neck.

He says, 'Little bitch got you all running in circles.'

A train steams towards Euston, grey smoke against the dark sky, thundering hard into my chest.

I move the pistol away from his head.

He senses the shift and says something under his breath that I don't hear over the engine whistle.

Consumed by noise, I point the gun at his left hand.

I shoot a bullet through the top of his palm and out through the other side of his knuckle. It cracks the night air.

Through the noise of the passing train I imagine a crunch of bone and a faint splitting of metal. I'm not sure what's left of the fourth finger on his left hand, but I doubt he'll ever wear a wedding ring again.

I drop the gun and oilcloth off a wharf at Regent's Canal and find a bomb site to shelter in for the rest of the night.

Sleep doesn't come.

In the morning I leave my greatcoat under the floorboards, making sure the pockets are empty.

I've saved two weeks' wages and have my marriage

certificate with me as identification, though I might use a different name that I haven't decided on yet.

In the washroom at St Pancras, I no longer recognise the man staring back at me in the mirror. He takes out a razor and shaves off the beard he started growing when he first went to prison.

Afterwards he looks a little more like someone he used to know, but the light in his eyes has gone. He's not the man he once was. He can't see what's ahead and no longer knows where home is.

He doesn't look like he'd survive five more years, let alone fifty.

He buys a ticket from the booking office in the station.

He sits at the window of the carriage and waits for his new life to begin.

The television room is quiet with the set switched off.

Everyone else has gone to bed.

It's even quiet out on Hammersmith Grove now the commotion is over.

Ros said I could sit up until she finished writing her reports, then she'd take me to my room before she went home for the night.

Not much she could do for the young woman hit by the van, she said.

It's been a day of misfortune, what with one thing and another.

So I thought I'd just sit in my chair, look out at the dark street and think about those we once loved, and those that passed us by.

The carriages jolt as the train pulls out of London.

The man listens to the slow rhythm of the wheels clattering over tracks as it picks up speed, rattled by points where the lines cross outside St Pancras.

He remembers putting a bullet through Vera's husband's left hand, late the night before.

He thinks of Kurt flying up from the trapdoors, held in mid-air for a moment. Flicking his head to throw off the noose like a footballer nodding a cross into the back of the net.

A black hole open in the floor beneath him.

The guards watch as the noose rides upwards over his chin, all of them thinking the hangman really fucked this one up.

The noose catches under Kurt's nose.

Gravity is about to win the battle with the flying man, which was always going to happen of course.

Kurt drops into the black hole with a sharp crack. He drops and swings and pisses himself in his final human act.

It takes a while for his body to stop moving.

He listens to silence for the first time in seventeen minutes.

PART FIVE

Thirty-Seven

He calls himself Francis Cooper.

Soon, people will shorten it to Frank, which he prefers.

He takes the train to Derby, then another to Cromford, which he remembers passing through once before.

He likes the sound of his new name.

It's still him but he's Frank Cooper now.

He picks up some second-hand clothes from a jumble sale in a small chapel near Cromford marketplace. He finds boots, a couple of shirts and a solid pair of trousers.

The jacket's too big but he doesn't mind that either. It's clean and warm and looks like it's hardly been worn. He considers getting the sleeves turned up, but he'll wait until after winter in case he needs to wear a jumper underneath.

He thinks about the men who used to wear these clothes. He reckons they didn't come back from the war.

The unlucky ones.

He finds a guest house for a few days to get his bearings and burns his certificate of marriage to the Hammersmith girl in the grate on the first evening.

A man in a pub tells him they're looking for workers at Chatsworth House and gives him the name of the estate manager.

He remembers a walk he never made through Chatsworth when he was in Bakewell before.

The estate manager is a kind and friendly man called Mr Willis, with large eyes and thinning curly hair, who speaks with a broad accent that's difficult to understand at first. They're the same age and both served in Bazentin during the Battle of the Somme in the Great War.

The two men talk briefly about Bazentin Ridge then move to easier topics. The estate manager asks why he moved out of London and Frank Cooper says there's nothing there for him any more.

Mr Willis asks to see his identification papers.

He tells him he lost them in a fire.

Mr Willis says he needs to see some identification as the maintenance staff work closely with the Duke and Duchess of Devonshire. He has to know they can be trusted.

Frank Cooper understands, thanks Mr Willis for seeing him and apologises for wasting his time.

They shake hands and he gets up to go.

Mr Willis asks how he's doing in his head and Frank Cooper says no one's ever asked him that before.

The estate manager says, 'We went to the second war without healing the scars of the first.'

There are shadows behind the eyes of both men.

Frank heads for the door.

Mr Willis says, 'Hold on a moment, Mr Cooper.' He scratches the side of his head and says, 'Let's see what we can do without them papers.'

He starts work the following week, digging pits and laying water pipes.

A few days later, Mr Willis introduces Frank to a man in a green oilskin jacket, swinging a pickaxe at a stone in a ditch, knee deep in muddy water, who turns out to be the Duke of Devonshire.

Frank offers to take over with the pickaxe and the Duke says he wants five more minutes to get the bugger out himself and if it still hasn't budged he'll let him have it.

In May, Berlin falls and peace comes to Europe.

Frank doesn't attend the street parties because he likes to keep his own company and never felt the second war was his.

The Americans drop two atomic bombs on Japan and he thinks of Evie stood outside St Stephen's Church many years ago.

He rents a worker's cottage in Edensor on the Chatsworth estate, which he'll live in for the next seventeen years, though it'll never feel like home.

He helps build fences for horses to jump over and even names one of them.

Being outside does him good. He feels himself getting strong again with the passing years. Feels his skin weathering in the country air.

In 1948, he listens to radio transmissions of the summer Olympics in London and remembers his father taking him to White City when he was eight when everyone hated the Americans for lowering the flag in front of the King.

He prefers to listen to the radio than watch television broadcasts.

Later that summer he thinks he sees Auntie Pam near the cakewalk ride at Cromford Steam Fair on a balmy

August evening, but realises the woman would be too young to be Pam. He rarely goes to Bakewell and doesn't try to find her when he's there.

He reckons Auntie Pam was as much of a tinker as she said his parents were, and being a tinker probably runs in the family blood.

Two young policemen visit the mess room in Chatsworth to check the identification of itinerant labourers. They say it's connected to the shooting of a man in London several years ago.

Mr Willis claims proper checks are done on all the staff but the policemen are looking to find false names.

The Duke of Devonshire appears in the mess room. Both police officers stand to attention in front of him and the Duke tells them he personally verified everyone's identification papers and if they get to the kitchen quick enough they'll be in time for tea and a Viennese biscuit made by the Duchess herself.

Once the policemen have gone, the Duke gives a wink to Frank Cooper and says, 'Break their bloody teeth on them too if they're not careful.'

Frank sometimes walks to the stone circle on Stanton Moor at the weekends where he remembers saying a prayer to the Nine Ladies, though he's learned that prayers mostly go unanswered.

He turns fifty and takes up fly fishing for a year or two.

In the evenings he listens to the BBC World Service and follows the Korean War and *The Goon Show*.

King George VI dies and Elizabeth II takes the throne.

Frank sees an end to rationing and the breaking of the four-minute mile.

Churchill resigns after a second stint as prime minister.

Frank listens to the reports of a war brewing in Vietnam and the Suez crisis, after which he sees the return of petrol rationing.

The Soviets launch the first satellite into space while the Americans put Elvis on the television sets.

In all this time he has three relationships.

The first is with a widow he meets in Hathersage, whose first husband was tortured and killed by the Japanese. It's more of a friendship, which develops slowly over a year or so then quickly fizzles out because she can never get over the loss of her first husband.

The second is with a local woman in Edensor. It quickly becomes physical but brings a quiet shame to both each time the act is over. They try to keep it secret, which doesn't help, and anyway, rumours will always spread through a small village like the plague.

The third relationship is a little more peculiar. It starts with a visit to a brothel in Wirksworth one afternoon. It's an ordinary terrace house that smells of bleach and prophylactics, with bead curtains hanging in the doorways and red Chinese lanterns in each of the small rooms. The lady is accomplished and kind and remains appropriately distant.

He tells her his name is Billy.

He makes the mistake of visiting her again the following month, and after that it's hard to break the habit over the next couple of years.

He realises his feelings for the woman are somewhat complicated but lets it run its course and is surprisingly grateful when he arrives one day to find the local police have raided the house and closed it down.

They were good, fine women, all three of them, but none of it was love.

Towards the end of the decade he feels the world get smaller.

Aeroplanes seem to crash with alarming regularity, including one carrying a young Manchester United football team in Munich.

In 1958, he listens to news reports of race riots in Notting Hill, between local Teddy boys and West Indian immigrants enticed to Britain for a better life.

He thinks about the streets where he used to live, sees them like the veins on the back of his hand and misses home for the first time in thirteen years.

Frank Cooper waits for the rest of his life to happen.

He waits and he waits.

He sees the sixties arrive in a blaze of colour and wonders again what London is like after all this time.

He knows the locals in Derbyshire will never forgive him for being born elsewhere and wonders if, in a year or two, he might decide to go back home.

Thirty-Eight

Gordon opens the large cardboard tube brought from the storeroom.

He unfolds the branches of the Christmas tree and stands it on the table near the garden doors, then argues with Mrs Akinyemi about hanging a string of decorations between two wall lamps. She says the string always falls down when a breeze blows through.

Gordon tells her to stop being a killjoy and Mrs Akinyemi goes back into her office.

When Mrs Chaudhry and Mrs Subram come in from the garden a few minutes later, the draught brings the decoration down and Gordon fixes it back up quickly before Mrs Akinyemi sees.

The next morning, Gordon and Mrs Akinyemi are still arguing, probably because the decorations fell down in the night. Sylvie has been talking to Ros by the table where they used to leave the morning newspapers before they got too expensive. Sylvie walks past looking upset and I wonder if it's something other than the paper decorations causing the bother.

They think because we're old we don't notice these things.

By her office Mrs Akinyemi says loudly, 'You say if you want, Gordon, but I'll have nothing to do with it.'

Gordon stomps over to the television set. He turns the volume down but leaves the picture on, which makes Mrs Bentley and Mrs Cutts grumble at him.

'Ladies and gentlemen,' he announces. 'May I have a few words?'

There's been an increase in empty armchairs since Jimmy Parris died, and only about ten of us in the sitting room.

Ros is standing by the door and Sylvie hasn't come back in yet.

Gordon stands on a chair and speaks loud and slow like we're naughty children. He says we'll be getting letters to inform us the new owners of The Cedars are working with a property developer to build luxury flats on the site. He looks at Mrs Akinyemi, smart as a churchgoer with a face like thunder.

'You'll all be found places by the company who lease the building. It's not been officially announced and we're not meant to say anything yet, but . . .' he looks across at Mrs Akinyemi, 'I thought everyone should hear now rather than in dribs and drabs. We're all in the same boat,' he continues. 'Some of our jobs aren't guaranteed either.'

Despite the serious look on his face, I think Gordon always enjoys a bit of drama. He says, 'Sorry for being the bearer, but in my opinion it's no way to treat anybody.'

He gets down from the chair a little awkwardly, walks past Mrs Akinyemi into his office and shuts the door. She watches him go with a face that could have been carved out of mahogany.

Looking around the room, I try to remember what Gordon just said to us all. Something about a letter and moving elsewhere. There's a few murmurs from the residents but everyone goes back to what they were doing before. There's not much else to say when you can't even take a piss without help. Our days of forming a riotous mob are over.

Ros turns the volume up on the screen and walks out of the room without a word. The news is on.

The news is never good. Trouble brewing somewhere in the world.

I sit quiet and look out of the window at Hammersmith Grove.

A girl in school uniform leans against the low brick wall talking to a friend beside her with a drink can.

They'll be cold without coats this time of year but school kids hardly ever wear coats unless it's snowing, which it isn't, despite the fact it's already December and Gordon's decorations have gone up.

I watch them talk excitedly, vivid with youth, and wonder what they're saying to each other.

It's a beautiful sight, their whole lives stretched out ahead of them.

The girl leaning against the wall turns around, still talking to her friend, facing the window. It feels like she's looking directly at me for a moment. Looking through the glass at a very old man sat in a chair looking out.

She stops talking, as if she knows I'm watching her watch me.

The most extraordinary thing happens.

She smiles.

She lifts her hand and waves at me.

A gentle wave.

I smile back, though I'm not sure she can see me smiling out on the street.

I've already used a lot of strength listening to what Gordon had to say, and I don't think I'm up to waving at the girl on the pavement right now.

She drops her hand and the two friends move off down the road.

I watch them disappear behind the wall, like the boy with the orange balloon.

Maybe she couldn't actually see me in here and was only looking at her own reflection in the window.

Maybe it was the view of herself and her friend she was waving to.

No matter.

It was a lovely sight, right in front of my eyes.

Mrs Akinyemi shuts the door of her office with a bang and the paper decoration hanging between the two wall lamps splits and flutters down.

I've come home from Derbyshire to get old.

It's summer 1962 and a heavy smog hangs over London, which feels connected to the death of Marilyn Monroe.

After moving in with Mr Hooper, the Hammersmith girl deposited money from the sale of the flat into an account for me, but the building society closed years ago and I can't get to it without a solicitor.

House prices have gone up in the seventeen years I've been away, but it's enough to live on for a while if I don't use it to buy another flat.

I find a boarding house near the railway depot in Old Oak Common with a sign saying *No blacks, no Irish*. The landlady is happy to let me stay long-term while I put my name down for a council flat. Dinner at six o'clock sharp every day, breakfast at seven.

No callers. No one to call.

My hands are weathered from working the land. I now have skin the colour of country folk, though my accent sounds like it never left London.

I take a part-time job in a furniture warehouse in Acton and scratch out my savings from the post office in Shepherd's Bush each week. Up from the old Empire, the Pavilion cinema has been rebuilt and renamed the Gaumont, with the Essoldo, a smaller cinema, sandwiched between the two.

The ornate iron street lamps have been replaced with ugly concrete poles.

There are still a few familiar shops, like Lyons coffee house and Palmers Stores, but most of the others have changed. Ellis's bakery long gone.

The roads have been resurfaced and my father's old tram tracks taken up.

Four new high-rise tower blocks are being built on the south side of the green.

Electricity burns constantly, even at night.

There's more colour now, in shop windows and on the

faces of the new West Indian residents, and I quickly tune my ear to the burr of the voices and my eye to the mix of people and the bright clothes they wear.

Shepherd's Bush market thrives, though Norland Road has been demolished for a new motorway that will connect the Westway at White City to Earls Court and Kensington, but will run out of money just as it gets to the green.

I no longer know the names of all the fruit and vegetables on the market stalls.

People seem to have money in their pockets, the austerity years now over, but I don't know where it's coming from.

The sky is full of satellites and space races. The Soviets have sent Yuri Gagarin up there, and John F. Kennedy promises the Americans they will put a man on the moon by the end of the decade.

Impossible to think of travelling so far away. I'm sixty-two years old and it's taken all this time to come back to the place I started.

My hair is grey but still growing, though my eyebrows could do with a tidy. The lines around my eyes match the cracks down my cheeks, a few broken veins observed while shaving. A small jowl like a turkey gullet now hangs in front of my Adam's apple.

I don't have much cause to see myself in a mirror, but it's definitely the face of an older man who looks back at me now.

It takes a year for the council flat to come through. One bedroom, a living room, kitchen and bathroom on the seventeenth floor of a new tower block on the south side of

Shepherd's Bush Green, which suits me well enough. The lady from the council says to inform them of any change of circumstance to prevent me renting it out to someone else.

I sign the forms and the place is mine.

The walls are painted the colour of an old folk's home. The furniture is grey and fawn. A sofa and armchair, pine table and two chairs, a bed with a wardrobe and drawers to match.

I spend the first night looking out at the people below and it feels like I've come home. Looking down at the changing world, a melting pot of cultures: the blacks and browns, yellows and whites.

Sixty-two years gone, just like that.

Shepherd's Bush spreads out beneath me and I think it would be pleasant, at this age, to have someone to share the view with.

Thirty-Nine

Lonely lady new to town, looking for gent & good times.

I draw a circle around the advert and put the newspaper on top of the television set. It's a small black-and-white from Radio Rentals on the Uxbridge Road but the picture's good with the aerial this high.

The news shows footage of American soldiers in Vietnam, and is followed by *The Good Old Days* with Leonard Sachs. I thought the audience sang 'Down at the Old Bull and Bush' because it's filmed nearby at the BBC, but it turns out to be made in Yorkshire.

Something about the lonely hearts advert draws me back. I try to decode the words to get an image of the woman who wrote it before turning my attention back to *The Good Old Days*. Mr Sachs bangs his gavel on a block, introducing singers dressed to the nines performing old-time music hall numbers. When the programme's over, I take out my Basildon Bond notepaper and write a reply to the box number in the advert, thinking I'm probably not going to send it in the morning.

The next day I put on my jacket and shoes.

The lift isn't working so I take the stairs to the ground floor and walk to the post office to buy a stamp. I drop the envelope into the postbox before calling at the market for carrots and cheap stewing steak from the Arab butcher.

There's a tin of potatoes somewhere in the kitchen, so dinner's sorted.

Time is passing and I'm getting slower with the quickening years.

A letter arrived this morning.

Mrs Akinyemi put it down as I was eating a small bowl of stewed fruit. I was excited to get it, hoping it might be news about Archie from the young man who pushed the shop trolley for the Duke of Edinburgh. Instead it was something to do with that business Gordon mentioned a few days ago, and I quickly lost interest having heard Gordon bang on about it once already.

I wonder if the Duke of Edinburgh and the Duke of Devonshire knew each other. It's a long distance between them if I remember my maps well enough.

Mrs Elliot, Mrs Pursglove and Mrs Wood have already moved from The Cedars to another home. They were nice enough and you'd hear them laughing together, but they didn't have much to do with anyone else, so it's probably fair to say it won't make a lot of difference now they're gone.

Sylvie says Mr Ozturk has a son no one knew about, who's now arranging for him to move to a home nearby. If he's lucky, it might overlook the blue sea where his wife and brothers were murdered. He'll be able to go back and fill in all the gaps in his own history.

It's a warm spring day in April.

I dig out my old jacket and my maroon army tie that requires fixing precisely so the little yellow flag can be seen in the centre of the knot. Moths have taken a few bites out of the jacket, which has a tear on the top pocket.

I'm sixty-three years old and my fingers work reasonably well, despite the gentle tightening of arthritis in my left hand when I'm feeling low.

I'm too old to go courting but the times they are a-changin'.

Walking up Lime Grove, four lads with long hair get out of a fancy car outside the BBC studio with a crowd of girls screaming at them. New houses have been built and it's difficult to locate the spot where Evie and I shared a kiss on a snowy night forty years ago.

Mr Putter has long gone, but there's a new tailor on the Uxbridge Road next to Radio Rentals, an Indian who works every hour of the day and charges less than Putter did. He can repair the moth bites and top pocket with blind stitching, he calls it, and steam-clean the tie.

When I collect them, they both look good as new.

I'm feeling apprehensive about meeting Mrs Jackson in the Portobello basement bar she suggested in her reply. Our courting has been done by post and we've yet to speak to each other as she doesn't have a telephone where she lives.

Her note was short and friendly, saying she was pleased to hear from me. She suggested meeting in a jazz club and didn't mind what I looked like. It felt churlish asking her for a photograph after that.

I sent a reply by first class saying I looked forward to meeting her there and I'd be the gent carrying a copy of the *Standard*, wearing a maroon tie with a yellow flag on the knot.

I suppose you get to the age where looks aren't as important as they once were.

The jazz quartet haven't started yet. A double bass lies next to a piano, with a small drum kit behind. I sit at a table in front of the stage with a gin and bitter lemon and a good view of the room. One last throw of the dice, I reckon.

A middle-aged black woman asks me something about my jacket that I don't catch because of her strong accent, so I tell her I didn't see the cloakroom when I walked in.

She says, 'What's that?'

I take off my jacket and hand it over to her, asking if I'll need a ticket.

She says, 'Mr Binns?'

Her voice is husky, rich and slow, like she curls all the letters around the roof of her mouth with her tongue. I wonder how she knows my name, thinking Mrs Jackson might have had to put it down on a list when she booked it.

She holds out her hand, says, 'I'm Betty Jackson. If you got a problem . . . with anyt'ing at all . . . I understan' if you wish to leave right now.' She speaks slow, like she's not afraid of running out of time. She says it like I'm doing her a favour.

I say, 'It's warm here,' hanging the jacket over the back of the chair like it was my intention all along.

I stand up to shake her hand a little more formally and, thrown by the manner of our greeting, tell her this is a very pleasant surprise.

She says, 'Well that's the introductions over with,' and smiles.

Over with, like the r between the two words is a long river flowing somewhere exotic.

It's difficult to guess her age, being unfamiliar with dark-skinned women, but I'd guess she's a few years younger than me. She wears a purple and cream patterned dress below the knees, with a white-ribbed woollen jacket and a black hat over dark, wiry hair.

Long white earrings hang down to her neck.

Her eyes are warm and smoky with make-up around the edges like white women wear. A smear of red lipstick has caught on her teeth.

She says, 'Nice to see a gentleman wearin' a tie.'

There's magic in her voice and it takes me to the kind of beach I've only seen in colour photographs, with palm trees and warm white sand.

I ask if she'd like a gin and bitter lemon.

She says, 'I never touch alcohol,' and laughs.

I'm thinking I should probably leave now.

She says, 'Surprise me with a *fruit juice*,' and makes it sound like a very hot day. She carries a sweet musk of sandalwood.

400

Before I go to the bar, Mrs Jackson says, 'Mr Binns, would you rather we sit here where everyone can watch a white man an' black woman on a first date, or at a table in the corner out o' sight?'

I wonder if it's some kind of racialist test.

I tell her, 'I don't mind where we sit, but perhaps you should wipe that lipstick off your teeth before people start talking.'

She throws her head back and laughs, and I know Mrs Jackson and I are going to get on just fine.

We ask a few questions, like on any kind of first date.

I condense my answers to details about Shepherd's Bush: working the railways, driving a bus in wartime and so on. I tell her I was in France in the first war and she says I don't look old enough.

I tell her briefly about the seventeen years in Derbyshire, which is a place she's never heard of.

She came to England from Jamaica with the first wave of immigrants in 1948. She holds down a cleaning job in Whitehall each morning, another in a clothing factory in Somers Town in the evening and works in a hotel kitchen on Oxford Street in between. At weekends she caters for private parties to help save money to get back to Jamaica one day.

I ask if she's been married before and she raises her eyes and says, 'Twice. I'm good at failed marriages.'

The band play and we listen. We haven't stopped talking since we met and already the curl of her tongue makes her accent the most natural sound in the world.

I'm not sure about jazz, but next to Betty it feels sensual, like something from another world. A lazy trumpet riffs over a bass and piano while the drummer shuffles along like he's playing in a different time. It's moody and slow and I can even pick out a tune once in a while. In sections where the rhythm holds steady, Betty sways her shoulders in a way I've never seen a white woman do.

Later, I walk her home through the streets that once belonged to Harry Coggins and his sister Peg, but time is passing and that's history now.

The neighbourhood is changing. A lot of houses have been rebuilt over the years but I wonder if the tree in the garden is still there.

Betty asks how old I am.

I say I'm as old as the century and she looks surprised and says, 'I ain't gonna be pushin' no old man in no wheelchair,' and laughs again. 'If it's a nurse you lookin' for, Grandad, hop along now.' She's laughing but I don't doubt what she says for a moment.

'You not gonna ask how old I am?'

I tell her there's things a gentleman never asks a lady and she smiles like she's secretly pleased.

We walk past the Walmer Milk Bar on Ladbroke Grove and I ask Betty Jackson if she'd like a cup of coffee before calling it a night.

Two black men look up but neither say a word. We sit on red stools by a counter along the wall. The coffee is warm and has a sweetness even without sugar, with a swirl of cream that leaves a light foam around the edge of the cup.

'I'm good at failed marriages too,' I tell her, stirring the froth into my coffee and talking a little about the Hammersmith girl.

She listens and doesn't judge me for my mistakes. Then she tells me how she first came here, when she was married to Mr Jackson.

Forty

Britain had asked for help from its Empire to fight the Nazis.

In Jamaica, Elizabeth Jackson's husband joined the RAF in 1942 and was sent to England to serve as a mechanic on Hawker Hurricanes for three years.

When the war was over, he moved back to the Caribbean. Betty was already thirty and afraid the war had stopped them having a family. They tried for a couple of years before he persuaded her to go to Britain with him to start a new life. They were offered cheap travel and repatriation to their mother country and so Betty said goodbye to her parents. They bought tickets on the first boat taking immigrants from the West Indies to London for twenty-eight pounds each, with the promise of a warm welcome and plenty of jobs waiting across the Atlantic.

It was 1948 and she was thirty-three.

There were nearly five hundred people on the *Empire Windrush*. Mostly men looking for work, some couples wanting a fresh start and Polish refugees going back to Europe after the war. A teenage stowaway was discovered on board and the other passengers paid for her ticket so she could stay in England when they arrived.

Betty sips her coffee slowly. She adds more sugar and takes a while to stir it in before continuing.

It took just over three weeks to reach Tilbury as the ship's engines kept breaking down. It was an old German vessel, torpedoed by the British during the war, and carried the scars to show it.

Arriving in the Thames estuary under grey clouds, they were greeted by a flotilla of small boats. The West Indian passengers lined the deck rails to wave at the welcome party but the crew told them it was a protest by the British, who didn't want immigrants in their country.

They sailed close enough to read the banners and hear them shouting, 'Wogs go home!'

At Tilbury Docks they were left to stand at the quayside for several hours. Betty hadn't realised it would be so cold and didn't have enough warm clothes. She wondered where the sun had gone. Eventually several buses took them to an underground shelter in Clapham, where they lived for the first few days.

She thought it was a mistake coming to the new world but her husband was keen to find work. He left the shelter saying he'd be back when he had a job and somewhere for them to live. Several days later, she was given a ration book. It was the first time Betty had eaten since arriving in England.

In two weeks her husband returned. He told her that instead of finding a home, he'd found the woman he'd been seeing when he was stationed here in the RAF. He said he was moving in with her, then turned and walked away, and Betty never saw him again.

She says the first few years were hard. She couldn't afford a ticket home and took any work she could get to start saving for a boat back to Montego Bay.

I say, 'That's an awful tale.'

She says, 'It ain't over yet,' with a twinkle in her eye.

Three years later, she met a swarthy Irishman called Ryan. She laughs when she says he was almost as black as she was.

She knew he was trouble but fell for his charm. She believed his excuses when he'd go off drinking for days. They got married and rented a room in Kilburn. He told her he'd like to move to Jamaica with her. Soon after the wedding, he disappeared for good, taking all the money she'd saved since her first husband left.

She laughs at her own history and says, 'I'm tellin' you this, Billy, 'cause I never had no luck with men. And I ain't looking for luck no more. Marriage an' bein' tied to one person, it don't work. I'm done with lovin' 'cause it done with me. Free love an' good times. That's all I'm expectin' these days.'

I say, 'I didn't have you down as a free love kind of person, Mrs Jackson.'

'Not free,' she tells me, laughing again. 'Paid for with old heartbreak. If you okay with that, we'll be jus' fine.'

We walk out of the milk bar and down Ladbroke Grove. She stops in front of the terrace where she rents a basement room, an argument in full flow behind a boarded window upstairs. Betty Jackson asks if I'd like to come in for the night.

I say I need time to think about it all, but perhaps we could meet the following week?

She offers to make dinner.

We shake hands and I walk back to the bus stop, regretting my decision not to spend the night with Betty Jackson.

There's no sign of the schoolgirl who waved at me some days ago with her friend. I'm hoping to see them again, sitting on the wall and enjoying being young.

I wonder if people ever enjoy being young. All that worry about what life will be like when you're older.

What makes youth precious is not knowing how precious it is. Staring at a puddle on a pavement holding an orange balloon, or playing with the marbles in your pocket, and it being enough.

Meeting Mrs Jackson felt like it was enough. Like it was me arriving in the new world. When it looked like the best years were over and the only thing left was a slow descent into infirmity.

Long way still to go, even back then. A few aches and pains on waking, especially the ankle on wet days. Occasional brushes with doctors dispensing wisdom in the health centre, most of whom I've outlived. Those who tell you to do less of this and have more of that. Or the others who say have more of this and do less of that.

If we jumped in a single moment from young to old, the shock of the change would kill us.

This place feels quiet since Mrs Pursglove, Mrs Elliot and Mrs Wood have gone to another home. It's a shame we didn't sit together more when they were here. Perhaps we could have got to know each other better over the years.

But not everyone wants to talk all the time. It's such an effort, all that listening and speaking, learning about other people's lives, swapping stories of the past and filling in the gaps.

Yes, it's definitely not the same here with those three ladies gone.

Her rented room is small and warm and smells of spice.

Mrs Jackson locks the door behind us with a crude padlock, saying the house is full of thieves. I leave my shoes by the door after walking in. The carpet's thread-bare but Betty thanks me for taking them off.

Her window looks out on a wall, a glimpse of the pavement above and a slice of sky beyond that.

A washbasin in the corner, a small table with two wooden chairs, and a single bed that I'm surprised she can sleep in. A small electric Baby Belling oven with a single ring and a griddle plate gives out a mouth-watering smell. Mrs Jackson feeds the electric meter with a stream of coins. She says you can't beat slow-cooking. The overhead light bulb gets switched off after Betty wipes a dusting of flour off the table. She puts out the cutlery, lights a few candles in the room and says the food will be ready soon.

She puts the daffodils I brought instead of wine into a small jug on the shelf and plays a record on her red Ekco record player. She asks what I'm thinking and I tell her the man sounds a bit whiny but I like the harmonica. She laughs and says she thought I'd prefer Bob Dylan to jazz. I tell her my wireless is set permanently to the World Service.

Betty says, 'What are you really thinkin'?'

I tell her I'm trying to understand what free love means.

She says, 'Don't worry about it.'

I say, 'Is it companionship with a bit of how's-your-father on the side?'

She laughs again and says, 'That pretty well sums it up.'

'As long as you don't end up having to push me around in no wheelchair.'

'It won't come to that, Mr Binns,' she smiles. 'Men always leave me long before then.'

Her warm chicken patties crumble in the teeth and melt on the tongue. The pepper sauce brings my forehead out in a sweat that isn't unpleasant.

She brings two pots out of the oven, lifts the lid off the steam and spoons ackee and salt fish from one and curry goat in a thick gravy from the other, with fried plantain, rice and peas, and hard-dough bread. The plantain tastes more like parsnip than banana. The peas are red and earthy.

I wipe up every drop of the curry goat with the hard-dough. Betty watches me soak the drips off my brow with a flutter of serviettes and asks, 'Are you sufferin' there?'

I tell her not at all and ask for seconds of the salt fish,

not caring if it'll play havoc with my digestive system in the morning.

Afterwards she crushes pineapple into a jug and adds apple juice and sweet syrup to settle everything, then sits and rolls a cigarette by the window using tobacco and dust crumbled from a lump of resin.

I ask where she buys it and she says it's easy when you know how.

She lights the joint, takes a long draw and hands it to me. It tastes sweet and thick and yellow.

My senses are awash and I feel alive and numb at the same time.

We talk about failed marriages and she says, 'It always hurts to fall in love.'

She asks where *how's-your-father* comes from and I tell her I've no idea, which we both find extremely funny.

We hold each other's gaze for a long while and I hold her hand across the empty plates.

After the first few moments of undressing, there's no awkwardness.

The single bed might be small but we fit together as well as any companions might.

I'm surprised how soft her dark curly hair feels to the touch.

There's kindness in her brown eyes, laughter at the ridiculousness of it all and life in the old horses yet.

The next time we walk out together, down Portobello the following weekend, I ask if it's all right for companions to hold hands.

She says some people won't like it and I soon see what she means.

Coon, wog, teapot, nig-nog, spade, sooty-fucker . . .

White teenagers make monkey noises passing by.

The American president is in the news talking about equal rights, but the sight of a white man and a black woman together clearly upsets a lot of people.

A black man calls me 'Patty', and the woman beside him hisses through her white teeth like a lazy snake.

An older white man approaches, well-dressed, carrying a briefcase and umbrella. He appears baffled at first, like we might have been friends at one time, and I'm wondering if we've met before when he spits out, 'Nigger-lover,' as he passes.

I try to find an appropriate response but nothing furious or funny enough comes to mind. Betty says to ignore it, so I decide I'm too long in the tooth to be fired up by names, and carry on walking regardless.

It's May, 1963 and we've been companions for a month. We spend each weekend together, except when she caters for a party in Woking. We sleep together but rarely kiss, as neither of us are fussy about being in love again.

We've seen the damage it can do.

If I'm careful with the pennies then my part-time job and small savings from the old flat in Coningham Road gets me through the week. Her long days working three jobs, from four in the morning until nine at night, make me want to look after Mrs Jackson, but ours is not that kind of relationship.

I struggle to understand what free love means for us,

other than harbouring the gentle ache that we're both holding something back from each other.

'D'you wear a tie every day?' she asks.

I tell her I like to look my best for her.

She says, 'We gotta get those buttons undone, Billy Binns, once in a while.'

On the way to my flat, she goes into a shop in Portobello for some groceries while I browse the exotic display of fruit and vegetables outside. She comes out without saying what she's bought.

We take our time climbing the stairs to the seventeenth floor and ignore the boys kicking a football on the landing behind us. Despite the pollen in the balmy air, I put on both bars of the electric fire, as Betty's always cold.

She likes to look out of my window at the evening sun with a blanket over her shoulders and tells me about the view she had from her veranda across Montego Bay.

Betty Jackson opens her handbag and unwraps a small piece of baking paper with a little blue pill inside.

She breaks the pill in two.

'Half a tab of acid each,' she says. 'To undo a couple of those buttons if you'd like.'

I tell her, 'My doctor says I get dyspepsia if I have more than one glass of wine.'

She says, 'It's a long life, Billy, to keep makin' the same mistakes. Repeatin' the same old choices.'

I say I'm not sure it's for me.

She smiles and says that's fine. 'We can jus' watch television instead. Up to you.'

She's right about making the same old mistakes.

I hold my hand out.

She gives me one half of the pill and slips the other into her mouth.

I watch her and do the same. She sits next to me on the sofa and holds my hand.

'What do we do now?' I say.

'We listen to sound of the cosmos, Billy.'

I'm listening hard but the only sound is buses on Shepherd's Bush Green below.

'The answers are all out there. Just gotta listen for them.'

An aeroplane above us and kids on the landing kicking their ball against the front door.

Thump thump thump.

A dog barking somewhere down below.

Always a barking dog.

'You wan' to kiss me, Billy?'

The ghost of someone else floating around.

We kiss while the cosmos cooks up answers to questions I haven't even thought of yet.

I look at my watch.

Thirty minutes since taking half the little pill and still no sound.

A red 88 bus is moving up the wall next to the window.

I trace its route along the plaster.

Two bells to stop, one for go.

Or the other way round maybe?

One for stop and two to go.

Two stops to the bell.

The bell stops and goes on.

The 88 passes the crack where the plaster has split.

The lower deck is empty.

Faces look out from the top, singing something on the wireless a moment ago.

I follow the bus past the tram cracks in the plaster, a circus strongman sat on the top deck.

Queen Elizabeth waves from a seat down the front but there's no sign of the Duke of Edinburgh beside her.

We get on.

Two bells for go.

I sit next to the Queen like I'm the Duke. She holds her sceptre in one hand, her crown perched on top of her Afro. Her black face smiles at her people waving through the window.

They say, 'Go back where you came from, Your Highness.'

My flat looks massive up there.

The Queen asks if I believe in free love.

I tell her I don't know what it means.

She says, 'Hmm.'

I tell her I've paid a price for love over the years and it's never done me much good.

She says, 'Young people nowadays think they can jump into bed with anyone but it won't do them no good because they ain't earned it yet.'

She says, 'There's no such thing as free love when you're young. Gotta pay for it first with heartbreak.'

I tell the Queen I paid for it a few times, once in a hayloft before the Great War, and years later with a professional lady in Wirksworth, though neither brought me much joy.

She raises her eyes to heaven and says, 'You should speak to my husband about that.'

My mouth is dry.

She says, 'Marriage is hard.'

We're like peas in a pod, me and her.

She waves at her subjects again then turns back to me and says, 'Imagine one goin' through life an' never havin' one's heart broken! One might as well say one's never lived!'

Betty Jackson throws her head back on the settee and shakes with laughter at something she just said.

I ask her to repeat it but it's hard enough concentrating on what's happening now without worrying about the past.

She has a twinkle in her eye and her hair radiates orange.

I wonder if my half of the pill has started working yet.

She says she doesn't like amphetamine because you only see people as outlines, but acid lets you see them as a whole, inside and out.

I know exactly what she means.

She says, 'You can take them apart and put them back together again.'

'Story of my life,' I tell her.

When she taps me on the arm a little later, just the two of us are here.

Mrs Jackson says, 'I'm not goin' to fall in love with you, Billy.'

I tell her, 'I know.'

'I paid the price. I expec' you did too.'

The air is moving but it's much slower now.

'Heart broken by affairs, loveless marriage,' she continues.

I tell her I reckon I've been in love four times and it only ever brought me pain.

'Better to keep meetin' new people. It makes us who we are. If we're more honest, no one gets hurt.'

'Not just one forever love?' I ask.

'This is the sixties, boy! Liberation. Make the most of it.'

'Free love?' I ask her.

'Paid for with heartbreak.'

'So how does it work?'

She shrugs like it's easy to explain. 'If you gonna want to love other people, you have to share the one you love.'

'Doesn't it hurt, sharing the one you love?'

'Not if it's somethin' you choose.'

'I don't know how to choose that,' I tell her. 'I'm too old-fashioned.'

She smiles and holds my hand. 'No need for lies or secrets.'

'What if sharing with someone makes me want to kill the man I'm sharing you with? What if I don't want to be shared?'

Betty Jackson smiles, still holding my hand. 'You know your problem, Billy Binns? You think too much.'

We're an odd couple, sitting here.

She asks, 'I thought you said you always end up gettin' hurt by love?'

I nod my head.

We both start to laugh.

It feels good when everything makes an odd kind of sense.

I look out of the window hoping to see the Queen again.

She's there on the pavement, against the wall, back with her friend.

Leaning against the bricks in their school uniforms, eating a bag of crisps.

It looks cold out there.

I wonder what they're talking about. What to do with the rest of their lives, or boys, more like.

I watch them like there's nothing else happening in the world. Despite the effort it takes to hold my head up for any length of time. I don't want anyone else to see what I'm looking at. A little secret to keep for myself, for these moments at least.

The girl turns towards me once more while her friend stays with her back against the wall.

The television set is on loud again but I manage to shut out its noise.

It gets dark early in the afternoon and I'm not sure I'll be able to see them out there much longer.

They finish the crisps. The friend with her back to me moves from the wall and turns to look through the window too.

It's like they can see me through the glass.

The first girl lifts her hand and waves like she did last time.

This time I raise mine and wave back. A silent motion, like the wave Vera gave me the very last time I saw her.

Her friend gives a little wave too and I feel a surge of delight, a wash of happiness pumping the powdery blood through the veins, down to the feet and back.

They turn and walk away, leaving an empty space on the pavement behind them, and everything now feels better because they were there.

After returning with doughnuts from the Middle Eastern man who keeps his shop open all hours, Mrs Jackson asks if I'll come with her to a party in Woking next weekend. It's hosted by Mr Thistlethwaite, who runs the factory she cleans in Somers Town, in the big house he shares with his twin brother. He pays her to do the food, she stays the night as a guest and clears up the mess the next day.

Even stoned, there's something not right about the arrangement.

She says, 'You can be my little chef.'

We're already onto our third doughnut.

I ask if I'd need to bring anything, like an apron or waiter's gloves.

She laughs and says, 'Just an open mind.'

I tell her, 'It's a long way to go for a house party.'

She says, 'It's a long life to keep makin' the same mistakes.'

Forty-One

Betty says Mr Thistlethwaite and his twin are identical except for a moustache sported by the one who runs the factory.

It's his brother who meets us at Woking station in a tiny Hillman Imp. He doesn't get out of the car but leans across to say hello through the open window. Not having met either of the Thistlethwaites before, I clamber into the back with the bags of food while Betty sits beside him in the front.

He's short and squat, wearing brown tweed trousers and waistcoat with a watch chain that makes him look like the rabbit in *Alice in Wonderland*. He doesn't speak much as he drives us to the house, his belly pressed against the steering wheel of the little car. The skin on his neck creases and unfolds every time he changes gear. Betty and Mr Thistlethwaite's twin brother don't seem to have much in common. In one of the silences I ask where he works. He says he drives up to his brother's factory in London to do the wages on Fridays, doesn't like the city, prefers the air out here.

The conversation stops again and I'm already thinking it'll take more than a few drinks to undo Mr Thistlethwaite's brother's buttons if the party's going to be as fresh as Betty says. She smiles over her shoulder and I look out at the trees beside the road, thinking how flat Surrey is after Derbyshire, like it's been cultivated rather than left to grow wild over the centuries.

We turn down a wide leafy street with large houses set back from the road.

The Thistlethwaite's home is red brick with stone pillars either side of the front door and looks like one of the Bayko buildings Archie and I might have progressed to had we got beyond the signal box. Mr Thistlethwaite's brother parks his Hillman Imp on the gravel by the front door and Betty and I climb out.

The old brickwork needs repointing and the window frames could do with a fresh coat of paint. The Hillman Imp looks too small for the driveway and I reckon the Thistlethwaites once had a good inheritance but aren't doing as well as they hoped.

Betty's been here before, of course. She leads me through a side gate, down a passageway to the rear garden, which backs onto a large common over the fence.

'Servants' entrance,' she tells me, though it's me doing most of the carrying.

We go through the kitchen door and unload bags of food into the refrigerator, which hums and rattles each time the door is opened. Betty puts me in charge of making the sandwiches from the tubs of fillings we prepared earlier that day.

'Nothin' spicy,' she whispers with a wink, as the pungent smell of boiled eggs and coronation chicken begins to clear.

She empties goulash from the Tupperware and warms the pan on the stove.

Mr Thistlethwaite's brother hovers around to keep an eye.

I tell him he has a lovely house.

He says, 'It's my brother's. I just live in it.' After a pause he adds, 'I'll be upstairs if you can't find anything.'

When he's gone, I tell Betty this isn't what I was expecting.

She says, 'You think too much!'

She says the twin brother never stays for the evening. I reckon he's probably got the right idea and wonder if I'll do the same once the food's out.

Betty reads my thoughts, touches my arm and says, 'Billy, you can do whatever you wan'.'

I'm not sure free love is right for me, faced with the reality of sharing the woman I came here with.

The other Mr Thistlethwaite is a better-drawn version of his twin. The moustache makes sense of his features and he smiles as he talks, which gives him an advantage over his dour sibling. His face looks redder than is healthy on a man his age.

He bounds into the kitchen with his belly tucked into his waistcoat and a small sheen of sweat glistening across his brow. His suit and watch look expensive and it's immediately clear who benefited most from the inheritance.

He kisses Betty on her cheek with his hand across her back, his trousers belted high like Billy Bunter.

Betty introduces me and says I'm her little chef.

He shakes my hand and leaves a damp film in my palm which I wipe dry once he's turned away.

He tells Betty four people have dropped out, which now leaves eighteen guests, plus four maybes including a nice Indian couple who've been before, and his fingers wiggle in anticipation of the long night ahead.

He curls a finger through the tub of egg mayonnaise, sucks a lump of egg off the end and reckons it could do with more salad cream, before sidling out of the kitchen to check on the bedrooms.

We spend the next hour on the food. I put out the quiche Lorraine and sausage rolls, make sandwiches and cut squares of cheese and pineapple onto cocktail sticks. Betty cooks a green pepper stew for any vegetarians who won't eat goulash. She prepares her rice and peas. The goulash, rice and pepper stew will get heated in the stove later to eat buffet-style, so once the cocktail snacks have been served to the arriving guests, our duties are pretty much over.

When my kitchen tasks are done, I tell Betty I need some fresh air and she says to take myself off through the back gate for a walk on the common.

It's five o'clock and the warm June afternoon promises a balmy evening to come. There's two hours before guests start to arrive and I'm having doubts about this new world Mrs Jackson has brought me to.

It looks very ordinary to me.

The appeal of sharing the one you love only makes sense in odd moments, in the complicated thrill of passion, but faced with the reality, in the warm light of day, I don't know whether to escape or stop thinking too much as Betty keeps telling me.

The back garden is unkempt and the grass needs mowing, which makes me think of the lawns at Chatsworth, cut the way the Duchess liked.

The house shrouded in trees looks like a place in a fairy story where either wonderful or terrible things happen. Stood at the end of the garden, I've no idea which it might be.

I open the high bolt on the gate and go through, pulling it closed before heading onto the common beyond, through the trees to a wider footpath, noting the way back to the house.

Following the path under branches, dry earth underfoot, to a small lake in the middle of the common. A man with a dog approaches, but he doesn't nod or say hello like the people in Derbyshire.

Ghosts among the trees.

Harry calls down from one of the branches while his mother swings on a rope below him.

Fifteen seconds, beginning to end.

I say hello to Mary but she doesn't nod or say hello either.

I stop beside a weeping willow, grateful for the sound of evening birds. I'm unsure if I've ever made a right decision in difficult moments or the good it's ever done me.

A misguided life.

I choose to see this through and find a new way forward as the times they are a-changin'.

Yes'n.

How many years must a man go through with nothing to show for love?

No forever girl.

No warm hearth or Sunday lunches.

No fire in the grate.

No grandchildren.

A breeze rustles the soft branches of the willow.

I hear Archie playing beneath the leaves and I'm suddenly afraid none of this is happening now, that I'm sitting in an old folk's home with my life fading away and the television set on much too loud.

I need to know what happens when you share the one you love, after all these years getting it wrong. To share what can never truly be owned in any case.

Walking a circle around the common, past the small lake, back towards the house where I started.

A metaphor for life, maybe?

It's a surprise to discover the gate of an old church at this late stage of the day. It's the kind of thing you imagine finding in the morning.

Another ghost, perhaps.

The gate is under a gable of black timber, which opens onto a path through a graveyard and up to the church door.

I wait beside the gate, knowing these places aren't for lost souls like mine.

Time is passing. Gin hour.

I'm about to turn back to the house. Instead I open the gate, walk under the gable and up past the gravestones.

The thick iron handle lifts with a solid bang. I stare into

the heavy silence of the church. It feels like God has taken a deep breath and refuses to let go.

I close the door behind me, washed in the chill of the air. A ladder of light falls across the altar beyond the weight of dark pews, blackened by centuries of unanswered prayers.

Peace hangs heavy. The outside world is forgotten here.

I walk to the front and sit on a pew, wondering if unbelievers are allowed a word with God in here.

Silence bears down like a hand pressing hard on my chest.

A magic of expectation.

Evening sunlight angles through the windows like sleet.

The last prayer I made was to the Nine Ladies on Stanton Moor half a lifetime ago.

I'm too old for a wife and child now, and I wonder what I might pray for these days. Strength to share the one I love, maybe? Forgiveness for those I let down along the way?

I close my eyes and listen to the silence. It's good to think without needing words.

The door opens, a middle-aged couple walk in arguing loudly and all the magic of the church has gone. With my prayer unsaid, I walk out of the pew and down the aisle like a bride retreating from her own story.

The early-evening sun is blotted by dark clouds and the weather is changing.

I nod at the gravestones, to the faces I've buried over the years.

Down to the gate and under the black gable, having lost all sense of time.

Betty will be needing a hand.

I pick up my pace and set off back towards the house.

A woman walks down the path towards me.

We're of a similar age. She wears a lilac coat and sensible shoes. Her hair's wrapped in a headscarf even though the evening is warm. I reckon she's one of those people who notes the change in the weather.

I wonder if she'll say hello to the stranger walking past, or ignore me like everyone else has this evening.

She doesn't look up but keeps her eyes on the ground beneath her shoes, worn for a walk in the country.

Something familiar about her.

Her name rolls off my tongue.

'Evie.'

Forty-Two

She stops, looks up.

Her face takes a moment to adjust.

She looks at me square on, her big eyes framed in an older version of the same face. They lift up over my forehead as if she's still looking for answers in the sky, as fresh now as the first time I saw her do it.

Her closed lips, paler now, that soft curl, beautiful and heartbreaking.

She was mine and I let her go.

I try to see her as she was, to make the age lines disappear, and for a moment she looks as she did, old to young in a single moment, like a short tunnel between two distant stations.

She says my name.

Silence between us.

A second or two, not much more, but enough to summon forty years of unspoken words.

I concentrate now on the changes in her face; the lines across her forehead and around her eyes. A gentle sag in her cheeks and a light greying of her skin. The years have been kind to her.

She says, 'How are you, Billy?'

I always knew I'd see her eyes once more.

I say her name again.

She smiles, and there she is in the creases, adorned with the hard-earned badges of life, worn and adorable.

She asks, 'What are you doing here?'

I tell her, 'I've just been to church,' but it sounds like an attempt to prove my worthiness, even now. The bells of St Stephen's and a walk in the rain down the Uxbridge Road in a wedding suit and new shoes meant for her, loud in both our memories.

'I mean, what are you doing in Surrey?'

'There's a party,' I tell her. 'I'm doing the food with a friend.'

I sound like a child that's been let out of a house. She nods like she's already heard enough.

'You look well,' I say. 'Not seen you since . . .'

The words catch in my throat.

She fills in the gaps. 'Since your wedding day, Billy. Forty years ago.'

I'm losing my footing, slipping on wet stones. My armour gone and the battle already lost.

Old wounds blaze in the heat of her eyes.

I ask, 'Are you on your own?' and it carries more weight than intended. My hands shake like dying fish at the end of hooks.

'I got married a long time ago, Billy.'

She sees my disappointment and senses the victory she's long waited for. 'To a doctor in Hampstead,' she continues. 'Albert.'

She stops, knowing the sound of his name is more than enough punishment for now.

428

'I'm pleased,' I tell her. 'You found happiness. You deserved it, Evie. I'm sorry . . .'

My words catch again. I take a second and change tack. 'Is your husband here too?' looking for him further down the path.

'Albert died a few years ago.'

I tell her I'm sorry to hear that.

'He was struck by lightning and fell out of a tree.'

I think of Harry and Mrs Coggins and the weeping willow. How everyone has a story to tell.

'We had some good years together,' she continues. 'But it wasn't . . . He was never . . .'

She looks down at her feet, brushes an invisible speck off the pocket of her lilac coat, then smiles. 'We make our decisions, don't we, Billy. Have to stick by them, I suppose. We had two lovely children, Albert and me, so that was good.'

I ask how old they are.

She says, 'Old enough for me to have grandchildren, who I see as often as they let me.'

'I'm sure you make a wonderful gran.'

'How's Alice?' she asks.

It takes me a moment to remember who Alice is.

'We separated twenty years ago. Not seen her since then.'

She says, 'Shame how it goes.'

'Are you living in Surrey now?'

'I visited a friend in a hospice and wanted to clear my head. I'm staying in a hotel nearby so I can see her again tomorrow. That'll be the last time, I reckon, though you never know. You may have an inkling but you never know for sure.'

'I'm sorry about your friend. Life doesn't get any easier, does it?'

She says, 'It was hard to start out with.'

A wood pigeon coos somewhere above us, a five-note phrase, over and over.

Evie says, 'Shouldn't you be getting back to your party, if you're helping a friend with the food?'

I smile and ask, 'So where are you living these days?'

'I moved, after ... To Belsize Park. When I married Albert, we bought a place in Hampstead. After he died, I wanted to come back west.'

'You're in Shepherd's Bush?'

'Not far from Dad's old bakery, gone now, of course. Small flat with a little garden off the Uxbridge Road. It's all I need.'

She sees the dark clouds above me.

'Do you think that's strange,' she asks, 'to go back after all this time?'

'I'm surprised I've not seen you there, that's all.'

She says, 'It's a big place.'

I tell her I moved to Derbyshire for a number of years and came back too, to a council flat above the green.

She smiles and I sense she's ready to go.

'I still think it's odd we never bumped into each other,' I tell her.

Her lips twist into a flat S again, a reluctant smile. She says, 'I may have caught sight of you, Billy, once or twice. Down the market, along the green.'

'And you didn't say hello?'

The old wounds, ripe and sore.

'We were never meant to be, I suppose.'

I see her hiding in doorways down the market, on her way to the Underground, not wanting to be seen. Afraid I'll stop and start talking.

Raw, unhealed.

'Why did you come back?'

'It's my home, Billy. Why shouldn't I? You're the one who left me.'

I look through the gable at the small church in the middle of the common.

I look at the trees and the sky, a low hum of traffic in the distance.

I look at the woman in a lilac coat on the path beside me.

All that history. Never knowing what comes next.

She says the name of the hotel. 'If you fancy a drink later. Catch up on all of our lives maybe.' She laughs at herself, like it's a ridiculous notion.

'Would you like that, Evie?'

She looks at her feet, tips her head, already regretting it.

I say, 'I'd like to catch up, very much. After the food. Would that be . . . ?'

She says, 'I'm not holding my breath.'

I tell her I'll be there by nine o'clock.

She says, 'Well then, Billy Binns.'

'Are you sure, Evie?'

'I once promised that if we ever spoke again, I'd make you do all the work.'

She smiles, her guards back on duty, then turns away.

We go in opposite directions down the path.

I look back to make sure it's her and not one of the ghosts in the trees but she doesn't turn around.

Mary Coggins, Evie, Archie, Vera, Betty Jackson . . .

One to the next, to the next, to the next.

It feels like everything in the past has led me to this single moment, being here now after meeting Evie again in the trees.

A new beginning, with Evie waiting at the end of the line.

Starting fresh.

Making sense of the chaos that came before.

A breeze catches the weathervane at the top of the church spire. Its rusting metal joint squeaks and scratches as it twists to a new position.

Evie says we never know the last time we meet in life. She reckons we may have an inkling, but we never know for sure.

Water pipes grumble behind the old plaster walls. Car lights arc across the ceiling like spaceships through the galaxy.

Seeing those girls on the pavement again has lifted my spirits, knowing they are out in the world somewhere with all their lives stretched before them.

Remembering Evie, too.

Putting some of that old agony to bed, those ancient regrets, knowing it didn't have to end on a wet day outside

St Stephen's Church down the Uxbridge Road when we were young and foolish.

I've even managed to drag myself over to the wheelchair in front of the small table, to the typewriter Ros brought in for me to use.

To get more of it down and remember what love feels like, before it's gone for good.

Tap click. Tap click.

Tap click.

Ding.

Forty-Three

The sky is black when I get back to the house and the lamps are on in the windows. It reminds me of an old people's home somewhere in the distant future.

My head is still cloaked in the quietness of the church and I'm not sure how much time has passed since leaving to walk around the common.

A low rumble of thunder in the distance, the overture for a coming storm.

In the kitchen Betty Jackson says, 'You look like you've seen a ghost.'

She takes a small tray of cocktail sausages out of the oven. She's changed into smart black trousers and a white blouse with several buttons left undone, make-up around her eyes and her thick hair tied under a wide blue ribbon. I've not seen her this beautiful before.

She says, 'I thought you'd run off an' left me.'

I tell her I'll put on a clean shirt and I'm all hers.

There's no one here under thirty, and I'm certainly not the oldest.

The doors between the two downstairs rooms are open to make one big space, the curtains drawn and candles lit. Lampshades cast muted colours up the walls.

More than a dozen men and women stand formally, drinking sweet Asti Spumante from wide glasses. The spools of a reel-to-reel play a compilation of songs from a shelf in the corner of the room. I recognise Acker Bilk's 'Stranger on the Shore' and the 'Theme from Dr Kildare'.

Rain has started battering the windows.

Women wear thin summer dresses in bright colours: yellows, greens and oranges. One lady in her forties has a tight red skirt with tassels and matching blouse that leaves little to the imagination. There's no shortage of cleavage on display. The men are more conservatively dressed in slacks, open-necked short-sleeve shirts and good shoes. One or two wear cravats with their shirt buttons undone and I'm already thankful I took Betty's advice not to bother with a tie.

Mr Thistlethwaite emerges from the hallway in a yellow open-neck shirt with a gold sleeveless knitted cardigan. He introduces a couple caught in the downpour between their car and the front door without taking his arm off the woman's shoulders. I hand them two glasses of Asti Spumante and fill the others nearby from the bottle. I'm content to be a waiter rather than a guest until my obligation to Betty is done, knowing already this new permissive sharing world isn't for me.

Knowing Evie is waiting on the other side of the common.

A man kisses the new lady as if they were behind closed doors, then turns back to his wife on the other side of him. She doesn't seem confused or hurt by the idea of sharing the one she loves, and I wonder if I'm the odd one out here.

I go back to the kitchen for the cheese and pineapple on sticks, and to pick up another bottle from the fridge. Betty is the only black person here except for a middle-aged Indian couple in their fifties, and it's a struggle not to look down the front of her white blouse as she passes with a plate of devils on horseback.

I wonder if Mr Thistlethwaite's twin brother has left the house or is hiding in another part of it.

Betty kisses me on the lips as she passes, and it feels like another betrayal to Evie that I'll have to square as collateral damage, the small final cost of a messy exit from this strange place.

A man in an orange cravat with a goatee beard is changing spools on the reel-to-reel. He introduces himself as I fill his glass, says he's in charge of the music and points out his wife across the room stood talking to a short man with a low fringe and sunglasses.

I tell him I'm with Betty Jackson and the man replies, 'Yes, I met Betty last time,' and I'm not sure whether to ask questions or change the subject. He tells me he's compiled several spools of music at three and three-quarter inches per second, ensuring a high quality of playback, plus some others at the slower speed of one and seven-eighths inches per second. He says these will play twice the amount of music with a slightly reduced quality of playback, but require less switching over later on when everything starts hotting up.

How quick the evening turns.

A couple by the door have already swapped partners, while the short man with sunglasses is undressing the wife of the man in charge of music, now passionately telling me how tape will outlast vinyl as an audio format.

No one else is paying much attention to what's happening in the room and it soon becomes bizarre and tawdry. It makes me think everyone here is just lonely and looking for something they don't have.

I can't see what it has to do with love, free or otherwise.

Betty comes over and asks how I'm doing.

I want to tell her I'll be saying goodbye when the food is served, but I'm not exactly sure what I'm saying goodbye to. Whether it's a relationship we have, or what companionship means.

There's love between us for sure, but not a love I understand.

But then I don't think I've ever understood what love is, which is why I'm trying to remember it now.

Perhaps it would be best to quietly slip away from Betty without saying goodbye, or is that something I'd only regret at a later date?

The coward's way out.

There's kindness in her eyes but it's not enough, and I know this isn't for me.

I understand the appeal of living outside the ordinary, against the rules. But what happens when it becomes ordinary itself and the appeal is gone? I don't need more time to find that out.

The years of sexual longing are over and it's a relief to be free. There was a time when it felt important because it wasn't happening, and the few moments it was were restless and unfulfilled.

These slowing decades have got the better of me.

I'm a man in his sixties, and the thrill of the wilderness is fading.

Saying goodbye to it now with Evie waiting across the common, a church and weathervane pointing the way through the storm.

I'll welcome the rain like a baptism.

Bringing me back to her as it took me away in 1923, forty years ago, with the sound of St Stephen's bells and the ache of new shoes.

It's time to go home.

I'll return, washed by the rain.

The understanding brings relief. It's what I've been looking for.

The man I hoped to become.

Evie sat quiet with her kind eyes, and the rest of my life falling into place, finally making sense at this late stage.

Knowing this is what love feels like.

I go upstairs for my jacket and overnight bag.

On the landing, a woman in a pale yellow dress sits on a chair smoking a cigarette, running the beads of her necklace through her fingers. The bedroom door behind her is closed.

I bid her good evening.

She says she's waiting for her husband. She makes it sound like he's getting ready to go out, but noises from the bedroom tell a different story: mattress springs, quiet yelps and a headboard bashing against a wall.

The woman smiles, but she's betrayed by the sadness in her eyes.

She interprets my silence as some sort of proposal and quickly states that Mr Thistlethwaite's parties are for her husband's benefit more than hers. She waves her hand as if she's fine with it all.

I tell her it's not for me either and walk to the room where I left my bag that afternoon. The woman is still sat on the landing chair when I come back a few minutes later, but the noises in the bedroom have stopped. The silence seems harder to bear, a quieter scale of betrayal.

I say goodnight again.

'Yes,' she replies.

Betty Jackson is in the hallway talking to a man with side-burns and a flowery shirt. She sees me coming down with my bag, excuses herself from the conversation and follows me into the kitchen.

'Not given up on me already?'

I tell her I bumped into an old friend on the common and she nods like she knew this would happen all along.

'Those same ol' choices. Repeatin' over and over,' she says.

I put my bag down, unsure whether holding her in my arms would be an intimacy beyond what's permissible here.

I settle for holding her hand beside the humming fridge and we both know this is goodbye.

'I jus' can't do the heartbreak no more, Billy.'

In the light of the kitchen, the lines on her face show through her make-up. Life hangs heavy on her dark skin. She looks like a fifty-year-old wearing the clothes of a younger woman.

I tell her, 'I'm very pleased I met you.'

She finds a smile but her eyes play dead. She hugs me like a friend and I think how hard it is to start a new relationship when you're old, with all the baggage picked up over the years.

It's warm outside despite the rain.

I turn my jacket collar up, walk down the garden and out through the gate in the twilight. Looking back at the house, soaked to the skin already, knowing it was never a place where good things would happen.

There's enough light to retrace my steps across the common, past the silhouette of the church against a sinking sky. The spire looks like one of those rockets the Americans have promised to send to the moon.

The street lamps lead me to the village, shrouded in drizzle, to a small hotel where Evie is waiting.

Darkness has come quick on the short walk, the rain is easing and the air feels fresh and cool. I stop outside the light of the hotel in my damp clothes.

I walk into the reception, through the bar, safe in the real world again. Past the restaurant to a hushed sitting room at the rear of the hotel.

Armchairs and carpet, the residents respectable, well-to-do. I've come a long way.

The life sentence I've paid these last forty years for those regrettable few minutes by the river with the Hammersmith girl.

In the void, I imagine the children Evie and I might have had together.

440

How different it would have been.

Sundays and firesides.

Those unlived lives, nameless, unfettered.

Knowing how life hangs on a sequence of tiny moments, each capable of shattering the rest like wartime bombs.

And here we are now, at the entrance of a sitting room in the back of a warm hotel.

Here she is, angled away from the door, side-on, quietly reading a magazine in an armchair.

As beautiful now as she was then. The light from inside, still with kindness in her eyes.

I know her.

She's turned herself away from the door to avoid looking over each time someone walks in. Sat in her own time.

I'm in the doorway thinking about forgiveness for all the things we shouldn't have done and remembering what love feels like.

She turns a page of her magazine.

I'm stood on the hotel carpet, rooted to the earth, waiting for her to turn and see me. Waiting for the moment she senses me here, as she soon will.

Held to the ground, waiting to see her face break into happiness.

I wait and I wait.

She turns another page.

I can't do the heartbreak any more, Billy.

Knowing I'll only do it to her again somehow.

Nothing changes.

A particular kind of love, but not one she needs to suffer.

Paid for with heartbreak.

Life spent making the same mistakes, those repeated patterns, over and over.

I hear Betty Jackson in my ear, knowing every word is true. It draws me down like an anchor, and I know what must happen.

I have to turn away from Evie before she sees me.

Before the anchor hooks the rocks and keeps me there forever. To uproot my feet planted firmly in the hotel carpet, knowing this time it must be for good.

She knew I wouldn't come, otherwise she'd have sat facing the door.

I choose to walk away.

To leave the warm hotel and its hushed bar, with its quiet residents and their well-to-do, ordinary lives that I'll never be quite right for.

I decide I must walk away, but my feet form a mutiny and refuse to rise out of the soft carpet.

I restate my order to leave and the rebellion subsides, a weak and cowardly opposition after all.

My heavy feet begin to lift and I start to move just as Evie turns her head to face me.

Her smile opens, bright, unguarded, like that snowy Christmas Eve when we kissed in an alley on Lime Grove. She smiles at me for the first time in forty years.

Pure tenderness explodes like a falling teacup. It shatters, sending fragments flying in all directions. The look between us lasts no longer than the moment of impact, but it's intense enough to dig its own grave and haunt us both for the rest of our lives.

My exit is in motion and it's too late to stop now.

No words will explain why this is happening.

We've gone beyond words.

Better to let the moment pass and the fragments fly and we'll worry about bumping into each other on the Uxbridge Road or down Shepherd's Bush market some other time.

I sense her watch me turn, but I'm unable to stop moving.

Unable to make good what I did to her before.

Still loving her in a very particular way.

Forty years looking to rediscover my forever girl, and it wasn't nearly enough.

I can't do the heartbreak any more.

She calls out, 'Billy?' as if I haven't noticed her in the armchair. She'll punish herself for doing this for the rest of her life, or at least until dementia takes away her pain.

But I'm already out of the doorway, back through the hotel, listening to the echo of Evie calling my name.

A large man sits alone at the hotel bar with a glass of whisky, doing a crossword. It takes me a moment to recognise Mr Thistlethwaite's twin brother, here to escape the tragic orgy in his house on the other side of the common. He looks up as I pass but doesn't recognise the man who sat in the back of his Hillman Imp earlier that afternoon.

I walk out of the warm hotel and across the road, back onto the manicured pathways in the shadow of the church, knowing I can't do the heartbreak any more.

On one of the beds Betty Jackson manoeuvres herself slowly between two men, one of whom is the rotund

443

Mr Thistlethwaite. The woman still sat on the chair outside the bedroom, running the beads of her necklace through her fingers, makes me consider that the other unclothed man in Betty's huddle might be her husband.

Betty sees me standing in the room.

She beckons me to join them, but I refuse the offer and approach a woman I poured drinks for earlier who is on the other side of the bed, wearing a red tassel skirt and nothing else.

I neither ask nor find out her name, despite what passes between us.

The shock of seeing Betty with other men quickly fades. A choice made easy when you disregard the rules made by people who haven't learned about life the hard way.

To my surprise, having decided the wilderness was over for me only that afternoon, I find intimacy with four different women the same evening. For once in my life, the desire is matched by capability.

Later, Betty's arms wrap tightly around me as we fall asleep together in one of the guest bedrooms, unbothered by the scent of others on our skin.

I send Evie a message through the airwaves as my eyes close. An apology of sorts, knowing she would never understand.

In the morning, I tell Betty what happened in the hotel and we lie together in the early-morning light, just the two of us, fired up by the recollection of the night before.

It feels strangely honest.

It feels free.

A particular kind of love.

Not one I understand, or even thought I wanted, but still a love nevertheless.

Sylvie helps me get into bed.

I'm exhausted from sitting up at the typewriter.

She says she's looking for work. A job's come up in another care home outside London but it's less money and a more expensive train from her mum's house each day.

She's meant to use the hoist to get me out of the wheelchair, but it's one of those evenings when everything takes too long. 'We'll be here all night,' she says. 'And you is all skin and bone, Billyboy.'

I lift my arm across her shoulder.

She tilts me forward and up from the chair.

The faint smell of her perfume reminds me of the old paraffin lamp I'd light on winter nights in my high-rise council flat overlooking the green. It was cheaper than feeding the meter and worked through the strikes too. A long wick and small metal hatch where you poured the paraffin.

It takes me back to the yards and hotchpotch alleys along Hammersmith Creek.

Not long now until we'll all have to move.

My final journey out of London, I reckon.

I won't return after that. Too much hassle getting back into the city.

My flimsy weight rests on Sylvie's shoulders as she does a skater's turn on the hard carpet to get me down onto the bed.

The pedal of the wheelchair catches under my slipper and the room takes an extra spin.

I feel weightless in the slow fall, like coming down with Flight Sergeant Cooper, the basket of the kite balloon above us.

Like Kurt floating down over London Colney into a farmer's field by a copse of trees.

Halfway down, I sense my knee buckle as if it were made of jelly rather than bone and cartilage. A tiny explosion of powder at the joint like the cracking of a crust on a fresh loaf of bread.

Spinning colours and a soft crunch as my head hits the firm carpeted floor.

Is this the end I was waiting for?

Is this how it happens?

We do not mend well at this age.

Sylvie says my name.

I think I'm replying, but she says it several times.

I'm looking up, watching her pull the help string beside the bed. Her arm across my shoulders, trying to scoop me up to the place we started.

I tell her, 'If you wanted a cuddle, you only had to ask.'

She laughs and says she thought she'd killed me.

I say, 'That won't look good on your job application,' and she laughs again, dark and throaty like she already smokes too much.

Tabor comes into the room.

I want them to put me in bed and leave me in peace, but Tabor says not until I've been checked for broken bones, and they both feel their way gently across my grey skin.

My bones are as fine as they'll ever be. It's deeper inside where the damage is done.

Tabor lifts me off the floor and says, 'There's nothing of you, Mr Binns.' His voice rumbles through his big chest.

He sits me on the bed and Sylvie helps lie me down. Tabor wraps the covers over my legs and up to my chin.

He says, 'Love those toenails, bro.'

I tell him, 'It's all the rage these days,' and Sylvie winks and says I'm a proper dandy.

She's going to write it up in the accident book.

I tell her not to fuss with all that.

She says she's got to report it and I say don't be daft.

She stands there for a moment and asks if I'd like the strip light switched off, but I didn't realise it was still on.

There's a dark, inky cloud across my eyes like a black umbrella pulled down low to shut out the top half of the room.

I nod yes to the strip light but don't see a change when she turns it off, and I suspect this will be the beginning of the end.

Forty-Four

Six years together, Mrs Jackson and me.

We leave Shepherd's Bush early, take a train to Derby and Matlock, then a bus to Youlgreave for a walk along Lathkill Dale in the late-afternoon sunlight.

It's July, 1969, and neither Betty nor I are in the mood for a sharing party. They've been on the wane for a year or two and much of the excitement has gone, along with my ability to keep up. A momentary thrill, quickly lost to the ordinary as the night wears on, but like most habits it's a hard one to break.

Only after I promised it wouldn't be cold in Derbyshire did she agree to leave the city and come for a picnic with me.

The sun is blisteringly warm. Mrs Jackson says she didn't know England could be like this.

I tell her a little about the years I lived up here, but it's not a weekend for memories and we choose to live in the moment instead.

There's a few people out walking the hills. Most of those we pass stare at Mrs Jackson like they've never seen a black woman before.

On a quiet stretch of the river I unpack a blanket from the bag and we help each other down onto the warm grass.

I'm sixty-nine and Betty's fifty-four and we both wish we'd brought cushions for our ageing arses.

I ask if she'd like a quick swim in the river.

She laughs and looks at me like I've lost my senses, saying she's only just getting used to not walking on a pavement as it is.

I open the picnic basket and we eat ham sandwiches and sweet potato patties Betty baked the day before.

The tea in the flask is sweet and still warm and we sit quietly watching the butterflies sipping on red and white campion, scabious, marjoram and water mint.

Men in the sky above will be walking on the moon in a day or two, which makes the universe seem a very small place.

I watch Betty Jackson eating a sandwich, looking at the insects on the water, and suddenly want to ask her if she'd like to get married.

The idea lands for a moment, like the butterflies, and it seems the perfect thing to do. I'm not sure how it sits with sharing the one you love, not to mention the potential for heartbreak at some point in the future, but I've learned not to worry about other days until they turn up.

I've learned to take things as they come.

I think about asking her the question, but the butterflies take off in the breeze and the moment passes.

Instead of asking her to marry me, I look up at the wide blue sky and think of all the people that led me here.

The people I have loved along the way.

And in those seconds I feel like an ordinary man sat next to an ordinary woman on a picnic blanket by a river with a basket of sandwiches and a flask of tea we brought up with us on the train.

An ordinary man living an ordinary life.

It feels right and good to be ordinary.

We stay in a little hotel for the night, not far from the coal dump where I once abandoned a stolen bus after running out of diesel.

The next day I take Betty for a walk around Stanton Moor and show her the Nine Ladies, thinking maybe one of my prayers was answered after all.

She's quiet on the train home.

I ask if anything's wrong, and she tells me she found a lump on her breast a couple of weeks ago that the doctor isn't too sure about.

I wake with an ache down the left side of my body and a swelling on my tongue where it caught in my false teeth.

My eyes are open but the dark umbrella is still there.

If I lift my head back, I can see daylight in the bedroom window.

Ros is on earlies and helps me get up.

She says I'm quiet today but doesn't mention the bruises when she gets me out of my pyjamas.

She wheels me into the breakfast room but I don't feel like eating this morning. Instead I tune my ears from the banging of spoons to the radio playing songs from the sixties, given that everyone is already sick of carols and it's not even the second week of December. One is about drinking to a pink lily that saved the human race, and another by a man amused they're taking him into a home.

Having heard enough of that nonsense, I tune my ears back to the sound of the breakfast room, like a barn full of ancient cattle waiting to be moved to a different part of the farm.

I sit in my usual chair, facing inside today rather than out onto Hammersmith Grove. Mrs Gibson sits a short distance away looking at the wall, a newspaper folded on her lap.

If I lift my head, I can see the small garden, remembering when Mrs Chaudhry scattered Jimmy Parris's ashes over Gordon's coat and hair.

Funny what stays with you in your mind.

Random moments.

Tiny fragments of memories, which are all we're left with, I suppose.

I look out at the garden and wait for Ros to bring me my morning cup of tea.

It comes quick.

She gets sent for tests and that's it.

Within two months it's in her blood and bones.

The weight falls off her, like leaves from the trees below.

She doesn't want to end up in hospital and there's little they can do for her other than relieve the pain.

Betty Jackson comes to live with me for a few weeks. I

move the bed in front of the window so she can look down at Shepherd's Bush Green, propped up with pillows.

'Not quite Jamaica,' I tell her.

'It'll do,' she says.

A couple of days later, I have several photographs of Montego Bay duplicated and tape them to the glass when she's sleeping that night.

When she wakes in the morning she laughs so hard it brings about a coughing fit that I'm afraid might finish her off.

A man from the council comes after a neighbour informed them a second person was now living in the property. They leave a form to fill in, but it's hard enough getting by without ticking boxes about everything too.

I sit with her when she wakes. Sometimes we talk, but mostly we just stay quiet.

A West Indian nurse from the medical centre comes every few days. When they speak, Betty's accent gets stronger again.

She tells me how much she liked Derbyshire. She says it was her last good day out and doubts she'll make it outside again.

I lift the glass so she can sip water.

The only thing she asks for is water.

I make sure both bars of the electric fire stay on beside the bed. A pile of coins kept stacked, ready to feed the meter.

Gordon stops beside me.

He says, 'This was handed into the office for you,' and puts a large brown envelope on my lap.

The opening has only been folded closed rather than stuck down, which is good for me as I'm not sure my fingers are up to opening envelopes today.

I feel for the paper inside, wondering if this now means I'll have to answer more of Gordon's questions.

'From two young ladies apparently,' Gordon says before disappearing, first into the inky umbrella and then, if I lift my head, back into his office on the other side of the sitting room.

I pull out a sheet but it doesn't feel like paper.

A pale yellow gauze made of soft fabric.

I adjust my head to make better use of the light and try and see the details forming on the cloth.

A tree in full bloom, like in summer.

Its brown trunk and thick green leaves.

The sort of tree I climbed with Archie that day, when two young lovers stopped below us. We shared an apple and I gave Archie his first pocketknife.

I brush the soft wool, imagining each blossoming branch beneath my fingertips.

It's hard to make them out at first, but words are forming next to the picture.

Each letter sewn in bright colours.

I move my head very gently to the side, letting the murky light in the sitting room pick out the shapes embroidered into the cloth until the words make sense.

It's a slow read but a beautiful story.

For the old man in the window.

*

Ros brings me my tea but I'm not in any state to keep leaning across to the side table, so I perch the cup and saucer on my knee and hold it firmly instead.

The soft fabric with the embroidered tree resting on my other trouser leg.

Ros says it's a lovely gift and there's always hope for the world when young people take you by surprise like that.

She says I'm asking for trouble holding onto my teacup and to make sure I keep it steady.

Motes are floating across the surface of my eyes in a wet mist.

I can't be sure if a dark cloud hangs low above the garden fence outside.

Mrs Gibson takes in a deep breath and lets it go.

She leans forward in her chair near the wall and puts her paper down on the floor beside her. She gets up very slowly until she's stood, bent over like a question mark.

She turns to face her chair and grabs the armrests with both hands. They're as thin, bony and blue-veined as my own.

She shuffles her chair sideways in small hops across the linoleum until it's next to mine.

I ask what she's doing.

She says, 'Moving a little closer to you.'

I tell her she'll do herself an injury if she's not careful.

Mrs Gibson laughs and says, 'It's too late for that, sunshine.'

She turns around and gently lowers herself back into her seat beside me.

The inky umbrella slips down a notch and another piece of the sky goes black.

Mrs Gibson says, 'You're looking pale today.'

I tell her I wasn't feeling myself but I'm much happier now.

With the lifts working again, the gentleman several floors below lets me borrow his wheelchair for an hour or two.

I bring it up to surprise Betty during what we call her good hour, late in the morning, soon after she's woken.

She objects at first but I don't take no for an answer.

I put two warm jumpers over her nightdress, a winter coat on top and a blanket over her legs.

We take the lift down to the ground floor and head out for a lap of the green.

She says, 'You're only makin' a point 'cause I said I wouldn't push you roun' in no wheelchair.'

I tell her, 'Next time get one of your other lovers to take you,' but she goes quiet and it feels like something I shouldn't have made a joke about.

We cross the road under the footbridge, heavy with fumes, past the Underground station and the old arch that once led to the white palaces and canals. Past where Lyons coffee house used to be.

It's hard work when you're not getting any younger yourself.

We cross Wood Lane, head down through Shepherd's

Bush market and onto the Goldhawk Road. It's difficult to talk while pushing a wheelchair, weaving through all the busy shoppers.

We return to the green, across the traffic lights on Shepherd's Bush Road, back to the flats and up to the seventeenth floor.

I help get her into bed and return the wheelchair to the man several floors below.

When I come back, Betty says she enjoyed her trip around the block, although later I wonder why I took her out in the first place. Maybe it did have something to do with what she'd said about wheelchairs. Maybe I was just trying to prove a point about what love is after all.

Mrs Jackson told me she wanted to be alone when she died, to curl up like an old dog and do it by herself, but when the time comes, she changes her mind and asks me to sit with her.

I tell her I'm not going anywhere.

Curtains drawn to keep out the clouds.

Lamp on the floor with a tea towel over the shade to hold off the light.

A brown ring on the tea towel where the bulb has burned through.

I take her hand.

The nurse is on her way but doesn't arrive in time.

Ten of us at the funeral.

All men the same sort of age, white and black, most of whom I've never seen before.

After the service, we stand in a cold room above a pub on Ladbroke Grove. Too many sandwiches for the turnout. Couple of drinks, not knowing what to say before going back to our lives.

I'm late with the rent and monthly bills.

I ignore all the letters about council regulations and notices of eviction.

One day I come home to a letter on the door saying the locks have been changed.

I'm not sure where to sleep that night but find my way down to the Thames and a bench in Furnival Gardens, near where Hammersmith Creek used to be.

I have an old winter coat with newspaper stuffed down the sleeves for warmth.

I look for old doorways to sleep in. Tonight there's only a light breeze and the stars are out over the river.

There are worse places I've slept.

This will do me now for a year or so.

Mrs Gibson reaches across, puts her hand on mine.

My other fingers grip the saucer and teacup, balanced cautiously on my knee, and I'm regretting not asking Ros to put it on the side table for me.

'Don't you worry, Billyboy. I'm right here.'

'Thank you, Mrs Gibson,' I tell her.

'Call me Evelyn,' she says.

I tell her I once knew a girl called Evelyn when I was young. We had a lovely home to live in and a lifetime of happiness ahead of us. We'd walk to White City holding hands and talk like it was the easiest thing in the world. I picked cherry blossom for our wedding confetti and kept it in a pouch at the back of my clothes drawer. Life was mapped out like a good dream, but I made a mistake and it disappeared in an instant.

She laughs and says, 'That's boys for you.'

I tell her she once gave me one of her father's old tobacco tins to put my cufflinks in, which I've still kept to this day.

She says, 'The smell never goes, even after all these years.'

I'm wondering if this is a conversation I've had before when my fingertips suddenly tingle as if they've been electrified, then numb in a frozen heat. I see the saucer perched under the soft crook of my thumb but sense the balance shift, not knowing if it's still secure in my hand.

The powdery blood churning to a halt.

One last trip then, down to the feet and back.

Forty-Five

I watch the teacup as it starts to fall.

A tiny slip, a rattle in the well of the saucer.

I watch it start to turn. The tea in ripples, lurching to the edge, perched on this frail knee, a joint in all but name.

The days long gone when it would bend and rise. Muscles worn to bone, a chalky dust. The human body coming to its end.

How we fussed over things that didn't matter. Worried over nothing. They say you don't miss the water till the well runs dry.

Long life, nearly over, almost done.

I would have liked to see another summer. Watch the rhododendrons come to bloom one last time. Purple in the corner of the garden, just outside the window here.

The embroidered tree across my trouser leg, words in the picture.

Mrs Gibson's hand holding me tight.

Evelyn, she said to call her.

Ros is serving tea on the far side of the sitting room as the teacup turns.

The aches from last night's fall draw down through my old bones. I've not seen Sylvie this morning. Lovely Sylvie. I don't want her to be worried.

Mrs Bentley next to Mrs Cutts, television set on much too loud. Mrs Greatorex lifting a biscuit to her mouth, doomed to fall as crumbs. Mr Buffery coughing and dribbling at the same time. He needs someone to go over and wipe his chin. The three Indian ladies in a huddle as usual, talking in a language I wish I'd learned to say hello in.

Mr Ozturk's empty chair.

The far corner where Mrs Pursglove, Mrs Elliot and Mrs Wood would sit around together.

Mrs Gibson stays quiet, holding my hand tightly from the seat where Jimmy Parris liked to read. Maybe she's remembering all those she loved. Lost in her own past, filling in the gaps.

Time slipping by, the best days behind us.

Mr Buffery's cough falls quiet again.

I lift the inky umbrella to see the wind rustling the treetops above the garden wall outside.

The first drops of tea spill over the edge of the cup like tiny pearls. Like some old film playing through, one frame at a time.

They rise over the rim into the air, escaping the teacup as it tumbles.

I wait for the smash of cup and saucer on linoleum, for the splashing of tea on the hard floor and the crash and roll of broken china, but it doesn't come.

Instead, a train of stories roll through my mind, watching the teacup still turning in the air.

Mary, Evie, Archie, Vera, Betty Jackson.

Is Betty done, like the rest of them?

It feels slow but goes quick.

We had good times, Betty and me. You don't expect to find love when you're that age, after all the heartbreak. Realising it doesn't have to hurt, sharing the one you love. Not if you keep to your rules and sod what anyone else thinks about it.

Not at first, anyway.

Drops of tea suspended as the handle lifts. A fraction of movement, enough to know which way the wind is blowing.

Yes'n.

The cup heading into space while the saucer shifts on my old legs, yet to follow on its own slow drop.

The embroidered yellow fabric sticking where it is.

A taste of metal in the roof of my mouth.

I wonder who'll have this chair when I'm gone. Not a bad spot if you're not fussy about seeing the television set. A good view out of the window of the cars and vans going by. You can see the blue lights when an ambulance rushes past and kids sitting on the wall after coming back from school.

Lift your head and you get a view out the back window too. The garden and the blue tarpaulin on the roof of the sheds next door. A new building going up over the wall.

Everything changes.

The beginning of the end, I reckon.

The teacup falling to the ground and I'm not sure, if I'm honest, if I ever really remembered what love was like.

The memories done; tea spilling over the rim, the saucer slipping off my old knee, soon to tumble as well.

Maybe Ros could ask her boyfriend to look at the pages I've left on the table and tidy up the loose ends when she gives him his typewriter back. Check the spelling and whatnot.

461

If I could choose what happens now, I'd lift my hand to stop the cup from falling. Grab it in the air and settle it back down. Catch the drops of tea so nothing gets spilled or broken and life carries on as it was.

These last moments.

The slowing heart.

Mrs Gibson looks across and upwards, over my head, with kindness in her eyes. There's never enough kindness in the world.

She knows what this is.

Five of them.

Mary, Evie, my boy Archie, Vera, Mrs Jackson.

Walking with me through the old white arch on the green. Through the exhibition palaces. Past the canals and gypsy caravans. Past the old Olympic stadium, the fairground with the Flip Flap ride, the water chute and up to the big dipper.

All five sat in the carriage behind me.

A gentle lurch and up we go.

Slowly upwards.

Climbing over London.

Notting Hill and the City to the east. North to Wormwood Scrubs. Hammersmith to the south, then the river. Out west across the fields where it starts turning green.

An empty seat beside me.

Maybe the magic is here, waiting for whoever is next. Like the grave of the unknown soldier, the vacant place a testament to those still to come.

Anonymous, hopeful, expectant.

The teacup passing my shin now, the saucer turned full circle.

The tea spilling onto my trousers but no time to feel the wetness coming through.

My powdery blood drawing to a halt.

The woman beside me in the armchair holds my fingers tight.

Evelyn, did she say?

I knew an Evelyn once. Evie for short.

She'll have to find somewhere else to live in a month or so when this place is gone. Maybe she could stay with her great-granddaughter, who comes to cut the ladies' hair and reminds me of someone I used to know, like an old story from way back.

Everything looks clear through the window. The inky umbrella has lifted.

I can see raindrops down the glass. It must be wet outside.

Evie lifts her hand, brushes it against my cheek and says, 'I can feel your breath on my fingers, Billy Binns.'

Her words clear as a bell.

Her warm touch on the back of my palm.

I know her.

We met someplace before, I'm sure.

There'll be gaps here and there, but Archie will make sense of the pages after Ros has taken the typewriter back.

He'll see what I've put at the start for him.

The dedication, like in a proper book.

He'll see the person I was.

463

An ordinary man who loved a few people in his time.

He'll see the mistakes I made.

How sorry I was for them all.

He'll know there must be loss, there must be letting go when there's always more to come.

The falling saucer turns in the air like a picture sent down from the moon. A tiny planet crashing to its end.

Last breath in.

Last breath coming out.

Wait.

Wait.

There's time enough maybe, before the teacup hits the ground and the saucer rattles on the linoleum flooring, to get a shave and find a tie that isn't stained with gravy. The maroon one with the yellow flag in the drawer that's difficult to knot, perhaps.

I'll dig out the cufflinks from my old tobacco tin.

Ask Evie out for a picnic, sat in the chair beside me now with kindness in her eyes.

Beauty in her face, still flowering like cherry blossom.

I'll take her for a drive. We'll get out for the day.

Somewhere not too far, to the countryside when the weather picks up. Feel the sun on our faces. Take a blanket and find a little spot by the river.

Under a tree, like the one I'm looking at now, sewn into the fabric below me.

Lie down on the blanket with the field in bloom.

The yellows, reds, whites and blues.

Butterflies sipping on scabious and wild campion.

We'll smell the marjoram and the water mint.

Drink some wine. The best doctors say never stop drinking wine.

We'll not bother dwelling on the past or talking about old loves. We've had quite enough of that, thank you very much, and I'm not sure it's got me anywhere.

We'll just be us, starting now, and everything will be fresh.

Eat our picnic, finish the wine and watch the butterflies float across the river.

Maybe even a kiss and cuddle in the warm afternoon sunlight.

And after we've kissed, we can lie back in the long grass and imagine we're stuck onto the bottom of the world, being held there by gravity. And instead of looking up at the clouds, we'll try to imagine we're looking down into the sky below.

Looking down as the world spins.

Just her and me, stuck to the bottom of the earth. Looking down at the sun in the sky below as we spin around above it.

And when gravity makes sense to us again, when everything in the world appears to be the right way up once more, we'll pick ourselves up from the long grass, walk to the edge of the river, strip down to our undies and jump in.

Mary Coggins, Evie, my boy Archie, Vera, Betty Jackson and the new lady sat beside me with skin like cherry blossom and a soft curl in her lips.

Six loves.

All the history within her face, those beautiful lines.

All the kindness.
All the life.
It's a long, slow climb to the top.
Up and up it goes.
And then.
And then.
We wait.
We wait.
We wait.
And then we fly.

for Archi e

The S ix Loves o

Acknowledgements

Thank you to the six. I hope you know who you are.

I was living in W12 in 1993 when I first had the idea for this book after seeing black and white photographs of trams on Shepherd's Bush Green in the old library (now the Bush Theatre), and a derelict white arch that stood idly beside the Central Line station before Westfield was built. I had the bones of Billy's story mapped out but quickly became daunted by the idea of researching the whole of the last century and worked on contemporary TV and radio scripts instead.

A few years later, in 2000, I discovered a series of booklets self-published by the Shepherd's Bush Local History Society. The secretary, Joan Blake, and her husband, Chas, invited me to their monthly meetings at the back of St Luke's Church on the Uxbridge Road. Over the next few months I listened to their stories of growing up in the 20s, 30s and 40s, ate their tea and cakes and watched slide shows of the canals and old exhibition palaces at White City. We discussed a proposal to develop the wasteland into what would become Westfield shopping centre many years later. Without the generosity of Joan and her friends it would have been impossible to get started. It took me the next eighteen months to research and write part one of the book.

Faced with more lengthy bouts of historical research for parts two to five, I decided again that I wasn't cut out for writing novels and abandoned the idea. Eight years later I was struggling to come up with a fourth play for Radio 4. I decided to submit a treatment for *The Six Loves Of Billy Binns* (cue Willy Russell's line in *Educating Rita* about how to resolve the staging difficulties of Ibsen's *Peer Gynt* by doing it on the radio). It still needed more research but writing a forty-five minute radio script was less daunting than persevering with the rest of the book. In 2009 Sir Tom Courtenay gave Billy a voice, and the radio play, of which I'm very proud, still gets repeated.

Eighteen years after writing the first hundred pages, and at a very different stage of life, I met Andrew Gordon at David Higham Associates who read what I'd started and encouraged me to finish it. I immersed myself in the Shepherd's Bush Local History Society publications again and took two years to complete a full draft. Andrew then introduced me to Jemima Forrester, who instantly became my agent and whose extraordinary clarity, wisdom and red pen were instrumental when it came to writing another draft to submit to publishers.

Imogen Taylor at Tinder Press wrote me a beautiful letter and offered Billy a home. I worked on another draft, very grateful for Imogen's inspiring and incisive editorial notes. Yeti Lambregt's beautiful design captured the spirit of Billy. Amy Perkins and all the team at Headline paid kind attention to detail through the proof-reading and marketing process.

Of course, age caught up and the Shepherd's Bush Local

History Society disbanded over time. Their legacy of invaluable publications include:

Shepherd's Bush Market – Markets and Traders from 1864 (Shepherd's Bush Local History Society, unknown year)

Shepherd's Bush Memories – Bill Goble, Life-long Rebel (Shepherd's Bush Local History Society, 1984)

Around the Bush – The War Years (Shepherd's Bush Local History Society, 1987)

The Scrubs (Shepherd's Bush Local History Society, 1998)

Around the Bush – A History of Shepherd's Bush (Shepherd's Bush Local History Society, 2000)

I also found a wealth of information in:

Hammersmith and Shepherd's Bush in Old Photographs by Jerome Farrell and Christine Bayliss (Alan Sutton Publishing Ltd, 1995)

Hammersmith and Shepherd's Bush Past by Barbara Denny (Historical Publications, 1995)

London Transport by Michael H. C. Baker (Shire Publications, 2016)

Holland Park and Shepherd's Bush Ordnance Survey Map, 1913

A number of other sources, including many friends and colleagues, provided historical details, but special mention goes to Big Wal (Valentine) and Claire Gould, who knew much about the price of fish, and other more dubious services through the ages. Hilton McRae helped illuminate the 60s. Kurt's life (and death) is loosely based on the harrowing story of Karl Richter who died in Wandsworth prison in 1941, though it's unlikely he shared a cell with Billy Binns. Albert Pierrepoint's informative biography *Executioner* provided many details on the hanging, though I've taken a few liberties to imagine events from his victims' perspective. I spent a lot of time in the London Transport Museum peering into bus cabs and asking the staff questions about fuel capacity. According to *The Greater London Bus Map* all bus routes in part four of the story were accurate at the time of going to press, 1940.

Thank you to my friends and fellow script co-writers, Paul Mari, Chris Niel and Katie Lyons, for invaluable writing lessons over the years. Thank you to Theresa Hickey at CDA and the Sue Terry girls for keeping me working so I could afford to write. Thank you to all those who read early proofs and kindly provided quotes.

Thank you, Sophie, for the wonderful curiosity table and the love we once shared, without which the story would not have been written. Thank you, Ernie and Walt, for growing up with me. Thank you, Mum and Dad, who watched me turn some difficult corners and all those friends who stayed close when times were hard. Thank you to my aunts, Karen and Rosemary, who bought me so many good books when I was a teenager. And thank you, Em, for lighting the way forward. Tap click. Ding.

Finally, Billy Binns is a somewhat unreliable narrator. I've gone to great lengths to ensure the historical accuracy of his recollections throughout the book, but any mistakes in the text are entirely his own.

RL, September 2018